"Malan's fantasy debut straddles two worlds, each detailed in vibrant colors and images. Believable characters and graceful storytelling make this a good addition to most fantasy collections." —*Library Journal*

"Blending the timeless enchantment of a Patricia A. McKillip fantasy and the epic narrative splendor of a Tad Williams work, Canadian author Violette Malan's debut novel is nothing short of superb. *The Mirror Prince* is—like the Newford saga by fellow Canuck Charles de Lint—a kind of urban fantasy, taking place simultaneously in the Shadowlands of Earth and the magical realm of Faerie. The book's surprising—and utterly satisfying—conclusion is well worth the build-up. Fantasy fans should brace themselves: the world is about to discover Violette Malan." —*The Barnes & Noble Review*

"Violette Malan's debut novel is everything a fantasy novel should be. There is adventure, there is romance, there is magic, there is danger and loss, love and sacrifice. There is lovely writing, and again, the promise of more to come." —*The Washington Times*

"Elves get yet another remake in this fantasy first novel ... it's a good read." —*Locus*

# THE MIRROR PRINCE

# THE MIRROR PRINCE

## Violette Malan

**DAW BOOKS, INC.**

DONALD A. WOLLHEIM, FOUNDER

375 Hudson Street, New York, NY 10014

**ELIZABETH R. WOLLHEIM**

**SHEILA E. GILBERT**

**PUBLISHERS**

http://www.dawbooks.com

First Paperback Printing, July 2007
1   2   3   4   5   6   7   8   9

DAW TRADEMARK REGISTERED
U.S. PAT. OFF AND FOREIGN COUNTRIES
—MARCA REGISTRADA
HECHO EN U.S.A.

PRINTED IN THE U.S.A.

For Paul

# *Acknowledgments*

I'd like to thank Joshua Bilmes, for asking questions until he was satisfied, thus making sure that I was satisfied as well, and Sheila Gilbert for welcoming me into the family. Tanya Huff and Fiona Patton, for setting such good examples, and for their support and friendship; Bill and Carol Mackillop for employing me when I needed money; special thanks to Sandra Beswetherick and Therese Greenwood for reading various versions of the manuscript; Steven Price for his support and advice, and his dad Charles Price for information about subways; David Ingham for his suggestions about apostrophes. Finally, my brother Oscar Malan for telling me, many years ago, to read *The Lion, the Witch, and the Wardrobe*. He was right.

# Prologue

## Seattle

MALCOLM JONES TURNED his battered old Mercedes into his driveway and pulled up as close to Jenny's Camry as he could get. It took him a couple of tries to get the emergency brake to engage, and he reminded himself—out loud this time, so he wouldn't forget—to get the boys in the garage to look at it when he took the car in on Friday.

Malcolm swung open the heavy car door, the chill, damp air almost a relief after the heat of the interior. He climbed out and reached back in for his briefcase, bending over to pick up his hat from where it had rolled off the front seat into the foot well on the far side of the stick shift. Suddenly he smelled oranges.

"Stormbringer," someone said.

Malcolm stood up, striking his head on the roof of the car. He backed out, hands holding tightly to the crown of his head, trying not to hiss, trying to puff his breath out to ease the pain, as they had told Jenny to do when she was in labor.

He squinted. The man next to the car was tall, as tall as Malcolm himself, though thicker through the shoulders, and with the ruddy skin, sun-bronzed hair, and soft hazel eyes of a friendly Viking.

"Where is the Exile, Stormbringer?"

"What are you talking about?" Malcolm glanced at his front doorway—just how close was it?—and saw that the house was dark. A cold hand squeezed his heart.

"Do not know, will not say," sang a liquid voice.

Malcolm whirled around. There was another tall man on the far side of the car. This one was dark, but with a Celt's fine-boned features, fair skin, and blue eyes. He smelled of freshly mown hay. He glanced up at the dark windows of the upper story and smiled.

Malcolm dodged around the man in front of him and ran toward the house. He expected them to stop him, and when they didn't, the chill holding his heart squeezed a little tighter.

Jenny was not in the living room. Only a third man, this one as fair as straw, holding Jenny's cell phone, punching in the buttons, holding it up to his ear and then smiling. The whole room smelled of hyacinths.

"Where's my wife?" He spoke matter-of-factly, as if he were asking one of the twins.

"So it is true," the fair man said. "They have *dra'aj* enough for that, the Shadowfolk. That will be useful to us, by and by."

"The woman and the children are upstairs," Oranges said to Malcolm. The man who smelled like mown hay closed the door to the street behind him and stood next to Oranges, blocking the front hallway. This time, as Malcolm tried to get around them to go upstairs, they stopped him, Mown Hay and Hyacinth, pulling his hands away from the railing, twisting his arms behind his back, their delicate, long-fingered hands as hard and as cold as talons. He would have bruises in the morning, if he lived. Oranges stood in front of him now, peering with cold interest into his face.

"We don't care about them," Oranges said. "Tell us where the Exile is."

"Let me see my family," Malcolm said. His whole body strained upward. If they had been human, he would have shrugged them off like old clothes, but he was not stronger than three of his own kind. Still, he tried to see some movement of shadows in the upstairs hallway. To hear some sound that would make the icy grip in his chest go away. "I'll give you whatever you want. Let me see them."

"Later, perhaps."

A smile came and went on Hyacinth's face, and Malcolm's heart grew still. Too late, he thought, remembering Mown Hay's smile outside, and the way his eyes had strayed up to the second floor. To the bedroom windows. Too late. No point now in trying to shield Jenny and the twins. No point in pretending that these people had made a mistake, that he was not what he was. That they were not what they were.

No point in buying time while he decided whether his Oath was worth the lives of his family. He could see it in Hyacinth's face. That decision had been made for him.

"We do not want you, Stormbringer. We want the Exile."

Malcolm shook his head. Their timing was badly off. Tragically off. It had been six years at least since the Exile had graduated from Seattle University, where Malcolm was a professor of history. "Why? Why now? The Banishment is close to ending—"

Malcolm gasped as the one who smelled of oranges took a fistful of his hair and pulled his head back hard enough to snap his neck, if he had been human. "Because our Prince has need of him now, that's why."

"You cannot . . ." But Malcolm could see from their faces that they thought they could. He shook his head, slowly at first until he found he could not stop. He *Moved, Traveling* away from the house that no longer held anything of value to him. Away from the life that was no longer his.

But when he opened his eyes, he had not gone anywhere. He was still in his front hall. They still held him fast, their long-fingered hands still bruising his arms.

"What are you trying, Stormbringer?" Oranges shook him a little. "Why not tell us? Your Oath is to protect him from humans during the Banishment." Oranges leaned in close. "Do we look like humans to you?"

Malcolm felt his lips stretch out in the parody of a smile. "Why don't you bring my wife?" he sneered. "My children? Threaten to hurt them if I don't tell you? Hmmm?" Their silence gave him the proof he had not needed. "You've made a mistake there, my brothers. You have no weapons now."

"Have we not?"

Malcolm laughed. His throat was raw and he felt like choking, but he went on laughing until his legs gave out and the only thing holding him up was their hands. There was a sudden, sharp pain on the side of his face.

"You're fools," he said finally. He tasted blood, and spat. "I would have told you," he said. "Not just to buy the lives of my wife and my children. Not just for that." He got his feet under him and tried to stand. Their hands tightened. "You could have stopped me on the street and asked me and I would have told you. I wouldn't even have asked if you meant him harm. Why should I? I would have told you."

"Yes, yes. And now you will *not* tell us, is that it?"

Malcolm laughed again, but stopped as Oranges raised his hand.

"Perhaps you *will* kill him. But perhaps he'll surprise you." Malcolm's arms didn't hurt anymore, and he found he could stand upright. "I'll tell you. I'll tell you more than you wish to know. You have named me Bringer of Storm, and in that you speak truly, a storm comes. But this storm will break over *your* heads. This storm will come as a dragon and devour you. Here is my curse on you, my brothers. The man you seek is called Ravenhill. You will find him to sunward in the place the storm gathers. The place called Toronto."

"Do you think we free you now?" Mown Hay breathed

in Malcolm's ear. "Do you think you buy your life with this?"

Malcolm shook his head. He bought nothing. Jenny was dead and they would kill him, and it did not matter. His children were dead, and his time in the Shadowlands was over. And that did not matter.

He saw movement over Orange's shoulder and the habit of living made him look. A rangy white dog with dark red markings came trotting out of the kitchen, smiling a toothy doggy smile, his tongue lolling out of the side of his mouth.

And even while part of him—the part that was still Malcolm Jones, Associate Professor of European History— wondered how so large a dog had managed to move so silently, the dog *changed*, growing grotesquely larger, its fur becoming scales, and its snout dripping. The part of him that was Stormbringer began at once to struggle in the iron hands that held him. That part of him recognized the dog. He was still ready to die. But not this way. He would rather live than feed the Hound.

Stormbringer gathered himself and flung out all his *dra'aj*. As his power left him, and the final darkness covered him, he heard a howling.

# Chapter One

CASSANDRA KENNABY REVERSED her rapier and placed it, swept hilt first, in her assistant's waiting hand. She grinned at her opponent, giving the girl's shoulder a gentle squeeze, before turning to where spectators' chairs were set up a safe distance behind a sturdy mahogany railing. Her friend Barb was leaning on the barrier, shaking her head, half smiling.

"You okay?" Cassandra asked, pulling off her mask. "You look a little pale."

Barb shook her head again. "For a minute there . . . the swords moved so fast . . . I thought you were going to kill her."

"That would defeat the lesson." Cassandra wiped her face with her sleeve. Her silver hair clip clattered to the floor and, cursing mildly, she retrieved it, pushing her gold hair back from her face. "Sarita's not fast enough to hurt me," she added, turning to watch her young opponent receive the congratulations of the other students. "And I wasn't planning to hurt her."

"I guess." Barb shrugged. "I don't think I've ever seen anyone fence with real swords before."

"Sarita's reached the stage where she won't learn anything further using foils and épées." Cassandra spoke over her shoulder as she led her friend down the narrow corridor toward her office and her private shower. "Fencing's an art, I grant you, but it's a *martial* art."

"It's not like watching a competition. I mean it is, but ..." Barb waved her thought away with an impatient twitch of her hand.

"We don't teach that kind of fencing here," Cassandra turned back to her friend. "Fencing isn't a way to score points, it's a way to kill people."

Barb laughed. "You tell the parents that?"

Cassandra shook her head, trying unsuccessfully to hide her own smile. "Some people can't handle the truth."

When all the students had gone for the day, and the street doors of the dojo were bolted, and even the practice swords had been locked away, Cassandra opened the long wooden chest that sat against the wall behind the old maple trestle table she used as a desk. The chest was made of ash wood and had been carved to her design by a master carver, long before she had come to Toronto with the old sensei to open a dojo in the western world. The carving showed a sleeping dragon, curled around a group of revelers feasting in a bright forest clearing, and was so detailed and so lifelike that occasionally people—including those who tried to open the chest for purposes of their own—found themselves unable to look away from the sight of the guests dancing, especially when the dragon winked and stretched out its curved claws like a lazy cat.

Cassandra slipped the battered leather case containing her dueling swords into the space left for it at the back of the chest. Her fingers brushed against a larger bundle wrapped in heavy folds of raw red silk and she felt a sudden tug of longing deep in her chest.

"You will need that, I'm thinking."

Heart in her mouth, Cassandra spun around, crouching to take advantage of the desk's cover, a throwing knife already in her hand, and found what looked like an eleven-year-old boy standing in the open doorway of her office. Long practice kept her face calm, her expression one of neutral interest. She took in the layers of baggy clothing, the beanie cap, and the wide skateboard. But this was not some child who had stowed away in one of the locker rooms, waiting for a chance to play with the weapons—or steal the computers. In his eyes the centuries showed, turning his child's face, his body, his clothing, and even the skateboard into parody. He would have fooled any adult human, but Cassandra knew that this boy had never been eleven. And never a boy.

Under her surprise, a part of her was almost glad to see him, even if he *was* a Solitary. It had been over a hundred years since she'd seen or spoken to any others of her kind here in the Shadowlands. The Basilisk Prince had been discouraging travel between the worlds for centuries and had finally set a guard around the Portals—something that had turned out to be a good thing for humans, who were less plagued by Ogres, Trolls under bridges, kidnapped children, and demon lovers. But something that made life terribly lonely for those Riders whose duties kept them here.

So a strange Rider would have been surprising enough, but a Solitary? And a strange Rider she would have felt behind her, would have sensed. A Solitary was like so much empty space. *And there are no Solitaries anywhere*, Cassandra reminded herself, *who can be trusted*.

"I greet you, Younger Sister," the Solitary said, his voice like shifting gravel. "You are Sword of Truth. Your mother was Clear of Light. The Dragon guides you. You are no kin to me, but I know you."

Cassandra inclined her head, once down, once up, slowly, careful to keep her eyes on the Old One's face. She had no trouble recognizing the ritual greeting, though, to her knowledge, she'd only met one Solitary before. Riders like herself didn't mix with Solitaries—not by choice anyway.

"I ask your pardon, Elder Brother," she said, giving one of the allowed ritual answers. "I do not know you."

"Say, rather, you do not recognize me, for you *do* know me. I am Hearth of the Wind, the Last Born," he said, "and the Earth guides me. The Shadowfolk call me Diggory," he added, and waited.

"Cassandra," she said, inclining her head once more in acknowledgment that she had, indeed, met him before—though then he hadn't looked anything like a young boy with a skateboard.

"And my people say that Riders have no sense of humor." Diggory bowed and turned his stone-colored eyes to the open chest. "For you're well named, then, Truthsheart."

Cassandra lifted her eyebrows and deliberately turned her back on him, though it made the fine hairs on the back of her neck shiver. She put out her hand to close the chest's lid.

"Best leave it open, I think. You'll have need of what you keep there."

Cassandra turned back to face the boy with old eyes. "You've said that already."

"I bring you word from Nighthawk."

Possible, Cassandra thought, since it was in the company of her fellow Warden that she'd met this Solitary before, but . . .

"Why send you?" she asked, her glance, before she could stop it, flicking to the phone on her worktable.

"Because he cannot come himself, and I am surer than the technology of humans." The Old One took a step closer to her. "Your Oath calls you, Warden. The Exile is in danger of his life. Take your weapons and go to him."

Cassandra's heart leaped, but she leaned back on the edge of the chest, crossed her ankles, and folded her arms. Offhand, she couldn't think of any reason why a Solitary would want to trick her into tearing off armed into the streets of Toronto, but that's exactly why she had to be careful. Being tricked by a Solitary was humiliating at best, fatal at worst—then again, be too careful and she might trick herself. Slowly, she had to go slowly.

"I find this hard to believe," she said.

Diggory smiled, showing far too many teeth for a human boy. "Of course you do. After all this time? When no steel has ever touched him, no bullets found him? Why," the Solitary leaned forward and lowered his voice as if sharing a secret with her, "even earthquakes and plagues wait until he has gone his way before they begin their feeding. He has forgotten his *dra'aj*, but it has not forgotten him."

"And so?"

"And so that was humans, and it's not humans my lord the Exile needs to fear and never was, there you're right. But the Banishment nears its end, and the Basilisk Prince moves his pieces upon the board, and they wear the shape of the Hunt. Do you tell me the Exile has nothing to fear from this?"

Cassandra stopped in mid-shrug, allowing the knife to slip back into her hand from its sleeve sheath. "The Hunt? I had always understood the end of the Banishment to be a good thing."

"And so it might have been. But the Basilisk Prince builds his Citadel in the Vale of *Trere'if*. Yes," Diggory continued as Cassandra stifled an involuntary movement, "he has dared so much. Now he knows that which he has sought to know this long time, and now he seeks to know what only my lord the Exile knows. And he cares not what means he uses to learn it. And it's for *you* to keep the Exile safe, as always." Diggory smiled like the sun coming through clouds and Cassandra almost found herself smiling back.

What he said was true. The Basilisk Prince had grown in power and importance since the time of the Great War; some said he was High Prince in everything but name. Even Cassandra, who had not set foot in the Lands of the People the whole time of the Banishment, had heard that much. Still . . .

There was only one thing the Exile might know that the Basilisk Prince wanted: the whereabouts of the Talismans—but that didn't make sense. What had happened to make that knowledge so important now? Frowning, Cassandra studied the open, guileless face of the Solitary.

"I come to you almost too late," the Old One said, as if in answer to her unspoken suspicions. "I do not need to tell you the end comes, but you *must* act or your Oath is forfeit. Come, Truthsheart, would I trouble to lie? To you?" Diggory shook his head. "You think it was a jest, what your mother named you? Younger Sister, listen to your heart. You know I speak the truth."

Cassandra studied the Troll eyes in the boy face. Even if she did know the truth when she heard it—and right now that seemed like a mighty big if—she wouldn't be quick to let this one know it.

"And what is the price of this truth, Elder Brother? Or has Nighthawk paid it?"

"I seek no payment," the Old One said. "I have given my all without need of bargain."

The cold spot in Cassandra's belly dropped several inches. What Solitary would give anything without bargaining first? "You want nothing, then?"

The Old One suddenly loomed over her, his disguise fading as his skin became a darker gray-brown, and his eyes lost their human irises and pupils. Cassandra was glad of the chest behind her—it stopped her from shaming herself by backing away.

"What do you know of what I might want? What would any Rider know, except the Exile?" He snarled with his mouth full of teeth, but he was already shrinking back down to human scale. "I will tell you this, Younger Sister. If you do not save the Exile, it will not matter one tenth part of an ant's whisker what you, or I, or any being wants. We will none of us be safe. No Solitary, no Natural, no Rider of any Ward. Not even here in this place—the Basilisk Prince will find even these poor Shadowfolk useful to his hand."

The room seemed suddenly cold, and Cassandra folded her arms again, hugging her elbows. "I will consider your words," she said.

"Don't take too long," said the voice of the skateboarder, as the Solitary gave her a last grin, turned on one sneakered foot, and was gone. Cassandra waited, listening to the clatter of his feet on the staircase, until she could be sure she was alone.

"Get a job, I said. See the Shadowlands, I said. What could go wrong?"

Cassandra rubbed her eyes and sank into the old oak captain's chair behind her worktable with a sigh. Her whole day had started out badly, startled awake, trembling and cold, out of a dream of storm and lightning. Thunder that seemed somehow to be calling her name. She hadn't been asleep long—it wasn't more than one o'clock in the morning when the dream's thunder woke her—but she'd been wired, so energized that she couldn't fall asleep again. Now here it was almost bedtime, and it looked as though she wouldn't get much sleep tonight either.

She gathered up her hair in one hand, snapping her silver hair clip shut over it. She closed her eyes and breathed in through her nose and out through her mouth until her hands were relaxed on the arms of the chair, her breathing slow and regular.

Her stomach was clenched like a fist and she could taste acid in the back of her throat.

All the old Songs told how Solitaries—whether Troll or Giant, Ogre or Siren—were liars and tricksters. How they were at their most dangerous when you could not see what they would gain from tricking you. There were questions she should have asked, questions she had not even realized she had until the Old One was gone. She knew truth when she heard it, fine and good. But what he'd told her couldn't have been *all* of the truth. Where *was* Nighthawk and why hadn't the old Warrior come himself? Or called? Did the Troll Diggory mean what he said when he named the Hunt? Was *that* the danger? But *how*—

And most important, what should *she* do, when she'd sworn her own private oath—Warden or no Warden— for her own private reasons, never to be in the presence of the Exile again?

Not that she was afraid to. Of course not. She was sure that so much time had passed since the last time she saw him . . . in fact, Cassandra considered, she hadn't seen him since he came to Toronto in his current persona. Still, she knew just what he'd look like. Just how green his eyes were when he laughed; just how his hair, raven-black, grew curled behind his ears. How his voice sounded in the dark. How his skin tasted of vanilla. How her lips could feel his heart beat in the hollow of his throat—

Cassandra jerked her head up out of her hands. Maybe she should be worried after all. She took another deep breath in through her nose, slowly, pushed it forcefully out of her mouth, and reached for the phone. Regardless of what the Solitary had said, she would call her *fara'ip*. Blood of her blood they might not be, but the other two Wardens were the closest thing she had to family here in the Shadowlands. Whatever this danger was, they would face it together. That was what being *fara'ip* meant.

Out of habit, Cassandra glanced at the clock on the wall. The six-hour difference made it all the more likely that Nighthawk was at home and in bed. She punched fourteen digits into the phone and waited, impatiently tapping the tabletop with her fingers until she realized what she was doing and stopped, laying her hand flat. Finally she heard the soft tuneful buzz that was a phone ringing in Nighthawk's flat in Granada. She opened her mouth when the click came, but caught herself when she realized it was the answering machine.

"Diego," she said, when the beep came, in case some friend or cleaning lady would be the one to pick up the message, "I've just had a visit from a gray man—a bridge builder—who said he'd come from you. Call me back as soon as you can."

Cassandra placed the handset back in the cradle and thought, lower lip between her teeth, before picking up the phone again and dialing another fourteen digit number, ready to leave the same message on Diego's mobile phone. The soft buzz was cut off not by the message service, but with a burst of static, from which all she could make out were the words "fuera de servicio." It was possible, she thought, as she cut the connection. There might be three or four places where mobile phones didn't work in Spain. But what were the odds that Nighthawk was in one of them? She glanced at the clock again. Even if she could Move that far—and she couldn't cross the ocean without a crossroads—if Nighthawk wasn't in his apartment . . . She punched another number into the phone, this one with only eleven digits. Malcolm's machine answered immediately, but the outgoing message was not in the voice she expected.

"If you're trying to contact Dr. Malcolm Jones," a gentle contralto instructed, "please call Detective Sergeant Sonia Rascon at—" followed by a number. Cassandra dropped the handset back into the cradle and drummed her fingers on the varnished tabletop. It looked as though the Old One was to be trusted after all. She stood up. It was dinnertime in Seattle, and Seattle she could reach without a crossroads.

She turned again to the chest behind her worktable, this time opening it and unfolding the layers of thick silk that covered her *gra'if* weapons. She hesitated over the swords but finally settled on a poniard, easy to conceal if she had to, and a pair of finely mailed gloves with attached gauntlets which she pulled on her hands. She had a leather suit jacket hanging on the back of her door, and she slipped it on before checking her reflection in the window glass. It was dark enough outside for the window to act as a mirror. She nodded. With the jacket on, her gauntlets could pass at a glance for ordinary driving gloves.

She stood, closed her eyes, and thought about Malcolm Jones' front door. In her mind was the image of her room. She began to erase the image, piece by piece. Subtracted the oak captain's chair, the carved chest. The little crystal paperweight in the shape of a dragon with its paw on a sword. The fountain pen leaking ink onto a pad of paper on the table. Subtracted the pad of paper and the table. The hand-knotted wool carpet under her feet, the oak floor under the carpet. Into the image she added heavy granite flagstones, neat short grass carefully edged, a prizewinning rosebush still wrapped in burlap for the winter. The wooden raised-panel door painted a bright raspberry, with its egg-shaped agate knocker.

The air CRACKED, the temperature dropped, and the wind blew raindrops into Cassandra's face. She shook her hair back out of her eyes. It was early evening in Seattle, but even with the overcast sky and the rain, it was much too dark. She stepped back and frowned when she saw there were no lights on in the house. Malcolm and Jenny wouldn't have taken the children out on a school night.

Cassandra reached for the doorbell and stopped. The luminescence given off by her *gra'if*-mailed hand was faint, but it was enough to show her the padlock on the door, the crime scene tape, and the police seal.

Once she'd twisted off the padlock, the seal presented no problem. She stepped into the foyer and held up her hands, waiting as her pupils adjusted to the soft glow. Even for her eyes there was not enough light to show color, but Cassandra didn't need light to tell her what color the dark areas on the floor and the spray of splashes up the staircase really were. *Blood somehow manages to have color,* she thought, *even when there is no light, and even when it's hours old.*

The Rider known to humans as Malcolm Jones was a Singer, more interested in tales and histories than blades, but he had stayed alive without difficulty for the whole of the Banishment, just over a thousand years. He was not slow or unskilled by human standards, and it could not have been humans who had killed him.

Of the three Wardens who guarded the Exile, only Nighthawk had started the Banishment as a Warrior, and he had spent much of their early years training the younger Wardens until Cassandra and Malcolm had met his standards. Cassandra had loved the art more than Malcolm, but she wasn't in Nighthawk's league and never would be. But he hadn't come himself; he'd sent the Troll. Was it possible that their time here in the Shadowlands had slowed him? Cassandra shook her head, the cold lump that had been in her stomach since the Troll came into her office growing larger and, if possible, colder. Would she find crime scene tape and evidence of slaughter at Nighthawk's home as well?

A whisper of sound to her left, and Cassandra slipped into a shadow, blade once again in her hand as she extended her hearing around her, making sure this wasn't a distraction to keep her from noticing as something snuck up behind her. A small white dog with dark red markings came into the room from the kitchen beyond, its claws ticking on the hardwood floor, passing through a shaft of cold moonlight that filtered through the sheers on the front window. The dog halted there, in the moonlight, moving its head from side to side, its muzzle wrinkled, smelling the air she had walked through. Cassandra grew more quiet, more ready, trying to breathe out the shock she felt.

No, the Troll Diggory hadn't lied. The Hound explained what had happened to Malcolm and his human

family. The Hound meant the threat to the Exile was
real.

Cassandra wished she'd grabbed her swords after all.
Both of them, no matter how odd it would have looked
if she'd been seen. She wasn't at all sure that she could
kill a Hound with her little poniard, *gra'if* metal or no.
The Hound took another step in her direction, morphing into something with longer legs and a toothier muzzle. It sniffed the air again and lowered its muzzle to the
stained carpet. If it wasn't Hunting for her . . .

As soon as its eyes were elsewhere, Cassandra Moved.

Max Ravenhill didn't think of himself as the kind of guy
who daydreamed about a girl. Not that there was anything *wrong* with it, exactly. It was just something a person
was more likely to do as a teenager, when daydreaming,
particularly while bored in school, and was part of a normal life. And Max was certain that if he'd had anything
like a normal life as a teenager, he'd have been daydreaming with the best of them. But since his normal life
waited until he was in his twenties to begin, perhaps it
wasn't so strange that he should wait until now to day-
dream about a girl, not because he was bored, but because he didn't want to think too much about the
meeting he had just left, where his first graduate student
had successfully defended her thesis. Max had found
reason to wonder, over the previous few months, how
professors who weren't experts in the history of warfare
managed all the strategies, the intrigues, and the rever-
sals that made up the average pursuit of a PhD.

Shari's defense was too recent, and the triumph connected with it too fresh, so as he walked along Queen
Street whistling, his hands in the pockets of his jeans
and the tails of his long open coat swinging behind him,
Max escaped into other thoughts, thoughts that until now
had been too exciting to indulge.

Three days before, Max had gone to his Department

Head's monthly wine and cheese party, and he'd seen someone. He'd recognized the feeling that shook him right away, even though he could say with certainty that he'd never felt it before. He remembered thinking, as he sipped his pineapple juice, that it must be some kind of racial memory, one that allowed people to understand without panicking when their bones and blood, heart and mind, woke up—to understand and welcome all the possibilities that stretched out from the moment that rang like a bell, the excitement, and the longing, and the fear that stops the heart.

Nothing else gave you the bell-ringing feeling so powerfully as that meeting of the eyes—across a crowded room, as it happened—when you saw your Beatrice, your Laura, your Dark Lady.

Except this lady wasn't dark. She was a pale honey-blonde, with eyes like a cloudy sky and skin like rich cream. And for that magic instant, seeing him looking at her, those stormy eyes had flashed, and that skin had flushed the merest rosy flush and her lips, a little too wide and a little too full, had begun to smile, before she'd gotten her face under control, and the mask of polite interest she'd worn before catching his eye slipped back over her perfect features.

It was obvious that Professor Hepworth knew this woman well, so Max had managed an introduction, and Cassandra Kennaby had again flushed that almost imperceptible color when they'd shaken hands. So he hadn't been too disappointed when she'd made polite small talk in her rough chocolatey voice and excused herself after the minimum length of time demanded by courtesy. Max was fairly sure that Cassandra had felt something very close to what he'd felt himself—not so sure as to be smug about it, but sure enough that he'd asked the Head about her (single, owned a martial arts dojo, medical degree though she didn't practice), looked up the number of the dojo, and had already called her twice, leaving one live voice and one voice mail message.

The voice mail he'd left only minutes ago, as he climbed the steps up from the subway, telling Cassandra his good news and asking her to help him celebrate. It was a good omen, his finding her the other night. With the success of his student's defense, his career had taken an important step forward. This was the kind of thing that practically guaranteed he'd get tenure at his next review. Everything in his life was finally falling into place, inching toward the true. Max didn't even notice the chill that an early April evening was bringing to the city streets.

He smiled as he caught his reflection in the darkened glass of a butcher shop. A scruffy white dog with blood-red markings was sniffing around the door and broke off to wag its tail at him. A young man who jostled Max's elbow while he and several others waited for the lights to change at the corner of Queen and Bond, smiled and apologized before walking off. Max shook his head in disbelief, feeling his smile stretch even wider. Everyone must be feeling good today.

The light changed, and Max stepped out into the road. He felt a heavy, warm impact on his left side, and a sharp blow on the back of his head. He heard rather than felt the crack of his knees as they hit the pavement. *Car hit me,* he thought, as the world began to darken. *Must have run the light.* His vision shrank down, down, until he was looking at a tiny image, like a TV screen at the end of a long hallway, surrounded by blackness. Max concentrated, and found that he could hear what people were saying, see what they were doing. The blackness got no worse, but the messages from his brain faded to nothing long before they reached his hands and feet.

He couldn't be badly hurt, he reasoned; he could feel the hands that took him up under the armpits, and lifted him to his feet. The hands on his left arm felt wrong somehow, as if the person was wearing mittens, or had his hands bandaged. The cold city air, scented with car exhaust, had an overlay of faintly rotting meat, and Max flashed on the image of his own reflection in the butcher shop's window. When he tried to pull away from the awkward grip, it became firmer. *I need to lie down,* he thought.

The people holding him folded Max into the backseat of what felt like a large car. *No,* he thought, *I need to lie down.* He wasn't sure whether he'd spoken aloud. The car door closed and Max felt hot, moist breath on his cheek. He turned and looked directly into the panting muzzle of a huge dog, inches away from his face, so close that Max recoiled, banging his elbow on the car door. He blinked, but his eyes refused to focus. The dog, light-colored with dark markings, at first looked short-muzzled like a bulldog, and then long and razor-mouthed like a wolfhound, the image blurring and flickering until Max felt nauseated. Only the eyes, black as holes and intelligently aware, never changed. The sickly sweet scent of old meat grew stronger and Max shut his eyes, willing the insulating blackness to grow thicker. The car rolled forward with a jerk that almost spilled Max to the floor and caused the dog to stand up on the seat. Saliva dripped on him from the dog's jaws, and Max's stomach lurched again.

They hadn't gone far when the door of the car was wrenched open and something yanked Max bodily out, knocking his head against the doorframe. A voice he strained to recognize called to him to run, and Max found himself able to stagger a couple of steps. On the third or fourth step the numbness abruptly disappeared, and the world came into sharp and normal focus.

He had no idea in what direction they were running, or even what street they were on, but the woman who had hold of his wrist seemed to know where she was going and that, at the moment, was good enough for him. His rescuer was almost his own height, wearing a black ankle-length coat. Her thick blond hair, crisply curling in the damp air, was held back with a silver clip, and she had a long leather bag with an ornate silver clasp slung over one shoulder. Max's right wrist was clamped in her gloved hand, and when she turned the corner onto a more deserted street, Max instinctively dragged back a little.

The woman increased the pressure on his arm, and at the same time turned her head to look at him. Recognition relaxed his muscles and Max exerted himself a little until they were running side by side, her hand still firmly on his wrist.

"Cassandra?"

"Run."

"Where are we going?" They had turned another corner and still she didn't slow down.

"This way."

The alley she pulled him into was about fifteen feet wide, long and dark, with a chain-link fence connecting the buildings at the far end. A motion sensor clicked and a light came on, showing Max a loading platform along the left side of the alley. Cassandra pushed him behind her into the shadow created by the platform and turned to face the entrance. She slipped the long bag off her shoulder and lowered it to the cracked concrete close to Max's feet. The way she handled it told him the bag was heavier than it looked. With a sound like a sharp whistle, she drew a sword out of the top of the bag. Max saw that what he had mistaken for the bag's elaborate closure had actually been the sword's hilt. Cassandra shrugged off her coat as well, leaving her in a dark red T-shirt, a pair of heavy black jeans faded almost to silver tucked into knee boots. She was wearing gloves as finely scaled as fish skin, the same bright silvery metal as the sword, with gauntlets that reached almost to her elbows.

"I saw only one, were there more?"

"What?"

Max dragged in a lungful of cold air. You always thought you were in great shape until you had to run for your life. Then you wished you'd spent more time at the gym.

"The Hound, I saw only one."

"Uh, yes, I think so."

Cassandra nodded, "We have a chance, then."

Max watched as she crept forward, her eyes focused on the opening of the alley. Light from the streetlamp touched the curve of her cheek like a lover's fingertip. Max took a deep breath and let it out slowly. Cassandra tilted her head, straining to listen. Max could hear nothing over the sound of his own breathing. He edged closer to have a look for himself. Without turning, Cassandra put her palm flat against his chest and held him back from the edge of the wall.

"Stay behind me."

"Cassandra, it's me, Max."

"I'm quite capable of recognizing you, Mr. Ravenhill, thank you." Her cool tone took Max right back to the party where they had met. He almost laughed.

"Just not capable of returning my phone calls."

She spared him a glance over her shoulder before returning to her look out. "Which would you prefer? That I stay by the phone ready to return your calls, or that I pull you out of the cars of people trying to kidnap you?"

"Well, if it's one or the other, I choose the bit with the cars."

"Everything's turned out well, then, hasn't it?" She flicked another glance at him. "Did they hurt you? Were you bitten?"

Max shook his head. "I banged my head, but I feel okay."

Cassandra took another quick look at the street and bent down over her shoulder bag. After rummaging for a moment she retrieved a short, thick-bladed knife and held it out to Max.

"Here," she said. "Watch the edge. You can cut off a finger if you're not careful. If the Hound gets past me, use it."

Max told hold of the knife, surprised to find how heavy it was, but how comfortable and familiar the hilt felt in his hand. "If you can't stop it with your sword, I should use this?"

"Not on the Hound, on yourself."

"Ah, that clears things up."

"Here it comes. Stay back, and don't look it in the eye."

Now Max could hear it, the soft sound of a dog's great paws, padding along the concrete. Faster than he could have imagined possible the large dog he had seen in the car rounded the corner of the alley, moving so quickly it almost lost its balance as its claws scratched for traction on the slick concrete.

Max realized that the trouble he'd had focusing in the car had not all been because of the blow to his head. The shape of the creature, of the Hound, was changing, flickering around the edges even when the central shape remained the same. It changed twice in the time it took to round the corner, its dog's fur morphing to leathery skin, to scales, and back to fur.

As soon as it saw Cassandra it leaped, and for a moment Max thought she wouldn't be able to get out of its way. Faster than he could follow, she ducked and twisted, the sword whistling through the air, but even as it leaped, the creature changed form. What landed was not hound, but a kind of chimera, its lion's head maned with snakes, and its dragon's tail spiked. After scrabbling to regain its balance, it headed straight for him. Max raised the little knife and, feeling how inadequate it was as a weapon, snatched up the only other thing to hand, Cassandra's shoulder bag, and threw it into the creature's face.

It stopped abruptly in mid-leap and fell back, but not from the bonk on the nose he'd given it. Cassandra had grabbed its spiked tail as it passed her and hauled back on it, slicing the tail off at the root with a quick downward cut of her sword. She wiped her glove clean on her jeans, and with the same motion pulled a long dagger out of her boot. The chimera turned its attention back to her, twisting in midair and flickering into yet another monster, hydra-headed with the body of a lizard, both heads and claws reaching out for her. But its injury transformed with it, leaving it tailless and bleeding. Cassandra struck off the left-hand head as it foolishly turned to look at its lack of tail, but even as blood gouted, spattering them both with hot drops, the head grew back. Cassandra held it at bay for a few moments, her blades at the ready as it circled her, looking for an opportunity to lunge.

"Stay behind me," she called, as she dashed forward to slash at the creature's foreleg, her hair flying loose. "It's trying to split us up." Max nodded and shifted his own position. The creature lunged again, and Max lost track of the action as Cassandra moved with blurring speed and the thing flickered through half a dozen further changes before settling into a leathery, scaled parody of a griffin. Max glanced around and spotted Cassandra's bag where it had fallen after bouncing off the Hound's face. He dashed forward and picked it up, wrapping the straps around his fist, and took an experimental swing. With any luck, he could manage a head blow.

In the meantime Cassandra, breathing hard, had landed another cut, this time to the creature's shoulder. Blood flowed freely, but its injuries didn't seem to slow it down. It kept circling, and Max realized that it was maneuvering the woman into the pool of blood.

"Watch your feet, there's blood on the ground."

Cassandra grinned as if he'd just given her good news. *I'm glad one of us is having a good time,* he thought.

Cassandra's right heel skidded, her hands went up, her blades flying into the air, and the creature lunged forward, snatching at her head with its neck outstretched. Desperately, Max swung the leather bag, catching the lunging beast on the side of its head. Its saucer eye flicked toward him, its clawed foot flashed out, but the beast continued moving forward, stepping into its own blood and slipping in its turn. Cassandra twisted on the heel that was still on dry ground, caught her blades in the opposite hands as they came down, stabbed her dagger into the creature's reaching limb, pulling it toward her, encouraging its slide, and simultaneously bringing down her sword left-handed on its outstretched neck.

The creature dropped in its tracks, momentum taking Cassandra down with it, its head bouncing off the wall and rolling to a rest at Max's feet. It flickered again, ringing the changes on every form Max had seen, and a few that he hadn't, until it finally took a twisted human form, a man's thin and wasted face, eyes staring, before it faded completely away. The alley was once again empty and quiet, as clean as it had been when they entered it. No beast, no blood, except what still steamed on their clothing. Cassandra was back on her feet with blades still raised to strike, breathing hard, and grinning, a tear in her T-shirt showing not skin but another gleam of metal.

"You did that on purpose," Max accused her, "made it think you'd slipped in the blood."

"They like to kill, it makes them too eager."

"How about you? Do you like it?" Now that the adrenaline was seeping out of him, it was all Max could do to control the shaking of his hands. How could she stand there, smiling?

She took a deep breath and looked at him, the light fading from her face, the smile gone.

"You're bleeding, where did it get you?"

"What? Nowhere . . ." Max's stomach clenched, and even as he spoke, his knees gave way for the second time that evening, but this time Cassandra caught him before he could hit the ground. He clutched at her arm, getting a handful of strangely warm metal gauntlet. A tremor began in his hand, moved up his arm, and claimed the rest of his body. Dimly he heard the knife "chink" as it fell from his other hand to the pavement. A spot on his left side, down near the hipbone, felt very cold, and the coldness spread, and a shhhhhhhhhh of static in his head grew louder and louder as his body floated farther and farther away.

Cassandra hissed, and Max felt her hand, warmer than the metal glove should allow, press firmly on the icy wound in his side. He could feel her arms cradling him, feel her shift on the cold concrete until his head fell back on her shoulder. She put her mouth on his lips and breathed. And breathed. And *BREATHED*. And his body soaked up her breath like a dry wick soaks up oil, filling itself with her warmth and air and sweetness, and still Cassandra breathed. Until Max began to fear that he would empty her, until the cold place in his side finally became warm and Max took a deep, shuddering breath.

"What the hell was that?" He'd been dying, he was sure of it, and somehow Cassandra had stopped it, had made it simply . . . go away. His side, under the torn and bloody cotton shirt, wasn't even sore. He cleared his throat. His voice sounded as though he hadn't used it in weeks, and he could feel the exhilaration of being alive already beginning to fade. Cassandra picked up the short-bladed knife from where it had fallen and tossed it into her bag as she walked stiffly over to where her coat lay next to the loading dock. She kept her face turned away from him as she crouched down on her heels, wiping her perfectly clean blades on the skirt of the coat. She glanced back at him as he got to his feet, but otherwise acted as if nothing had happened. As if she hadn't just saved his life. Twice.

"Do you know what I mean when I say the Hunt?"

Max blinked as he mentally changed gears. If that was what she wanted to talk about, he was willing to play along. But soon she'd have to explain what it was she'd done . . . and how.

"Well, folklore's not my field, but I believe there are several schools of thought—" Max broke off as Cassandra raised her eyebrows. "Okay, I take it you mean the Wild Hunt? So there's huntsmen, horses, hounds—

some say human spirits—but most agree it's something to do with the Sidhe." Max leaned back on the edge of the loading dock as if it was the chalk ledge of a blackboard and crossed his arms.

"Specifically the Trouping Faerie, yes? They hunted some kind of supernatural prey, didn't they?" Max shook his head slowly. It was crazy, it was impossible, but he had seen what he had seen. "That's what *that* was? One of the Sidhe?"

Cassandra put her coat back on and slipped the long thin dagger back into her boot, her hand trembling ever so slightly. "It's the same with all the stories, a little bit right, and a little bit wrong. The Hunt is not made up of what you call the Sidhe, it *hunts* the Sidhe."

Max handed Cassandra her bag, but took a step back instead of helping her as she slung it over her head and adjusted it until it hung along her back. Of all the crazy— "I don't get it. You mean that thing was after *you*?"

Cassandra gave a final shrug to her bag and turned until she was looking him in the face.

"No, my lord. It was after you."

# Chapter Two

"I'M GOING HOME," Max said, relieved to find his voice steady, if not his hands. He moved his head slowly from side to side, lips pressed tight. None of this was happening, and he'd stop thinking about it as soon as he could. "I appreciate your help, but you've got the wrong guy."

"If they're not there already," Cassandra said, "home's the first place they'll look."

Max looked down at the blood on his clothes, his own already drying, tacky and chill, the Hound's blood still wet and gleaming where it had splashed on him. He raised his head. The sidewalk at the end of the alley looked so ordinary. Any minute now his legs would move and he'd walk down there, turn right and go on down to King Street, catch the streetcar, go home, and put on the hockey game.

"You doubt they're after you?" she said, her voice brittle. "Maybe I should have left you in the car a little longer."

"All of you people are making a mistake," he said, eyes fixed on the world he'd always known. "Whoever it is you're looking for, I'm not him." He looked back at Cassandra to find her nodding at him, as if they were sitting over coffee, discussing the Peloponnesian conflict and she was considering his point, finding a polite way to tell him he was full of it.

"We can talk about that when you're safe," she said. "You didn't seem inclined to argue with the Hound," she added, when Max opened his mouth.

Once again Max felt the Hound's misshapen hands, pulling him into the car, saw the look of feral recognition in the beast's eyes as it approached him, felt the coldness in his wound before Cassandra had healed him, and he shivered, whatever argument he was about to offer dying in the cold. She was right, he wasn't inclined to argue with the Hound.

"And, frankly," Cassandra added, ignoring his trembling as if she hadn't seen it, her voice neutral again, matter-of-fact, "I would prefer not to argue with whoever sent the Hound either."

"Oh, I don't know," Max said, forcing a lightness he didn't feel into his tone. "Maybe we could get all this straightened out." Cassandra hitched up her shoulder bag and looked away. "Okay, then, you seem to have all the answers." His voice was harsher than he intended. "Where to?"

Cassandra turned back to him and took his hands, standing so close that Max thought she was going to kiss him. He parted his lips and inclined his head.

A SLAP! of air sucked the breath from his lungs and a loud CRACK! like a thunderclap deafened him.

"What the—" The darkness was so complete Max couldn't tell if his eyes were open or closed. Suddenly there was a great rumbling overhead, and a rush of movement filled the darkness around him, followed by a subdued moaning howl. Disoriented by the dark, it took him a minute to place the sound as metal wheels hugging metal tracks around a curve. *Streetcar?* he thought. *No, not a streetcar, the subway.*

"We're safer *here?*" From the hollow echo, the space they were in was quite large, and quite empty. It also seemed at least ten degrees cooler and much damper than the alley.

Max heard Cassandra sigh in the darkness as she let go of his hands. He clenched his fists against the urge to grab at her and took a slow, careful breath.

"So where are we?" he persisted.

"If you're going to be distracted by unrelated matters, this is going to take much longer than it needs to."

Max reached toward her voice and grabbed a handful of sleeve.

"Remember me?" he said around the tightness in his throat. "I'm the one who doesn't know what's going on. How do I know what's related and what's not?" he asked the darkness around them.

"We're in the abandoned Queen Street Station." Once again her voice was drowned out by a roar, and a rush of air as somewhere nearby an empty station was suddenly filled by a hundred and eighty tons of subway train.

"Can I ask why?"

"We need a crossroads," she said, taking hold of his wrist and freeing her sleeve from his hand. She spoke like a teacher, as if she were repeating the same lesson for the hundredth time but still found it interesting. The tone was familiar, soothing, and Max was surprised to find the muscles in his neck and shoulders loosening. He felt more than heard her move away from him in the darkness. "In this world, the land's *dra'aj*—its magical essence, for want of a better term—concentrates in Lines, so to Move any real distance quickly, we need a crossroads. And to be safe, we'll need to put some real distance between us and the Hunt."

Max gestured in the darkness. "This is a crossroads?"

"Union Station is the crossroads. Using it is tricky. We can't just Move straight to it because there's a Portal to our Lands there as well, and we don't want to trigger it by accident, so we'll have to walk from here."

Max shook his head. Some of that made a kind of

sense. What were train stations but huge crossroads, and Union was the largest and busiest of Canada's train stations. He wanted to get somewhere safe as badly as Cassandra did, maybe more so. He just wasn't sure they had the same idea of safety. He needed time to think, to find out what they wanted with him, and—most of all—time to figure out the flaw that made them think he was one of them, the flaw that would free him. But how were they going to get anywhere in this darkness?

"Couldn't we have come straight here? How come you didn't Move—" he tried to give the word the same emphasis she had, "us away from the Hound?"

"What, you think I should have stood still in the middle of Queen Street? Tried to Move us from there?" Judging from the tone of her voice Cassandra was rolling her eyes to the heavens. "Besides," she added more evenly, "once the Hunt is on a trail, it can follow you through a Move. You can't leave it alive behind you."

Max nodded in the darkness. That figured. He blinked rapidly, realizing that he could now make out a soft glow, just beyond arm's length. As his eyes adjusted, he saw that Cassandra had taken off her coat and pulled off her T-shirt. She was on her knees beside her leather shoulder bag, taking the sword out and placing it to one side so she could rummage through the bag. Max saw that the glow came from the mail shirt he'd caught a glimpse of through the tear in her T-shirt while they were in the alley. Soft as it was, the light was clear enough that he could see the skin on her arms forming into goose bumps. He shivered again.

Lit from below, Cassandra's features were sterner, the color washed out, the hollows of her cheeks and eyes darkened into angles until her face resembled an old bronze mask of the Athene Nike that Max had once seen at the Royal Ontario Museum. Then the mask moved, and Cassandra's human face returned. Max pushed himself back from her, finding himself unexpectedly close. *Except she isn't human,* he thought.

"You're a faerie," he said, not sure until she looked up that he'd spoken aloud.

"We don't call ourselves that," she said, starting to take cloth-wrapped bundles out of her shoulder bag, one of them another, shorter sword, and laying them next to the long sword already on the dirty pavement.

"So what *do* you call yourselves?" Max said, when it became apparent she had nothing further to say.

"The People, of course, same as any other sentient race."

Max stepped closer to her. "You know other sentient races?"

She sat back on her heels and looked up again.

"Well, I have my doubts about humans, now that you mention it." She frowned. "What humans call the Trouping Faerie—beings like you and me—we call ourselves Riders, because we . . ."

"Ride?"

"Yes, actually. We're social, we live in groups and we Move. Solitaries . . . well, that's self-explanatory, isn't it? They're the People who live alone, Trolls, Ogres, and Giants are the ones best known to humans. Then there are Naturals—they're like Solitaries, but they live in one place, mostly Trees and Water People."

"And would I be right in thinking that you all live together, in harmony?"

"You're the professor of military history, you tell me."

Max nodded, not really surprised that she knew so much about him. He would have liked it better, however, if she knew things about him because she was a normal human woman, interested in a normal human man, instead of a . . . a *Rider,* mistaking him for something he wasn't. "How much like humans are you?"

She stood, holding something round, flat, and thick, still wrapped in its protective cloth. "Imagine Riders are like Men—we have our own races, too, Sunward, Moonward—" she pointed at him, "—and Starward—" she pointed at herself, "and Solitaries are, say, dolphins, whales, and sharks. Naturals are the Everglades, the Oceans, the Rain Forest. How well do you figure we're getting along?"

"Ah," Max said.

"Exactly." Cassandra untwisted the cloth in her hands to reveal a heavy silvery torque, almost as bright and obviously made of the same metal as her mail shirt. She placed the torque around her throat so that the ends rested on her collarbones. As soon as it touched her skin, it glowed brighter.

Now Max could see that they were standing quite close to the edge of what could have been a subway platform, if you took away a century's worth of dirt and damage. The wall close to their backs arched over their heads—though not very far over, he thought. Either of them could easily touch the ceiling with a little stretching. But on the other side of the sunken tracks there was no matching platform. Instead, the space opened out, farther than he could see in the light given off by Cassandra's armor. He could make out no ceiling, just a couple of round columns thick as old oak trees, thick enough to hold up the whole city over their heads. Faint gleams showed where water lay still and silent between the old pillars.

"I've heard about this place," he said, his voice sounding louder somehow, now that there was more light. "People say it's a myth."

"People say that about us, too."

Max turned back to her, his wonder once more replaced by irritation. "Look, before this goes any further—why don't you just tell me what's going on? I know you've got the wrong man; I could clear this up in a second—"

She was on her feet, her face suddenly inches from his own.

"You're a Faerie Prince. You lost a war and were Exiled. Now, for some reason, they're trying to kill you. Does that clear it up for you? Happy now?"

"But I'm not—" Max stopped talking as she raised her hand, palm up, placed his own palm against hers and kept on. "You're making a mistake, you only met me the other night."

Cassandra lowered her hand and pressed her fingers to her eyes, took a deep breath, and let it out slowly; it fogged in the underground air.

"*I* don't have the wrong man. *They* aren't hunting the wrong man. I didn't just meet you the other night," she said, biting off the words. "We've met many times. You just don't remember." She let her hand drop from her face. "I know you have a thousand questions," she said, her voice low and tight. "I swear to you, I will give you all the answers I have. *Somewhere safe.*"

Max hesitated. It *couldn't* be true. He knew who he was. But she was so certain, and she sure wasn't human, she had that part right and . . .

"You could have *died* in that alley," she said. "I only killed one Hound; do you bet your life there are no others? Shall we still be standing here arguing when the Hunt finds us?"

For an instant Max felt again the bone-deep chill that almost claimed him in the alley.

Max studied Cassandra's face. The mask of the goddess of battles was well and truly gone. Cassandra's hair had crinkled further in the damp, and there was a smudge of dirt and bright blood on her face. He was raising his hand to wipe it away when he remembered whose blood it was. The Hound had been real, he reminded himself. And the woman in front of him was real. More than real, somehow. As if the world came into focus around her. As if everything close to her was somehow . . . *truer*.

"I believe you," he said, hearing the truth in his own voice. And he did believe her. She would tell him everything she could . . . once they were safe. He would have his chance to figure it out, explain how they got it wrong. He pulled in a ragged breath of his own, looking away from a face that had become somehow more frightening than the face of Athene.

Cassandra held still a heartbeat longer before turning back to her open bag. "Did you ever go in for any weapons training?" she asked.

"That's a funny way to put it," Max said, glad of the change of subject. "But no."

"None of this will be of any use to you, then," she said, frowning at the cloth-wrapped bundles she'd taken out of her bag. Now that he looked closely, Max could see by the shapes that some of the items at least were daggers, and others looked like arrows, though he could see no bow.

"What, no guns?"

"Guns won't kill the Hunt, only *gra'if* does, and god knows where yours might be."

"That what this is?" He brushed the tips of his fingers against Cassandra's body armor. "Got any more?" He'd been dying to see what it was made of, but he found himself somehow reluctant to actually touch it.

"Mine won't work for you."

"What makes it glow?" The light, moving as Cassandra moved, prevented Max from seeing much more of what was in her unzipped shoulder bag.

"My personality."

"Smart-ass."

When he looked up, Cassandra was smiling the first genuine smile he'd ever seen on her face. He found it easy to smile back at her.

She pushed her hands through her hair, and her smile slowly faded.

"What is it?"

"My hair clip." She knelt and scanned the ground around their feet. "I must have dropped it in the alley."

"I hope you're not planning to go back for it." Max crouched to help her hold the side of the bag open. "What's this?" he picked up a light helm that lay to one side of the bag, loosely wrapped in silk. It was warm, and it seemed to hum with the faintest of vibrations, as if a charge ran through it. Odd, but not unpleasant. She was quite right, he thought, this wouldn't fit him. Even in the uncertain light, Max could see the helmet, very little more than a coronet hung with fine mesh, was fancifully carved, with a beast's face on the guard that would rest just above and between Cassandra's eyes. Max found that he could make out even the finest of the carved scales, even the teeth in the beast's mouth.

"My Guidebeast," she said, taking the helm from him and sliding it into the bag.

"A dragon?"

"You have good eyes."

Anther rush of air, another roaring moan overhead. Max looked up. This time a smell came with it, a smell like an old dirt-floored cellar. It was ancient but curiously clean, damp earth and wet concrete. Still, the ceiling was so close above his head that even those huge pillars didn't make him confident that everything wouldn't come crashing down.

"Okay, so if we want Union, we go that way, right?" Straightening to his feet again, Max pointed south.

Cassandra shook her head. "There's no direct route, not anymore. We'll have to go around the long way."

Max shook his head, rolling his eyes to the damp splotches on the tunnel's roof. "Why am I not surprised?"

Cassandra packed the last of her daggers back into her shoulder bag, zipped it almost shut and slipped in her longer sword before slinging the bag once more over her shoulder. She would have liked to have the sword in her hand—that's where it felt most natural—but she'd need her hands for other things. Besides, anything that came at them faster than she could draw her sword—well, she wasn't going to worry about it.

She glanced once over her shoulder, checking to see that Max followed, before leading the way past a bricked-over opening that had once been intended as a pedestrian exit from the platform. The concrete underfoot was uneven and cracked. Rough-poured and left untiled in the first place, it was now showing the signs of years of water damage and uneven heating.

Cassandra took a deep breath and rotated her shoulders as she walked, trying to relax muscles as tight as steel cable. She couldn't remember the last time she'd had so much trouble saving someone's life—well, actually, she could, and now that she thought about it, it was the same someone. The Exile always thought he knew better, no matter who he happened to be at the moment. Fine, he was often right, but he never realized that there were some situations you couldn't talk your way out of. She hadn't meant to lose her temper, but somehow she'd known it was going to happen ever since she'd seen Max Ravenhill at the cocktail party. Their eyes had met, and she'd felt that familiar jolt, as everything in the world rearranged itself around them. She'd spent the last two hundred and fifty years—six of his lifetimes—avoiding that feeling, and fighting the urge to experience it once more.

He was too much the same, and different enough that the sameness couldn't help her. As usual, his response to strange events and stranger beings was more curiosity than confusion—he'd always been able to adapt easily. Malcolm, who was Stormbringer the Singer, had wondered whether this, too, was part of his fundamental nature, something left over from when the Exile was the Prince Guardian.

Right now Cassandra felt as though she hadn't slept since Diggory the Solitary had come to give her warning. Her shoulder hurt, and she knew that soon the long muscles in her thighs would start to twitch and cramp. She'd been running on adrenaline since pulling the Exile out of the blue sedan, and killing the Hound—she pushed that thought away. She could think about that later when she had leisure to be terrified.

Still, half an hour, give or take a few minutes, and they would be close enough to the crossroads for her to

Move them. Once in the Australian outback, they'd be safe. The Portal there was long destroyed, in the last Cycle according to what the Songs told, though the crossroads still existed. No Rider, and precious few humans, would think to look for them there.

Of course, then, instead of collapsing into a warm bed to nurse her bruises and rest her sore muscles, she'd have to think about what to tell the Exile. Anyone else would be satisfied with having his life saved, but not him—oh, no. All the answers she had, she'd promised him. She'd told him the truth before, more than once, and he'd believed her, every time. But something told Cassandra that Max Ravenhill wasn't going to be so easy to convince. In the old days, perfectly ordinary people were ready to believe in the strange truths that were outside their own experience. In this day, even bards and prophets weren't likely to recognize truth when they heard it.

Besides, she'd promised herself that she'd never tell him this particular truth again.

Cassandra reached the end of the platform and peered over the edge. She was prepared to jump down into the track bed, but though the old iron ladder was much rustier than she remembered, it held firm when she gave it a good kick. She swung herself around and let herself down, rung by rung, and waited at the bottom of the ladder so that Max could see his way down.

Enough light shone from her armor that Cassandra could just make out, about two yards away, the bottom of the narrow, concrete steps leading up out of the tunnel into the maintenance shaft for the station adjacent to this one, the real station. Cassandra squinted. Was there a shadow where one had never been before? She let go of the iron ladder and walked closer to the steps.

"Hey."

Cassandra ignored him; even concentrating as she was, she could tell Max was annoyed, not scared. Let him move faster if he didn't want to be left in the dark.

*Damn.* One of the support columns *had* crumbled since the last time she had been through here and blocked the opening at the top of the stair. She took a step back and bumped into Max.

"Can't you Move it?"

It took Cassandra a second to realize what he was saying.

"We're Riders, we can only Move what lives." She touched the rubble gingerly, laying the palm of her hand carefully on a large chunk of concrete. It was old, and there was enough natural rock and sand in the mix that a Troll could probably shift it, she thought. Where was Diggory when she needed him?

"Well, we won't shift this mess ourselves," Max pointed out, in a warped echo of her own thinking. "Not without a backhoe, anyway."

Cassandra worried her bottom lip between her teeth. As much as she might feel like it, there was no arguing with that. And where there was a choice between two dangers . . .

"There's another way," she said as she turned back to retrace their steps, "but we'll have to go through a tunnel that's in use."

"Somehow I had a feeling that was coming."

Max followed Cassandra in silence as she led him back up the ladder to the platform. When they reached the bricked-over opening, she slipped out of her shoulder bag and handed it to him.

"We're going to pull *this* down?"

She ignored his tone and answered his question. "Can you see up there, at the top of the arch? That bit where it's darker? Whoever bricked this didn't bother to fill in the very top. They knew the passageway behind this was being filled, so they were sloppy about it."

Max watched, holding her bag, as Cassandra moved nimbly up the wall, finding finger- and toeholds in the crumbling mortar between the old bricks.

"What use is this to us if it's filled in?"

"There's a crawl space." She looked down at him, hanging by fingers and toes. "What, no smart remark?"

Max's lips twisted in irritation, and only partly because he *had* been trying to come up with something to say about Riders having to crawl. What did she want from him? Here he thought he'd been holding up pretty well, given the number of impossible things he'd seen and done in the last few hours.

"I'm not saying I wouldn't rather be sitting in a nice pub with a pint," he said. "But if my alternative is the Hunt, I'm willing to concede that there are worse things than crawling in underground tunnels."

Cassandra grinned at him. "Glad to see you haven't lost your sense of humor," she said, as she reached the top.

Max fought down another wave of irritation. Whether or not he believed her preposterous assertions, Cassandra certainly acted as if she knew him inside and out.

And didn't like him much.

He watched her wriggle into the dark hole at the top of the arch; her legs waved in the air a couple of times before disappearing. A second later her face appeared in the opening. There was a new smudge obscuring the blood on her left cheek.

"Pass up my bag."

Max picked up the bag and held it up above his head at arm's length, just high enough for Cassandra to reach it and pull it into the hole with her.

"Need any help getting up?"

Max didn't need to see her face clearly to know she was smiling again. Or smirking, more like it. He shook out his arms and legs and, bending his knees only slightly, jumped up and hooked his fingers in the top layer of brick, inches from Cassandra's face. He drew himself up, careful to breathe normally, until their noses were almost touching.

"Want to give me some room here?" he asked, pleased that his voice didn't show the strain his arms were feeling.

With the only available light attached to Cassandra, crawling along in the semidarkness took longer than a history professor could have imagined. There wasn't enough space to get on his hands and knees, and dragging himself along was hard work on the elbows. Max had time to think about the tons of rock—and steam pipes, and rusty support columns, and maybe subway trains—above them, and time to wonder what they would do if they found the other end blocked. It didn't seem likely that he would be able to turn around in this confined space, and he could only hope that Cassandra could Move them somewhere from here.

Preferably somewhere aboveground where they could walk to Union Station in the upper air. Or maybe take a cab. Crawling was much harder work than he would have thought, and at one point they passed a spot where they were separated from what must have been live steam lines by only a few inches of concrete.

Once a train passed nearby, deafening them with the screaming of wheels, and sending an earthquake-sized rumbling through their little space.

"Finally some luck," Cassandra said, her voice pale in the quiet left by the train. "That train went through the tunnel we're heading for. It will be clear for us."

Max grunted, trying to keep his breathing steady, and continued to shuffle forward. After what seemed like another mile, he bumped his nose on Cassandra's boot-heel, and swallowed a curse.

"Here we are," she said over her shoulder, "Are you ready?"

"As ready as I'll ever be," Max said. He thought about the spot on his side where the Hound had wounded him and wondered if Cassandra would be able to fix him if he were hit by a subway train. Of course, if they were both hit, it wouldn't matter.

Max heard a soft thump that could only be Cassandra's shoulder bag hitting the floor of the tunnel below them. The space had narrowed here, but somehow Cassandra managed to wriggle around so that she could go out feet first. She hung by her fingers for a second before she let go. Max moved forward as quickly as he could so as not to lose the light. He peered out over the edge at her. She was wiping her hands on her jeans.

*Exercise in futility*, Max thought; they were both as filthy as crawling through rubble-filled, hundred-year-old tunnels could make them. With some relief Max saw that the electrified third rail was on the side farthest from their exit hole.

"Max, we haven't got a lot of time."

Max came out of his reverie with a start. "There isn't enough room here for me to turn around," he said. Even if he was limber enough to do it, which he had been when he was six. Maybe. His only option was to go out head first.

He looked more closely at the wall beneath him and snorted. Of course, the hole they were coming out of was at center of the tunnel, with no wall or support column anywhere near.

"Wriggle out," she said. "I'll catch you."

"The hell you will," he muttered. But really, what choice did he have? He edged forward until he was hanging by his hipbones, the edge of the rough cement cutting painfully into the tops of his thighs. He craned his neck to look at Cassandra, but that movement arched his back too much for balance and he started to slip—

"Don't look at me, just reach down."

He did as he was told. Two hands clamped painfully around his upper arms, and before he knew it, he had been dragged out of the hole and was being shoved upright.

"There, that's better."

Max was glad she thought so; he was going to have bruises on his arms to match the ones on the front of his thighs. He looked around. This tunnel was the tidy younger brother of the one in the abandoned station. There were lights here and—

And a rumbling.

"Oh, shit," he said, even as Cassandra knocked the breath out of him, pressing him against the wall with her own body. Max wrapped his arms around her and hung on for dear life.

Max had an instant to register the feeling of Cassandra's body pressed against his, thigh against thigh, breasts flattened against his chest; to breathe in the saffron scent of her hair, to realize that her armor was pliable and ever-so-slightly warmer, not colder, than her skin— then the wall of air pushed through the tunnel by the train behind it slammed into them.

Some indeterminate time later, the world stopped shaking.

"Max."

"Hmmmm."

"You have to let go of me."

Max loosened his grip just enough to be able to look her in the eyes. "I know what you're thinking."

"Of course you do," she said in a tired voice. "Bards and Poets always think they know what other people are thinking."

"Well, I'm a history teacher, so what does that prove?"

"It proves you study the wrong kind of history, not to know that Bards and Poets were the history teachers before there were people like you."

Max shrugged without letting go of her. She had moved her hands so that her palms were flat against his chest, but she wasn't pushing him away. "Were they usually right, or wrong?"

The look Cassandra gave him was as good an answer as any, and Max smiled.

"Very well, what am I thinking?" she said.

"You're thinking that this," he tightened his hold and moved against her ever so slightly so that she could be in no doubt as to what he meant, "is just a reaction to almost dying . . . several times. It isn't." Max's voice lowered as his teasing tone died away, and he knew that he'd never been more serious. "It isn't."

He felt Cassandra begin to tremble. By the time she was actually laughing out loud, Max let her go and she collapsed to the floor, holding her sides and trying to draw in enough air to take a deep breath.

"I didn't think it was that funny."

"I'm so sorry, really, my deepest apologies, it's just," she took another deep breath. The laughter faded slowly, but it did fade. "That isn't at all what I expected you to say."

"Which was?" Max held out his hand and drew her to her feet.

"I expected you to tell me what I was thinking."

*"Which was?"* he repeated through clenched teeth.

The echo of her laughter reappeared for a moment on her face. "Oh, no, Bard you may be, or history teacher as you prefer, but you don't get my thoughts as easily as that. When we reach safety, I said, and that's what I meant."

"You might reach safety a little faster, Truthsheart, if you were less noisy about it."

One second Cassandra was facing him, smile fading on her face, the next she had her back to him, knees bent, sword drawn and point raised to eye level. Max tried to step around her—or at least beside her; whoever it was seemed ready to talk, after all—but no matter how he moved, she managed to stay in front of him.

The person coming toward them through the shadows created by the uneven lighting loomed grotesque and misshapen. A Gargantua that dwarfed a tunnel big enough to contain a subway train. Max couldn't shake the chilling feeling that what he saw was actually an indescribable distance away, making the figure horribly larger than he could imagine. And yet, through some trick of perspective, the giant seemed to become smaller and less misshapen as it neared them. Until it stepped into the clear soft light cast by Cassandra's armor and became much shorter than either Max or Cassandra. Became, in fact, a small boy, complete with beanie cap and skateboard.

Max shook his head. "I must be more tired than I thought," he said.

"Are you well, Younger Sister?" The boy's voice was the soft croak of a kid with a cold.

"A little startled, Elder Brother, but otherwise well, I thank you. I thank you also for the true warning you gave me."

"You guys know each other?"

"This is the third time we have met," Cassandra said.

"Third time lucky, so they say." With those words the boy tilted his head to look at Max. "Like yourself, my lord Prince, I am not entirely what I seem."

His voice deepened into gravel while he spoke, and by the end of the sentence the childlike seeming had fallen from the boy like a discarded cloak. Max took a step backward as the figure grew taller, wider, until it had to stoop, its shoulders pressing against the top of the subway tunnel. He was the pale gray of limestone, even his eyes, with only the pupils black, even the inside of his mouth, even his sharp teeth.

*Troll*, said a voice in Max's head.

Max's lungs felt tight, and then he remembered to breathe. Cassandra touched him on the arm, and he managed not to flinch.

"Max," she said, "this is Diggory."

Max managed to incline his head to the Troll's shallow bow.

"How did you find us?" she said.

"Think where you are, Truthsheart. The Earth guides me."

"And can *they* find us as well?"

*Damn good question*, Max thought, glad of something else to think about. Those were awfully sharp teeth.

"There are no Solitaries among them, but Those Who Hunt eventually find, and this time I think sooner rather than later. Knowing you make for the crossroads, they are already in the tunnels. I think you must use the Portal; they will not expect that."

"I cannot take the Exile through the Portal," Cassandra said. "The end of the Banishment may be near, but it is not ended. His life would be forfeit and mine as well."

"His life's forfeit here, if the Hunt has its way. Those Who Hunt will follow your Moves, but they cannot follow through the Portal, not without a Rider to help them. Even with my help," he added when she still hesitated, "you cannot kill them all. It may be that you have no choice."

"Wait a minute, no choice about what?"

Diggory grinned as Cassandra looked back and forth between them, frowning.

"You've said that the Prince's safety had value above all other things," she said finally. "Do you hold to that now?"

"Younger Sister, I do. I will guard your back, Sword of Truth. But we must go now."

Cassandra waited a long moment before nodding. "Very well." She turned to Max and laid a gentle hand on his arm. "Please, trust me."

"But—" he turned back to the Troll, and wasn't really surprised to find the boy Diggory back, skateboard and all.

"I see you are full of questions, my lord Prince, but I advise you to follow your Warden. The time for answers has not yet come."

"That's what *she* keeps telling me."

With Diggory right behind him, Max caught up with Cassandra just as she reached the iron ladder that would let them up onto the platform. He could tell from the color and shape of the tiles, even before he was close enough to read the signs, that they were already at the subway station at Union, only two levels and maybe a hundred yards away from the train station proper.

At first he was surprised to see the platform empty, but once they were all off the ladder and he could make out the platform clock, he understood. Somehow it had gotten to be after two in the morning; the theaters that kept the downtown streets crowded were long closed, and the bars would have given last call. The train that almost got them must have been empty, on its way to bed in the yards.

As Cassandra headed for the exit at the far end of platform, Max edged closer to her. Maybe there were *some* questions that could be answered now.

"Why does he look like a little boy?" Max kept his voice whisper quiet.

"The better to lure my prey, my lord Prince." Though he'd reverted to his boy shape, Diggory's voice was still gravelly and booming.

"What kind of . . . oh." It didn't take much imagination to figure out what could be lured into dark alleys by a young child. "So is it children or child molesters?"

"Ah, I had not thought of that." Max could swear the Troll was laughing. "Has to be the one or the other, does it?" The Troll made a gusty sound that Max realized was a chuckle, but said nothing more.

"Ignore him," Cassandra advised. "That's all the answer you're going to get. He's trying to distract you."

"And he's good at it," Max said, shaking away the images in his head.

Cassandra had almost reached the exit, with Max close on her heels, when she skidded to a stop, reversed her direction, grabbed Max by the elbow, and propelled him back the way they'd come.

"What the—" Max looked back over his shoulder, and what he saw encouraged him to run faster.

"Go," Diggory growled as they passed him. "These are mine." As he spoke, he was already changing, and by the time Max looked back again, the little boy was gone, and the Troll was back.

They rounded the corner on the platform's other exit and were pounding up the stairs when the screaming started.

Max stopped, hesitated, and took two steps back.

"Max."

He looked up to Cassandra, above him on the stairs. She was smiling a grim smile.

"Trust me, that's not his voice." When Max still didn't move to follow her, she added, "He's buying us time to get away. Let's not waste it."

It didn't seem right to run away. Smart, but not right.

Max followed Cassandra up the stairs to the street level, and through the one-way turnstiles. She banged through the plate glass street doors so fast he almost didn't realize they'd been locked. They ran across the deserted street, and, watching now, he saw the locks "pop" as Cassandra wrenched open the doors to Union Station. This end of the station was the shopping level, and they ran past closed and darkened storefronts, heading for the exits on the far side that led to the train levels.

Now it was Cassandra's turn to hesitate.

"What?"

"This should be close enough, but . . ." She closed her eyes, forehead wrinkling in concentration. "We'll have to go up another level." She headed for an escalator, motionless now, and once again Max followed, by this time thoroughly confused. Street level at the subway end of the train station wasn't street level through the whole station, he realized as they went up.

They had reached the top of the escalators and passed into the lower level of the train station proper when they heard the howling, and the skittery sound of paws with ragged nails against the terrazzo floor. Max glanced back in time to see a large, light-colored dog with liver markings come into sight at the bottom of the motionless stairs. Behind it, incredibly quickly and silently, moved the Troll. When he saw Max looking at him, Diggory grinned and placed his huge clawed finger against his lips. The Troll then reached forward and grabbed the Hound by its tail, exactly as a small child might grab a pet dog that was trying to get away from it.

Max hoped never to see a child do to a pet dog what the Troll did to the Hound.

"Max, over here."

Max was happy to turn his eyes away. Cassandra was beckoning from behind an ornate marble counter, once part of the original ticket booth and now, from the evidence, used as a combination condiment and lunch counter by the nearby fast food outlet.

Cassandra had sheathed her sword once more, and held out both her hands to him. "Quickly, look into my eyes."

Max clasped her offered hands and waited while Cassandra took a couple of deep, steadying breaths. Out of the corner of his eye, Max saw a flash of movement just as Cassandra pulled him roughly to the left. A long dark arrow pinged off the marble next to Cassandra's elbow and fell to the ground. Max was still staring at it, open mouthed, when Cassandra dragged him away.

They ran, crouching over, to the end of the marble counter. Any farther and they would lose what cover it was giving them. Ahead of them on the right the marble floor became an inclined ramp, leading down in a gentle slope that was easy on travelers' legs and luggage. Still holding on to his arm, Cassandra looked first toward the incline, then back toward the far end of the counter, her lower lip caught between her teeth.

"How bad is it?" Max asked her. And where was Diggory, he thought, just as the Troll dived around the counter to join them. He had shrunk to fit, but there was still uncomfortably little room. Max wondered if the arrow shaft protruding from the Troll's leg was impeding him at all.

"Are you familiar with the expression 'out of the frying pan, into the fire'?"

"That bad, huh?"

"I'm afraid so."

"You must use the Portal, Truthsheart. It is your only chance. Even you cannot Move here."

"There are Riders with them," Cassandra said. "The Hunt can follow."

"I will create a diversion," the Troll said. "By the time I am finished, you will be gone." Diggory smiled, and Max looked away from what was stuck between his teeth.

Cassandra looked at the Troll, her brow creased and the corners of her mouth turned down. Finally, she nodded. "I thank you, Hearth of the Wind, Last Born."

"You are my *fara'ip* now, Truthsheart, truly my sister. Tell the others what became of me."

"I will, Brother," she smiled stiffly, "so long as the same fate does not befall me." She turned to Max. "This way, my lord Prince."

Max didn't move. "We can't leave him."

"Do not take this from me, my lord." Diggory sketched a sign in the air between them and without another word, leaped up on the counter, cracking the marble and scattering boxes of straws and stir sticks.

As the Troll began to roar, Cassandra grabbed Max's hand and, still doubled over, dragged him running for the ramp. When another arrow shot past them, Cassandra drew her sword again and used it to knock two more arrows out of the air before they could reach them. Then they were down on the lower level, where short passages along each side of the concourse held the escalators that led to the train platforms.

They did not take any of the escalators, however; they ran straight down the center of the vast hallway, their footsteps echoing loudly on the granite floor. A set of tall double doors with the words "Panorama Lounge" etched into their frosted glass panels blocked off the far end of the concourse. Cassandra ran toward them, and Max thought that she intended for them to make their stand there, with the doors behind them, or perhaps in the lounge itself. But she didn't slow. When she raised her sword, Max realized that she was planning to cut them a way through the glass, and his steps faltered.

Cassandra tightened her hold, and Max felt the bruising grip of her fingers just as a giant fist grabbed him around his middle, crushing the air from his chest, and threw him toward the door.

The air was sucked out of his lungs until they ached and the world around him blackened and the blood began to roar in his ears. A great pressure squeezed him like a snowball in the hands of a giant, smaller, smaller, until suddenly the pressure released and he soared free.

Then he was lying on a flat, cold surface, stars impossibly bright and impossibly high overhead. The air was warm and humid, nothing like as cold as it should be for the stars to be so bright, and Max could smell flowers. Cassandra was pulling herself to her knees and crawling over to him. Max heard the sound of pounding feet, and the last thing he saw was the shadow above her, knocking Cassandra on the head, and the last thing he felt was the weight of her body as it fell on top of him.

# Chapter Three

THE BASILISK PRINCE, Dreamer of Time, looked to his left just as a shaft of sunlight warmed the small golden bell enough to make it ring. He smiled and pushed away from the worktable and its layers of drawings. The Singer across from him—a Starward Rider, as it happened, her carefully braided golden hair three shades lighter than the color of the bell—relaxed back into her chair. The Basilisk Prince smiled again, and the Singer dropped her eyes.

"That will be all for today," he told her. "You will remember where to begin tomorrow?" He stood up and walked over to the window without waiting for her to answer what had not really been a question. Of course she would remember, that was what Singers were for. He found his workroom warm again today, despite the opened windows. He looked down at the Garden below, laid out to match the drawings on his table, each section with its own peculiar character. Almost finished. In the years since the War, he'd had every Rider who visited his court—not that they'd known then that it was his court—interviewed by a Singer. And he'd sent Singers out to interview other Riders, whether influential or unimportant, Sunward, Moonward, or Starward. He had given each Singer precise instructions, to use his or her unique ability to record, from each Rider met with, descriptions of the parts of the Lands they knew, the places they'd visited, passed through, lived in.

And while these descriptions were being collected, synthesized, and refined, the Prince had asked his Warriors, those Riders who had fought for him against the Exile, to cleanse the Vale of *Trere'if* for him. And then, he smiled, he had sent for the most renowned Builders to come and create his Garden. The Lands in miniature he had told them the Garden was to be. From his vantage point, the Prince could see how neatly each section was divided from the rest by white pebble paths. The final touch, the Dedication, only waited for him to be declared High Prince. Then, as a symbol of his new power, he would use those pebbled paths as guides to create walls of *dra'aj*, his *dra'aj*, and from that moment visitors to his court would have to Move from section to section. Only he would be able to walk through the Garden like an ordinary Rider. It would be ordinary only for him. It was important, he thought, that all the People who came to his Citadel, especially the Solitaries and the Naturals who came to what would then be the court of the High Prince, be reminded of who and what commanded here. Riders. The only race of the People who could Move unhindered through the Lands. This place, this Garden, would be a symbol of that Power.

Almost finished. Just the last few pieces to fall into place.

A little tune played its way through the back of his thoughts just as the shaft of sunlight rang the second golden bell on his worktable.

He turned back into the room and clapped his hands sharply, making the Starward Singer jump. "Come!" he said. "It is time to visit the Garden. You will accompany me."

"I thank you, my lord Prince," the Singer said, rising to her feet, "but my other duties—"

"You have no other duties but to serve your Prince." The Basilisk found it hard to talk around the sudden constriction in his throat, and the tug in his viscera. Normally he could be patient with these small annoyances, but lately . . . perhaps he was tired. The Griffin Lord had told him to rest, and he should have heeded his friend's advice. He could feel, almost *see,* the glow of *dra'aj* in the Singer, luminous and thick as cream. Beads of sweat formed on his upper lip, and he willed them away before they would be noticed. He motioned her to precede him through the room's arched doorway, careful to stay far enough from her to resist the pull of her *dra'aj,* watched her cross the landing and let her get two steps down the wide staircase before following.

He needed her alive, he chided himself, unfaded. Would need her until at least tomorrow, when she could tell him where they had left off today. After tomorrow? Well, he would see.

He waited until they were passing the empty Council Chamber before he trusted his voice enough to ask her about a detail that had caught his notice. "What do you know of the discipline called 'writing'?"

The Singer put her hand out to the railing as she turned her head to answer him.

"A tool of the Shadowfolk," the Singer said. "I believe there have been attempts to create a written form of our language, but none have succeeded."

"Why?"

The Singer walked down several more steps away from him before she realized he had stopped. The knuckles on the hand holding the rail had turned white, and he nodded, waiting.

"It is not known, my lord Prince." Her blue eyes were so beautiful, almost dark in her suddenly pale face. "We can read and write in the Shadowtongues very easily, once we are taught. We need not even be taught the different tongues, it is as if they were all the same for us. It is only our own tongue that we cannot 'write.' It is thought that our language is too pure to be physically reproduced."

"Yes, that is likely," the Basilisk Prince smiled as a new thought occurred to him. "From our tongue came all other tongues. We are the seed, the beginning." That fit what he had long believed about the Shadowlands and its connection to the Lands. He signaled to her and continued his descent. "Still, it is not possible that the Shadowfolk have a skill we cannot match," he told her. "When the Garden has been Dedicated, this will be your new task."

"Yes, my lord Prince." This time, the Singer did not turn around.

Almost immediately, he regretted his impulsive words. The project was much too important to leave in the hands of a Starward Rider. Surely there must be a Sunward Singer among the many Singers of the People. But, if he chose a Sunward, would there not be discontent? Once or twice his friend the Griffin Lord had advised that he divide his tasks and responsibilities more evenly among the three Wards. The Griffin had many failings, but for all that he had an excellent understanding.

Nevertheless, good advice could be hard to follow. Though it was only natural, it would not do to show too much favor to Riders of his own Ward. His purpose was to unite Riders against Solitaries and Naturals, to put an end to the petty squabbles that traditionally arose among Moon, Sun, and Stars—not to add to the factiousness. They were all Riders, after all, and had much more in common with each other than they had with any other beings. They were not so much at odds when Guidebeasts were still seen, the Songs told, when Riders still had *dra'aj* enough for their Beasts to manifest. Then there was less talk about which Ward a Rider claimed. *Then* honor and status came from the strength of your Beast, not from the color of your skin, hair, and eyes.

Still another proof, if he needed it, that Riders had fallen, another sign that the end of the Cycle was near, that changes had to come. He had done all he could, more, he thought, than anyone else could have done to solve this final problem, to restore Riders and all the Lands to their proper glory. There was only one thing lacking, one missing piece to the puzzle, and that would be supplied by the Exile.

The Starward Singer had waited for him in the entrance hall at the foot of the tower. Now was not the time to be thinking about all he had left to do. This was his time for relaxation, for recreation. At his gesture, the Singer turned and opened the doors into the Garden.

Several of the Riders assembled outside the Basilisk Tower, most in the deep magenta colors of the Basilisk Prince, tried to catch her eye as she came through the doors, but the Prince was much too close behind for Twilight Falls Softly to risk any kind of signal. There were those present who might betray her for even a change of expression, even a frown due to too bright a sun. It was hard to be in the Basilisk Prince's *fara'ip*, difficult to win a place, more difficult still to keep it. None here had anything to fear or gain from her; as a Singer she had her own *fara'ip*, the bonding closer than blood, and wanted none of the Basilisk's, but there were many who would not believe it.

She moved quickly down the wide stone steps and turned when she reached the flagstones at the bottom, turned in time to bow with the others as the Basilisk Prince appeared in the doorway at the top of the steps. The doors closed behind him of their own accord, framing him in brightness as their golden wood caught the rays of the sun and gave a special glow to the burgundy of his hair.

Twilight discreetly edged backward, hoping to lose herself in the group of waiting Riders. It wasn't unusual, she'd been told, to feel uncomfortable in the Basilisk Prince's presence—that was the price of exposure to great power—but his direct regard was beginning to terrify her. Too many people who'd received that regard were seen no more, as if the weight of the Prince's notice removed you from the notice of all other Riders. Once or twice she was sure she'd seen a look of hunger in his eye. She'd learned to identify the danger signals, the sudden pallor, the minute trembling of the hands, the almost imperceptible dampness of brow and upper lip.

Were her nerves powering her imagination, or was the Basilisk Prince paler than usual today?

Twilight fell into step with the others as the Basilisk led the way down the first path. He liked to stroll through the Garden every afternoon and check the progress of the Builders, and he liked to take a select group of Riders with him. These thought of themselves as his *fara'ip,* but privately Twilight wondered whether the Prince was capable of such a bond. The group, always small, was frequently made up of the same Riders—today Twilight saw the Singer Snow on the Mountain and her own kinsman Patience in Time in the group—though not always the Prince's current favorites. Twilight Falls Softly had been told—Singers heard everything eventually—that sometimes the Basilisk Prince took a special guest to enjoy the Garden privately with him, but the Prince always returned alone. No one but the Naturals living in the Garden knew what happened on those occasions.

As the Basilisk Prince led them near a fountain, the chuckling water leaped, forming a crystalline tower in the air, subsiding only as the Prince's steps passed by. Twilight murmured and smiled with everyone else, each of them careful to catch the Prince's eye so that he could approve of their pleasure in the manifestation. Twilight had to admit it; it *was* impressive, the grace of it, the perfect melding of space and time and movement.

More than anything else in the Basilisk Prince's court, it showed how real his power was.

A small woman, thin as a stem, skin like pallid moss, pale violet of hair, stood ankle-deep at one side.

"You have done well," the Basilisk Prince told her, his voice ringing like silver bells. "Tell your people."

"Thank you, my lord Prince," she said, her voice as crystal as the water, as she bowed her head and disappeared once more.

The promenade continued, and Twilight found herself able to make small conversation—about the Garden—with her kinsman Patience, who introduced her to another Rider, a Sunward, whom she did not know. As she relaxed, smiling freely at a remark the Sunward Rider made, she realized how very tense the day's work with the Basilisk Prince had made her. She might be just as tense tomorrow, but for now the Basilisk Prince was pleased, chuckling his delight as the Garden acknowledged his passing, each section in its own way, here with sounding waters, there with a light fall of snow, with flowers that bloomed as he approached and closed as he walked out of their meadow. The Prince laughed aloud as the party was caught in a sudden shower of rain, and Twilight laughed with him.

In the silence of the next section of Garden, Twilight could hear running water splashing and tinkling over rock, and a voice light as a rainbow singing in accompaniment to the water.

"What do you here?" There was no laughter in the Basilisk Prince's voice now.

Sudden silence and the water stopped, the singing stopped. Twilight was almost sure that her breathing had stopped, and that even her heart had stilled.

"Come forth," the Basilisk said. "Do not make me compel you." A small Natural, a Water Sprite almost the image of the one they had already seen, stepped to the edge of the water. Pale green as a lily pad she was, hair like jade, eyes the rich hue of emeralds.

"You are not to sing, not to let your waters play, except in my presence." The Prince spoke in sorrow, like a father to a wayward child. Twilight slipped her hand into the crook of her cousin Patience's elbow, needing suddenly to feel something solid and warm. All around her the group of Riders stifled their movements, becoming as still as the water they were near.

"My lord Prince," the crystal voice rang pure, true notes, "the Garden is large, and you come so seldom . . . it is my Nature to sing and play."

"Your Nature? Your Nature is bound to me. You have no Nature unless I will it." Even now his voice was gentle and soft. Twilight did not relax, and the muscles in her kinsman's arm were like *gra'if* metal.

"But, my Lord, we—"

"*WE?* There are others? You conspire to disobey me? Who are these others?" Now was his voice a terrible thing, and Twilight closed her eyes, unable to bury her face in Patience's sleeve as she longed to do.

"No, my lord," the little Natural chimed. "I mean, I mispoke my lord Prince, there are no others. I—"

"It makes no matter." The Prince's voice was once again calm, and Twilight let go the breath she was not aware of holding. All would be well, she'd been frightened for nothing.

"You *will* warn them, you yourself will serve as warning to any 'others' who might think to defy me."

Quick as a cat, the Basilisk Prince seized the Water Sprite by her fragile upper arm and pulled her out of the water. Twilight winced when she saw the little Natural's unformed feet; she was never meant to stand on a dry surface. The Prince turned to the Rider next to him, the nice Sunward Warrior Patience had just introduced her to, and pointed to a patch of rocky ground, well away from the little Natural's pool.

"Stake her there," the Basilisk Prince said, thrusting the Water Sprite to the ground. "Let her dry. Let her *dra'aj* return to the Lands."

Twilight sank her teeth into the inside of her bottom lip, hoping her face was impassive, hoping she had even managed a small smile and small nod of approval. She doubted it very much, but she hoped. The little Natural would dry slowly. Her pool would shrink with her until eventually, after hours or days, she would be only a thin film discoloring the rocks, and then the wind would blow even that away.

"Let us continue," the Basilisk Prince said, smiling, as he led them past the struggling Natural.

Twilight thought about meeting the Prince in his workroom on the morrow, and forced a smile to her lips.

The group passed into a formal garden within the Garden, where stone paths and neat hedges separated carefully placed flowers and topiary. The Basilisk Prince quickened his pace as he glimpsed the figure making its way down the path toward them. *The Griffin Lord,* Twilight thought. If only he'd arrived earlier, the little Natural might still be alive. The Basilisk Prince's wrath could be deflected, if caught early, but nothing could persuade him to undo what had been done. These days it seemed that only the Griffin Lord's opinions had any effect on the Basilisk Prince's behavior. The Griffin came striding toward them, purposeful and sure, pausing with a beautiful movement of his hand at the required distance. The Prince, rather than gesturing the Griffin to approach, stepped forward himself to meet him.

Twilight edged forward, her Singer's curiosity overcoming her caution. She had seen the Griffin Lord at a distance, but this was her first opportunity to observe him closely. Like herself, the Griffin was a Starward Rider, distinguished by his pallor, his dark blue eyes, and his elaborately braided hair, blazing platinum like a cloud of starlight. Like the rest of the present group, he affected the current monochrome fashion of the Basilisk's *fara'ip*. His breeches and boots, his tunic, cut long enough to reach the knees and divided for riding, were a deep forest green, and heavily brocaded with griffins.

However, unlike the others, who wore no jewelry whatsoever, the Griffin Lord displayed his individuality, or his recklessness, in the shape of a jeweled ring, worn in the left ear.

The Griffin was not, Twilight noted, the only one present who did not wear the deep magenta colors of the Basilisk Prince. But he was the only one who looked comfortable doing so.

"My lord Prince," he said, his voice light, as if he'd found a way to whisper and speak aloud at the same time. He lowered his eyes and bowed with another graceful gesture of his hand. The Basilisk Prince reached out and touched the Griffin's cheek with the back of his fingers as the Rider straightened.

"What news do you bring me, my dear one?"

"We have the Solitary who gave them warning, and this." In his right hand the Griffin held out a hair ornament about the length of his thumb.

Twilight strained to see as the Basilisk Prince took hold of the little clip, turning it over in his fingers. Small as it was, it was extraordinarily detailed and lifelike, a three-dimensional depiction of a dragon asleep, its nose buried beneath its tail like a cat napping.

"Is it *gra'if?*" A murmur among those watching quickly stilled as the Basilisk Prince lifted his hand.

"No, my lord, the ornament is made of what the Shadowfolk call silver."

"Do we know to whom it belonged?"

The Griffin Lord shook his head. "Two of the Wardens were Dragonborn. We do not know which of them dropped it."

"If it is coincidence, I must say that I do not like it." The Basilisk Prince turned the small silver dragon until it caught the sun. Twilight took a step back, getting several of the others between her and where the Basilisk stood with the Griffin Lord. She'd had her fill today of what the Basilisk Prince did not like.

"She often knows more than it seems possible for her to know," the Griffin reminded the Prince. Twilight winced. No telling who the "she" under discussion was, but it sounded as if she should be more careful. And as for the Griffin Lord, he spoke boldly, more boldly perhaps than was safe. Twilight glanced around and saw that the other Riders were looking carefully at the fountains and shrubs that surrounded them. They all knew that the Prince loved the Griffin Lord, but others had been loved, and were seen no more.

"Where is he now?"

"They passed through the Portal, my lord. What would you have us do?"

The Basilisk turned to face them once again, and Twilight prepared her best smile. He inclined his head, and she bowed with the rest. As she raised her head, she caught the eye of the Griffin Lord. Something in his face . . . some unexpected look. The jewel in his ear flashed in the sunlight. Was he shaking his head at her, or had it been just a tremor of the light? As he turned his face from her, Twilight thought of the little Natural, staked out to dry within sight of her own pool, and wondered how far she could get from the court if she left now. Was it even worth the attempt? Was there any safe place for her to go? She thought again of the Water Sprite. *No,* she realized, an unexpected freedom in the thought, *and it's just as dangerous to stay.*

She'd go, then. Her heart beat so loudly she was sure the Basilisk Prince would hear it and question her.

The Basilisk Prince felt the muscles in his face loosen, the tightness in his stomach—almost a cramp—die away. How much he enjoyed seeing the brightness in their eyes. He turned his back on the *fara'ip* and walked with his beloved friend toward the now distant tower.

"I had to discipline a Natural today, a little Water Sprite," he said.

"Did you?" his friend answered. "I suppose it couldn't be helped."

"Most definitely not. But now, of course, there's a gap in the Garden, and that will have to be taken care of before the Dedication."

"As I have said, you do too much. Let others take care of these details."

"Ah, how like you, dear one," the Prince shook his head, smiling. "But it is the details that count." A few more of them, he thought, and all would be accomplished. Soon now, very soon. He looked at the silver dragon in his hand. The tools he needed to make every Rider, every Natural, and even every Solitary as obedient as was the Garden through which he walked were almost in his hands. It only wanted the final piece, the Exile.

There had been those, the Prince recalled, placing his hand on the Griffin's shoulder as they walked, who suggested—carefully, where they thought he would not hear of it—that everything he did stemmed from being passed over for the Guardianship, but it was not so. True, back before he was the Basilisk Prince, when he was only Dreamer of Time, he would have been content to Guard the Talismans, to hold the heart and good of the People as his charge. When his cousin, Dawntreader, was chosen instead, the Basilisk Prince had known that his was another, more difficult, path.

All the Songs agreed that the Guardian of the Talismans was the one Rider—the one among all the People—who could never be High Prince. It was *that* task which Dreamer of Time knew to be his own, but Dawntreader had refused him the Talismans. *Refused* him. Even now, the Basilisk had to consciously refrain from forming fists at the thought. Even at the end of the War, when Dawntreader had surrendered, and Dreamer of Time was hailed for the first time as the Basilisk Prince, he had been unable to act. He'd quietly tested his allies and had seen that there was no heart left in them, at that moment, to force Dawntreader to their will. Renewed conflict—and forcing the Guardian would have meant exactly that, as the arrogant son-of-Solitaries well knew— would have been the result. Dawntreader's surrender had achieved what a war he could not win had not: it had gained him time. Or so he had thought.

But the passage of time had changed many things. Now very few gave thought to the welfare of the Prince Guardian, and the state of his Banishment. Many, if asked, would not even know if he lived. And now, now that the Basilisk Prince had all the allies he could want, he no longer needed them. The little tune threaded its way through the feelings behind this thought. Now he had the means to force Dawntreader to do what was needed.

The Prince stopped to stroke the ornamental grasses that grew against the Citadel wall. He drew the stems through his hand, inhaling the clean green scent of the crushed plant. This time, the Prince Guardian would agree to give the Lands the High Prince they so badly needed. This time he would not be able to refuse. The Prince drew his hand back sharply. The edges of the grass had cut his hand. He smiled. He should have re-membered the greenery did more than look pretty. He turned to the Griffin.

"Find them. Bring them to me," he said, looking at the blood on his fingers. "The child of the Dragon is not to be killed, mark that."

"And the Solitary?"

"I will see him now."

"It shall be as the Basilisk Prince wishes."

~

Cassandra dropped Max's hands and covered her eyes with her palms, biting back a scream of frustration.

"What's wrong? Why isn't it working?"

Cassandra shook her head. "I don't know!" The words came out louder than she had intended. Abruptly, she turned from him, scanning the room.

"Maybe you should try to relax."

Cassandra squeezed her eyes shut, her hands in fists. Could she, for heaven's sake, have two seconds' peace to *think*? Was that too much to ask? At times like this, she felt that only her Oath kept her from slapping him silly. Max's tone had been gentle, the rough velvet of his voice comforting, but his advice made it all the clearer to Cassandra just how little he understood, and just how alone she was. She rubbed her eyes, feeling the pull of exhaustion. Just how long had she been awake? Had she had *any* sleep since Diggory had come with Nighthawk's warning?

"I just can't focus on the room," she said, resenting the tremor she heard in her voice. She took a deep breath and looked around her once more, trying to concentrate on the details. The room looked strangely familiar, considering how long it had been since she'd last visited a Rider's fortress. It looked as though whoever had brought them here meant them to be comfortable. There were thick rugs on the polished stone floor, darkwood chairs like most of the elder lords had, the kind that would conform themselves to your shape without the aid of cushions or padding. There was a spread of wine, juices, fruit, and cheeses on the inlaid table, each item in its own never-empty plate, basket, or carafe. The walls were covered in brightly embroidered tapestries that looked as soft as flannel and smelled like laundry dried outside on a warm breezy day. There was even a fire burning in the grate, warming the room and filling it with the smell of apples. Altogether a pleasant, comforting place, Cassandra thought, taking her lower lip between her teeth, but if she were unable to form a picture of it in her mind, she could not Move them.

Max picked up a carafe and carefully sniffed at it.

"I suppose this will be poisoned?"

Cassandra shut her eyes again. Couldn't he tell she was trying to think? "If they wanted to kill us," she said through clenched teeth, "we'd be dead already." She opened her eyes to find him looking at her, a softness she hadn't seen before in his eyes.

"Listen," he said, in his voice like velvet. "I was serious. If there's nothing we can do, we need to put it out of our minds and relax."

Cassandra turned her back on him and continued her examination of the room. The Exile had always been full of advice, and she'd heard that particular piece before. But that was when they were dealing with humans; things had changed now, as the never-ending supplies of food reminded her. And besides, she wasn't convinced there *was* nothing she could do. Just because she couldn't Move didn't mean they shouldn't try to get out by ordinary means. And get out they must, that was clear. A room with no exit was still a cell, no matter how thick the carpets and how good the wine. The Troll Diggory had given his life that she might keep the Exile safe, and that was a sacrifice she had no intention of wasting. The Troll had been right all along, she thought; something *was* terribly wrong. What did the Basilisk want with the Exile, and why couldn't it wait until the end of the Banishment, especially now that it was so close?

Cassandra rubbed her forehead with stiff fingers. *One problem at a time,* she instructed herself, hearing the echo of her voice saying the same thing to her fencing students. If only she found herself as easy to obey as they did.

"What kind of animal is this?"

Cassandra spun around. Max was pointing at the tapestry with the wine goblet in his hand. Cassandra's hands clenched again, and she closed her teeth on the curse that rose, heated and furious, through her throat. How could he stand there admiring the artwork when everything had gone so radically wrong? Without another thought, Cassandra stalked over to his side of the room, grabbed a double handful of cloth, and yanked with all her strength.

Max leaped backward as yard upon yard of heavy fabric pulled loose and collapsed into a pile at their feet.

Cassandra froze, her hands still gripping fabric, her frustration-fueled rage draining away, replaced by a shiver as understanding dawned. She stared at the lines of onyx and darkmetal, some of them as fine as hairs, some as thick as her wrists, which a great use of *dra'aj* had blasted into the walls behind the arras. She pulled down more of the material, though she knew what she would find.

"Wow. Look at this workmanship—why would anyone *cover* this?" Max's fingertips were centimeters from the darkmetal when Cassandra came out of her trance.

"Don't touch it," she said, knocking his hand up. "The room is Signed."

"Which means what, exactly?"

Cassandra pushed her hair out of her face, longing for an elastic or even a piece of string to tie it back, avoiding Max's eye as far as she was able. She was acutely aware that she had just lost her temper in a violent and embarrassing way in front of a man she was supposed to be protecting. And she was more than a little irritated to find that now that there really was nothing she could do, she *could* relax.

"A Signed room," she said, trying for the steady voice she used to teach the youngest students, "falls from the mind, everyone's mind, except the one whose *dra'aj*," she waved her hand in the air to beckon the words to her, "*powers* it." She couldn't think of another way to put it. "I've never been in such a room, though I have heard of them." The Songs told of all things, her father used to say, back when he still cared for such things as the Songs told of. "There's an old Song that tells of two lovers—or they may have been rebels—who were sealed into a Signed Room. The Rider who had sealed them, so the Song goes, was killed on her way to report the deed to her Prince." Cassandra shivered as she reached out and touched the stone wall between the lines of onyx and darkmetal. The stone was warm. "As a child I used to wake up in the middle of the night, wondering how long they had chosen to live, those two. Or if they were still alive, somewhere, waiting for the Signs to be opened."

Max merely nodded, rubbing at the back of his neck and said, "Now I know what Schrödinger's cat felt like."

"Then why are you smiling?" Now that her frustration was fading, Cassandra found her irritation disappearing as well.

Max pulled out one of the chairs at the table and sat down, shifting over until he could put his feet up on another chair, ankles crossed. His black cowboy boots were dusty, and there was a bright smear of blood on the pointed toe of the left one.

"I know I should be terrified," he said, "but I find it strangely reassuring to learn that you can lose your temper. That's maybe the third time a normal, feeling person has shown through that yeoman-of-the-guard shell you're wearing, and I'm glad to see her. Which one is the real you?"

Cassandra pulled out another chair and sat down, one leg folded under her. "Both, I suppose." She frowned at him, hiding a yawn with her hand. How was it he managed not to look out of place, even dressed in his torn shirt, old jeans, and cowboy boots? He had slapped most of the dust and dirt from his clothes, but there were smudges on his face and hands that only soap and water would remove, and the Hound's blood still glittered wetly where it had spattered him. He looked tired, too, no matter how lively his voice or his questions; his face was a stark white, even the silvered strands in his hair seeming whiter somehow among the black, as if everything about him was tired and drawn thin. Only his green eyes retained their sharp focus and bright jade color.

"When did you sleep last?"

Cassandra jerked upright in surprise.

Max let his feet down with a thump. He indicated the layers of tapestries with a jerk of his head. "Want to stretch out?"

Cassandra looked over at where the thick pile of fabric beckoned. Her eyes were scratchy. "More than anything in the world."

"But?"

"I said I would give you all my answers." Cassandra pulled the platter of food toward her, tore off a piece of the bread, and broke off a slab of cheese to go with it. "This may be our only opportunity."

Max poured some wine into the second goblet and passed it to her. "I wish you hadn't said that."

"We certainly don't appear to be in any immediate danger," she said, finding herself reluctant to begin.

Max picked a fruit from the bowl between them that looked like an apple but smelled like a ripe peach. Now that she was about to give him "all the answers she had," he found he wasn't sure he wanted to hear them. Though her gray eyes glittered, Cassandra's face was drawn with exhaustion, the delicate bones more prominent, adding for the first time an alien cast to her beauty.

*If her ears were pointed,* he thought, *she'd look like a Tolkien elf.*

"Tell me something," he said. "Why do I annoy you so much?"

"I beg your pardon?" Her chocolate voice rumbled, almost too low to hear. She'd looked up, but not quite enough to look him in the eye.

"Look," he said, leaning forward on his elbows and turning the fruit around in his fingers, "the person you're pissed with, that's not me. You've got me confused with someone else—you *must* have."

Cassandra slowly chewed a mouthful of cheese and washed it down with a swallow of wine. When it became apparent that she wasn't going to say anything, Max tried again.

"I know who I am. I'm Max Ravenhill. I've never met

any of you people," he held his hands up as she opened her mouth. "I know, I know, you say I don't remember. But that's just it. I *do* remember. Look, history's my field and we're talking about *my* history. And I remember all of it. No blackouts, no time unaccounted for. No amnesia. You see what I'm getting at?"

Cassandra looked away from him, her lower lip between her teeth. Finally she seemed to come to a decision.

"Max Ravenhill is a construct," she said, "a fiction. Your memories, everything before the last fifteen years, are fake."

"Impossible." Max smiled, feeling the weight fall away in relief. This was the wildest thing yet, no one could expect him to believe this.

"More impossible than the Hound? The Portal? Check the level of the wine, has it gone down? Are there fewer pieces of fruit in the basket? More impossible than that? Than *this?*" Cassandra Moved suddenly to the Signed wall and by the time his eyes had shifted to her, startled, she stood behind him, hands on his shoulders. When he flinched, she removed her hands and was once more facing him from her seat across the table, the air faintly cracking around her.

"That doesn't mean—" he began, with the feeling of a drowning man clutching at a piece of floating wreckage.

"Think of a memory," she said, tucking the curling strands of her hair behind her ears, "something no one else could know."

Max licked his lips. He didn't need to think very long. He wasn't kidding when he said that he knew his own history. Forget it and you're doomed to repeat it, that's what Santayana said, and if there was anything Max didn't want, it was to repeat his own history. And of all the events of his life, there was one that even now Max could barely bring himself to think about, let alone say aloud. But he had to be sure, and this was the one incident Cassandra couldn't possibly know. Max had been the only one there, and he had never been able to tell anyone, not the police, not his friends, not the grief counselor.

He found he could not look at her when he finally spoke.

"What was Franny singing?" he asked, his eyes flicking to Cassandra's face, pale as ivory, even as he willed them away. She had shut her eyes, but not before he'd seen the light in them change, not before he'd seen a depth of sorrow in them that shook him. Max began to tremble.

" 'Someone to Watch Over Me,' " she told him, in her voice like melted chocolate, her eyes still closed, as if she could not face him.

Max turned away, raising his hands to a face suddenly numb with cold, even as he was shaking his head in useless denial. As if he were watching a scene in a play from his seat in the audience, he saw himself falling forward from his chair, hands over his face; saw Cassandra in front of him, her hands out to catch him; felt her fingers biting into the rigid muscles of his upper arms.

"No." His voice was so hoarse it seemed to come from someone else. "You can't know this. You can't."

"I do know. I was there when we gave you the memory, that one and many others."

He pushed her hands away and stood up. Cassandra remained on her knees for only an instant before she got slowly to her feet. Max had raised his arms to ward her off when he realized that she wasn't reaching out for him.

"You *gave* them to me? How could you do this? What kind of sadists are you?" His lips trembled, his throat closed on a sob. How could they have given him the sight of Franny in the bathtub, her veins open?

"I could tell you that they are human memories, no better and no worse than those of other humans. It would not be a lie, but it would not be the whole truth."

"Oh, by all means, let's have the whole truth!" He

threw himself back in his chair, fighting to take an even breath, and glared at her.

Cassandra sat slowly down in her own chair, an expression of weariness and, Max thought, regret, on her face. *Good,* he thought, gripping his chair arms fiercely. He didn't, he *couldn't* believe her, but that she could even *pretend* what she was saying was the truth . . .

Cassandra picked up her glass and drained it. Max concentrated on the movement of her throat as she swallowed.

"We learned we couldn't make things easy for you," she said at last, replacing her goblet on the edge of the table. "You weren't a man to whom ease could be given. You accepted it only if it was hard won, and at your own hand."

"How convenient."

"I make no excuses," she said, her storm cloud eyes focused on the goblet. "I tell you only what is true, whether you like it or not. When the Banishment began, and we Wardens arrived here to accept your custody, we found you had no memory—a side effect, we thought of the Chant of Binding that made the Banishment possible. We told you who you were—why not? Your *dra'aj* had been bound, but you'd be sure to notice that you didn't age and die like humans. It was the simplest way to explain what we were, and why we were with you. But after time passed, you began to forget what you'd been told, forget who we were; you began to act . . . erratically, as if your mind was being erased."

"Alzheimer's?" Intrigued despite himself, Max leaned forward.

"Not exactly, but . . ." she shrugged. "We thought it must be because you were separated from the Lands, and from your *dra'aj*. You're the Guardian, after all; who could know what effect leaving the Lands could have on you? When we realized what was happening, we—well, we gave you a set of memories to replace the ones you were losing. It seemed to be the only thing that would help. We couldn't give you *your* life, but giving you a whole life—as if you were human—that worked. But the pattern repeated, and after the passage of time, the memories would fade, the . . . erratic—" Max had the feeling Cassandra was using that word as a substitute for something much worse that she didn't want to say aloud, "—behavior resurfaced, and we would give you a new life again."

"How . . . ?" Max found he couldn't complete his question.

But she knew what he was not asking her, and that told him more than he wanted to acknowledge about how much truth she was sharing.

"Thirty times at least," she said, "maybe more. And we tried, many times, to give you memories of happiness and contentment. We were never successful, they wouldn't take. These memories—like Max Ravenhill's memories— painful and soul-searing as they may be, are no more than the echoes and shadows of your own true struggles. We found we could not change your fundamental nature, but must reproduce it as best we could. You *can* be happy and content, but only if you do it yourself." She looked across at him. "Tell me, would you have wanted your life different?"

Max opened his mouth to say of course he would. But then he found himself closing his mouth, the words unspoken, as if, having heard the truth from her, he could give her nothing less than the truth himself. What would he change, exactly, about his life? Which memories to save and which to trade in? Would he choose to keep Franny alive, knowing how hard life was for her, knowing that it wasn't what she wanted herself? This was by no means the first time he'd thought about this, not even the first time someone had asked him the question. Everyone who ever examined their own lives considered these questions eventually. They were fairly easy to answer when there was no way to relive your life.

But this woman was telling him it might have been

different. That they—whoever "they" were—might have given him a different life, had they been able to change his "fundamental nature." Today's Max Ravenhill might never have existed. He'd always said, glibly he now realized, that no one would knowingly choose the life he'd had—but he'd always acknowledged that his past, even Franny's suicide, had helped to make him the person he now was. And dammit, he liked that person. He couldn't imagine being someone else. He didn't *want* to be someone else. And he'd fight to prevent becoming someone else.

*Shit!* he thought. *I'm acting like I believe her!*

He sank his head into his hands. His skull felt as if it would explode. It was impossible, but . . . no, a world in which Franny didn't die was a world in which she'd never existed.

Max jerked his arm out of the reach of Cassandra's hand.

"Why don't you get some rest," he told her, forcing the words out through the tightness in his chest and throat. "I don't think I want to hear any more of your truth just now."

# Chapter Four

PEACE AT DAWN BRUSHED a spot of dust from the sleeve of his new shirt with a careful hand. He had dressed with great attention for this watch, and for the first time in the magenta of the Basilisk Prince. He was not sure if he was frustrated or relieved that his newly forged darkmetal glaive, blade still un-blooded, was not likely to be needed. Guarding the Solitary had not turned out to be quite as formidable a task as Peace at Dawn had half hoped. Tricky they were, so all the Songs told, but this one, a Troll, looked to have had all its trickiness beaten out of it. Peace had long suspected that the Solitaries' reputation for being keep-both-hands-in-sight clever was highly overrated, if not a thing of Song only. Peace hadn't met many Solitaries—there were none in the Garden yet—but he had always thought that they could not be so *very* dangerous.

Like the Basilisk Prince, Peace at Dawn was a Sun-ward Rider, and he believed the rumor that Sunwards were able to resist the tricks and machinations of even the wiliest of Solitaries much better than Riders of the Star or Moon. He'd also heard the rumors that the Basilisk Prince favored those of his own Ward over others, and while it would not do to say so aloud, Peace himself was sure of it. It only made sense, as the Basilisk Prince himself had said, that you trusted your own first. The very fact that he had been given the task of guarding the Troll proved that Peace had been noticed, and was therefore in line for important things.

The Troll was *bound*. The way he was caught—Peace did not like to think about the Hunt; none of the guards did. No matter that they came only to the Basilisk Prince's call. When the rumors first flew that the Basilisk Prince was using the Hunt, many had simply not believed them. Indeed, many still did not. Peace himself took care with whom he discussed such matters; only the truly trustworthy could know. Not all could see that it was necessary to use the right tool to achieve the right end, and the Hunt was clearly the right tool in this matter. Why, Peace had heard that even the Exile had been found, when everyone knew that son-of-Solitaries, Peace carefully spat into a corner, had been successfully evading capture for years, after he'd treacherously tricked and killed his Wardens. Probably with the help of the very Solitary Peace at Dawn was guarding. Brought from the Shadowlands, they'd said, and what could a Solitary have been doing there?

Peace stiffened as he heard a noise behind him like a throat clearing. He knew a trick or two himself, he thought, his lips twisting into a smile. This Solitary wasn't going to find him easy to take in. Slowly he reached into the tiny inside pocket of his purple leather waistcoat and took out a small mirror, held it up near his right eye, and adjusted the angle of reflection until he could clearly see the Solitary behind him. Everything possible had been done to prevent the Troll's escape. The chamber itself was large, the walls easily ten spans to a side and almost as tall, made by the Basilisk Prince himself of some smooth unjointed stone. The Child of Earth was suspended in the middle of the chamber, his limbs spread by the chains fixed to each wrist, each ankle, so that no part of his body touched the stone of the walls or floor, or anything that had come from the earth, and might therefore aid him.

The Troll had been carefully searched for *gra'if* when he was captured, and the chains that held him now were ordinary darkmetal, though Signed, of course, by the Basilisk himself. Only the Basilisk could free the Old One now, supposing anyone would want him free. It was not safe to have *gra'if* metal around a Solitary, everyone knew that. After all, it was the Solitaries who made it, no one knew how. And who knew what tricky spells might be lying in wait for the unwary? No one who wished to follow the Basilisk Prince wore *gra'if* nowadays, even if they might have a suit of it hidden somewhere in their home.

Peace remembered his older sister having *gra'if*, and how proud of it she had been. Peace never admitted to anyone that as a child growing up he had envied his older sister, and that his major ambition had been to have *gra'if* of his own one day. There was no knowing where his sister was now, which was a good thing, otherwise Peace would have to tell. He sighed and slid the hand mirror back into his pocket.

"Has the prisoner given any trouble?"

Peace jolted to attention, almost dropping his glaive. If the Basilisk noticed how startled he was . . . but a stolen glance showed him that Dreamer of Time was looking over Peace's shoulder, at the suspended Troll.

"No, my lord Prince." Acutely embarrassed by the croak in his voice, Peace cleared his throat as quietly as he could. If he did not know better, Peace thought, he would think the Basilisk had been running. He was breathing in shallow, uneven gasps, and Peace noticed a light beading of sweat on his lord's forehead and upper lip. Instead of the normal, ruddy complexion of a Sunward Rider, the Basilisk was pale, his skin blotchy.

"Are you well, my lord Prince?" he ventured.

"Yes, my boy. Yes. Come here a moment, would you?" The Basilisk Prince gestured and Peace approached him, head bowed. The Basilisk laid his arm around Peace's shoulder, leaning on him. The boy slipped his own arm around the Basilisk's waist, realizing that his lord needed steadying, regardless of his reassuring words. Why, the Basilisk's hand was bleeding.

"What's your name, boy?"

"Peace at Dawn, my lord. My mother is Light in the Sky, and the Dragon guides me."

"Dragonborn are you? Ah, well, it can't be helped." The Basilisk patted him on the shoulder, and Peace felt bold enough to raise his head.

"My lord?"

"Nothing, my dear, nothing. Look into my eyes."

Puzzled but happy, Peace at Dawn turned his head enough to look at the Basilisk Prince directly, eye to eye, as the great lords did. He was being *Seen* he thought, his heart pounding fiercely in his chest. He could hardly wait to tell his father.

"................" the Basilisk said.

Peace opened his mouth, but he could not form the words to apologize for not hearing what his lord had said. Neither could he shut his mouth again.

"..............." the Basilisk said, and Peace felt the brush of warm breath on his cheeks, smelled the faint, not unpleasant scent of the wine the Basilisk had taken that afternoon.

The Basilisk Prince leaned toward Peace, his own lips parted, and gently sucked the air out of Peace's lungs in a long hiss.

"................" the Basilisk said. As Peace began to tremble, the Basilisk's eyes burned red, and his arms tightened like vises around Peace's shoulders.

*No,* Peace thought, *wait.*

"......."

But the Basilisk Prince was still speaking, his tongue flicking in and out of his thinning lips and Peace stopped struggling to find his own voice. He couldn't interrupt the Prince, could he?

The Prince's face seemed to grow longer, his nose sharper and his eyes impossibly large, and red, and still. The Basilisk Prince went on speaking the lines Peace at Dawn could not hear, as he felt his limbs stiffen and his blood grow still. By the time he thought of struggling, of calling on the light that perhaps lay within himself, of calling the fires of his own Beast, those fires, deep within him, had turned to stone.

～

Twilight Falls Softly waited to leave her chambers until after the late meal had been served, when she could be reasonably certain that everyone in the Citadel would be about their evening amusements. The Basilisk Prince had not been seen since he'd gone off with the Griffin Lord, though gossip had *that* lord already back to the stables and gone. No point in waiting until full dark, she told herself, glancing out her open window to where the clouds blew over the moon. There would never be a moment when the whole court would be asleep—and if there were, what explanation could she give for not being asleep herself? One of the guards-in-arms who was always patrolling the Citadel itself would be sure to stop and ask her. No, better to go now, while there were still Riders out and about in the Garden, enjoying the small freedoms that night brought, even here in the court of the Basilisk Prince . . .

If only she were able to unlock her knees and stand.

Twilight knew that if she stayed, she would only become another one of those never seen again, never spoken of. She would never make it through another day with the Basilisk Prince without betraying herself, not with the image of the drying Water Sprite always before her eyes. Twilight wrapped her arms around herself and shivered, even though a fire burned in her hearth. If only she could stop trembling. And if she were to go, it had to be now, tonight. Even if somehow she could avoid the Basilisk Prince tomorrow, if she waited until the Garden was Dedicated—and that event was not far off, messengers had been sent with invitations and Riders were even now gathering at the court—she would not be able to simply walk away. Only Movement would take her out of the Garden then. And no one Moved within the precinct of the Basilisk's court without his feeling it, without his knowing, somehow.

She forced herself to relax, sitting up straight on the edge of her bed, her ankles crossed as her mother had taught her, hands clasped in her lap as if she sat at her lessons. Her fingers entwined, she starting tapping her thumbs to the music she was playing in her head. She thought again about taking her new gown. Made in the traditional rainbow hues worn by Singers, she had worn it only once since coming to the Prince's court. But whoever it was the Prince would send to her rooms when she did not arrive in his workroom at the appointed hour would take careful note of what was there, and what was not. So long as there was no evidence of flight, if her rooms did not look as though she had run away, they would waste time looking for her in the wrong places, time she could use to get well away. She must take nothing with her, absolutely nothing except what she was wearing now.

And she couldn't wear the rainbow-colored gown now, not and expect to go unnoticed.

Twilight's hands stilled as her eyes turned once more to her darkwood harp. No, she told herself for the fourth time in as many minutes. *Absolutely nothing.* She sat up straighter, squaring her shoulders. Even that must stay. Especially that. Her work with the Prince did not call for her harp, and if it were missing in the morning, it would not look as if she had been on her way to him. With her most precious possession here in her rooms, everyone would think she had merely stepped out of them and was somehow detained about the Citadel.

She took a deep breath, and another, as if she were about to Sing in company. She forced herself to stand up before she could think of any further reasons not to and marched to the Chimera-carved door. Her hand on the jeweled latch, Twilight glanced back once more at her harp. No! She turned away, resting her forehead against the cool darkwood of the door. She let the music she was thinking flow down into the muscles of her throat, opened the door, and stepped through. She hummed a little louder as she neared the bottom of the tower steps and heard the murmur of voices ahead of her. Hearing her humming music, no one she passed in the Citadel, or in the Garden once she reached that far, would speak to her, or interrupt her in any way, believing that she made a new Song.

There were only two guards gossiping in the hall at the base of the Chimera Tower. As she expected, they merely nodded politely and turned away as she walked beyond them to where the courtyard door stood open to the night air. In minutes she was through the courtyard and the gate beyond it, and some of the tension left her neck and shoulders. As she expected, there were other Riders out strolling in the Garden, and she was congratulating herself on escaping their notice when a Sunward Rider looked at her sharply, an unexpected look of concern on his face, and Twilight realized with a jolt of terror that she had stopped humming. She forced what she hoped was a reassuring smile to her lips—it felt like Death's own grimace—and hummed a short motif over twice, with a small variation the second time, as she passed him by. He smiled and nodded, turning back to his own companions, persuaded, Twilight hoped, that whatever he'd seen on her face was nothing more than Singer's block. She focused once more on her music, and relaxed the set of her shoulders, letting her arms swing naturally in time to her humming as she strolled along the paths.

She wanted to run, but she let the Song she was humming govern the speed and pacing of her footsteps, just as it would if she were really making a Song. Any direc-

tion would do for now. As for when she reached the
edge of the Vale of *Trere'if*—she was not going to call it
the Vale of Basilisks ever again—well, there had been a
rumor of Wild Riders to the Windward, and she supposed that was as good a direction as any. She did not
know how large the Vale was, but she would walk all
night if necessary. All day. Until she was free. Or until
they found her.

Twilight shivered and pushed that thought from her
mind. She went on humming, even though there was no
one near her, allowing the simple, everyday task to
relax her. She had never been particularly powerful, her
*dra'aj* was nothing out of the ordinary, but she'd always
felt invigorated after Singing. She'd heard it was the
same for others with special talents, even Healers and
Warriors, that they felt stronger after they'd used their
gifts.

When she realized where her feet were taking her,
she stopped, heart hammering in her chest, even the
Song dying away in her throat. It seemed she could
leave her harp, but there was something else—someone
else, she corrected—she could not abandon. Leaving
the harp bought her time, it was a step toward a safety
that was precarious enough as it was . . . surely stopping
to free the little Water Sprite would undo all of that? It
was madness, and dangerous madness at that.

Her feet were carrying her forward, even as she de-
bated. Apparently she had made up her mind without
knowing it. In fact, now that she actually thought about
it, stopping to free the Natural would take only a few
minutes, and the act itself wouldn't add much danger to
her flight. Who would even notice? Twilight strode forward with more purpose. No one would go to check on
the little Natural. Only those who had been present this
afternoon knew about her staking, and none of them
would have reason to do it. Even the Prince, supposing
anyone would remind him, would not order such a
check. There would not even be a guard posted to prevent

interference, and all for the same reason: it would never occur to anyone that someone would defy the Basilisk Prince by setting the Natural free. As soon send someone to see if the sun had risen.

Twilight walked a little faster down the pebbled path, but when she came to the next cross path, she hesitated, teeth gnawing at her upper lip, as she turned first one way and then another. She had set off in the right direction without being aware of it, but now, now that she was consciously trying to find the right way, all the paths, all the trees, rocks, and hillsides looked the same under the moonlight. Her heart beat faster and she bit down harder to prevent the whimper that rose in her throat from escaping. For the first time in her life she wished that she were a Warrior, and not a Singer. If she'd been born a Warrior, she'd have freed the Water Sprite and been halfway to the Wild Riders by now. No Singer was going to Make a Song out of *this* daring escape; Twilight wasn't even out of the Garden and she was already lost.

She stood still, heart stuttering, breathing uneven. If she panicked now, she'd be done for certain. She threw her head back and filled her diaphragm with air. Years of training relaxed her muscles, her breathing exercises quelling this panic just as effectively as it had ever done her stage fright. She had not particularly noticed their path this afternoon, she had been too busy watching the Prince. But she was a Singer, and she could not forget what she'd once known. Her heart slowed, she began to Sing the Song of the afternoon's tour. She was careful not to let her voice grow louder as she grew more confident. Verse after verse came to her tongue, each little couplet and beat of rhythm a footstep on her journey. She saw where she had turned the wrong way, and retraced her steps into a meadow of sleeping flowers and began again. Here there had been snow, and here a shower of rain.

As she Sang, and her *dra'aj* rose and fell with the

words, and her feet followed the notes along the familiar route, Twilight found herself wondering for the first time just where the *dra'aj* for the Garden came from. She had been told that it was the Vale itself, *Trere'if* that was, which provided the needed *dra'aj*, but if that were true, Twilight thought as her voice rose and fell in a whisper just loud enough for her own ears, then why was not *her dra'aj* stronger as well? Why not everyone's *dra'aj*? Why only the *dra'aj* of the Basilisk Prince?

The clouds parted again as she rounded another turn in the path. The moonlight showed her just where they had heard—

Twilight stopped with a sharp intake of breath as she stepped into a shallow pool of water. She looked frantically around, but of course, she thought, breathing deeply again, if the pool was still here, then the Water Sprite had to be.

"Where are you?" she whispered, her voice barely louder than the wind in the trees. "Can you answer me?"

Twilight thought she heard a sound to her left, and as that seemed to match the picture she had in her head, she turned that way. She inched forward, feeling with her toes, fearful of stepping on the little Natural as she had stepped into the pool. A darker patch on the rocky ground, a sound of dry, hoarse breathing. Or was it just dry leaves blowing in the wind?

Twilight knelt and carefully felt in front of her. A whimper of sound told her that the brittle stick under the fingers of her left hand was no tree branch. Carefully she felt her way with soft finger touches along the Water Sprite's limb until she found the rope fastening, tight above a joint. She pulled her belt knife out of its sheath and cut the rope from the stake end, unwilling to risk breaking the delicate limb by exerting pressure any closer to it. Freeing the limbs on the far side of the sprite was trickier, as reaching over the little figure put Twilight at a bad angle, but even with the moon's light she was afraid to get up and move around, afraid she would step on the little Natural and shatter her like a pile of twigs.

She sat back on her heels, waiting until her hand stopped trembling before shoving the knife back into its sheath.

"I'm going to try to get you into the water," she whispered, knowing that if she said it aloud, she would have to find the courage to do it. "I'm sorry if I hurt you. Can you make one sound, one sound only, to say if you agree?"

Again the whimper came, just once.

Twilight maneuvered her hands under the brittle rib cage, scraping the backs of her fingers against the rock beneath the sprite, afraid to handle her too much. It was like picking up a doll made of the driest twigs and dressed in cold silk. Twilight's hands felt large and clumsy, and sweat trickled down her nose as she heard her own voice whispering the word "sorry" over and over. She got her hands under what she thought were the sprite's armpits and lifted. The little arms reached up then, trailing their bracelets of rope, and hugged Twilight around the neck. The little Sprite's hair broke and crumbled as she laid her head on Twilight's shoulder.

*Oh, Hydra that guides me,* she thought, careful not to whisper her prayer aloud, *please may I not break her.* She turned as quickly as she could and this time stepped deliberately into the pool. She knelt and tenderly lowered her burden into the cool liquid. The water thrashed around her ankles, reminding her of the time her father had taught her to catch trout with her bare hands, and suddenly she was knocked backward onto the ground as two strong wet arms were around her neck and her face was being covered by wet kisses.

As she swallowed a sob, Twilight realized that not all the water on her face came from the Sprite.

"Oh, my sister," said the Sprite in her crystal voice. "Oh, thank you, my sister, thank you."

"Can you leave here?" Twilight asked. Her heart sank.

A fine adventurer she was, for certain. Until this moment it had not even occurred to her to wonder how the Water Sprite was to leave. She *couldn't* go back to the Citadel for something to carry her in. She *couldn't*. They would both be caught, and what good would that accomplish? But how could she leave the little Sprite now? Twilight was so taken with her own fears that she almost missed the Water Sprite's answer.

"*I* can leave, but what of you, my sister? Surely you will not stay?"

"Oh, no, but—will you manage? I must go quickly—I took so long to find you—" Twilight was ashamed to be so relieved, but if the Sprite had no further need of her . . .

"Wait, my sister, are you not afraid that the Hunt will follow you?"

"The Hunt is not here," Twilight said. But her Singer's ear heard the question in her words.

"Do not be willful, my sister, do not deny what you know to be true. Come with me, it is the only way."

"If I Move us, the Prince will know—"

"But he cannot know if I go! And you are my *fara'ip* now, my sister, and so can travel with me. I will keep my waters flowing, and none shall see you. What is your name?"

"I am Twilight Falls Softly," Twilight said. Sister to a Natural? Why not? "My mother was Stars Unchanging, and the Hydra guides me."

"The Hydra? A water beast! You are well-named and we are well-matched, my sister. I am Tear of the Dragon, and Water is my guide. Come, take my hands, and we will go together from this place."

Twilight drew in a deep breath and took Tear's hands.

Cassandra added a palmful of fragrant leaves to the pot of water heating near the fire and remained there on her knees, as if the tea needed her supervision to steep.

Like the stone carafe that was always full of wine, and
the basket that was always full of fruit, the fire burned
without benefit of added fuel. How strange, how mirac-
ulous after all this time; and yet, how ordinary, here in
the Lands. She looked around. There wasn't even a fireplace poker for her to play with. Which, now that she
thought about it, was probably a good sign. That the
poker was missing meant that someone—someone who
didn't want it to be used as a weapon against him—
would be along to confront them.

Not that she was looking forward to the confrontation,
exactly. Without turning her head, Cassandra stole a
glance at the table where Max sat sound asleep, his head
pillowed on his crossed arms. So far her confrontations
weren't going very well. Still, if she was lucky, enemies
with weapons would show up and give her something
easier to do.

She released her breath in a long sigh. There was no
telling how much time they had before someone *did*
show up, and past experience told Cassandra that she
and Max needed to finish talking. She'd hoped the tea's
spicy smell would wake Max up, so she wouldn't have
to. She was perfectly aware that her reluctance to wake
him had nothing to do with his needing his rest, and
everything to do with not wanting to see that look on
his face again. She shuddered. Had he ever looked at
her with quite that mix of anger and disgust before?
*Come on,* she told herself, *it can't get worse.* If only she
believed it. She stirred the pot. The tea was ready, too
much longer and it would be stronger than Max liked it.

"Max."

He came awake and alert immediately, as he always
did, and Cassandra's heart turned over. Too much the
same . . . and not enough. His eyes narrowed as he saw
her, but thank all gods the look she dreaded was no
longer in them. She poured his tea, carried the delicate
cup back to the table, and set it near him.

"Truce for now?" she said, sinking into the chair she'd used before.

He rubbed his face, shaking off sleep. "What you told me doesn't change anything," he said finally, the velvet of his voice rough and broken. "It's not proof. I mean, you're Sidhe, Faerie. Nothing's beyond you, not even—"

*Not even,* Cassandra thought, seeing in the stiffness of his face what Max was unable to say, *knowing what song Franny had been singing as she bled to death.* Her hands gripped the arms of her chair under the edge of the table, where he could not see. She should have known he would have thought things over before he fell asleep, and he would have told himself that of course she knew secret things about his life. It would take him a while longer to reach the next conclusion, that if she was Sidhe, and could do anything, then it also followed that she could do what she had told him had been done, and that therefore everything she had said to him could be true.

"There's no harm, then," she said, keeping her voice carefully neutral, "in my telling you the rest of the story, the events that bring us to this room."

"Go ahead," he said.

Cassandra drew a goblet toward her. As she expected, it was clean, no residue of wine left dried to the bottom. As she put her hand on the pitcher, Max raised his eyebrows, warming his hands around his mug of tea.

"Wine for breakfast?"

"We don't get drunk," she said as she poured, her eyes carefully watching the dark red stream as it flowed from jug to goblet, "and as you pointed out, we're not human." She set the pitcher down slightly to the left of where it has been, so that it was no longer precisely between them. She leaned back in her chair, focused her attention on a bloodstain near the neck of Max's T-shirt—she couldn't quite make herself look into his eyes—and began.

"The Songs tell us," she said, "that long ago, closer to

what was probably the middle of this Cycle, you were called Dancer at Dawn, or Dawntreader. Your mother was Light at the Summit, and your father was Raven of the Law. The Phoenix guides you. It was said then that you always knew the why of things, understanding their beginnings in a way that others could not. Then the Choosing came, and you became the Prince Guardian, the Talisman Keeper."

Max cautiously sniffed at the tea in his cup before taking a sip, apparently satisfied. "Wait a minute. What's the choosing?"

Cassandra found she had to consciously stop from speaking in the rhythms of Song telling, "When a Guardian feels her *dra'aj* Fading, or his, of course, though it's almost always a woman, she chooses an apprentice to be the next Guardian."

"And what does that mean, to be a guardian?"

Cassandra studied the leaf pattern glazed into her wine goblet as she turned it around in her fingers. "Not *a* guardian, *the* Guardian. The People have four sacred Talismans. There is *Ma'at*, the Stone of Virtue, which cries out when the High Prince steps upon it. There is *Porre'in*, the Spear of War. Whoever holds it leads the People in battle. There is *Sto'in*, the Cauldron of Plenty, font of *dra'aj*, from which comes all life, and all living things in the Lands, and there is the Sword of Justice, *Ti'ana*, which is never defeated. The Guardian keeps these Talismans safe until the High Prince comes."

"So he's a kind of regent?"

Cassandra risked a glance at his face, but Max was not looking at her. Instead, his eyes were narrowed into a very familiar frown of concentration. His Bard's look. What he would, no doubt, call his history teacher's look.

"In a manner of speaking," she said. "There's been no High Prince in my time, or the time of my father. It's possible for Riders to go their whole lives—and we live very long lives, by human terms—without ever knowing a High Prince. The times of these Princes are told of only in the Songs, and the Songs say these Princes come only toward the end of each Cycle, to guide the people into the new time. I doubt there are any now living who have seen the last High Prince."

There were times, Cassandra thought, when she had sat across a campfire from this man and watched him tune his harp as she told him this story. At this point, he usually asked about the Songs of the People, recognizing that they were histories, as were the epics of the Bards, but not this time. This time he only nodded for her to continue.

"You had not been the Prince Guardian for long when the Lands began to . . . darken. This darkening was more than the Fading our parents had long spoken of, as they told us of the glories of their youth, the glories we young ones had never known, when the *dra'aj* was plentiful and Guidebeasts were still seen. The Hunt appeared and grew stronger, though no one knew who had called it, and with it other monsters and abominations. Heroes did not return from quests. Two of the Nine Portals collapsed and shut, and there was not *dra'aj* enough to restore them. Places, some of them well-known places, changed so that they could not be found by Moving, one had actually to Ride there, only to find them blasted almost beyond recognition.

"A Rider called Dreamer of Time came to you saying that the Cycle was clearly turning, bringing with it the time for a High Prince. And Dreamer asked you to let the Talismans speak, certain that they would choose him. You refused."

Max frowned in concentration, putting down his cup and leaning forward on his elbows. "Why?"

"So far as the Songs tell, you shared your reasons with no one. Many supported you, saying that the Guardian alone could offer the Talismans. And many supported Dreamer, saying that the times were turning dark, and that a High Prince was needed to save the Lands."

"So came the war."

Max sat back abruptly. "Typical. Country's in trouble

and the best thing these two idiots can think to do is have a war."

Cassandra smiled. "You were one of those idiots, my Prince."

"That's what *you* say." Max shook his head. "You don't have to tell me. I lost, right?"

"You lost." Cassandra couldn't keep a small smile from escaping her control. Max had just spoken of himself as the Prince. It didn't surprise her. He *was* the Prince, however much he denied it.

"Speaking hypothetically," he added.

She nodded, his tone wiping the smile from her lips. Prince or not, Max Ravenhill was still a historian, trained to think objectively.

"Of course," she agreed. "Some called for your death, calling you a traitor to the People, the cause of war since you refused Dreamer the Talismans. But the majority of Riders were against that. It was one thing to disagree with your decisions, they thought, quite another to kill you. After all, who could know what might come of it, if the Guardian was killed? Then Dreamer himself, now called the Basilisk Prince after his Guidebeast, spoke for your Banishment, and prevailed. And here was this other world, the Shadowlands, to which you could be sent."

Max nodded, considering. "Okay, banishment. Good thinking. But it doesn't explain why I don't remember any of this."

"How could they Banish one of the Traveling Folk? A Rider who can Move where he wills?" Cassandra shrugged. "The Basilisk Prince knew of a Chant that would remove your *dra'aj*. We Wardens were sent, under Oaths, to protect you, lest, in your changed state, you be killed by humans. As I've said, we found that your memory had gone with your *dra'aj*, and though it was unexpected, it made a horrid kind of sense. Without *dra'aj* you couldn't return, without memory you couldn't rally your followers or be used as a tool by them," she pointed out sourly.

"But we've had very little to do over the years. You have some very powerful luck working for you. Hearth of the Wind, the Solitary who called himself Diggory, said that it was your *dra'aj*, awake inside you even though you did not feel it."

"Today hasn't felt very lucky, somehow."

She smiled and shrugged. "We still live."

Max waited, watching the warm firelight play across Cassandra's ivory skin, until it became apparent that she had finished speaking. He shifted a little under her steady gaze. Though she'd avoided meeting his eye, all along she'd been looking at him with a teacher's special patience, or as if she was taking him through his lines in a play she knew too well.

"So what's changed now?" he said. "Why come after the Guardian now?"

She spread her hands. "Diggory said it was because of something that only you know. That can only be the location of the Talismans. And that makes no sense." She frowned in concentration until Max coughed softly. "Your followers agreed not to oppose the Banishment so long as the Talismans remained safe, which is to say in hiding, until it was over. Only you know where they are."

Max shook his head slowly, barely able to stop himself from laughing out loud. Only the look on Cassandra's face stopped him. "But *I* don't know where they are."

For a moment Cassandra merely looked at him. "Then, regardless of what you believe, you'd better do your best to help me convince them you are the Prince Guardian. Otherwise, they may kill us out of hand as being of no use to them."

Max rolled his eyes upward. "Great," he said. "My life just might depend on my actually being someone else. So to save my life, I have to give up my life. You people are just charming, *so* glad I ran into you. Death by Hound is looking better and better." He pushed aside his mug of tea, cold now, and sat forward, leaning his right forearm on the edge of the table. In this light Cassandra's hair looked like old gold, and her eyes were dark as agates. Only her skin remained the palest of ivories. He could see where a fold of cloth had creased her cheek while she slept.

He knew nothing about her, Max realized, beyond that she had saved his life several times in the last day. No, not his life, he amended, the life of this Prince she claimed he was. This Prince she'd known for hundreds of years. The story she'd been telling explained what had brought him—if he was this Prince—to this room. She hadn't really explained what had brought her to this place.

"What's your name?" he asked her.

She looked up, startled into finally meeting his eyes. "My Rider name is Sword of Truth, or Truthsheart. But Cassandra will do, if you don't find it too ironic."

Max frowned, but only for a second. Of course she would name herself after the Trojan princess who tricked Apollo, who then cursed her, saying she would always speak the truth, but never be believed. Of course she would find it ironic.

"Did you know him? Is that why you're so sure about all this? Were you . . . friends?" Looking back, something in the way her voice changed at parts of the story told him this might be true. Even now, her face showed a subtle sadness as if it cost her some effort to answer him.

"I did not know the Prince Guardian," she said, her eyes fixed on a pastry her fingers were pulling into crumbs. "We Wardens weren't chosen from among those who knew you, my lord. We were from neutral families, small families, old, but with little *dra'aj*. My father withdrew from the conflict when my mother died. That was as much darkness as he was able to deal with. I don't think he actually remembered that there was a war, unless he was reminded. The world and its concerns had stopped for him."

Max's next question went unasked.

A soft bell, like the note of a bird, heralded a change in the movement of the air around them. The smell of applewood faded as fresh air spun through the room. Cassandra rose to her feet and drew Max to the side of the table, so that they stood with the fireplace to their backs. She tried to edge herself in front of him, but he stopped her with a hand on her arm.

"I would rather stand beside you, if I might."

She gave him a careful stare, and nodded.

The tapestries on the far side of the room shifted, billowing out slightly to allow the passage of a young Rider dressed in green. Cassandra saw that he was a Starward Rider like herself, pale, blue-eyed, with hair so fair it was almost white.

# Chapter Five

WHEN HE HEARD THE SOUND of axes,
Windwatcher bit back on the curse that rose
to his lips, and tried to ignore the chill spot
just below his heart. The sudden tightening of his muscles made him jerk back on the reins, and his Cloud
Horse swung her head in protest. But that was safe
enough, he could always claim to have been startled by
the noise.

"Coming here is not the cleverest thing we could
have done, my lord," Horse of Winter said quietly, shifting as if uncomfortable in his borrowed colors. "We
should have Moved directly to Griffinhome."

"So I believe you told me, Horse of Winter." *Would
that I had listened,* Windwatcher thought as he saluted
with a casual wave of the hand the Sunward Captain of
the Guard overseeing the men who wielded the darkmetal axes as they rode by. "You were right, this is a mistake, but I would have felt a coward if mere rumors had
kept us away." Curiosity could kill even so old a cat as
himself, he acknowledged, worrying at the inside of his
lip with his teeth, but when Horse of Winter had come
to Windfast with his urgent summons to Griffinhome,
Windwatcher had been on horseback already, going to

see with his own eyes what rumor had whispered to him. And it was true. The hollow cold spread until Windwatcher had to look down to make sure his hands still held his reins. The Stories told that Naturals lived through many Cycles, perhaps even through all of them, from the beginning of the world. This would be the last Cycle for the Natural of *Ne'agal* Wood.

Windwatcher forced his shoulders down and laid his left hand loosely on his leather-covered leg, not far from his sword hilt. The picture of idle curiosity—he hoped.

"What do you think it has done, the Natural of these Trees, to have merited this cleansing?" Horse asked.

"Who can tell? Undoubtedly committed some folly, real or imagined, which has forfeited the promised protection of the Basilisk Prince."

"Perhaps it merely ventured too close to the citadel of whatever pet of the Basilisk's has the disposal of this holding." The younger Rider murmured between lips carefully smiling to hide the feelings Windwatcher saw in his eyes.

The older Rider nodded as if in reply. He was careful never to complain about the Naturals in his own holding of Windfast. *Thank you, Roc that guides me, that I do not know the name of this poor Natural.* His cheeks grew hot, as Windwatcher acknowledged his relief. But without the name on his tongue, he need not stop to make inquiries, and Riding here was reckless enough without that.

The guard captain, watching them as they rode by, lifted her hand in belated acknowledgment of Windwatcher's salute, letting them pass without remark, but he knew himself a rash fool for coming this route. The path through *Ne'agal*, already less shaded than it had been, was long, and now that he and Horse of Winter were watched, they would have to Ride down every tortured span of it. Moving now would draw down the wrong kind of attention. Attention he could ill afford to draw, considering what he was wearing under his ruby-and-saffron tunic. It seemed to him likely that any-one looking at him would see the presence of his *gra'if* shining in his eyes.

"Is there nothing we can do?"

Windwatcher could hear the suppressed rage in the younger Rider's voice.

"Nothing but die with it, which itself achieves ex-actly nothing." The older Rider eyed the young mes-senger. "We are on our way to do what we can for all the others," he added when he saw Horse press his lips together.

At first, there had been general protest when the Basilisk's men began to move against Solitaries and the more active Naturals, but those who spoke had a habit of disappearing—Faded some said—and that was a lesson speedily learned. Not that Windwatcher had any love for Solitaries himself, no sensible Rider would, but when had the feeling against Naturals become so strong?

The instant they were out of sight of the workers, Windwatcher and Horse of Winter Moved into the court-yard of Griffinhome, the fortress of Honor of Souls, where servants in Honor's green-and-gold livery were already waiting. One helped Windwatcher dismount, taking his gloves and Riding cloak, while another took the Cloud Horses around to the stables to be brushed off and fed.

Horse of Winter exchanged the borrowed ruby-and-saffron cotte he had worn as Windwatcher's squire for the gold and green of his true colors as Herald of Honor of Souls, and started up the shallow, wide stone steps that led to Griffinhome's main doors. Windwatcher care-fully loosened the lacing at the collars of his waistcoat and shirt to reveal his *gra'if* mail, his eyes drawn upward to the turrets and domes of the fortress with a sense of seeing them for the first time. Fortress it was named, but battlements and barred gates notwithstanding, it had been built for beauty and charm, not to withstand any kind of attack.

"My lord?" Horse waited patiently at the great doors carved with their guardian Griffins.

"Griffinhome will not have Changed since my last visit."

"No, my lord." Horse exchanged a quick glance with one of the guards still in the courtyard.

"When I was young," Windwatcher said, his eyes still admiring the flight of the turrets, "I had a cousin living close to the Shaghana'ak Abyss, who was to be married. He caused his fortress to Change every time one crossed a threshold. The entire visit became a game of hide-and-be-found." Windwatcher shook his head slowly, still in awe of the magnificence of his cousin's feat. "When it came time for the ceremony, every door opened into the marriage room, delivering the guests to the correct place at the correct time."

"I have heard stories of such things, my lord, but none so elaborate as that."

Windwatcher drew his gaze down from the skies to the young Rider's face. "Now you wait to escort me through your fortress from courtesy, and policy, not from necessity."

"And did my lady, Honor of Souls, Change Griffinhome often in the days before?" the young Rider turned to lead Windwatcher through the open doors.

Windwatcher ran his hands through his mane of red hair, smoothing it into some semblance of order. "I would not have been a welcome guest of your lady in the days before the Great War. I supported the Basilisk Prince's claim to the Talismans, and she, as you well know, being of her *fara'ip,* is sister to the Prince Guardian's mother, and so one of *his* most loyal supporters."

He could feel the young Rider stiffen as they walked through the second, inner doors and into the interior of the fortress. Windwatcher waited for the inevitable question, but when it came, it was not was he expected.

"What became of your cousin?"

"One day, after the Great War, the Abyss widened, taking house and cousin with it."

"The Basilisk?"

"It was wise not to speculate upon such matters, even then."

"And does no one Change their fortresses now?" The young Rider's voice was wistful, as if he would have liked to see such a thing himself.

"It is not safe now to show the power of that much *dra'aj*. It might earn you a visit from the Basilisk Prince."

Horse of Winter nodded and turned into a narrow corridor.

"With respect, my lord, I find it hard to think that you once followed the Basilisk."

Ah, there was the expected question after all.

"Easy to see when the game of Guidebeasts is over exactly how one's pieces were swept from the board." A shame he had not been a better student of the game before the War, he thought, as they rounded the turn and began to climb a darkwood stair, each step inlaid with small green stones making a pattern of leaves and flowers. Like every other elder house, Windwatcher had had the choice of backing either the Prince Guardian or Dreamer of Time, who became the Basilisk Prince. He'd made his observations, examined the pieces and the moves . . .

"I expected the Guardian to lose, but," he shook his head. "There's a way of losing that is not losing . . . and a way of winning that has no triumph in it. I should after all have backed the Red, and not the White, however logical my choice seemed at the time. But in truth it was not logic that influenced me, but prejudice and personal dislike."

"Dawntreader must have seemed an odd choice for the old Guardian to have made, given his upbringing."

The older Rider looked sideways at the young one, but there was no criticism in Horse's face, only the willingness to understand. "The last Rider who should be chosen, many of us thought. And so, when the old Guardian Faded, and the new one refused Dreamer of Time a chance to offer himself to the Talismans, many of us were shocked that Dawntreader, the new, the untried Guardian, would refuse him. Arrogantly and without seeking counsel, without even recourse to the Talismans."

"Did no one think it suspicious that Dreamer of Time should be so quick to offer himself?"

"Give us credit for some few wits, Horse of Winter. No one doubted that the Cycle was turning, that the times did indeed call for a High Prince. Already there were fewer births, and mysterious changes to the Lands, inexplicable losses of *dra'aj,* and disappearances, as people, even places Faded. Some thought it the end of the world.

"And many of us, myself among them, believed we understood the Prince Guardian's motives all too well. We saw in Dreamer of Time a good candidate for High Prince . . ." Windwatcher let his voice fade away, not needing to say what Dreamer of Time had become.

"And in the Guardian you saw a Rider raised by Solitaries, a Rider you believed could not have the welfare of his own People in his heart. You saw a Cycle coming in which Riders would become the unimportant third," Horse finished the thought for him. "And so the War?"

"And so the War."

The War had been long, so long that everyone was grateful for an end to hostilities, though there were those who saw surrender in the Prince Guardian's request for a cease-fire. When it became evident that the Guardian did not feel that way, these same Riders would have had him compelled. The Prince Guardian had not feared them, saying that they could not force him without killing him, and that he knew they would not kill him. It was at this point that the Basilisk Prince, Dreamer of Time as he was still, came forward with his plan of Banishment. Let us give the Guardian time, he had suggested. While he thinks quietly and undisturbed, let us do what we can to ready the Lands for the turn of the Cycle. We will be prepared when the Guardian is ready to act.

Even the Guardian's followers saw wisdom in this, so measured and reasonable it had seemed, asking only that the Talismans be well protected in their Guardian's absence. So Dreamer of Time was listened to, and commended for his wisdom, and began to be called the Basilisk Prince.

But what was seen as wisdom had shown itself to be wiliness and cunning.

"The Banishment has been so much longer than any of us believed possible," Windwatcher said. "All of your life, which has been long, young as you are." Horse of Winter opened a chamber door and Windwatcher entered, turning in the doorway to complete his thought. "The Lands worsen, as if the Cycle turns faster now. And the Basilisk Prince gathers more and more power as those who would speak against him disappear, Faded or gone into hiding. He has long closed the Portals to the Shadowlands, so that none may visit the place of Banishment, and the Prince Guardian is spoken of no more."

"Except darkly." The younger Rider made no move to leave.

"Speak on," Windwatcher said.

"What of the Basilisk's strange malady?" Horse of Winter asked. "It is said that he is occasionally seen sweating and pale, his hands shaking."

Windwatcher shrugged. "I have heard this also, and I have heard that Riders disappear from his very court, even from his *fara'ip,* and nothing is done, no voice is raised. They say the Hunt is about him always now, fawning on him and doing his bidding."

"Surely not?" There was no mistaking the shock in the younger Rider's suddenly pale face.

"Who will speak against it? More and more are of the Basilisk's mind. They see nothing wrong in using Hounds to Hunt down Riders, see nothing wrong in killing Naturals. Somehow they cannot see that the Lands grow not more prosperous, but more poisoned."

Horse of Winter pulled out a cushioned chair and Windwatcher lowered himself into it with a sigh. He only hoped the news that had made it imperative to summon him was good. He thought he could guess why the Prince Guardian had refused the Basilisk on the Talismans' behalf. Given the chance, he thought he would now do the same himself. There were worse things, after all, than the end of the world. If they did not find a way to stop the Basilisk Prince, they would all, very soon, learn what that was.

Max found it difficult to swallow past the lump in his throat and the sudden dryness in his mouth. He never thought he'd look back with fondness on the attack of the Hound, but there was something to be said for events that moved so quickly you didn't have time to feel afraid.

Not that the smiling man standing before them, left thumb tucked in his belt, right wrist resting negligently on the basket hilt of a sword dangling unsheathed from the same belt, exactly inspired fear. In fact, the Rider looked enough like Cassandra to be her taller, fairer cousin. His eyes were a dark blue, their depths enhanced, if anything, by the color of his clothing. Belt, knee-high boots, breeches, short tunic, even the points of the laces closing the full sleeves of his shirt, were dyed an identical shade of rich emerald. His platinum hair was elaborately braided off his face, and hung down his back below his waist. He wore a single silver ring with a green stone in his left ear, and though his smile was open, it made Max conscious of every smear of dirt on his own skin, and every splotch of wet Hound's blood on his clothes.

The man turned his smile on Cassandra and inclined his head. "I am Lightborn," he said. "Honor of Souls is my mother, and the Griffin guides me."

Cassandra inclined her head once, never taking her eyes from the pale Rider's face, but did not speak.

Lightborn waited, lips compressed, until, with the smallest of shrugs, he turned and took a step toward Max, his hands outstretched as if in welcome. Cassandra slid between them, noiseless on the thick carpet, and Lightborn froze, backed off slowly, and lowered his arms.

"Your Warden almost killed three of my people," he said, his eyes flicking to Max over Cassandra's shoulder, "before we knocked her down." When his thumb was once more hooked in his belt, Cassandra eased back to her position next to Max.

"She'll do better next time," Max said.

Lightborn threw back his head and laughed. "Well said, my brother. And how did you enjoy the wine I left for you?"

Max hesitated, his heart suddenly pounding. He was fairly certain Cassandra would have mentioned a brother, if only as a way to offer him more proof.

"Are we brothers?" he said finally.

The man's smile died away as he shot an uneasy look at Cassandra. "You have been kind enough in the past so to speak of me. I trust I do not now overstep the Prince Guardian's good grace."

"Look—"

"Forgive me, my Prince, but my mother comes."

The tapestry was pulled aside by unseen hands to allow the entry of a formal party. Two of them, simply dressed in green and gold, with plain swords sheathed, took up positions next to the opening in the tapestries.

The lady who came smiling toward them was dressed in a green-and-gold gown that fell in a long drape to her feet, leaving her arms bare. She was clearly related to Lightborn, with the same delicate hawklike nose and beautifully arched eyebrows. And, like Lightborn, the

smile she gave Max was full of warmth. But Max would
have expected someone at least in her sixties, and this
woman looked no older than the man claiming to be
her son. Early thirties at the most would be Max's
guess, no older than himself, or Cassandra.

Max raised his eyebrows. Of course Cassandra claimed
that she was over a thousand years old, and that Max
himself was older still.

*These people aren't human,* Max reminded himself,
returning her smile with a shallow bow, *they can look
however they want.*

The man with her, foxy-haired with bronzed skin, and
dressed in deep ruby red and dark yellow, looked to be
in his late forties. His topaz eyes narrowed as Max
looked at him, but not in challenge. Max felt chilled, but
he bared his teeth in a grin just the same. He'd once had
a professor in graduate school at Seattle University with
that same calculating gaze, someone who made you feel
unprepared no matter how much you'd studied. Max's
stomach sank as it occurred to him that Professor Malcolm Jones might be part of his false memories. *Not
now,* he told himself, *think about that later.*

He glanced at Cassandra out of the corner of his eye.
She stood relaxed, feet shoulder-width apart, hands
hanging loose, knees slightly bent, lowering her center
of gravity. She had edged away from him again and
turned slightly, so that she could keep everyone in
sight. Her eyes were bright, and she seemed on the verge
of smiling.

Max had seen that almost smile on her face in the
alley, as she waited for the Hound to arrive. He stood a
little straighter, squaring his shoulders and taking a full
breath. They'd come out of that in one piece.

The lady in green-and-gold bowed, and as if this was
a signal, both the older man and Lightborn put their
hands on their sword hilts and began to draw. Fast as
thought, even while their blades were still clearing their
scabbards, Cassandra was in front of him, kicking the

sword out of Lightborn's hand, leaping to snatch it out of the air as it came down, and, landing on her toes, holding the point not at Lightborn, but at his mother's throat.

Lightborn took a step toward his mother before freezing into immobility, but the lady herself only smiled, her eyes sparkling as she slowly lowered her hand.

"My Prince," she said in a voice like silk on glass. "A word."

"A word," Max agreed, his eyes flicking between Cassandra's face and the point of her sword, millimeters from the older woman's neck.

"Fealty," said the lady, and at that word Lightborn sank down to one knee. After a slight hesitation, the older, redheaded man knelt also, and, keeping his gaze fixed steadily on Cassandra, reversed his sword, offered it hilt first to Max. Max stepped around Cassandra, careful not to crowd her, took the offered weapon, and backed away once more.

"I have no need to offer you my sword, my Prince," Lightborn murmured, "since your Warden holds it already."

Cassandra slowly lowered the blade she held, but did not back away.

The lady inclined her head. "You are right to be cautious, Truthsheart. You will not remember it, but you are known to me. Your mother was Clear of Light, and the Dragon guides you. You were one of the three Chosen-to-Watch. My name is Honor of Souls, my mother was Eye of Evening, and the Hippogriff guides me. My son you know, and this our comrade and adviser is Watches the Wind, he is Roc-guided. I knew your mother well, Truthsheart, and I welcome you to Griffinhome."

Max cleared his throat and touched Cassandra lightly on the shoulder with the fingertips of his free hand. "Perhaps if we put the swords away, there'd be less chance of killing someone by accident."

Honor of Souls turned back to him and her smile deepened as her eyes took on a soft glow. "From the look of Truthsheart," she said, "I doubt it would be an accident."

"Cassandra . . ." Max began.

"Who set the Signs on this room?" she said, ignoring him.

"I did," said Honor of Souls, her voice caressing. "For your own safety. My spies tell me that those who searched for you have returned to search the Shadowlands, not finding you here."

"There are not many still with *dra'aj* enough to Sign a room." It was impossible not to recognize the pride in Lightborn's voice.

His mother waved away his words. "I would give all I had to keep safe the Prince Guardian, even were he not the child of my sister."

Max flashed a look at Cassandra, but she looked back with eyes wide, shaking her head minutely. If he read her right, this was news to her as well. He looked back at Lightborn. Not brothers then, but cousins.

"You are not the ones who sent the Hound?" Cassandra's dark chocolate voice was softly hoarse, as if tense throat muscles were only just beginning to loosen.

"Indeed, we are not." It was impossible not to recognize and believe the tremor of distaste in Honor's voice.

Cassandra studied the older woman's face and nodded, satisfied. She took a step back, and lowered the sword. When Lightborn advanced with his hand out, however, Cassandra shook her head.

"I will trade you, sword for sword," she said, and Max jumped as Windwatcher tossed back his red hair and laughed out loud.

"By the Wards, she is right," he said, smiling and shaking his head, his voice rough and warm. "She knows none of us and we've taken her *gra'if* from her, helm and sword. Until we give it back she has no reason to trust or treat with us. And from what I see," he said, nodding at Max, "at this moment she speaks for the Prince."

Honor of Souls gestured to the two men standing

guard and one lifted his hand in casual salute before pushing his way through the folds of the arras. Honor turned back to Cassandra.

"I give you my word on the love I bore your mother that your *gra'if* comes."

Cassandra sketched a bow, reversed her grip on the sword and held it out, ornate hilt first, to the older woman. Honor took it with a smile and handed it to her son.

Once again Max found everyone, Cassandra included, looking at him, waiting for him. This time he wished he could make them look away. Max took another deep breath, and handed the older man his sword.

"I thank you, my Prince," Windwatcher said.

"Don't be so sure," Max said. He took a deep breath and let it out slowly. "I've got something to tell you."

"Where are your friends, Old One?"

The Troll known as Diggory spat out a mouthful of rock-gray blood and wished that he could have stained Dreamer of Time's pretty purple tunic with it. But that Basilisk spawn had already learned not to get too close. Diggory grinned.

"You may not be smiling very much longer," the Basilisk said, a hard edge showing through the melody of his voice.

"Perhaps not," the Troll agreed amiably. "But then I won't care, will I?"

"You will stop smiling long before you die, Son of Earth."

"So far, it seems I'm to die of boredom." This was fun, in its way. Diggory shifted his shoulders as well as he could, considering that he was hanging suspended in front of a darkmetal wall. The Basilisk and his inquisition had found that, effective as hanging him in midair might be if they intended merely to keep him, it was impossible to really torture a person unless there was something to push against. The last twelve hours had had their painful moments, but the inquisitors were discovering that it took a great deal to hurt a Troll. Even the parts of him which were now dragging on the floor didn't hurt. Much.

"Tell me what I wish to know, and all I will do is kill you. Refuse me, and I can do much worse."

Diggory laughed, more because he knew it would annoy the Basilisk than because he found anything funny. Almost, he *was* beginning to be bored. "You are stupider than you look," he finally said. "Nothing you wish to know can be learned from me. Where is the Prince Guardian? I don't know. Where are the Talismans? I don't know. Who does know? I don't know. I've just come from the Shadowlands, you idiot, and I can't tell you what I don't know, no matter what you do." He spat again, wincing at the sudden pull of a torn muscle in his chest. "You'd have been smarter to let me escape and then follow me."

"So you would know how to find him, if you were free?"

Diggory fell silent. He had forgotten that the Basilisk had always boasted of his little knowledge of and less congress with Solitaries. He would not know, therefore, that, Earth-born, Diggory could find anything that touched the earth. Even in the Shadowlands he had been able to find Truthsheart and the Prince Guardian in the subways. If his friends had touched the earth anywhere here in the Lands, Diggory would have a starting point for his search.

"If all I wanted was my freedom," he said finally, "I could be still in the Shadowlands, eating prey and building bridges."

"I would give you safe conduct to return there."

"You talk a great deal of what you'd give me. So far, all you've given me is a look at my own bowels."

The Basilisk gestured at the floor. "You could be mended. Find me the Guardian and you would have a Healer *and* your safe conduct. You have my word."

This time Diggory stopped the smile before it reached his lips. He knew exactly what that word was worth. The heat he felt rising in his blood was not all due to the Basilisk's lies, however. That was too old a story to fuel much fire. But that the ignorant spawn of a stone-faced Basilisk thought that *he* could trick a Solitary.

As if Diggory didn't know that if the Basilisk set him free it would be only for long enough to hang Max Ravenhill on a darkmetal wall. As if Diggory would trade his freedom, or anyone's freedom, for that. Better they were all dead, as his *fara'ip* believed him to be. His *fara'ip*. Now the Troll did smile. The Basilisk thought himself a trickster, did he? Well two could play at that game.

"What of my *fara'ip*?" he asked. "I would want them about me. Would you give them safe conduct as well?"

"Your *fara'ip*?"

Diggory could almost see the Basilisk's thoughts turning, could almost see him examining the idea, looking for a flaw. Was it possible? Could the Basilisk Prince's ignorance be deep enough to suppose that Solitaries were just that? Solitary?

"Yes, of course," the Sunward Rider said finally. "I would extend the safe conduct to your *fara'ip*."

Diggory stopped his by now unconscious struggle against his bonds and felt his abused muscles truly relax for the first time in hours.

"*All* my *fara'ip*?"

"All.

"You let me go, I find him for you, and you give me and all my *fara'ip* safe conduct; we may go wheresoever we please?"

"Yes."

"Done! IbindyouIbindyouIbindyou." Diggory laughed aloud, his glee wiping out, for the moment, any pain he might feel. The look on the Basilisk's face, half doubt, half suspicion, was tastier than many a human morsel had been.

"Of course I am bound," the Basilisk said smoothly, if with a trace of doubt in his voice. "I gave my word, did I not?"

"Ah, but what did you give your word to? You said you would give my *fara'ip* safe conduct. Did you even ask what *fara'ip* I might have? Or did you, foolish Rider that you are, think I had none? Do you even know who I am?

"I am Hearth of the Wind, you fool, the Last Born. The Earth is my *fara'ip*, and it is bound now, too, with your words. If you free me and go back on your word, you will never set safe foot to Earth again. The Prince Guardian is part of my *fara'ip*, and has been since I found him beside his dead mother. Free me, O Prince of Basilisks, and you free him. Give me safe conduct, and you give it to him."

Diggory laughed again. Now he knew why the Basilisk chose purple for his colors. It was because he turned such a lovely shade of it when enraged.

". . . . . . . . ." the Basilisk Prince said.

Diggory waited for his laughter to subside, shaking his head. "What? You're going to suck the *dra'aj* out of me like you did that poor Sunward fool yesterday? Why don't you try it and see what it gets you?"

The Basilisk turned an even darker shade of magenta. His skin seemed to swell and he grew taller, his breath escaping his lips in a hiss of foulness. His hair lifted, forming a crest, and his eyes grew red. Diggory did not even try to look away. Instead he spat again, and this time got the Basilisk right in its curving beak.

━━━◆━━━

Windwatcher slammed his palm down on the table with enough force to rattle the wine cups.

"Everything is changed if he does not know who he is."

Max opened his mouth but held his tongue when Cassandra placed her cool fingers on his wrist. She was right, he supposed. His opinion wouldn't change anything for these people. He might as well keep it to himself.

Windwatcher turned to Cassandra, "How long has he been like this?" he growled. "When did he lose his memory?"

"My lord," Cassandra's tone was chill, her courtesy sharp enough to cut. "He has always been as you see him, since the beginning. We Wardens assumed it was part of the Banishment," she continued, outlining the theory she had already shared with Max.

Max watched the three Riders look at each other as they took in what was evidently a surprising and unwelcome bit of news.

Finally Lightborn spoke. "Could this be the Chant of Oblivion?"

Honor nodded, eyes narrowed, her silver-white hair catching glints of light as she moved. "That, or some other binding, one we were not told of." She looked up. "One of the many things, it seems, the Basilisk did not tell us."

"This is not the time to rehearse the Basilisk's perfidy," Windwatcher growled. "It will not take us any farther down our road."

After the initial outcry, Lightborn had persuaded everyone to sit down at the table and see what clarity nourishment might bring to the discussion. Cassandra's *gra'if* had arrived, and everyone, including Max, had looked away as she had clutched at her battered shoulder bag, so ordinary and human looking in this perfect room. Other servants had arrived bringing platters of food. Honor of Souls had taken a seat at the center of one long side of the inlaid table, and had the two men to either side of her. Max sat facing her, with Cassandra on his right. Between them on the table lay the remains of yet more fruit, as well as spiced meats and sweet rolls. Max had tried something that looked like a chicken leg, and tasted like nothing he'd ever eaten. He found it difficult to keep his eyes away from platters which never seemed to empty, no matter how much people ate, and concentrate on the discussion.

"None who know me will doubt that I have no love for the Basilisk Prince," Windwatcher was saying, "nor have I reason to suppose that any here does. But I have a question. I did not know the Prince Guardian well—he was no intimate of mine," the man added with a nod to Lightborn and his mother. "There are many others like me among our present allies, and so you may take my question in a good spirit. How sure are we that this is the Prince? Your pardon, Truthsheart," he said with a small bow to Cassandra, "but I can suppose that in your zeal to protect the true Prince, it might occur to you to pass off another Rider, or even one of the Shadowfolk with a passable resemblance, to use as a lure for the Prince's enemies."

Max sat back in his chair, exhaling sharply as a wave of—was it relief?—surged through him. Of *course* that's what she'd done. That would explain everything, from his own certainty that he was no more or less than Max Ravenhill to her adamant refusal to even consider the possibility of a mistake. Not, he realized, sinking back down to earth, that he'd ever felt that Cassandra was lying to him. Mistaken, yes, but sincere.

Cassandra leaned back in her chair, raising her head from her tented fingers. "An excellent idea. I wish I'd thought of it." Her tone was one of speculation and interest. "But he has never had any memory of being the Prince Guardian, unless . . ."

Everyone waited politely for her to finish her thought, but Max thought he knew what she was thinking. Unable to change his fundamental nature, she'd told him. But what would that prove?

"What have you thought of, Sword of Truth?" Windwatcher was unable to contain his impatience.

Cassandra shrugged, shaking her head in dismissal. "If we had his *gra'if* . . ."

Lightborn clapped his hands and laughed. "That is what *I* call an excellent idea." He leaped to his feet, his platinum braids swinging as he went to the entrance and spoke quietly to one of the guards standing there. He waited until the man had nodded and left before returning to the table.

"If you give me but a moment, Windwatcher," Lightborn said as he sat down again at his mother's side, "I think I can provide the proof you need."

At first those at the table kept silent while they waited for the guard to bring Lightborn's proof. Then Windwatcher turned to Honor of Souls and, in a voice too quiet for Max to catch, began speaking urgently to her. Clearly the redheaded man was disturbed. Lightborn smiled at Max and seemed about to speak, but Cassandra shifted, drawing the younger Rider's eye, and he kept silent.

Max found his hands had formed fists, and he forced them to open. They couldn't have any proof, he told himself. He wasn't the Prince, so they didn't . . . But he couldn't help wondering what kind of proof Lightborn believed he had. What kind of proof would these people find acceptable? And what, if it came down to it, would he accept as proof himself? *Nothing,* he thought. They were all making a mistake, Cassandra included, and with any luck, this little demonstration of Lightborn's would convince everyone of that, and Max could . . .

Could what? Go home? Somehow that wasn't as attractive as it had seemed only a few hours ago. He looked to where Cassandra sat leaning back in her chair next to him, right ankle crossed over left knee, completely relaxed, as always. She'd saved his life—*no,* he thought, *she saved the Prince's life.* If he wasn't the Prince, she'd have no reason to stick around. But could *he* walk away from *her?* Did he want to? Say he could, and he wasn't so sure about that, could he walk away without knowing what would happen? Warfare, the political stresses and social tensions that led to armed conflict, was his life's work. Could he walk away from the chance to study it for real?

He smiled at himself. Listen to him, was his interest really so purely academic? Max was too old to kid himself that way. Could he really just go home and not try to help these people? Go home and wait for this Basilisk Prince guy to win? Tell himself he was minding his own business? And then what, wait for the Basilisk to show up back home? The Nazis had names for people who stood back and minded their own business.

"Your strategy's wrong," he said aloud. Everyone turned to look at him, but now he was in lecture mode, and thoroughly calm. "You need to get rid of this Basilisk Prince. Once he's dealt with, it won't matter where the Talismans are."

The three Riders across the table glanced at each other.

"Two things wrong with that, my Prince," Windwatcher said. "For one, we cannot, as you put it, 'deal' with the Basilisk. We are not strong enough. We need you, or the Talismans, or both, to rally support. Second, even should we rid ourselves of the Basilisk, the Lands need a High Prince, and for that, soon or late, we will need the Talismans."

"There's a third thing," Cassandra put in. "If it's the Basilisk who used the Chant of Oblivion against the Guardian, we must get him to remove it before we 'deal' with him."

The return of the guard, accompanied by two unarmed servants carrying between them a small chest made of flame-colored wood, put a stop to Max's reply. The chest was about five feet long, eighteen inches high, and two feet wide. Cassandra let out her breath in a slow whistle and stood as soon as she caught sight of it.

Lightborn and Cassandra between them cleared a spot on the table, and the servants put the chest down in front of Max. He looked at the faces around him and saw nothing to indicate what he should do next. Windwatcher was entirely impassive—the man might have been watching a chess game between moves. Honor of Souls patted Lightborn on the arm, pleased approval apparent on her face. Lightborn wore a sardonic smile, as if he were waiting for Max to respond to a dare and was certain that he knew what the outcome would be.

Only Cassandra looked at him with that same shadow of lingering sadness he'd seen in her face before, as if she knew that he was about to be made very unhappy. She had no doubts, Max thought, she never did have. For the first time since waking up, he began to wonder himself.

"Go ahead," she said. "Open it."

Max turned back to the chest, giving it a good long look. *Proof for them is proof for me,* he decided, feeling the truth of it settle on him. *I have to know.* His hands were on the lid, and his thumbs on the catches, before he even knew he meant to move. The carving was intricate and deep, as if the chest were a solid block of wood. Max blinked to give his eyes a chance to focus and saw that the carving represented scenes, and not just geometrical patterns. In one part people appeared to be gathered at a feast around a great cauldron; among the feasters were a group of young men fencing, the crowd around them cheering them on. Farther over he saw another crowd, some watching and some participating in games of spear throwing, archery, and more fencing. At the center near the bottom, between where Max's two hands rested on the catches, people and strange beasts looked on as a beautifully rendered bird rose out of its nest. As Max squinted, trying to see whether the nest was indeed made of flames as it appeared, the bird turned its head and slowly blinked one eye.

Max jerked his hands back as if from an electric shock. Cassandra closed her hand around his wrist. Her fingers warmed as if picking up heat from his body, and he turned to find her eyes fixed on his face.

"Is it supposed to do that?"

"When the right person touches it, yes."

Max looked back at the chest. He told himself again that these were Faerie, making carvings move wasn't beyond them. Yet he found there was a part of himself that wanted to be the right person, the person who could make this carving, this wood, live.

"Open it." Cassandra repeated as she released his wrist, her fingers lingering.

Max took a deep breath, thumbed open the catches, and pushed back the lid of the chest. A smell like baking apples rose from the heavy flame-colored damask inside. Gingerly, he pushed aside the wrappings, using only the very tips of his fingers, but he could still feel a trickle of power tingle its way up his forearms.

The sudden light made him squint, and the first thing Max saw as his eyes adjusted was a sword. Without thinking, he lifted it out, hefting it in his right hand and feeling how perfectly the hilt fit his grip. It felt warm, like a living thing. He held the blade up to his face, tested the edge with his left thumb, and pulled it back, bleeding. He grinned at Cassandra over the edge of the blade as he stuck his cut finger in his mouth, tasting the clean copper taste of his own blood. He put the sword down in the lid of the chest and lifted out a mail shirt like the one Cassandra was wearing under her filthy T-shirt. Or not like hers. Max looked more closely at the tiny fitted plates. Where Cassandra's were shaped to look like scales, these looked more like tiny feathers. He smoothed his hand along the metal and found it warm, like the feathers of a living bird.

He lifted it to pull it on over his head.

"Max."

He looked at Cassandra over the fold of metal.

"It goes next to the skin."

He grinned at her. Of course it did. That was where Cassandra was wearing hers. The other people in the room seemed far away as Max stripped off his own torn and dirty T-shirt and pulled the pliable warmth of the mail shirt over his head.

Max had once had a pair of gloves made for him by a master glover. They had fit so well that he had at times forgotten he was wearing them. The mail shirt made those gloves feel as if Max had been wearing ski boots on his hands. It didn't fit like a second skin, it *became* his skin. He could actually feel it adjust to fit, hugging each ridge of bone and muscle, until it was as much a part of him as his eyes or teeth.

Suddenly Max choked, shaking his head in an effort to clear it. *No,* he said, but the word couldn't pass the constriction in his throat as the mail shirt seemed to tighten. He wasn't the Prince after all, and this thing was trying to smother him, to kill him for daring to usurp its master's place. Part of him felt gleeful triumph that he was, after all, right, and everyone else wrong. Part of him felt a sorrowful loss.

He heard movement, and the voices of the others, but knew that even Cassandra wouldn't be fast enough to save him. He caught a flash of anger in someone's blue eyes.

The last thing he felt was the slam of the table edge as it hit his forehead.

# Chapter Six

STUPID, STUPID, STUPID. Cassandra finished counting Max's pulse and laid his arm back by his side on the heavy damask coverlet. Sitting down on the edge of the bed, one leg tucked under her, the breath she took shuddered, and she had to try again, and again, until her own breathing was as steady as Max's. He'd only fainted, after all. He was a little pale, but his pulse was strong and regular. She hadn't been so frightened since the Hound. She rubbed her eyes with the tips of her fingers. She'd thought she'd known what to expect—she was certainly familiar enough with the physical demands of wearing *gra'if*—but the psychological effects became so unconscious over time that she'd forgotten all about them. In his own mind, Max was a human being, but his body knew what he really was, and the conflict between what his mind knew and what his body knew . . . well, it was simply more than Max could take just now. Those who wore *gra'if* were more closely connected to their Guidebeasts, according to what the Songs told, and while the sensation of pulling it on was, by all accounts, nowhere near as consuming as meeting with that Beast, they might still have killed Max with this little experiment. Not that warning him would have made the least difference. That he would wake up only stiff, sore, and with a blinding headache was more luck than she deserved.

The room they'd been given in the guests' tower of Griffinhome was smaller and more intimate than the Signed room; a place for privacy and sleeping, not a conference room. The walls were covered with sandalwood paneling—darkwood, of course—instead of tapestries; the table was smaller and had only two chairs, but both of these had cushions and arms; the fireplace was cold, though there was wood laid ready to light. The real differences were the bed, piled with silk-covered cushions and down-filled bedding, and the two windows open to a sun-filled sky. Between the windows hung a drape of bright linen, thickly embroidered with a Phoenix rising from its nest of flame.

A noise in the hall drew her attention to the closed chamber door. There would be someone waiting there, more servant than guard, in case she or the Prince needed anything. It had taken a bit of persuasion, once she was sure Max wasn't choking to death, to get the older Riders to let her take Max to the rooms Honor of Souls had ready for them. Lightborn especially had wanted her to wake Max up, but in Windwatcher Cassandra had found an unexpected ally.

"Let him sleep," Windwatcher had said, his baritone growl causing everyone to turn and look to where the Sunward Rider still sat at the table. "Truthsheart is his Warden, and a Healer as well. At the least we know now who he is, not that we are any better off. Unless," Windwatcher had looked at Cassandra, "the *gra'if* . . . ?"

Cassandra leaned back against the bedpost at the foot of Max's bed, drawing her knees up and resting her forehead on her crossed arms. She had no more answer now than she'd had then. Though it *would* solve their problems, wouldn't it, and hers, too. If being reunited with his *gra'if* was enough to undo the effects of the Chant of Oblivion, if he woke up the Prince Guardian, and no longer Max Ravenhill . . . at the very least a good part of her personal difficulties would be ended. And at the most? She'd known the *gra'if* would recognize Max, and she'd said so, but whether it would do anything more . . .

Cassandra should have known that Windwatcher would understand; she'd seen the *gra'if* mail showing at the open collar of his red tunic, and the wavy-bladed dagger hanging at his belt. As Riders who had been fitted for *gra'if*, they shared a bond of experience that excluded Lightborn and his mother. *Gra'if*, arms and armor, was made by Solitaries, forged by a special process known to very few even of them, using the intended bearer's own blood. Not everyone was able to sustain the making of a complete set of *gra'if* armor and weapons; no one knew why, though there were plenty of theories. Some Riders had only a single *gra'if* gauntlet, or a dagger, but whatever pieces were made, they were literally an extension of the bearer's body. Those who had not undergone the process could have only a dim understanding of the bond between a Rider and *gra'if*.

She rolled her shoulders, loosening tight muscles, and ran her hands through her hair. That bond was something she'd have in common with the Prince, if Prince it was who awakened. But that was all they would share. Even if Max Ravenhill didn't remember her, didn't remember all the lives they'd shared together, at least they had the experience of living a human life in common. They might not have anything else, but they had symphonies and subways, the Inquisition and the Pieta, traffic jams and Titian, Shakespeare and rock and roll. Waking up and realizing it was the weekend, and even though the alarm had gone off, you didn't have to go into work today. Sunday morning crosswords and—

Cassandra looked up, her cycling thoughts stopped short by movement at the head of the bed. Max was waking up.

The first thing he sees is his own hands, holding a freshly sharpened goose quill pen. The parchment on the table, marked with the small symbols he uses to show the deployment of men, has been scraped clean for reuse several times already, and he hopes he won't have to do it again. The only way the duke can use his cavalry is to bring them in from the left flank. He knows the duke won't like to hear that, but it is the only way.

The candles flicker as a young man, tall, pale, with honey-gold hair and slate-gray eyes, closes the chamber door and smiles at him with Cassandra's mouth, and his heart turns over. When they're alone, she can leave off looking like a young man, passing herself off as his servant and squire. She couldn't be always with him, ready with her sword or her memory of how many other campaigns he had guided, if they knew she was a woman. He preferred not to think about what would happen if it came out that she was not even human. Their sharing of that secret is part of what binds them so closely together. But only part, and the smallest part, he thinks, as he watches her move scrolls and parchments from a chair. He loved her before he knew she was Faerie. He knows that he has loved her in other lives that he does not remember, and that he will love her again. And he believes that even when he returns to his own life, when the Banishment she has told him of is over, and he becomes his true self once again, he will still love her. She does not believe this, he knows; it is something that gives her a sad look from time to time. But he understands that his love for her is one of the few Truths about herself and the world around her that she does not see.

"Max," she says, and he knows she is speaking to him, even though his name is not Max, "You need to wake up now," she says. "Wake up."

And he does.

Max stamped his right foot to set his bootheel and turned to where Cassandra stood slouched, eyes closed, resting the back of her head against the door, her folded hands a pad for her tailbone. They'd both taken the time to wash and change their clothes, and she was dressed much the same way—though not in the same colors, he noticed—as he was himself: breeches made from a glove-soft leather tucked into riding boots whose heels rang on the wood floor as he walked toward her. His pale yellow shirt was cut close to the body, and over it he wore a cotte of flame red, thickly brocaded with phoenixes. Over the cotte was a harness, almost a vest, light, but elaborately woven from thin gold leather, meant to hold his weapons and other gear. Cassandra's shirt and breeches were silver, her cotte a dark blood-red, brocaded with dragons. Over it she wore a harness like his, but hers was made of fine strands of black leather, and supported a short sword on her left hip. The sword that should have hung down her back, the long sword she'd used to kill the Hound, was leaning against the stone wall, close to her right hand. Both cotte and shirt were open at the throat to show her *gra'if*.

Max touched his fingers to where his own *gra'if* lay under the fine cloth of his shirt. He had been intrigued when Cassandra had told him he didn't have to remove it to bathe. Less intrigued when she told him why. The *gra'if* had been made out of his own blood, it was literally a part of him—no wonder Cassandra's had always felt so warm, touching it was like touching her.

Proof for them was proof for him, he'd said when he was opening his *gra'if* chest, and no matter how much he still told himself it wasn't so . . . his skin and bones and blood knew that it was. This *gra'if* had been made for him—*from* him if what Cassandra said was true—and that meant he was the Prince.

Well, as *right* as the *gra'if* felt, as *True,* it didn't change what he wanted. His own clothes, his own bed, his own life.

"They're waiting for us, Max."

Max looked at Cassandra without lifting his head. "Are we ready for them?"

His heart lifted as she smiled. "Are *they* ready for us?"

⤙

The three Riders waiting in the bright sunny room all looked up as Max followed Cassandra in. As if they'd rehearsed it, their eyes flicked first at Max, and then at Cassandra. She shook her head minutely, and Max began to have an idea of how important it was to these people that the Prince be restored by the way the light died out of their eyes and their shoulders fell. Honor of Souls was slow to turn, and she offered Max the thronelike chair at the head of the table almost as an afterthought. She'd been hoping, he realized, that she could offer it to a restored Prince, but whether he had his memory or not, he was still the Prince.

Max came around the table, his boots clicking on the intricate parquet flooring. "Please," he said, putting his hand on the back of the chair to the right of the one Honor of Souls had offered him. "That should be your chair." He waited until she was seated at the head of the table before sitting down himself.

Windwatcher nodded, and sat down to Honor's left, across from Max, with Lightborn next to him. Cassandra sat forward on the edge of the chair to Max's right. Lightborn and Windwatcher both looked at Honor of Souls, waiting for her to speak, but the older woman was staring absently into the middle of the room, eyes unfocused.

"My lords," Cassandra said, and again, Max thought, it was a measure of their preoccupation that all three of the Riders jumped slightly at the sound of her voice, "why did you bring the Prince Guardian here? Why does the Basilisk Prince want him? What is it that could not wait until the end of the Banishment?"

Windwatcher narrowed his eyes, as if he wanted to

protest her right to speak up, but the older Rider sub-sided when Cassandra turned to him and raised her eye-brows. Max covered a smile with his hand. It was as if the words "Don't try it, buddy" had been said aloud.

"Does your Oath still bind you?" Windwatcher asked.

Cassandra sat up straighter, placing her hand lightly on Max's wrist. Max, unsure what Windwatcher meant by his question, found his heartbeat returning to nor-mal, relaxed by her touch.

"Here's the thing," she said, leaning forward to tap the polished inlay of the tabletop with one fingernail. Max smiled to hear her fall into the cocky familiarity of human speech. *She's here for* me, he thought, *she's on my side.* "He's safer with me than he is with any of you—always will be, Oath or no Oath. So unless you tell me what's going on, I'm out of here, and he goes with me." She glanced at Max, and when he nodded, cocked her head at the other three and raised her eyebrows. "Clear so far?"

"We would stop you," Lightborn said, the steel in his tone at odds with the smile on his face.

"You would try," agreed Cassandra. She sat back in her chair, and folded her arms, the picture of stubborn resistance. But Max had seen her slipping two bright *gra'if* daggers into her sleeves, and knew she was ready to back up her words. He squeezed his eyes shut. This was all he needed.

"Stop," he said without thinking. Honor of Souls, who had been gently drumming the side of her wine cup with her fingertips, keeping time to a tune only she could hear, froze in midtap. Windwatcher and Lightborn both sat back in their chairs. Only Cassandra did not move. Max swallowed, his mouth suddenly dry. "If you chil-dren are through checking whose sword is longer, maybe we can get back to the matter at hand." He turned to Honor of Souls. "You were about to tell us why you brought us here."

A curious smile, a twinkle in her eye, and Honor opened

her mouth to speak, only to have Lightborn cut in before she could begin.

"The Basilisk Prince wants the Talismans, and the Prince Guardian is the only one who knows where they are."

A little muscle jumped at the side of Cassandra's mouth as she shook her head. "When the Banishment ends, the Talismans will reappear, and everyone will know where they are. Try again."

This time Honor of Souls raised her hand, and Lightborn subsided, leaning back in his chair, eyes on Cassandra.

"The Basilisk Prince does not wish to wait," Honor said, in her cool silk voice. "He wants the Talismans now, and if that is not possible, he wants the Guardian in his hands and captive when the Talismans appear, not free and a rallying point for others." Honor looked around the table before focusing once more on Max and Cassandra. "The Basilisk has found the Chant of Binding."

Max looked at Cassandra, ready to take his cue from her reaction, but this time her face was blank. A cold spot in his stomach, there for so long he'd started to ignore it, expanded to twice its size. He already knew Cassandra well enough to know that showing nothing but calm wasn't good. He glanced quickly at the others, and saw nothing there to reassure him. Lightborn had a hand to his ear, twisting his earring. Windwatcher leaned forward on one elbow, chin on his fisted hand, but the knuckles of that hand were white.

"What does that mean?" His voice trembled with the beating of his heart, but no one else seemed to notice.

"According to the Songs which touch upon it," Honor said, "the Chant of Binding goes back to the very first Cycle, or at the least to the Cycle when the Talismans were made, if they are not the same." The elder hesitated, her eyes searched Max's face. "It is for the Guardian only to know it, for it can be used to bind the Talismans."

"To *bind* the—" Cassandra's voice climbed higher as

she bit off her words. Max realized that the pain in his wrist was her hand, clamped so tight that he had reached across to grab at her fingers before he was consciously aware of moving. He forced himself to stop trying to pry her fingers loose and instead laid his hand gently on hers.

"What? What is it?" he said through clenched teeth.

"The Talismans cannot be bound by force," she said, loosening her grip. "They cannot. They *must* not."

"Okay, okay. Take a deep breath and explain it to the human guy. What's the real problem? The Talismans get bound anyway, don't they?"

A bit of color returned to Cassandra's face as she breathed more slowly. "You don't understand. These aren't just symbols like a human king's crown and scepter; the Talismans are the manifestation of the Lands themselves. The Guardian has the responsibility of protecting the Talismans, of preserving them and through them the Lands and all the People: Rider, Solitary, and Natural. When the time comes, and the High Prince is chosen, the Guardian binds the Prince to the Talismans, to the Lands, with mutual consent." She shook his arm. "Do you see? The Prince is bound *to* the Talismans—not the other way around. What will happen if that binding is reversed, so that the Basilisk Prince became not the servant of the Talismans, but their master?"

"That is what the Basilisk seeks," Lightborn said, his tone for the first time without the lilt and archness of his courtier's voice. Part of Max noted how much he preferred this voice. "Dominion over all the Lands. Not to lead, but to drag by the throat."

Max bit his lip. Part of him wanted to laugh, to say, "Ah, yes, the old world-domination trick," but he remembered the Hound, the touch of its paws, the cold focus of its eyes. His fingers moved as if by themselves to touch his *gra'if,* rubbing until he could feel the tiny scales. It was all real. All of it.

"That's not all," he said, his voice sounding hollow

and strange to his ears. "You say the Talismans will manifest at the end of the Banishment. Will the Banishment end if the Prince Guardian dies?"

"No," Windwatcher said firmly. "Indeed, that was the very reason Banishment was chosen—to protect the Guardian's life."

"But he doesn't have to live beyond that." Max looked up, seeing the truth in their faces.

Windwatcher nodded. "If the Basilisk Prince succeeds, it means the end of the Lands as we know them. He is already making of them a twisted blight, and . . ." the old soldier looked as though he were about to spit, remembered where he was, and refrained. "There are no children of this generation, neither Rider nor Solitary nor Natural," he said finally. "Without the Prince, if the Cycle does not turn, this will be the end of the People." Windwatcher clamped his jaws tight.

"We cannot have the Basilisk as High Prince, we cannot allow him to bond with the Talismans by force." Honor's voice sank to a thread of sound. "Better the Cycle turns without us. We *must* keep the Talismans out of his hands, we must take them now, ourselves, and destroy them, if need be."

"That is our purpose," Windwatcher said. He leaned forward rapping the table with his knuckles, looking from Max to Cassandra and back again. "We bring back the Prince Guardian before his Banishment is ended, that he may serve his purpose. That he may protect the Talismans."

Cassandra sat back, patting the arms of her chair with her open palms, staring at some spot high up on the opposite wall. There was nothing there but a pattern in the paneling. "And that's the reason for the Hound, and the others—no one is trying to kill him, just to bring him alive to the Basilisk." She lowered her gaze and looked at the others, searching their faces in turn, her eyes narrowed. "To keep him until it's time to kill him. Or even to make him tell where the Talismans are."

"Yes."

"How long do we have?" Cassandra said.

"One turn of the Sun," Lightborn said.

Cassandra gripped the arms of her chair.

Max looked from face to face. "Explanations please."

Eyes lowered, Cassandra spoke through trembling lips. "A little more than a week," she said, "and the Talismans will be revealed, and the Basilisk will simply take them . . ." Her voice faded away and she licked her lips.

"Is there a way to restore him?" Windwatcher growled. Max's heart jumped in his chest. This was the real question, wasn't it? The one he was more than half afraid to hear answered.

"I will not trouble to deny," Windwatcher was saying, "that you did not have my support before the Great War, when Dreamer of Time asked to be Tested. Like many, I mistrusted that a Rider raised by Solitaries was a true Rider. Well, I will fight beside you now; I would fight beside even Solitaries, and I am not the only one whose heart has changed in this way." The old Rider's eyes narrowed, and such was the man's focus that it seemed Max was alone in the room with him. "You would not give your reasons for refusing Dreamer of Time—an action we took to be a sign of your arrogance, and your holding yourself apart from Riders, your true people." Windwatcher lowered his gaze and frowned before looking Max once more in the eye. "Many of us can guess at your reasons now. Since we are speaking truth," Windwatcher looked at the other faces around the table, "I have said I would now give the Prince Guardian my backing, nor will I withdraw it, not for the Hunt, or any other peril." Windwatcher touched his *gra'if* with the first two fingers of his right hand, and Max felt a sudden thickness in his throat, knowing that he'd just seen the man swear an oath. "But I know what others will say. Some who would give their support gladly to the Prince Guardian will not fight without him. So, I ask again, can he be restored?"

"There may be a way," Lightborn said.

Cassandra looked up into the silence that greeted Lightborn's words, aware of the sinking of her stomach, aware yet again of the imminence of loss. *No,* she reminded herself, *this is good, this is what we want.* Even though a part of her refused to believe it. Sure, she'd told herself years before that there could never again be anything but her Oath between her and the Exile, but . . . knowing that something was coming wasn't the same as facing it. With the end of the Banishment, she would finally be free. And alone.

"There is someone who knows a great deal about the Chant of Oblivion," Lightborn said. "It is possible she might have a suggestion."

The others fell silent as Lightborn left the room. Max was flushed, and it was all Cassandra could do to stop herself from laying her hand against his cheek to check for fever. Instead, she rubbed her own face, her eyes feeling gritty with exhaustion. Maybe if this was really over, if her Wardenship was done, she could beg a bed of Honor of Souls and get some sleep.

"You said he was touched by a Hound," Windwatcher said. "What of that?"

Cassandra roused herself, blinking. She should have known it would be the old warrior who would pick up that point. "I killed it," she said, ignoring the challenge in the older man's lifted eyebrow, "but if there are more—if the Basilisk Prince is using the Hunt . . ." she lifted her own brows, making it clear she was waiting for Windwatcher to tell her what he knew.

"People have not wanted to believe it," Windwatcher finally said, his baritone rumble almost too soft to hear.

"I hear you," Cassandra murmured, remembering the Hound's blood on her jeans, still fresh and liquid, as it would always be. Liquid and fresh—

Cassandra sat up straight. "Our clothes," she said. "Where are they?"

"Taken to be burned, I hope," Honor of Souls said.

"No," Cassandra said, sitting on the forward edge of her chair. "That was Hound's blood, and we can use it to lure them here."

"For what possible purpose?"

"To kill them," Cassandra said.

"Of course." Max saw where Cassandra was going with this. "We've got to assume that they'll be sent after us again, right? This way we control the when and the where. We can be ready for them when they come."

"Not possible." Windwatcher shook his head.

Cassandra knew what was behind the older Rider's words. For most Riders, Hounds, indeed the Hunt itself, had been only something the Songs told of. Her own father had seen the Hunt once, years before she was born, and some said that Max's mother had been killed by the Hunt, leaving him to be brought up by Solitaries.

"I assure you they *can* be killed. I was taught by the Wild Rider Nighthawk, who was Warden with me in the Shadowlands. He had killed one in his youth, and he taught me the method, seeing that I bore *gra'if,* as he did." It was Nighthawk who had warned her not to look it in the eye, stressing that she must keep striking, no matter what form it took. "Kill it, or make sure it kills you," the grizzled veteran had said, "and whatever happens, do not let it feed while you still live."

"And where is your fellow Warden now?" Windwatcher asked.

"I don't know," she was forced to answer. Had he followed his own advice? she wondered with a sudden shiver. Could she hope that the old warrior had killed the Hound that found him, and was even now somewhere in the Shadowlands, hiding from the rest of the Hunt?

"I think we will burn your clothes, Truthsheart. Anything else is too dangerous."

She was marshaling her thoughts to continue the argument when Lightborn returned, ushering in with him a young female Rider. Another Starward, Cassandra noted without much interest. Once such things would have made a difference to her, but after years among humans, petty distinctions of coloring and—

"Oh, god," she said, her heart thumping. "Moon?" Exhaustion forgotten, Cassandra rose to her feet.

The younger woman had stopped in her tracks, staring at Cassandra. The next moment she was in Cassandra's arms sobbing out the words, "Sister, my sister."

Cassandra held Moon fiercely, breathing in the familiar poppy scent of her hair, having time to marvel that the girl was so much taller than she had been the last time Cassandra had held her in her arms.

"Charming as this is, we are under a pressure of time." Cassandra was sure that she could hear a whisper of real feeling under the rock-hard tone of command in Windwatcher's voice. "Are we to understand, Lightborn that your expert is of our Warden's *fara'ip?*"

"Indeed, I am Walks Under the Moon," the young Rider said. She loosened her hug only enough to turn and face the Sunward Rider. "My mother was Clear of Light, and the Manticore guides me. You may say, that my sister being a Warden is what made me an expert." She inclined her head to Honor of Souls. "You will forgive me, my lady," she said. "I was told there was a Warden with the Prince, and I hoped, but . . ." She turned back to Cassandra and this time gave her an almost shy smile. Cassandra took her sister by the shoulders and kissed her, once on each cheek, and once on the forehead.

"We will talk later," she said, unable to suppress a smile as she led her sister to the table.

Walks Under the Moon took the vacant chair next to Cassandra, sat up straight, and folded her hands primly in front of her.

"Lady Honor of Souls has provided me with Singers, and I have spent the last seven turns of Sun, Moon, and Stars searching through the Songs we have of this Cycle and the last, as well as those fragments we know to come from Cycles past, though we do not know how far past. I looked for the true Song of Chants that holds within its Choruses and Verses what we know of all the Chants of the People. I reasoned that if we could learn from it the source of the Chant of Oblivion—"

"We could get the Chant ourselves," Cassandra said, patting her sister on the girl's folded hands. It had been long, so long she had thought herself forgotten, but it was good to know that when Max—when the Exile was lost to her, she would not be alone. She would have her *fara'ip* again.

"Precisely. The Song of Chants is long, and some say as old as the Cycles themselves, and has as many versions as there are Singers," Moon continued in a voice very like that of an old professor of medicine Cassandra had once heard lecturing. "It has obviously become vulgarized over time, mixed with other Songs, new verses added when the memories of the Singers grew faulty. I needed to compare hundreds of versions to finally unite all the true pieces of the Song. As many as seven Singers have taken the better part of three turns of the Moon to teach me these true Verses."

Cassandra saw Max nodding out of the corner of her eye. Of course, Moon's words would make sense to him as a historian; even she had seen, over the years she'd spent in the Shadowlands, how even poems that were written down developed variations, and she'd seen how scholars' research could sort out the true from the false.

"Is there a point to this?" Max asked, chin in hand. He looked so much like a professor listening to someone's research proposal that Cassandra could almost hear the rustle of paper and the coughing of students.

"One Chorus of the Song of Chants tells us that, among others, the Chant of Oblivion can be found at the Tarn of Souls. Another Chorus tells that a journey was made to the Tarn four turns of the Moon before the Great War."

Cassandra felt a sudden chill, as if somewhere a door

to winter had been opened, and an icy blast had entered the house. "By the Basilisk Prince?"

"Is it possible?" There was something perilously close to admiration in Windwatcher's voice. "Could he have laid his plans so early?"

"So I believe," Moon said, eyes fixed on her folded hands, "though the Song tells no names. If it was the Basilisk, however, he obtained three Chants in all, each of which works on the *dra'aj* in some way. One he used to bespell the *dra'aj* of the Prince Guardian; one is the Chant of Oblivion, which makes one forget the *dra'aj,* and with it oneself; the third one I am not so sure of, it appears to free the *dra'aj,* separating it and allowing it to be . . . harvested."

"What?" Cassandra could see from the elders' faces that however diffident Moon was, this last possibility was not news to them.

Windwatcher and Honor of Souls traded looks, but this time it was Lightborn who spoke. He cleared his throat and shot a glance at Max before turning to Cassandra, his mouth twisted a little to one side in an apologetic smile.

*He's embarrassed,* she thought, surprised.

"The Basilisk keeps his *fara'ip* close about him." Lightborn's eyes finally found something to focus on at the far side of the room.

*Not embarrassed,* Cassandra realized. *Ashamed.*

"From time to time, a malady overtakes him. He becomes pale as the moon—he's a Sunward, did you know that?—and his face is drawn, sweaty. Lately, his hands shake and jerk, and his lips tremble. He seems unable to eat." Lightborn shook his head and took another breath. "Or uninterested. When this happens, he chooses someone, usually some servant, but not always. Not always," the Rider cleared his throat. "When the Basilisk returns, alone, he is restored, stronger even, than he had been before. And the other Rider is never seen again."

*Drug addict,* Cassandra thought. *No,* dra'aj *addict.*

"We think this third Chant allows the Basilisk to eat *dra'aj*," Moon added, when it appeared that Lightborn would not continue. "It has even been said that a Basilisk has been seen in his Citadel."

Cassandra nodded stiffly, torn between horror and awe. Of course, his Guide was a Basilisk, that was the source of his title. If he were indeed eating *dra'aj,* it *could* be possible, she supposed, for him to become strong enough for his Guidebeast to manifest.

Max knew from the pallor of their faces, the way Lightborn tore apart the napkin he held in his hands, that this was bad, but it made no sense to him. "What is it? What does this mean?"

Cassandra wet her lips before answering him. "No one has enough *dra'aj* for their Guidebeast to manifest. No one. Not in our time. If the Basilisk Prince can do this—"

"There are some who swear," Lightborn said, through stiff lips, "that they have seen it. That the Basilisk drinks the *dra'aj* of others, there is no doubt."

The silence was heavy enough to feel.

"So he's a kind of, what? Vampire?" Max asked, his brow furrowed.

"I think it may be worse than that," Cassandra said. "I've seen this type of behavior among humans," she glanced at Max again, "we both have. The sweats, the shaking, the loss of appetite. He's addicted now, dependent on eating *dra'aj.*" She pushed her hands through her hair. "He'll go on needing more and more, just to feel normal."

"And this is the Rider who would be our High Prince." Windwatcher's voice was heavy.

And there it was. The part of Max that was the history professor rubbed its hands in academic satisfaction. This is what made for interesting study. But most of him felt hollow and cold. Political ambition and savvy wedded with instability, perhaps even insanity. An Alexander would have been bad enough, but a Hitler?

"We must go ourselves to the Tarn of Souls," Moon was saying, leaning forward, "taking the Prince Guardian with us, and obtain there the Chant that will free him."

"Is this possible?" Cassandra asked.

"How can we know, until we have the Chant?" Moon said. "The Basilisk learned how to use it; we may do the same."

"I do not see an alternative," Lightborn said dryly in his light voice.

"Where is the Tarn?" Windwatcher asked.

"We cannot Move there," Moon said. "The Songs tell of no one except the Basilisk Prince who has actually been there. But there are many Songs that tell of the Tarn of Souls, and how one might find it, who wishes to speak to the Lady there. We would have to Ride, but we should be able to find the Tarn before the next turning of the Moon."

"A small company of Riders," Honor suggested. "Large enough to defend against those Solitaries and Naturals who may seek to attack us, but small enough that we may hope to pass unnoticed by the Basilisk's men."

"Best if *we* do not Ride then," Windwatcher said to Honor. "I have been summoned to court, to witness the dedication of the Basilisk's Garden, as I am sure you have as well?" Honor of Souls agreed with a grimace of distaste. "Then I will think which of my Riders will not be missed."

"I will Ride." Lightborn looked around the table. "The Basilisk will not think to see me for some days, knowing that I visit my home."

"See you be sure of that," Windwatcher growled.

Lightborn's face hardened, and for a moment he looked as if he might speak, but the touch of his mother's fingertips resting lightly on his hand kept him silent.

"It does not matter which of us is willing, unless the Prince will go." Lightborn finally said, turning to Max.

A shock ran through Max as everyone at the table turned to look at him.

"Whoa, whoa, wait a minute," he said, raising his hands palms outward. There was a tightening in his chest as it was brought home to him where all this talk was leading. He'd let himself get distracted by the political puzzle, lost in thinking about these lives and their problems in a haze of academic abstraction. He'd forgotten that they were actually talking about him. About *his* going to this Tarn, about this Chant being used on *him*. He knew what his answer had to be.

"I can't do this."

"Max—"

"No!" Max flung away Cassandra's reaching hand. He couldn't believe this. Here they had been talking about him, deciding about his life, as if he weren't even in the room. As if they didn't realize what they were asking him to do.

"I'm sorry, but I can't do this. If you had even a clue what you were asking, you wouldn't." He pushed back his chair and stood, looking from Lightborn to Windwatcher and back. Would either of them try to stop him? He looked back at Cassandra. Would she? "You're asking me to . . . to . . ." Fists clenched, shoulders hunched against the raised voices behind him, Max pushed past the guards in the doorway.

# Chapter Seven

CASSANDRA WAS HALFWAY to the door when Lightborn grabbed her by the arm and spun her around.

"What was done to him, there in the Shadowlands? That coward's answer is not the Prince's."

Muscles twitching with tension, Cassandra very slowly lifted her hand from the hilt of her shorter sword and held it open, fingers spread. She had seized it out of reflex, and she had to be certain everyone saw her letting it go. Lightborn, his face strained and pale, took a step back from her, though he rested his hand on his own sword seemingly by accident as he moved away.

Cassandra waited for him to draw, released a deep breath when he did not. "Better you should ask the Basilisk what was done before we had him, or perhaps I should say what *else* was done. This is nothing of ours. He is no coward, but he is not the Prince you knew."

Honor of Souls and Windwatcher were both on their feet, both in their own way maneuvering to stand between her and Lightborn. Only Moon, her hand to her mouth, had not moved from her seat at the table.

"Come, we must have peace," Honor of Souls said, holding out a hand to each of them. "If we fight among ourselves, the Basilisk will win. Lightborn, that you would even pretend to draw on a Rider bearing *gra'if* shows you lack the sense your Guidebeast gave you. Truthsheart, for the love I bore your mother, take your seat again, I beseech you. Let us finish our council, and when we have a plan, that will be time to speak again with the Prince Guardian."

Cassandra squeezed her eyes shut against a stab of headache. She wished she could simply Move Max back to Toronto, away from all these people, give him back his life as Ravenhill, the life he wanted. But even if these people would let her do it, she knew the Basilisk would not. He would hunt Max down until he found him. What was it Max had said? In order to save his life, he had to become someone else? Well, it looked like he was right. They were out of options. They had to keep the Talismans from the Basilisk Prince. They couldn't leave the Lands, and all the People in it—Rider, Solitary, and Natural—in the hands of an uncontrolled addict. She saw that clearly—but would he see it the same way?

"I will speak with him," she said. "Time for plans when he has agreed."

---

Lightborn left the council room as soon as he decently could, his face flaming hot at the memory of his exchange with the Warden. He made his way down to the stables, taking his time, walking more slowly as he calmed down, reluctant to take his temper and his anxiety—he swore by his Guidebeast that it was not fear—to disturb the Cloud Horses. The stables were his refuge, the calm of the great horses his balm, but there was more to his purpose now than the regaining of his own equilibrium. The Tarn of Souls was no ordinary place, and the journey would have its own perils. He had raised these horses from birth, and they would do whatever he wished without question. Still, it suited him to ask.

After he had spoken to them, each one individually, using their secret names that only he knew, and receiving the answer he expected, Lightborn turned to the other tasks necessary for the Journey. He was checking equipment, testing the fastenings on each saddle, the buckles of the delicate bridles, when he heard Honor of Souls enter the stable behind him.

"Did you make that?" she asked him, laying her long graceful fingers on the jeweled buckle in his hand.

"Long ago," he said. "It shines with a different brilliance when it is under the Sun, the Moon, or the Stars."

"Like the cloak pin you made for me?"

Lightborn nodded, smiling.

"So well you think of your mother, then, that you make her the same jewelry that you make for your horses?"

Lightborn shook his head at the old joke.

"Did you tell him?" she asked.

"You were too quick, I had no time," he said, turning away from her to set the buckle down.

His mother waited.

"He does not know me," Lightborn said finally. "How can he trust me now if I tell him the truth of it?"

"Better you should tell him now than that he learns of it from others."

"What others? There is only one other who can tell him."

The silence in the stable was broken only by the shuffle of hooves.

"Not so," Honor of Souls finally said. "I can tell him."

Lightborn covered his eyes with the heels of his hands. "What if he need never learn of it? How if it should come to pass that way?"

For answer his mother took his wrists, gently pulling his hands away from his face. She stroked his cheek with her cool palm. Lightborn closed his eyes.

"The path you walk is so narrow, and the fall so very far should you misstep," she said softly.

"I will be careful," Lightborn promised.

His mother believed that he was through with all deceptions, Lightborn thought as he followed her across the starlit courtyard and back into Griffinhome. Lightborn wished that it were so. What if they could not restore the Prince? They could not let the Basilisk find him. A problem with only one solution is no problem, his father used to say.

How could Lightborn tell his friend the truth, when he might have to kill him?

Walks Under the Moon gripped the edge of the table she sat on and looked down at her swinging feet. The table trembled with her movement, but that was part of the fun. Her soft leather slippers were the same silver-gray color as her sister's eyes, her gown the silver, red, and black of their *fara'ip*. She refused to wear the monochrome dress of the court dandies. Her lip curled back. Let everyone take her for a lesser house, unaware of court fashions; she knew her true value. Moon pointed her toes out, then in.

She smiled, swinging her feet separately, feeling the table shift to accommodate the difference in her movement. She'd only had leisure for short visits home for, oh, many turnings of Sun, Moon, and Stars, but that would all be changed now. Now that Truthsheart was returned, and they were a *fara'ip* again, they would go home to Lightstead, and it would *be* their home once again, restored.

Once Truthsheart was freed of her Oath.

Moon sighed, disappointment pressing her lips together. She had seen her sister at last, that was something, and more than something. She closed her eyes and saw again that look of special sunny warmth that only Truthsheart had ever shown her. But Truthsheart was still bound. Moon frowned, her feet still.

Surely once the Exile was restored, Truthsheart would be free, released from the Oath their father had forced her to take.

They had found their father in his tower room. His favorite room since his wife, their mother, had died. Moon did not know where the room was, exactly—since her father's Fading she had never been able to Move there again.

They had stood, hand in hand, and watched quietly until their father turned from the window, which that day had looked out over a bank of clouds. When he faced them, Truthsheart spoke.

"I will go, Father," she had said. Little Moon had pressed her face into her older sister's side, trying not to cry.

"You may refuse, Truthsheart," her father had answered. But not, Moon remembered, in a voice that said he wished her to refuse. And not, Moon supposed, that Truthsheart had really been able to refuse. Already a *gra'if* wearer, she was a Healer, after all, a rare Gift even among the Dragonborn. A good choice to accompany the Exile and his Wardens to the Shadowlands.

"I will go, Father," Truthsheart had repeated, and Moon felt again in memory how her sister had stroked her hair with her warm, *gra'if*-metaled hand. And he, who was their father, had nodded and turned back to his window.

Moon had cried then, but she had managed, jaw clenched tightly, not to beg her sister to stay. She knew very well, even then, that Truthsheart would never have left her if their father's illness, and worse, his indifference, had not made it necessary that someone act to secure their *fara'ip*'s future. Truthsheart's actions had put all Riders into their debt, as they were in the debt of all three *fara'ip* that provided Wardens for the Exile. Everything Moon had now—her standing among Riders, her freedom to pursue her researches, Lightstead, the fortress of her *fara'ip,* even her unfashionable gown—had been bought by her sister's sacrifice.

Well, that had gone on long enough. Now the Banishment was ending, and there would be a High Prince, and she would get her sister back. *So much fuss,* she thought, looking back over the council in Griffinhome. What did it really matter who became High Prince? According to the old Songs that told of it, it was simple enough to tell who the chosen one would be—and it seemed to Moon now that there was only one obvious choice. A pity others did not study the Songs as thoroughly as she did. They asked her for the answers they wanted, never asking for her opinion. It was true that no one liked the Basilisk Prince, but who else could it be? Well, her feet stilled as she considered. What about the Griffin Lord? But after a moment she shook her head. The game *he* was playing was so deep not even Moon could make it out.

A noise and she hopped down from the table, shook out her loose flaxen hair, and crossed the cold stone, inlaid with tiny basilisks, to the padded bench, where she sat, carefully arranging the folds of her red-and-silver gown, folding her hands neatly in her lap.

The door opened and Moon rose to her feet, heart pounding. A Sunward Rider stood in the doorway, thinner than when she had last seen him, smiling a smile that shook her bones.

"My child," he said. "A great pleasure to see you."

"My lord Prince," she said, as she felt the cool touch of his finger under her chin and lifted her gaze to look directly into his hazel eyes.

He gestured, the fall of his hand as light as smoke on a breeze, and Walks Under the Moon followed the Basilisk Prince into his rooms.

~

"So, that went well." Even to herself, Cassandra's voice sounded thick and tired.

Max rounded on her from where he had been staring out the window, his skin paled to bone, dark smudges showing under his eyes. "What did they expect me to say? What did *you* expect me to say?"

Cassandra ignored him, propped one hip on the edge

of the table, and rolled her head back and forth, stretching the muscles in her neck.

With her eyes closed, Cassandra linked her fingers and stretched out her arms, arching her back like a cat, rolling her shoulders individually, and then arching her back the opposite way. She swung her right leg completely onto the tabletop and reached for her instep. It was more important than ever that she stay relaxed and calm; if she couldn't sleep, she could at least stay loose.

"Well?" he said finally, stalking toward her.

Cassandra turned her face enough to look at him, glanced pointedly at his fisted hands. "Put those away," she said, her voice squeezed from the angle of her throat, "you might hurt yourself."

Max lowered his eyes and relaxed his hands. "Aren't you going to try to persuade me? You know, appeal to my better nature, that sort of thing?"

Cassandra let go of her right instep and stopped pressing her cheek into her kneecap. She looked up and wrinkled her nose.

"Wouldn't dream of it," she said, straightening until she could look him in the face. "So what now?"

He shook his head minutely. "Now?"

"Well, correct me if I'm wrong, but I believe you're the military history expert? So I'm assuming you have some strategy to suggest?" Max opened his mouth, but when he said nothing, Cassandra turned to face him more squarely. She leaned back against the table, crossed her ankles and folded her arms, tilted her head, and smiled. The very image of the courteous underling awaiting instructions.

The corners of Max's mouth turned down. "Look," he said, biting off the word. Cassandra raised her eyebrows and nodded brightly, stifling a smile when his hands balled into fists again . . . and then relaxed. "I'm no threat to this Basilisk Prince, not as I am anyway, not as *me*. If I disappeared, couldn't we . . . wouldn't he just let me go?"

Cassandra straightened, pushed her shoulder bag out of the way, and pulled Max's Phoenix-carved *gra'if* chest toward her. Her hands hovered over the lid for a moment, but when Max said nothing to stop her, she pushed it open. Max was wearing his mail shirt, but his helm, like hers only with a Phoenix's face on the forehead piece, his torque, gauntlets, and both swords were still in the chest. She pulled out the torque, held it out to him.

Max looked from the *gra'if* to her face and back again before taking the torque out of her hands. He slipped it around his throat one-handed, with a practiced motion, but clearly without being aware of the ease of his own actions, automatic, as though he'd done it hundreds of times before, as indeed he had. Cassandra let out her breath; what she had to do would be easier the more he was touching his *gra'if*.

"You may be no threat," she agreed, "but the Basilisk may not see it that way. We'll go if that's what you want, but we'll go armed—we may need to fight our way out." She reached into her shoulder bag and pulled out her greaves, propped her right foot on the edge of one of the armchairs, and began fitting the piece of *gra'if* to the front of her shin.

"You don't have to come." Max tossed his helm back onto the table. Cassandra turned her head to look at him. He still wore the torque.

"Don't I?"

Max's lip curled back. "Oh, that's right. I forgot about your Oath. Well, you can go home, I release you. Hell, you *are* home."

Cassandra felt heat rise into her face and turned away, concentrating on the laces of the greave on her shin. It didn't help that she'd often wondered how much of her love for him was an effect of her Oath. What better way to make sure that she would keep him safe? No, she told herself for what felt like the hundredth time. None of the other Wardens had felt this way.

"Look," Max said, his voice so soft he must have meant it as an apology, "you don't understand. You're asking me to . . . to agree to abandon my *self.* You tell me that I've done this before, that I've been other people, and it isn't that I don't believe you. Not anymore anyway. But, you're asking *me*—the only me I've ever known—to die."

"This isn't about you," she said, tying off the lace and switching legs.

"What the hell are you talking about?" Max said, color rushing to his face.

"Not about you, not about me. Not about what you want, or what I want." Cassandra took a deep breath and straightened to her feet, mouth open to tell him. Serve him right, the arrogant, self-centered son of a bitch. Oh, she could explain to him she knew intimately what loss was, knew it down to the last tear, down to the echo that sounds months, even years later and shows you that what you thought was the last tear wasn't even close. Yes, it was hard to die, but each person only does it once. She'd had to watch him die over and over. Watch the self that knew her, that loved her, die out of his face. To have him look at her—as he was looking at her now—with a stranger's eyes. She felt a thickness in her throat, and the stinging burn of tears behind her eyes. She told herself that the trembling in her muscles was exhaustion, not frustration. She took a deeper breath, and then another. Because she couldn't indulge her anger. She couldn't tell him all that they had once been to each other, that they had spent almost half a millennium together, eighteen of his human lives. That they had been lovers, not once, but many times, and that she had lost him over and over again.

The first time had been an accident.

It was back in the early days, when the Prince Exile was in his fifth or sixth human life. His Wardens had already started taking turns watching over him, secure in the knowledge that his luck protected him as well as they could, but unable to leave him completely because of their Oaths. Cassandra had been paying her usual visit to Stormbringer, then playing the part of a country lordling, acting as the Exile's patron. On Stormbringer's advice, she had come down to the great hall to watch the Exile's performance. He had been a Bard then, keeper of his people's history and traditions, witness to their great events and adviser to their lords. Curious, she had stayed to hear him sing, to watch the audience watch him, and to find to her amusement that he watched not the audience, but her. And curiosity, she told herself, had kept her with him for that night, and the next. Eventually, she had told him what she was, what he was, and he'd believed her, and laughed, and made a song of the exiled prince and his demon lover. He had made her swear to come and find him again, in his new life. He made her swear every time. And she had sworn, every time, until the last.

At first, it had been wondrous. She had known, over and over, the best of love, from the first intoxicating euphoria, through to the strong sustaining passions. Who would not want the person they loved to fall in love with them, over and over? But every time it became less joyful, every time less magical, as every meeting was colored by her awareness that the parting must come. And every parting grew more painful. Every first meeting, when he looked at her without recognition, without love, without any memory of their lives together, less bearable.

Until at last, that final time, she had made no vows to him, and when the Wardens met again to give him the dreams that would shape his new life, she had walked away, promising herself that she would watch, she would keep her Oath, but she would never meet the Prince again. And for his last six lives, until the Troll Diggory had appeared in her dojo, she had kept her promise. No, she couldn't tell him. Because she was about to betray all that they had once meant to each other, though Max

Ravenhill would not know it, would feel no sense of betrayal. She was going to use all that she knew about him, all that their many human lifetimes together had taught her about how the Prince's mind and soul—the parts that never changed no matter what life the Wardens gave him—about how that part of him worked. She was going to use what their love had given her to persuade Max Ravenhill to become the Prince Guardian while there was still time.

And if he knew afterward what she had done, well, she was prepared to pay for it then.

She pulled her hair back off her face and began braiding it behind her head; it seemed to be longer now that she was back in the Lands.

"Do you remember," she said, "in the subway tunnels, you asked me why I was annoyed with you?"

"You didn't answer."

She started to smile, and froze. Even her face muscles hurt. "It used to be a lot easier to convince you that you were someone else, and that in twenty or thirty years' time you'd stop being Homer, or Musashi, or Bacon, and you'd become someone else again. It didn't use to frighten you so much then. Maybe in those days people expected to die and be reborn as someone else." Cassandra found she couldn't look him in the face after all. She stood up, turned to face the table, and began sorting through the *gra'if* still lying there. Having something to occupy her hands would help her do what she had to do. Max's Phoenix helm had become mixed in with some of her *gra'if*, she saw, her heart sinking with the irony of it.

"You forget," she said, concentrating on the familiar motions of her own hands as they repacked her weapons. "You will stop being Max Ravenhill, whether you choose it or not. I believe the Chant of Oblivion will go on working, even here, until your own *dra'aj* is restored." All the daggers on the table were hers, marked with the dragon's scales. The Prince Guardian must not have any. As she began to set them to one side, Max took her wrist firmly in his hand. She looked up.

"Just tell me," he said.

"Threat or no threat, the Basilisk Prince *will* find you. The Hunt will go on looking for you, feeding on those who get in their way, until you are found. That is the cost of Max Ravenhill's remaining life, my lord, and whatever new life I might be able to give you. Will you pay it?" she said coolly, glancing at him from the corner of her eyes, seeing the stubborn skepticism on his face.

She turned to face him fully, leaning her hips against the edge of the table, crossing her arms. "The Basilisk wants you, and he will never rest until he has you. Even after he's taken and bound the Talismans, he'll still look for you. You will always be a danger to him. But then it will be too late to help these people. Too late to stop the destruction of the Solitaries and the Naturals, to save the Lands that give us all—even you, my lord—life. So perhaps the real question here is not whether Max Ravenhill will die—that death is coming, whatever we might do. The real question is whether that death will have meaning."

The silence that fell when Cassandra's rough rich voice stopped was the deepest Max had ever known.

"Nice to have everything clear," he said, more to break that silence than anything else. He rubbed his face with his hands, looked with longing at the bed, where the soft covers were still thrown aside as he'd left them when he woke up. The pillows still showed the imprint of his head. Maybe the whole thing was a dream and he would wake up. Were these really his options? Disregard the cost and spend the rest of his life on the run? Or give up his identity entirely? Die, and stop this world's Holocaust, this world's Gulag? Seemed simple, looked at that way. His fingers strayed once more as if on their own to touch the torque at his throat, his *gra'if,* feeling its warm and almost feathery texture. He felt calmer somehow, and sat down in the window seat, his back to the sun setting outside. He was barely aware of

Cassandra, leaning against the table, her arms crossed, both swords within reach.

"Tell me something," he said finally. "What will you do if I say no?"

Cassandra nodded, frowning, as if she was thinking his question over, thinking through her options. The slight movement emphasized the blue shadows under her eyes. She looked at her sword, at the weapons still on the table, and nodded again.

"The Banishment won't end unless you're alive. Killing you would keep the Talismans hidden," she said finally. Max's heart stopped beating. "It won't take long for someone else to think of that, if they haven't already. Lightborn probably has—he looks like he's hiding something. So we wouldn't be safe even here, we'd have to go into hiding."

"Just like that?" Max's heart started beating again.

Now a ghost of a grin flitted over her features. "Well, it won't be easy, but yes, just like that. This room isn't Signed. We could Move from here, though passing through a Portal might be a bit more difficult. We couldn't count on anyone tricking the guards for us again."

"No, I meant, 'just like that' for *you*." He didn't know why it mattered so much what she thought, but it did.

"As you have reminded me, my lord, I have my Oath." Her face was bleak, and she turned away from him as she said it.

His restoration would liberate her, he realized, among all the other things it would do. Until then she was bound to him, whether she wanted it or not. She would never just be with him, he would always wonder. Max opened his mouth to say the words that would free her and his breath was sucked away as the air CRACKED! and a dark-haired, purple-clad woman carrying a sword appeared directly in front of him.

# Chapter Eight

BEFORE MAX COULD DO more than take a
step backward, Cassandra's long sword was singing through the air, and the strange Rider's head
rolled into a corner as the body collapsed to the floor
like a wet paper sack. Max swallowed and looked away
from the blood spreading over the parquet floor.

"You sure that wasn't a friend?"

"Want me to wait and ask next time?" Cassandra
didn't sound particularly concerned as she wiped off her
sword on the dead woman's sleeve.

Max shrugged, a little surprised at how steady he felt,
how calm. *Swim or drown,* he thought, *too late to worry
about getting into the water.* His nose wrinkled as he
edged around the dead Rider's spreading blood and
joined Cassandra at the table, where she was stowing his
*gra'if* into a pair of leather saddlebags. Besides the helm,
and the torque and mail shirt he was wearing, there were
greaves, gauntlets, two swords, and one or two pieces
whose use he wasn't sure of. Max was reaching for his
sword when Cassandra picked up his gauntlets and began
to roll the fine mesh into a compact bundle. Shivering,
Max felt the ghost of her fingers on his own hands and
wrists.

"Cassandra," he started, but a raised finger stopped him from going any further. She was right, he thought. Whatever his decision might be, they'd need their weapons just the same.

Max glanced at the dead Rider and stepped back fast enough to bang jarringly against the table. The floor was empty. No body, No head. No blood.

"Cassandra," he managed through stiff lips, but she had already whirled around in the direction he was facing, clearly expecting, from the look on his face, to see another enemy.

"Oh," she said, turning back to him. "It's all right. I forgot that would happen, it's been so long."

"*What* would happen?"

"She Faded," Cassandra said. "Her *dra'aj* returned to the Lands." She made a face. "At least, I hope it did. I have an idea the whole process used to take longer."

"Oh—kay." Max slipped to the far side of the table and picked up his long sword, felt again the buzz of warmth as it fit into his hand, and gave it an experimental swing. It in no way resembled the smooth arc of Cassandra's stroke, but it made him feel better all the same.

Cassandra shook her head and offered him the shorter sword.

"Take this one," she said, "we'll be in close quarters out there, and the long one will only get in your way." She took the longer sword from him and, crossing behind him, slipped it into the back of his harness, where the weapon hung, swaying slightly, the long hilt just visible out of the corner of his eye. Her own long sword flickered in her hand as she sheathed it through her harness so that it, too, hung down her back, handy, but out of the way. "The long sword is for battlefields and for keeping people at a distance. The shorter sword is for fighting indoors and on horseback. Watch out with it, it's sharpened at the point and along the edge of the blade as well."

Max held the shorter sword and felt the same almost sentient response.

Cassandra reached out and changed the position of his thumb on the hilt. His grip was instantly more comfortable; the sword had felt alive before, now it felt awake.

"You've done this before," she said, drawing her own short sword and turning to stand beside him, shoulder to shoulder, "and wearing your *gra'if* will make your body remember its old skill, if you give it a chance. So relax, try not to think. Aim at the midline of your opponent's body, and try to cut straight down, or straight sideways. When you defend, keep your movements to small, short arcs," she swung her blade to demonstrate, "tap away your opponent's blade without taking yours too far from the central point. Use both hands whenever possible." She showed him the grip, and he did his best to imitate it. "There is a snap to the wrists, see? You've got the reach on most people, even here, but be careful just the same."

"Never would have thought of that," he muttered under his breath as he hooked the sword on the belt loop in his harness.

Noise and movement at the door caused them both to turn around. While Max was pleased to see that his own sword was up and ready almost as quickly as Cassandra's, the relief when he saw that it was Lightborn proved that he wasn't as ready for slaughter as he thought. The pale Rider made a quick face, as if he smelled the body and the blood that were no longer there to be seen.

"Are you safe?" he said. "Warriors have been appearing throughout the keep. Who would have thought so many of the Basilisk's Riders knew Griffinhome well enough to Move here?"

Cassandra shrugged, closing the zipper on her shoulder bag. She adjusted the strap to its full extent, and slipped her head and shoulders into it, making sure the strap passed under the long sword hanging down her back. The bag hung low behind her left hip, where it would stay out of the way of her sword arm.

"Come, my mother holds the main stairs, but we must make our way quickly to the stables before more of the Basilisk's warriors arrive." Lightborn opened the door and looked out, keeping flat against the wall.

"Can't we Move there?" Max said. He picked up his own saddlebags, and Cassandra helped him balance them over his left shoulder. For all that they were full of metal, they seemed very light.

"We must rejoin my mother first, my Prince," Lightborn said, "I cannot leave her to defend Griffinhome alone, not even for you. Do you follow me, Warden, and the Prince can be eyes-behind."

"Lead by all means, my lord. But the Prince will be safer between us." The look on her face was exactly the thinly disguised irritation of any professional who had been given instructions by an amateur. Max had often seen that look on the guy who did work around his house. Lightborn looked astonished—like a teacher corrected by a student. He covered up quickly, but not before Max noticed, and started wondering how much he actually liked the man. Max stepped into position between them to forestall any further discussion. He was ready to get moving; all this talking was just delaying things.

"Were we betrayed?" Cassandra murmured as she motioned Max to follow Lightborn through the door. Her voice was a mere breath in the relative darkness of the castle passage. "Where is Windwatcher?"

*Good question,* Max thought, but his attention was drawn by the sounds of fighting in the distance. It amazed him how quickly the room behind them had come to seem a refuge, even though the sudden appearance of the woman soldier proved that doors and walls weren't much of a sanctuary where Riders were concerned. Still, being in the passage made the fine hairs on the back of his neck lift up.

"I would not think it possible," Lightborn said firmly.

Cassandra shrugged. "He has changed sides once already," she pointed out.

"Many have done so, since the Great War—time you have spent safely in the Shadowlands, Warden."

Cassandra's only answer was a nod that Lightborn couldn't see.

Before they had gone more than halfway toward the corner of the passage, they were struck by a blast of cold air. Lightborn put a hand to the wall as another wave struck them. Caught in midstep, Max overbalanced, and only Cassandra's arm kept him upright. As they clung to each other, yet another wave came, bringing with it a sound so low it seemed to resonate in his bones. He smelled a fleeting but familiar whiff of old blood and rot. His stomach twisted, and he felt a sudden sharp pain low on his left side, where a scar marked his encounter with the Hound.

He looked at Cassandra once the sound wave had passed them, but she shook her head, eyes wide.

"It is the Horn that calls the Hunt," Lightborn said, dragging in air like a diver coming up out of the depths. "Some favorite of the Basilisk's is here to use it."

"Run." Cassandra pointed forward with her sword, and drew the long dagger she had used against the Hound out of the top of her left boot.

Running now, they followed Lightborn the short distance down the rest of the passage, around the corner and down another, identical except for the arched window openings on the left side. Max caught a glimpse of a night sky, a moon, half full, near the horizon, and the sky almost devoid of stars. Surely there had been sunlight coming in the window of their room only moments ago? Max skidded on the smooth tile floor as Lightborn slowed, and lifted his finger to his lips. They were nearing the end of the windowed passage, where it joined another, wider hallway. Lightborn turned toward them, jerked his head up, and pointed to the right. Max nodded, took a firmer grip on his sword, and followed Lightborn around the corner.

They found themselves at one end of an open gallery

from which they could see the top of what must be the main staircase of the fortress. The stairs themselves, wide and shallow, were made of some green-gold stone like marble; the staircase was wide enough for five people to stand abreast, and in that space Honor of Souls stood with two guards, all three with swords out. Moon stood behind them, a dagger in each hand. A quick glance told Max that at least nine purple-clad Riders were trying to come at them up the stairs. Honor and her people were helped by the height the stairs gave them, Max saw, and by the fact that their opponents were too crowded together to rush them. But even as Lightborn ran forward, the man to Honor's right, already bleeding from a wound in his right leg, went down, and Lightborn leaped into the space beside his mother before the successful enemy could flank her.

Max and Cassandra took up positions one to each side of Moon. Pale to the point of fainting, the young Rider gave her sister a stiff smile. Max moved around to Moon's left, and returned Cassandra's nod with the best grin he could manage. He hefted the sword in his hand, trying to regain that feeling of oneness he'd had when he'd first picked it up.

He had a moment to feel his skin get cold as his blood retreated from the surface, preparing for injury. He wished he'd had time to put on more than his mail shirt, as he glanced at Cassandra, a blade in each hand, her bag swinging off her left shoulder. Max remembered using that bag as a flail against the Hound, and shrugged off his own saddlebags, but found that without a strap there was no way he could conveniently use them as a bludgeon. He let them drop and pushed them behind him with his foot. As well-packed as they were, they were bulky, and he needed complete range of movement. And if he had to run, well, the stuff in the bags was no use to him unless he lived.

How much time did they have before the Hunt arrived? Honor of Souls took a step back onto the landing at the top of the staircase, and Cassandra called to her to step out, that she would take over. Before the woman could answer, the sound of running feet made them look toward the left. The Basilisk's soldiers had found a way around the main stairs after all and were coming at them from the far end of the gallery.

A shadow flickered at the periphery of his vision, and Max was moving even as Cassandra cried out a warning. His quickness meant the blow landed on his *gra'if*-protected shoulder and not on his head as his assailant intended. Max's numb right hand almost dropped the sword, but he remembered Cassandra's instruction just in time and brought up his left hand, instinctively continuing the movement into a sweep that sank his blade into his attacker's neck, knocking the man to his knees.

Max was staring openmouthed as the man's life spilled out onto the floor when he was shoved from behind. He flinched, turning to bring his sword to bear, but instead of striking at him, Max's new assailant grabbed him by his upper arms, dragging him backward away from the fighting. Max fought to dislodge the hands, desperate to prevent his attacker from getting a good hold, while he tried to maintain a grip on his own sword.

Max heard Cassandra call out behind him, but her shout ended in a grunt. Max set his teeth and clung harder to his sword as more gloved hands tried to wrest it from him. Feeling was just tingling back into his right hand, and Max tried not to think of what would have happened if he hadn't been wearing armor. The hands holding him shifted their bruising grip yet again, and Max, remembering that the edges were sharp as well as the points, planted his feet, shrugged his shoulders and twisted his wrists, thrusting out firmly with his sword. The man trying to take the sword from him sprang back with a cry, holding bleeding fingers. Max immediately threw himself backward, pushing off the floor as hard as he could with his legs. He knocked the unprepared man holding him to the floor, landing on his chest, pushing the air out of him, and rolled himself free.

He looked down, dragging air into his own lungs, and while he hesitated, the man on the floor kicked out and swept Max's feet out from under him. Max crashed against the stone balustrade of the gallery, banging his abused right arm again and numbing his shoulder. The man on the floor was just rolling to his feet, triumphantly grinning, when Cassandra dashed up and, twisting her double-handed grip sideways, swept off his head with one blow.

*Must like that headless look,* Max thought.

A slap as an arrow bounced off the stone floor and Cassandra ducked as another whistled past her head. Lightborn killed the man in front of him, kicked the feet out from under the man in front of his mother so that she could cut his throat, and stepped back toward Cassandra and Max.

"Kill as many as you can, and then back the way we came," he yelled over his shoulder as another of the Basilisk's Riders swung at him.

Max scrambled to his feet. Now that the first rush of excitement had passed, he found that he settled automatically into a routine of thrust and parry. He relaxed, letting his sword hand move, and he felt an unexpected detachment settle over him, at once distancing him from the fighting and narrowing his focus to the Rider in front of him. He was aware of Cassandra, behind him to his left, and how she moved like a dancer; he saw the flicker of Moon's dagger. Then he realized that the woman he fought now was no more trying to kill him than the guy who had grabbed him from behind, and that realization made him falter.

Before he could recover from his hesitation, Moon stumbled, falling with almost her full weight against Max's lowered sword arm. He took a step backward, but trod heavily onto his own saddlebags. In the moment it took him to lose his balance completely and fall, he had time to feel really stupid.

Max hit the ground hard, the breath knocked out of him. A weight, someone heavier than Moon he thought, as he fought to inhale, fell on top of him, and hands once more clutched at his arms. Max heard Cassandra's voice and struggled to turn toward the sound when—

SLAM!

# Chapter Nine

MAX DREAMS THAT a dog licks his face. It's more than a little unpleasant, the tongue is rougher, and much hotter than he would have expected. And talk about dog breath! Gagh! This dog must have been eating rotten meat. *How can I be dreaming,* he thinks, *when I'm not asleep.* Passed out, maybe. Too many Moves, beating him with images—a stone-walled room, the stones covered with moss and dripping water; the middle of a snowstorm, sleet cutting at his face; a wooded hillside, leaves just on the point of turning; a dripping rain forest unbearably hot, smelling of dying vegetation; a sun-drenched beach at low tide, and three times a grassy lawn circled with huge standing stones—like sitting too close to the screen in an action movie. Too many CRACKS! and SLAMS! taking his breath away as he passed from place to place, until his lungs and his brain just shut off. Do you dream when you're passed out? The dog goes on licking his face. Max wonders why he couldn't dream of Cassandra instead of this Hound—

"Rest, there is nothing for you to fear now." The voice was musical, soothing; the hand that had been stroking his face withdrew.

Max blinked and looked around him. He was lying on a long chaise piled with cushions in a large, circular, wood-paneled room. The linen-fold paneling was warmly golden, reflecting the light from the room's round windows. What he could see of the floor was covered with a scattering of small rugs, each complexly patterned. From the slant of the sunlight, it was late afternoon. He felt an unfamiliar ache in his right wrist and forearm and the stiffening of muscles that undoubtedly was the result of using a sword. He wondered how long he'd been asleep.

"Dawntreader."

Max turned toward the beautiful voice.

There was no doubt in his mind that this was the Basilisk Prince. Once, as a young man, he'd met Trudeau, when he'd been Prime Minister for several years, and this man had that same quality of power and arrogance. He moved with the awareness that he was the most important person in the room, and he would always move that way, no matter what room he was in. The Basilisk was a Sunward Rider, Max had been told, and this man had the same red-gold, sun-touched look that Windwatcher had. A long face, too thin, with a prominent nose slightly hooked, wide mouth, full lips. But, like all of the Riders Max had seen, beautiful.

"You are safe now, my brother, you are home again." His eyes dancing, the Basilisk took hold of Max's right hand in his left and laid the back of his own right hand against Max's cheek. The palm of that hand, and part of the fingers, were covered by a silky bandage. Max realized that the Basilisk was not sitting on a chair, but right on the edge of the chaise that Max himself was lying on.

The odd thing was, Max thought later, he really did feel safe at that moment. Warm and drowsy and content. The only uncomfortable note was the heat in the man's hands. As if the Basilisk was burning with fever. Max had to school himself not to pull away.

"All alone in that Land of Shadow, how did you stand

it?" The voice was resonant and warm, with an under-lying note of deepness. If he wanted to, Max thought, the Basilisk could raise his voice and make the win-dows vibrate.

"It's not such a bad place, when you get used to it." That came out growly, and Max cleared his throat. He did his best to push the remnants of the dream from his mind, but they were stubborn. From the way the Basilisk Prince was talking, it seemed as if he didn't know about the amnesia.

"You were always the bravest of us. That is what no one else remembers."

"What about what *I* don't remember?"

The Basilisk Prince nodded, as if he'd been expecting that. *He knows all right,* Max thought.

"I swear to you, I will make all things right." The Basilisk patted Max on the shoulder. And again, almost against his will, Max felt comforted.

"I cannot know what your captors have told you, though I can guess." The Basilisk shrugged, a rueful smile on his lips. "Hear me now, my brother. I need nothing from you. *Nothing.* This is the truth. Rather, tell me, Dawntreader, tell me what can *I* do for *you.*"

Max frowned, trying to concentrate. He hadn't thought of Lightborn and Honor of Souls as his captors, but it was true that none of them had asked what he wanted. And they hadn't exactly rushed to give him op-tions. He didn't mean Cassandra. Cassandra was differ-ent; she already knew what he wanted, and she *had* said that she would get him out if that's what he decided, but still . . .

Max found that he believed the Basilisk. The Rider's voice, his intonations, his face—all held the same qual-ity of credibility, of *veracity*, that Cassandra's held. Max wanted to help the people here, sure, of course he did. But of course he should weigh all the sides, consider all the possibilities. And really, more than anything else . . .

"I want to be Max Ravenhill," he said, the words out before he was aware he'd meant to speak them. The same instinct that told him the Basilisk spoke the truth prompted him to do the same.

The Basilisk nodded, squeezing Max on the shoulder as he stood up.

"I can do that," he said, still nodding. "I can let you have your human life again, once you've helped me . . . but I hope you will not ask it of me." He looked around for a moment, moved a glass that sat on a small leather-covered table and stood frowning down at it. "The People *need* Dawntreader and what he knows, I know you understand this. But I also," his eyes lifted to look past where Max lay on the chaise lounge at the round windows, "I miss my friend. No one understands me the way you—the way *he* did."

Again, the quality of *truth* was heavy about him. For a moment Max saw the burden of the Basilisk's loneliness, the same that could sometimes be seen in the faces of children who had lost a parent, whose childhood is lost also; children who realize they now face unimaginable responsibility. A loneliness tinged with despair.

"I hear we weren't always in such harmony." Max was careful to keep his voice neutral.

The Basilisk bit his lip and nodded again. "Perhaps." He looked back at Max. "But you and I, we are the only ones who can know what passed between us. And I am not in the least afraid to have you restored. In fact, I seek it. We will come to an accord, I am certain."

"You Banished me."

"And saved your life doing so. There were many who sought your death, and you *would* have died had there not been this alternative."

It was possible, Max nodded, considering. There was nothing in what the man said that actually contradicted what Cassandra had told him.

"What about my memory?"

The Basilisk shrugged, as if at a small thing. "I am

offering to restore it. That is more than the others can do for you. And if, as you say, you prefer to be the human person you are now . . . once I have the Talismans, I can offer you that as well."

The Basilisk's face was open and serene, his eyes a warm topaz in the late afternoon light. *This would be so easy,* Max thought. *Let him have what he wants, and then I get what I want.* He wouldn't even have to do anything, just let what was going to happen . . . happen. And then he'd be himself again.

"Whatever the others may say," the Basilisk's soft voice continued when Max did not speak, "the War was not caused by any enmity between us, and when you are restored, you will know this. We disagreed, yes, but left to ourselves, we would have come to terms. We both had enemies, and these others created war between us." He stood and walked to the window, continuing to speak to Max as he looked out through the arches. "You saw clearly all along," he said, "I know that now. I was misled. I allowed my pride to keep us apart. All of this," he swept his arm toward the world outside the windows, "I prepare for the High Prince, whoever that might be. I wish—I hope, that it might be me." He turned back to face Max, his eyes now hazel, clear, and direct. "But our first concern must be the People, and the Lands. Why should we wait? Let me end your Banishment now! Let me restore you, and together we will find the Talismans. They *must* be allowed to do their good offices, or all will be lost. Will you help me?"

Max squeezed his eyes tightly shut. It *could* have been a misunderstanding; human history was full of wars started over stupider things. Cassandra and her friends could be wrong . . . couldn't they? After all, Cassandra hadn't even been here, she only knew what she'd been told, and while Honor of Souls and her allies seemed very plausible, well, so did this man. The changes that were happening to the Lands *could* be just the Cycle ending. And as for what the Basilisk had been accused of, again, the years Max had spent studying taught him that sometimes rulers did things that seemed pointless or even cruel to those who didn't have access to the whole picture.

It was the Talismans that were important, everyone agreed on that. *You could help him find his Talismans and go back to being Max Ravenhill.* It was really very simple, when you thought about it. All he had to do was wait, and then go home. Home to his books, and his classes, and his students.

And Cassandra, would she come home with him?

"You smell like a Hound," he said in a hoarse whisper. Strange. He hadn't even been aware he was going to say that.

"I've given you too much to think about." The Basilisk turned until he had his back to the window. With the light behind him, Max couldn't see the man's face. Couldn't tell whether the Basilisk had heard him.

"Rest now. Nothing need be decided until the Sun turns. A fitting time for Dawntreader to return, if that is what you decide. In the meantime, rest, think, consider. I will have food brought to you." The musical voice was wistful, and before Max could move, the Basilisk Prince had bent over him and kissed him softly on the forehead.

Max watched the Basilisk leave and then lay back, shutting his eyes, feeling the tremor of reaction set in. The man had sounded sincere, but that was easy, wasn't it? Anyone could sound sincere, if he really wanted to. Hell, Max did it himself all the time. Besides, it was possible that he could be a monster and still miss his friend. Could smile and smile and be a villain.

Max didn't realize, until he heard the quiet shuffling sounds, that the Basilisk had not left him alone in the room. He turned over to face the door again and found another Rider standing there, this one pale and dark-haired like Max himself, leaning with his back against the closed door. The Rider was white-faced and breathing hard, his lips compressed into a thin line. As soon as he saw Max looking at him, he spoke.

"Sitting pretty, you think?" His voice was a husky caress. "You should have said yes, spawn of Solitaries. You should have fallen over yourself and thanked him for the opportunity to say yes, while you had the chance. Then he might have been kind, he might have been quick. You don't deserve his kindness, and you won't get it." Suddenly, before Max could prepare for it, the Rider had crossed the room and planted his fist squarely just below Max's rib cage. His *gra'if* mail shirt hardened instantly, deadening the blow. Max found that he was just able to make his lungs draw in air.

"Does this mean no breakfast?" he gasped.

The Rider cursed, backhanding Max across the face with his closed fist.

"Your Solitary's tricks won't help you here," the Rider said, spitting out his words. He snapped a set of dull metal manacles to Max's wrists as Max struggled, unable to turn away in the angle of the chaise longue. "You won't rule here, not when we're through with you. I'm to take you to a place where you can 'rest' and 'consider.' " Max didn't like the Rider's smile.

The Moonward Rider dragged Max from the chaise, across the floor, and into the doorway before he could even think to fight back. He was on his back, stretched out at full arm's length, the entire weight of his body pulling against the cuffs digging into his wrists. He tried to hook his heels around the doorframe, but the dark Rider merely kicked at his head and groin until he stopped.

And SLAM! they were in another corridor, this one much darker and colder.

Here there were no wood floors, but cold gray flagstones perfectly fitted so they seemed smooth as marble. The dark Rider kicked open a door and dragged Max through.

As soon as the door was open, Max's nose was assaulted with a horrible, acrid smell, like a sewer burning. His eyes began to smart and he coughed roughly, his nose wrinkling. The Rider pulled him almost upright, and before Max could get his feet properly under him, the chain that bound his wrists was shackled to the wall. The room was dark, and at first Max couldn't see what was causing the smell, even though the slack in the chain gave him plenty of room to twist around. His eyes took a few moments to adjust to the dim light entering through slits in the stone walls high over his head. Here the stone was the same carefully fitted smooth gray rock as the floor, veined, Max now saw, like marble, unremarkable except for a wide blotch where something obscured the reflection of the light. He twisted around the other way, squinted to get a better look, and whirled back around to face the still open doorway, gagging, stomach trying to climb up out of his throat. It couldn't be. His mind tried to reject what his eyes had seen, but it wouldn't.

Against his will, his head dragged him around again and his eyes forced him to look at what was stuck on the wall. He could tell that it had once been alive—Max prayed to whatever gods were listening that it wasn't *still* alive—but the only thing he could be sure of was the front half of a skateboard sticking out to one side of—he gagged and turned away, dragging in great shuddering breaths until his stomach sank back into place and stayed there. He looked back at the dark Rider, but the soldier wasn't looking at the thing on the wall. His pale eyes were fixed on Max himself.

"We only need you until the Banishment ends," the Rider said, his voice as matter-of-fact as the weatherman's announcing a clear morning with seasonal temperatures. "After that," he paused and jerked his head toward the abomination on the wall. "Consider it while you 'rest.' "

Anger and disgust choked him, and without thinking Max swept the Moonward Rider's feet out from under him with the same move that had been used on him back in Honor of Souls' upper hall. Once he was down, Max smashed him in the forehead with the manacles around his wrists and wrapped the slack of the chains around the Rider's throat.

Max probably wouldn't have done what he did next if it hadn't been for the skateboard.

⤙

Cassandra poured warm water over the back of her neck and set the jug down on the stone hearth. She squeezed the excess water out of her hair and straightened, tossing it back off her face, feeling it drip on her back.

"I tell you, my lady, we must flee," an older Starward Rider was saying. He wore the green-and-gold leathers of a senior man-at-arms. "If we go to the Shadowlands, we can close the Portals from that side. We know where the Prince Guardian has been taken, and," the man took a hesitant breath before continuing, "the Lands are already lost to us."

Moon handed Cassandra a towel, and she lost what else the Rider said in the rustle of cloth as she dried her hair. They had made it into the Signed Room inches in front of their enemies, and held the door while Honor of Souls activated the Signs. It was the safest room in Griffinhome now that it was Signed from the inside, and Cassandra was not the only one taking advantage of the quiet moment to wash off blood. She wrinkled her nose in disgust. One or two spots were never going to dry. There had been only one Hound, and she believed she had killed it, but at the very least, their enemies were on the other side of the door.

"We cannot remain here, that's certain," Lightborn said. "They may have achieved their purpose when they took the Prince, but the Basilisk will not leave us be. Not for long."

"I agree." Cassandra handed the towel to a waiting

servant and reached both hands behind her head to braid her hair. "But I don't think it's time for the Shadowlands quite yet. Pick another place, and I will bring the Prince."

"If you can do this, then all may yet be saved," Honor of Souls said, exhaustion showing in her beautiful liquid voice. "Will your Oath guide you?"

Cassandra didn't answer. She had no answer. She knew that it was stupid to go tearing off, throwing open every door and turning over every rock, screaming Max's name. Stupid and a waste of time. But that didn't mean she didn't want to do it. Or that she had a better idea.

"If you do find him, you can at least give him his *gra'if*." Lightborn put his hand on Max's saddlebags, sitting on the long table near the wall. Cassandra hadn't seen it, but the pale Rider must have picked them up as they were running to safety.

As she listened to the others turning over suggestions for safe places to meet, Cassandra unbuckled the bags and thrust both hands inside, feeling calm spread over her like warm water in a bath. The demands of her Oath still tore at her, but touching Max's *gra'if* was almost as good as touching Max. Absently, she named each piece as she counted them, broke off, and began to count them again with more attention, panic rising like acid in her throat, until she saw again in her memory's eye the way he had twisted his torque around his throat while they were still in the bedchamber, and relaxed. It was all right; Max's torque was not missing.

She'd had hers stolen from her once, she remembered, lifting her hand to her neck to touch it, brushing her fingertips against the fine scales. It was in the early days of the Banishment, when she and the other Wardens had been traveling with a small group of horsemen across the plains of what was now Mongolia. They hadn't always worn all their *gra'if* in those days, it was too noticeable. One visitor from another band of horsemen had noticed her torque, somehow, and had ridden off with it. She'd been able to find it, though, and deal with the thief, too. She had Moved to it. She had heard that, back when the *dra'aj* was strong, the great ones of old, like the Prince Guardian himself, perhaps, could call their *gra'if* to them. It was logical, in the human sense. After all, *gra'if* was made from a Rider's own blood; why shouldn't it have the properties of Riders? Why wouldn't it be able to Move? But Max Ravenhill couldn't call his *gra'if* to him, she thought, even if it occurred to him to try.

She picked up Max's Phoenix helm, ran the tips of her fingers over the fine metal feathers, stroked the beak of the Fire Bird. It was part of Max. It would want to be reunited with him. It wasn't able to Move on its own, but suppose *she* Moved it? Given the chance, wouldn't it take her straight to him?

"Just a minute," she said, interrupting the discussion that still was being waged around her. "I have an idea." She watched the faces change, hope growing in some, dying in others, as she outlined her theory.

"This is madness. You will kill yourself, and for what? The Basilisk has the Prince, and our part in this Song is over," Walks Under the Moon spoke into the silence that fell when Cassandra finished, her voice trembling.

"Not necessarily," said Lightborn from his perch on the edge of the long table. "We have until the Banishment ends to make the attempt. The Basilisk must keep him alive until then, if he is not already dead."

"He's not dead," Cassandra said, her hands still smoothing the warm feathers of the Phoenix helm. "His *gra'if* would feel different if he were."

"It's too dangerous," Moon said, shaking her head. "What if you had to . . . wear it?"

What, indeed? She'd be very surprised if wearing it wasn't exactly what she had to do. Cassandra had never heard of any Rider wearing the *gra'if* of another. It would be like wearing someone else's skin. She wanted to take Moon in her arms, soothe away her fears as she had done when her sister was still a child, but it was hard to offer comfort when she felt the same fear herself. "If anyone has a better idea, let me hear it."

"Let me at least come with you," Lightborn suggested. "My knowledge of the Basilisk's Citadel may be of some use."

She acknowledged his offer with a sharp nod. "Very well."

Crossing back to the table, Cassandra put Max's helm to one side, and repacked the other pieces in the saddlebags—gauntlets, greaves, even the sword Max had dropped when he was taken. Cassandra closed the bag again and hesitated, her hand still on them.

"We should take his *gra'if* with us," Lightborn said, coming up on her left side, "and all your own weapons as well. What if we are unable to return for them?"

That was good advice. Honor of Souls would have to unSign the room for the short time—Cassandra hoped very short—that it would take them to Move, and Sign it again once they'd left.

"Check outside while the room is open," Cassandra said to Honor, "if you can do it without endangering yourselves. You'll have to Move from here eventually. Wait," she added as another thought occurred to her. "Do any of your people bear *gra'if?*" Honor nodded and gestured as a young Sunward guard moved forward, drawing a *gra'if* blade as she came.

"Should there be another Hound," Cassandra said to the young guard, "it will be for you to kill it. Listen carefully."

"Moon," Lightborn called out as Cassandra completed her instructions to the now white-faced guard. "Can you Move to the stables and wait for us there?" He turned to Cassandra. "She'll be safe enough there. They won't be expecting us to Ride. If we find the Prince Guardian, we will need Moon to guide us to the Lake of Souls."

"I will wait until you come," Moon said, patting her

sister on the shoulder. "With or without the Exile, come to me there."

Cassandra nodded, pulling Moon into a tight hug before handing Lightborn Max's swords and dumping the contents of her shoulder bag out on the table. The easiest way to carry everything, she'd learned long ago, was to wear it. And where they were going, she might be glad that she had. Her greaves she was already wearing, strapped to her shins, and she checked to make sure that they didn't interfere with the daggers in her boot tops. Because she wore her mail shirt next to the skin, instead of over her clothing like a cuirass, she had to attach the jointed tassets, and the pauldron and vambraces to her leather harness so that her abdomen and upper thighs, and her shoulders and upper arms were now covered with light, finely scaled armor. She checked that her throwing daggers were in place in her gauntlets, and pulled them on. The last thing she put on was her torque.

Silence made her look up. One by one, everyone in the room had stopped what they were doing to look at her.

"Your pardon, Truthsheart," Lightborn said, almost whispering. "It has been many years since we have seen so much *gra'if*."

"It is easy to see you are Dragonborn, my dear," said Honor of Souls, coming to Cassandra with her hands outstretched. "What other could sustain all this?"

"I have known others to bear more," Cassandra said, turning away from the light in Honor's eyes. To Lightborn she added, "Are you ready?"

She tied her Dragon helm to the front of her harness and helped Lightborn balance the saddlebags loaded with Max's *gra'if* over his right shoulder. As she took up her position, ready to Move, she wondered whether she was going about this the right way. Other than the time she'd Moved to her stolen torque, and that was like looking for a part of yourself, she always Moved to some*where*, never to some*thing*. Could she do it when it wasn't a part of herself she was Moving to? But if she could Move herself to where her own *gra'if* was, and people could Move their *gra'if* to them ... Shaking her head, she picked up the Phoenix helm and nodded to Honor of Souls. She could chase her thoughts around in circles all day, or she could ...

... concentrate on Max, blocking first her awareness of her sister, Moon's low voice still murmuring her protests. Then Lightborn's hands on her shoulders. She subtracted the carpet under her feet, the darkwood and stone flooring, the smell of the applewood fire in Honor's Signed Room. The fireplace, the Signs, and the hangings that covered them. Added Max as she'd last seen him, dressed in his flame colors, his *gra'if* mail showing through the opening of his shirt, the curved Phoenix torque around his throat. His jade-green eyes blazing, his long face framed with raven hair dusted with silver. She added the feel of his mouth under hers as she breathed *dra'aj* into him, the touch of his lips on the hollow of her throat. She lifted his Phoenix helm and fitted it onto her head.

In an instant she was in the heart of an inferno, her skin stung by flames. She felt herself fall to her knees, though she couldn't have said what surface was under her. She struggled not to breathe, feeling the flames lick at her mouth, her nostrils. Her lungs strained, and she knew that soon she was going to open her mouth and suck in the fire, that she wouldn't be able to stop herself. Vaguely, she wondered where Lightborn was, whether his hands were still gripping her shoulders. This was the Phoenix nest, she realized, the heart of Max's Guidebeast. Where else would his *gra'if* bring her? Would it know that she was trying to help? Or would it burn her for her presumption in donning Max's *gra'if?* Suddenly, the burning torment faded, and Cassandra wondered if her nerve endings were gone, seared away. The flames continued to caress her, light as feathers now. She felt the heat, and the kiss of the flames, but they were not consuming her. Something inside her awoke and began to sing, the notes flickering in time with the fire, which now was strangely welcoming. *Nothing to lose,* she thought. She forced her muscles to relax, opened herself to the flames, breathing deeply until the heat filled her. She exhaled—WHAM!

⤙

"Max. Max can you hear me?"

It was Cassandra's dark chocolate voice.

"Is he injured?" Another voice. Familiar, but . . .

"No. It's as if he doesn't want to wake up. He hears me, but—"

"What does a guy have to do to get some sleep around here?"

The rusty croak of his own voice forced Max's eyes open. He blinked, but this time he wasn't dreaming, it really was Cassandra. Lightborn's concerned face hung over her shoulder. Max smiled and started to stand up, winced as his shoulder muscles complained.

"What happened here?" Lightborn toed the dead soldier's body where it lay as far from Max as he'd been able to push it.

"He pissed me off," Max said. He'd had time, before exhaustion had claimed him, to face the fact that he'd killed a man—not in self-defense, not in the heat of a fight, but in a rage of disgust and fear. Max swallowed. It was lucky his stomach was empty. He was hoping that after a while, the fact that the man was going to kill him would feel less like a rationalization and more like a good reason.

"Why hasn't he Faded?" Cassandra said.

Lightborn shook his head, still looking down at the dead Rider. "*Dra'aj* works strangely at times, here in the Citadel."

"Who placed these manacles on you?" Cassandra was running her fingers lightly over the metal around Max's wrists and the point where the chains joined the wall.

"He did," Max said, indicating the dead guard with a tilt of his head. "He hasn't got the key on him, I already looked."

Cassandra and Lightborn were looking at each other in a way that Max didn't like. "What?"

Lightborn bit his bottom lip. "There is no key," he said. "These are darkmetal, keyed to the guard himself."

"They open and close when he wants them to," Cassandra added when Max looked at her, eyebrows raised. She continued examining the ring bolt that attached the chain to the wall. She glanced at Lightborn and shook her head. Max looked from one ivory-pale face to the other.

"You mean I killed the only person who can get me out of them?"

The way they wouldn't look at him was answer enough.

"Well, it seemed like a good idea at the time." He squeezed his eyes shut. "What now?"

"Don't look at me," Cassandra said, taking a step back from them, her hands raised.

Lightborn gave a bark of laughter. "Truthsheart, I did not expect you to succeed in bringing us here and yet you did . . . so why not this?"

"It might be possible to Move him," she said, sitting back on her heels after examining Max's wrists again. "But I think he would lose his hands."

"Let's try that last," Max said, unconsciously flexing his hands in their metal prisons.

"Show some backbone," Lightborn said, still smiling. "She would be able to Heal you. You would, would you not?" he added, turning to Cassandra.

"Probably," she said, nodding slowly.

Max glanced at the hideously decorated wall. He noticed for the first time that both Cassandra and Lightborn had positioned themselves with their backs to it. "If *that's* my alternative," he said, pointing with his chin, "I'm willing to try it."

Cassandra glanced over her shoulder, her eyes following

his gesture. She stared for a moment before getting to her feet and crossing the stone floor, steps slow, lifting her hand and stretching out her fingers. Lightborn turned so that he, too, could watch her. *How can she bear to look at it,* Max thought, *let alone stand so close . . . touch it?*

"He's smiling," she said when she was close to the wall; her voice broke a little and she cleared her throat. "He tricked the Basilisk somehow, the old Troll. He angered the Basilisk with his last act. This," her nail ticked against a twisted dark gray limb, "this is stone now. True work of the Basilisk."

"So he went down fighting?" Max said, finding that he, too, could now look.

"Oh, yes," Cassandra breathed, still looking upward at the face.

"Protecting us," Lightborn whispered, his voice gentle and reverent.

Cassandra bowed deeply at the thing on the wall, touched it once more with her fingertips, before turning back to face them. "I have an idea," she said.

"Truthsheart." There was a warning note in Lightborn's voice now. Max glanced away from Cassandra's frowning concentration to find the pale Rider had moved a few steps nearer the door. "I think we must hurry."

"Wonderful." Cassandra opened Max's saddlebags and took out his gauntlets. "Can you get these on?"

Max thought there was no way she could force the cuffs of the long metal gloves under the shackles on his wrists, but he was willing to try anything.

"What do you think this will do?" he asked, holding out his right hand.

"I'm hoping that the *gra'if* will form a barrier between the darkmetal and your hands. It *is* part of you, but it's a part that's supposed to protect you."

If the *gra'if* had been formed pieces of metal, like the armor used on Earth, they could never have done what was needed. But it was more supple, like stiff leather, or like the finest of chain mail. Max knew of several of his students who would have loved to have clothing made of it. Once Cassandra had forced the edge of the gauntlet under the darkmetal cuff, the rest followed smoothly, as if the *gra'if* understood what was wanted and was cooperating. Finally getting the actual glove on his hand was the easy part.

"Quickly," Lightborn said from the doorway.

"I'm dancing as fast as I can." Max and Cassandra exchanged thin smiles. Hers faded quickly, and Max thought he knew why. Once he became the Prince Guardian, these little human jokes and references, this special camaraderie would end. They would no longer have the common background of the human world. He reached out with the hand she'd finished and touched her face. For a moment she held perfectly still, then she moved her face away, bending over his left hand until she had worked the other gauntlet under the darkmetal cuff.

Max stood up.

"Where to?" Cassandra caught his eyes and held them.

"If they have managed to leave the Signed Room, Walks Under the Moon awaits us in the stables of Griffinhome," Lightborn said over his shoulder, thinking Cassandra had spoken to him, "but we must hurry."

Cassandra still held Max's eyes with her own. In that moment he remembered that she still didn't know what his decision was, that they'd been interrupted before he could tell her. His throat closed, and he drew in a deep breath through his nose. He knew the question she was really asking, and he knew that she was the only person who was actually leaving it up to him to decide.

Max looked past her shoulder again, to what was left of the Troll Diggory on the wall. What was his real name? Hearth of the Wind, something like that. If he took Cassandra's unspoken offer and ran, they'd be followed. *Hunted down,* he thought, tasting the ironic bitterness of the image. And he'd eventually end up like the Troll, stuck to the wall with his own blood and then turned to stone.

And Cassandra would, too, if she lasted long enough. Along with everyone else who had something the Basilisk wanted.

Even if the Basilisk Prince did love his old friend, and Max shuddered at the memory of that hot hand on his face—even if the Basilisk didn't just kill him out of hand once he had the Talismans—Max couldn't put more power into the hands of someone who could do such things.

At that moment an armed soldier ran though the doorway—and impaled himself on Lightborn's ready sword.

"Now," Lightborn said, pulling his sword free.

Max caught Cassandra's eyes with his. "Stables it is," he said.

Lightborn and Cassandra each took one of Max's upper arms in their free hands. Cassandra turned to face the open doorway, her sword drawn. Just as Max nodded in response to Lightborn's questioning look, he saw movement out of the corner of his eye.

Cassandra swung up her sword and—

A SLAM! of air and the sudden quiet told Max it was safe to open his eyes. The smell told him they had reached a stable. They were standing in a clear area between empty horse boxes.

"Max, your hands?" Only when he heard Cassandra's voice did he realize that he held Lightborn's left arm in a tight grip. His gauntlets had dark dust around the wrists, but his hands were fine. He was about to say so, when he realized that Lightborn was sinking to his knees.

The barbed head of an arrow jutted out through the left side of his chest.

"Leave me, go!" Lightborn said, pushing at Max weakly with his hand.

"Cassandra?"

She was nodding at him when Walks Under the Moon came running in from outside. "Why are you—oh!" She froze, her hand halfway to her mouth.

"Do you have the horses?" Cassandra sheathed her sword and took Lightborn's dangling arm.

"Outside, but—"

"No time."

Cassandra helped Max maneuver Lightborn to where six horses were saddled and waiting just outside the wooden doors of the stable building. They were half again the size of the riding horses Max was used to, almost the size of workhorses, but as delicately boned and as daintily hoofed as Arabians. Clearly, these were Cloud Horses, all a soft dappled gray, their manes white, long and curling. They looked with interest at the Riders, one of them coming forward to snuffle at Lightborn with its delicate lips.

Max's heart sank a little. The saddles and bridles seemed to be made of jeweled cobwebs.

"Mount," Cassandra said. "I will pass him up to you."

"Can't you Heal him now?"

"The Basilisk's Riders are in the fortress, maybe even another Hound."

Max stopped arguing, waited until Cassandra had the man firmly in her grasp before turning to the horse waiting for him. He placed his booted foot into the delicate stirrup and kicked off, lifting himself into the saddle as gently as he could. To his surprise, the gossamer threads held him as firmly as any leather saddle he'd ever used. He settled himself and turned back to Cassandra.

She had broken off the arrowhead sticking out of Lightborn's chest, and was snapping off the fletched end as Max reached down to her. The shaft she left in the wound, Max knew, to prevent the gush of blood, and the loss of blood pressure, that would follow when she pulled it out. She was murmuring softly to Lightborn, who was paler than usual, but still conscious. She lifted him up to Max, and he took Lightborn under the arms, trying not to hurt the man further as he lifted him onto the saddle in front of him.

When she and her sister were mounted, Cassandra turned to the younger woman. "Where?" she said.

"The Turquoise Ring."

Cassandra nodded and held out a hand for Max. Making sure he had a firm grip on Lightborn, and that his knees were clamped as tightly around the horse as he could manage, Max extended his right hand. As soon as their fingers were linked, he was hit by the now familiar SLAM! of displaced air and they were outside, under a roof of stars. Max took a deep breath of air that didn't smell of metal or blood or manure. They were in the center of a level field surrounded by huge dolmens, bands of light like auroras shimmering between the stones. Max glanced around, his eyes narrowing. He'd seen places like this on his way to the Basilisk's stronghold.

His Cloud Horse shied, and Max fought to maintain his seat without dropping the man in his lap.

In front of them were six men on horseback carrying spears.

# Chapter Ten

"NEXT TIME CAN WE go someplace where people *aren't* pointing weapons at us?" Max muttered, shifting Lightborn's weight on the saddle in front of him. He hoped the Rider was unconscious. If it came to fighting, he thought, he'd sling Lightborn across his knees to get his weapon hand clear. Probably not the best thing for a man in Lightborn's condition, but Max's getting killed wouldn't do him any good either.

Max was surprised that Cassandra, usually so quick to draw a blade, or three, had made no aggressive move. Her hand was near her sword hilt, carefully and obviously not touching it, as she studied the horsemen as coolly as they appeared to be studying her.

These Riders were a marked contrast to the men-at-arms Max had seen in Honor of Souls' fortress. There, even the servants had a brightness about them, and the guards had worn more silk and brocade than armor. The people in front of him now were wearing plain leather, dusty and cracked, and looked as if they had been sleeping in their clothes. Their swords and spears and armor were mismatched and discolored with use, except for the man, clearly the leader, whose sword, gauntlets, and

helm—shaped like a bird of prey—gleamed with that
peculiar silvered light that Max recognized as *gra'if*. There
were only a few other *gra'if* helms and weapons, and
here and there a piece of armor, scattered throughout
the small force. Their faces, male and female alike, were
beautiful and cold, and though this band was less shining and polished, it seemed more like the Faerie of leg-
end to Max. Inhuman, hard, and dangerous.

The bird-helmed leader walked his horse a few paces
closer to them and stopped. He pushed his helm back
off his face and leaned forward on his raised saddlebow,
wrists crossed—like any movie cowboy, Max thought
with an inward grin—looking at them over his horse's
head. He was easily the tallest man Max had ever seen,
towering over the rest of his company. He was also the
first Rider Max had seen to show visible signs of age.
His face was lined as if with exposure to the sun and
wind, and his black hair was more than half silver. And
he was thin, his flesh so pared away that only his inhuman beauty was left. There was something familiar
about him, and Max wondered if he was one of the
Faerie who had spent a great deal of time on Earth.

"I do not know you." The man's voice was a whisper
of rough silk, as if it had been very melodious once,
and he had strained it by screaming. Looking at the
man's face, Max could well believe it. "I am Blood on
the Snow," the man said, looking between Moon and
Cassandra. "I was once Raven of the Law, and the
Simurgh guides me."

Moon drew in her breath in a small gasp, and Cassandra sat up straighter.

"I am the Warden Sword of Truth," she said, "and the
Dragon guides me. My companions are—"

"Dawntreader." The tall man urged his horse closer,
close enough that Max could see the gray of his eyes
even in the uncertain light of the auroras. Cassandra did
not answer. His Cloud Horse shifted under him as Max
involuntarily tightened his knees.

"We have a man dying here," Max said, trying to keep his voice even. "If you're not going to kill us right away, you might let us look after him."

Blood on the Snow rode his horse right up to Max, until their knees were almost touching. The old man gripped Max's upper arm, his hand warm and hard even through the layers of metal and sleeve. There was a bedraggled bit of blue cloth tied above his left elbow, still showing metallic threads in the weave. It was the only color about him. Max looked up into the old man's ash-gray eyes, and the impulse to pull away died before the light he saw in them. As he watched, however, the light dimmed, and the very slight smile on the old man's face faded as he let his hand fall back to his saddle horn.

"Your cousin will take some time to die yet," Blood on the Snow said of Lightborn, before turning to face Cassandra.

"He does not know me," he said to her.

"He knows no one," Cassandra said. "His memory has been taken from him. We take him to the Tarn of Souls, where the Songs tell we may restore him."

Blood on the Snow nodded slowly, his shaggy hair floating around his face even though there was no wind.

"I had heard that this Ring is one of the stations of that Road," Blood said. "Though if the Carnelian Ring is on your route, take warning that you must travel around it. The Land has shaken there, and the Stones are fallen and broken." One of the other Riders behind him made a murmur of sound, too low for Max's ears to pick up the individual words.

The old man lifted his hand in acknowledgment. "Take heed of this also. We Rode here to use this Ring ourselves and found in it a company of men, dressed in the colors of the Basilisk. We watched them, and they did not Ride, but stayed hidden in the Ring, plainly waiting to surprise the next ones who used it. We have no love for the things of the Basilisk, we Wild Ones, and so we took the company and killed them. It is hardly coincidence, I think, that you and the Exile were the next to appear."

"We thank you for your warning, and for the help you may have given us against our enemies," Cassandra said. "Will you not come with us to the Tarn? We would benefit from your wise counsel."

Max looked at her, surprised. Just who *was* this guy?

Blood on the Snow took his time to answer. "I cannot leave my people," he said finally. He looked searchingly at Max, his face once again stern and unyielding, before turning back to Cassandra. "It is good that the Guardian has returned. When he is himself again, tell him he can call upon me, and all who are mine. He will know how to find me."

*I'm right here,* Max thought, *you can tell me yourself.* But with a sudden sinking of his stomach, he knew why the old man had spoken as he did. The Prince Guardian might not remember the things that Max Ravenhill knew.

"I will do so, my lord," Cassandra said.

The old Rider nodded again, his eyes focused inward, before looking up at Cassandra once more. "What of the other Wardens?"

"The Moonward, Stormbringer, is taken by the Hunt," Cassandra said. "The Sunward, Nighthawk . . . I cannot say. He sent warning to me, and was not seen again."

Blood on the Snow sat so still that even his Cloud Horse seemed not to move. "The Nightflying Hawk is of my *fara'ip.* I will trust that he still lives, until I hear otherwise."

"Wait, my lord. I may yet have other news," Cassandra said as Blood on the Snow turned his horse away. "Do you have, as Nighthawk has, acquaintance among the Solitaries? I have news to give the *fara'ip* of the Last Born Troll, Hearth of the Wind."

Once more the older man paused before answering, his gray eyes turned cold as iron. "I am myself of that *fara'ip.*"

Cassandra nodded, as if hearing something she'd expected. "As am I," she said. "His final words to me were to name me his sister."

"Oh, my dear sister, do you say his *final* words?" The old Rider's voice was a faded whisper on the night air. "Is the Last Born truly gone?"

Max could see the gray eyes were tightly shut, the hand that held the delicate reins trembling.

"My lord." Cassandra edged her horse closer to Blood on the Snow, her hand stretched toward him. She stopped as the old Rider straightened, the cold gray eyes opening once more.

"Our brother was the Last Born, do you understand?" Blood said. "Not the Last Born Troll, but the Last of the Solitaries born in this Cycle. The youngest of all, and the hope of all. Now there will be no more young ones among the Solitaries unless the High Prince comes, and the Cycle turns."

"My lord," Cassandra's voice was as hollow as the emptiness in Max's chest. "We did not know."

Blood on the Snow inclined his head once. "How did our brother die?"

Cassandra hesitated long enough that Max knew she was seeing the same image that had flashed before his eyes. The image of the Troll's remains on the wall of the Basilisk's dungeon cell.

"Fighting his Prince's enemies," Cassandra said.

Max found himself nodding. Not just fighting, he thought. Winning.

"As he would have wished," Blood said. "One day I trust that we will have leisure enough for you to tell me more."

"As you say, my lord." Cassandra bowed her head.

Blood on the Snow and his followers saluted them with their spears before spinning their horses around in unison like dancers in a perfectly choreographed ballet and galloping off, gathering speed. They never reached the outside of the circle; the aurora flashed and they were gone.

Max found he was holding his breath. Watching a dozen horsemen ride into nothing was a little more startling than doing it himself.

"Who was that guy?" was all that he said aloud.

Moon seemed about to speak, but she hesitated, looking at her sister. Cassandra had moved her horse next to Max's and was feeling for the pulse in the side of Lightborn's neck.

"Your father," she said, without looking up.

Max stared into the empty space where Blood on the Snow and his Wild Riders had been. His father? His *real* father, he supposed he should say. He didn't know much about his human father—and the few memories they had given him hadn't inclined him to learn more. Obviously, Dawntreader, the Prince, had felt differently. The way Blood on the Snow had ridden right up to him, had taken hold of his arm, it looked as though they had been on good terms, the father and the son. Max wished Cassandra had said something in time, wished he had spoken to the older man while he had the chance. Blood had seemed like the kind of man Max would have liked to know.

But what would be the point? Max pressed his lips together. Soon it wouldn't matter what Max Ravenhill knew. It wasn't much consolation that the Prince had had a life, people who cared about him.

"He still lives," Cassandra was saying to Moon, "but he is sunk very low. We must get out of the Ring if I'm to help him."

"There's no time!" Moon looked at Lightborn and back at her sister. "We must away quickly. They will look for the Riders the Wild Ones killed. We must be gone from here before they come."

Cassandra hesitated, lower lip between her teeth. She looked up at Max. He knew what was going through her mind. They should run while they could, and yet—the image of the Troll's death was too fresh—letting Lightborn die when they might have saved him . . . Okay, he thought, he might as well make some decisions while he still could.

"Save him," he said.

"You're sure?"

Something in the way Cassandra asked the question told him he'd said the right thing. He nudged his horse toward the perimeter of the Ring. "You told me I was here to save people. Start with this one."

Once beyond the Ring of stones, Max found he had been holding Lightborn for so long that lowering the man into Cassandra's outstretched arms was almost more than his stiffened muscles could manage. Good thing it hadn't come to a fight after all, he thought. He dismounted slowly, carefully, stood holding his horse's bridle, the light webbing as cold in his hand as if it were made of metal. Moon, her objections put aside, was helping Cassandra ease Lightborn to the ground.

They hadn't ridden far, just enough to be out of the circle of stones that marked the Turquoise Ring. The dolmens still towered over them, black against the star-filled sky. The auroras had fallen dark now that there was no one in the Ring to activate them, but the stars were bright enough to read by, if Max'd had anything to read. He looked up, expecting to see the full moon, but there were only the stars, more than he had ever seen. He had never been much of a stargazer, but even for him it was disorienting not to see any of the well-known constellations overhead.

He looked down just in time to see Cassandra grasp what was left of the shaft of the arrow that transfixed Lightborn firmly in her right hand and, bracing him against her knee, draw it out with one smooth, steady pull. Blood gushed from the wound, and Cassandra placed her palm against it. With Moon to balance her, Cassandra shifted until she was sitting with Lightborn in her arms, his head on her shoulder, one hand on the entry wound, the other on the exit hole in his chest. Max found his fingers straying to his left side; he remembered what came next, and wondered whether he would be able to watch.

Walks Under the Moon had never seen a Healer at work before; that it was Truthsheart who Healed only served to make it more interesting. Healers appeared only among the Dragonborn, and so were rare among Riders, who usually had to go to some Solitary, or even a Natural, for those few injuries and illnesses that their own *dra'aj* could not cope with—not that any did so openly now. And in these times there were very few people left with enough *dra'aj* to help others. That was one of the things the Basilisk Prince had told her he would change, when he became the High Prince, one of the ways they would all be turning back to the golden days the Songs told of.

Moon frowned. Truthsheart had enough *dra'aj* for Healing, even without the help of the Basilisk. If her sister had never gone away, perhaps their father might have been saved, though there was no way to know whether his malady would have responded to Healing. One more question that would never be answered, thanks to the Exile.

Who did not look altogether content himself, watching Truthsheart with Lightborn in her arms. Good, Moon thought, this was all his fault. If there were any way to make him even less content . . .

"This may not be the best action for us to take," she said, and waited for the Exile to drag his eyes away from Truthsheart's Healing. "Someone betrayed us. Can we be sure it was not Lightborn? We could be bringing the source of our betrayal with us."

The Exile shrugged. "Then we'll have to. I'm not starting out by doing something that I couldn't live with."

Moon turned away, fighting to keep her face from showing her distaste. This person had none of the Prince Guardian's memories, she reminded herself. There was irony but no hypocrisy in his saying that there were actions he could not live with. She must try not to be unfair.

"Besides, if this Basilisk guy is as smart as you make him out to be, he had ambushes set up at every Ring along the Road in case we showed up. That's what I would have done."

With a cold certainty, Moon believed him. The Guardian was more like the Basilisk Prince than anyone suspected, she thought, strings from the same harp, leaves from the same tree. Each determined to get their own way, each sure of his own correctness and the other's error. Each willing to destroy everyone around him to gain his ends. After all, she realized, hugging herself, even now he was endangering everything, their whole plan, merely in order to satisfy his own image of himself. Max Ravenhill was no more than a thin veneer on the Exile. It was still his fault her sister had to go away, leaving her with their mad father.

She could slide over to him right now and slip a knife between his ribs. By the time Truthsheart finished with Lightborn, it would be too late to save the Exile. And her sister might not want to, Moon thought. After all, once the Exile was gone, her Oath to serve him was gone as well, and her sister would be free. Moon's hand was on her dagger and she had taken a step toward the watching Exile before she stopped. If she killed him before the Basilisk's men caught up with them, what would she have to trade the Basilisk for her sister's life? She needed him alive. How could she buy back her *fara'ip* without the Exile?

By the time Cassandra looked up from the man in her arms, Max thought he would start to scream. He was conscious of every small noise, the rustle of grass, the creak of insects. He'd had time to rethink his decision several times, and he was glad that Moon's presence prevented him from changing his mind. It was a lucky thing that she hadn't pressed her point about betrayal. Max wasn't sure that he would have been able to resist stopping the healing process and dragging the two women away.

Cassandra eased Lightborn off her lap and stretched him out on the ground. She joined her hands above her head and stretched until Max could hear the ligaments in her shoulders creak. She drew her legs under her and started to stand, only to lose her balance. Max's longer legs let him reach Cassandra's side before Moon could, and he slipped his arm around her waist to help her stand. She was shivering, and her skin was clammy to the touch. Without thinking, Max folded her into his arms.

"We should be going," she said, her voice tired and muffled in his cotte.

"I know."

# Chapter Eleven

MAX ROLLED OVER and stretched, the muscles in his back and hips protesting. Riding a horse was like riding a bike, he thought. You didn't forget how, but your muscles and your backside weren't happy to be reminded. He rolled out of his bedding as quietly as he could; no point in waking everyone up. They had stayed together in the lodge's great room, sleeping around the banked fire on the central hearth. The fire was large enough to keep the room warm despite its size and its vaulted ceilings sporting vast wooden beams. The lodge had plenty of sleeping chambers, but no one had felt like splitting up, and Max had helped Cassandra and Moon carry all the feather bedding they could find to this main room.

Cassandra opened her eyes as he tiptoed past her, but closed them again when he held a finger to his lips and pointed out through the open doorway to the passage that led to the windowed gallery outside.

Like the similar passageway in Honor of Souls' fortress, this was an enclosed gallery, like a hallway in a house with arched windows cut out all along the exterior wall. Here the passage, walls, and floor were all of wood rather than the stone found in the fortress of Griffin-

home. Even this part of the lodge was obviously meant
for the pleasure of travelers, as the bench all along the
wall under the archways made clear. Max eased the
door to the great room shut behind him and went to the
nearest unshuttered window. It took him a minute to realize there was no glass. He stretched out his hand, but
nothing stopped it. There *was* a barrier, he thought, a
point at which the relative warmth of the passage
stopped and the cold winter air outside the window
started, but what made the barrier he couldn't tell. Max
smiled, settling himself sideways on the wide bench.
This was the first piece of magic he'd seen here in the
Lands that wasn't trying to kill him.

The snow they had ridden through from the Morganite Ring, fat flakes like white moths landing gently on
the ground, had finally stopped falling. He thought the
drifts were maybe a little deeper, the branches of the
dark pines bowed a little closer to the ground, but on
the whole, there was no more snow than there had been
when they had arrived, guided to this travelers' lodge by
a weak-voiced but conscious Lightborn.

The moon was full, and the snow-covered landscape
sparkled, sharp and clear. Max frowned, leaning forward on the broad window ledge to take a closer look
at the scene outside. The moon had been full when
they'd arrived, and Max could swear that it was even in
the same position in the sky. How long had he been
asleep? He couldn't have slept through the whole day.
For one thing, he didn't feel anywhere near enough
rested.

A noise made him look away from the moonlight.

"Should you be up?" he said, standing and taking a
step toward Lightborn.

Lightborn waved him back. He still looked a little
paler than he had before, his skin more pearl than al-
mond, but other than the tears in his clothing and the
dark bloodstain down the left side of his body, there was
no other sign of his wound. It had taken Cassandra

some time the night before to persuade the man that he wasn't well enough to Ride. They had finally compromised and advanced only as far as the Morganite Ring, the next stop on the route Moon had worked out to the Tarn of Souls.

"I have told Truthsheart that I am not ready for a fencing lesson, but I am much better than I could have hoped. She looks as though she could give fully as thorough a lesson as your father used to give us." Lightborn's voice was light, precise, as if he was breathing very shallowly still.

Max sat down again, his back to the bright snow outside the window. "Did you know my father?"

Lightborn studied Max's face a moment before answering. "I find it easy to forget, now that I see you in your *gra'if*, dressed to Ride, that you remember none of us."

Max shook his head.

"I know Blood on the Snow," Lightborn said, sitting down as Max shifted to give him room on the bench. "As well as anyone could be said to know him."

"Did I know him better?"

The pale Rider made to draw up his left knee, winced, and set his foot down again. "There was a certain coolness between you and your father, and I am afraid to make too much of it in the telling. There was always a great love, and a great respect, but I believe it is easier to show respect than to show love."

Max glanced at the other man, but Lightborn wasn't looking at him. Instead, he seemed lost in his own thoughts, brows drawn in and mouth slightly twisted to one side. Somehow, this puzzled Max. Lightborn was a much more likable guy than the arrogant princeling he'd been before his injury.

"Tell me," Max said.

"Your father was not present when you were born, and for many years it was thought that you had died along with your mother. Only your father did not believe it. He did not rest until he found you. I remember as a child watching this grim-faced Moonward stranger ride into Griffinhome, always at night, never in the day. Sometimes he would have other Wild Riders with him, and sometimes my mother could persuade him to stay a few days to rest. Not that he did—I remember him training with the guards and soldiers of our *fara'ip*. But usually he would be up and gone with the sun."

"How did he know I was still alive?"

"He never spoke of it. My mother thought it was no more than guilt, from causing your mother's death."

"What?"

"No, no," Lightborn said, waving the idea away with his long-fingered hand. "It is just that both parents must be present when a child is born, or the babe will drain the mother's *dra'aj* completely."

*Great,* Max thought. *He didn't kill my mother, I did.* "What happens if the father's dead?"

"Usually, the mother stops the pregnancy." Lightborn gave him a searching glance. "Your mother chose to save you."

Max sighed. He supposed that should make him feel better, that she had chosen this, but . . .

"I do not think I ever knew *exactly* what it was that delayed your father," Lightborn continued. "He had left his Wild *fara'ip* behind him for the love that he bore your mother. And, for her sake, he was about some business for the Council of Elders when her hour came unexpectedly. By the time your father knew of it and had returned to her, she was gone. She had tried to Move to him—no one knows why she could not do it—and was lost. As were you."

"How long?"

"I cannot say. You are older than I. Blood on the Snow's searching was a fact of my early years. He had always been searching, as far back as I could remember. And then one day, he brought you to my mother's house.

"When he found you, you were not yet grown. But

you wore *gra'if* already, and the white hair," Lightborn gestured at Max's head, "you had that as well."

Max frowned, studying the other man carefully. "I don't understand," he said. "Why your house?"

Lightborn looked sharply at him, mouth slightly open, eyebrows raised. "Again I forget," he said. "Your mother is the sister of mine. Family by blood, as well as by *fara'ip*. As were we, in our time."

Lightborn fell silent as footsteps approached and Cassandra entered the passage from the great room. She tossed each of them a small packet that turned out to have a rich cake heavy with fruit inside.

"I'd forgotten how Riders packed for a journey," she said, tilting her head toward the room she had left, where the night before they'd dumped the leather-wrapped wicker panniers that formed the four packs carried by the extra Cloud Horses. There was exasperated amusement in her voice. "There's food, but no spare clothing; wine, but no water. You'll have to stay in your bloody clothes," she said, turning to Lightborn.

"It is preferable to dying in them, I assure you," Lightborn said, as they followed Cassandra back into the great room. There the fire had been built up, and Walks Under the Moon looked over from where she was repacking the panniers.

"Dawntreader—" she began.

"Just a second," Max said, raising his hands. "Can we keep things simple for the human? I'm Max, she's Cassandra," he pointed at her. "You're Lightborn, and you're Moon. Okay?"

"Her name is not Cassandra," Moon said, frowning.

"Indulge me." Max was aware of a certain bitterness in his tone. "It won't be for long."

Moon nodded, but something about the stubborn set of her mouth gave Max the idea that she wasn't happy.

"We should be on our way," Moon said to Cassandra as she closed and retied the wicker lid, "before the snow begins again. This is time we cannot afford to lose."

"Wouldn't it be better to wait until morning?" Max said around a mouthful of travel cake.

All three looked at him, Lightborn and Moon puzzled, Cassandra with the small smile he was beginning to find irritating.

"It's always midnight here," Cassandra said. "This is one of the unchanging Lands."

Max decided not to ask.

Lightborn insisted on helping Max carry gear down to the stables, but Max suspected it was more to give the man an excuse to visit the Cloud Horses than for anything else. The animals recognized them both, but they were particularly affectionate with Lightborn, blowing air in his face and shaking their heads at him.

"They were born in Griffinhome," Lightborn said, laughing, as he ran his hands along the flanks of the horse nearest him in evident delight. "My own horses."

"Are they . . . magic somehow?"

"Many say they have no *dra'aj*," Lightborn said, "but I am not of that mind. They have *dra'aj* in their own way, as does everything in the Lands. They are sensitive to Movement, and they take pleasure in the Ride. How could they do this, if they had no *dra'aj*?"

"In my world people argue over whether animals have souls," Max said. "Over whether they should have some of the same rights as humans."

"Perhaps I should visit the Shadowlands, when this is over."

"I'll take you," Max said, "if I can."

"When this is over," Lightborn repeated, giving the horse's flank a final stroke.

"Can you get us around the broken Ring?" Cassandra was saying to her sister as Max and Lightborn returned to the great room.

"I believe so," the younger woman said. "The Songs tell many stories about the Lands around the Rings. I should be able to piece together a pathway, though I wish I had my Singers with me."

"Can't we just Move to where we're going?" Max found his muscles protesting at the thought of more riding.

"Only the very powerful can Move to a place they have never been," Moon said as she fastened the ties on her own saddlebag. "And I think now they live only in the Songs. For the rest of us, the common run of Riders, we must know a place, and sometimes know it well, before we can Move there. The Ring Road," she continued, gesturing to the outside, "any Rider has sufficient *dra'aj* to use it, since it opens only to another Ring, another point on the Road. And it is used for Riding on a first journey, when one is not familiar with one's destination. The Songs tell that the Basilisk Prince found the Tarn of Souls using the Ring Road, and it is those Songs we follow now."

Max shook his head. "If we know which Rings to use, why don't we just Move to the one nearest the Tarn?"

"Movement to a Ring," Lightborn said around the piece of sweet cake in his mouth, "always takes you to the one nearest you, and so sets you on the Road."

"So it's not the Road that's in a Ring?" Max said.

"The Rings make up the Road . . ." began Lightborn.

"There is no Road," Cassandra interrupted, recorking a stone bottle and replacing it in her saddlebag. "There are only the Rings."

"Very Zen," Max said after a moment. "But no explanation."

Cassandra shrugged, that same half smile on her lips. "They're like Portals that open only to another Ring. The road is the road. No shortcuts."

"It is the destination that determines the order in which the Rings must be traveled," Moon added.

"So when the Basilisk wanted to find the Tarn of Souls . . ."

"He tried each combination of Rings, one at a time, until he found the one that would take him there. Once there, of course, he could Move there anytime . . ." Cassandra's voice died away.

"So he could be there now, waiting for us, since he

knows that is where we need to go." Lightborn let his hand, the sweet cake still in it, fall to his side.

Max looked around at their faces. "He won't do it," he said after he'd had a moment to think. "From what you've told me, he can't spare the time to lie in wait himself, and he won't want the rest of his people to know where the Tarn is."

Moon and Lightborn looked at Cassandra. Finally, she nodded.

Max hung back as they followed the others to the stables.

"You weren't very quick to agree," he said.

Cassandra smiled as she slung her saddlebag over her shoulder, careful not to catch it on any of her weapons. "The Songs all tell that the Prince Guardian was a more-than-able military commander," she said. "All I know for sure after Warding you for a thousand years is that you're very good at putting yourself into the minds of opposing generals. You have an intuitive grasp of strategy, of the balance and pull of forces. But even with this, you haven't always won."

"Do you have a better idea?"

"No."

"Then let's get on with it."

The Basilisk Prince turned from the Garden view outside the round window of his workroom to his guard captain, on one knee before him. Two others, each high in standing among the guards, knelt behind their captain. As if bad news came more easily to the palate from fools on their knees.

"I have sworn to withhold my hand from the Dragonborn Warden," the Basilisk Prince reminded them.

"In return for the Exile, certainly, my Prince, but we . . . you, do not have him." The Captain of the Guard, a flaxen-haired Starward Rider, lifted his eyes to the Basilisk's face.

The Basilisk smiled, though his teeth gritted from the cramp that suddenly clutched his right leg. "Young Walks Under the Moon is more clever than you, I think. She did not trade me her sister for the Exile, but for his whereabouts. The bargain is a true one, unbreached."

"But, my Prince—"

The Basilisk stared him into silence, one hand raised. He had glimpsed an idea, but exhaustion kept it hovering just out of his grasp. He had not had a chance to refresh himself after awakening feeling pale, when they had come to him, afraid to tell him that Dawntreader was gone—afraid not to tell him. Roused from his bed, it was all he could do to hold himself upright in the low chair before his dressing table. Now it seemed that he could feel his skin hardening, his lungs filling with heat. He forced his hands to stop trembling, his lungs and throat to unlock; he took two deep breaths, the second steadier than the first. He was tired, that was all. He was far more tired than he should be; there was so much to do, and he had to do it all himself. So many details, and he could not afford to let any of them slip away.

Then, as he lowered himself into his chair, the elusive thought came clear. Of course! He had thought to find the Guardian, to hold him until the Talismans manifested, but surely now that he was here in the Lands, there was no need? To have the Talismans before the end of the Banishment would be more than convenient, but not *necessary*. The little Moon had said revealed they intended to take Dawntreader to the Tarn so that he might be restored and so fetch the Talismans from their hiding place. Well, then, why should he not wait and let that happen? Why not let the Talismans be found, and then simply take them away? He would use the time to rest and strengthen himself. After all, he would always know exactly where the Guardian was. He could put his hand on him at any time. Still, he thought as he eyed the Riders

on their knees before his chair, that did not excuse
what had happened. While he could relax himself,
there was no reason for laxness among his followers.

"The fault lies not in Walks Under the Moon," he said
to them. "The fault lies here, in you. The Exile was lost
from here, from my very Citadel by your carelessness,
and you . . ."

The Basilisk's throat closed over the words, his breath
choking in his lungs. Once more he forced himself to
relax.

"You," he continued, "have not even suggested a way
to regain him. Fixing blame brings us no closer to solv-
ing this problem. Unless the problem is of a different
kind?"

"No, my lord Prince," said the Captain of the Guard,
his eyes lowered.

The Basilisk relaxed still further. People changed sides,
there was the thing. Perhaps even little Moon. It was always better to be certain. Always better to take precau-
tions. The Exile had few friends left, but even those
were too many. Here was a chance for a lesson to be
taught.

"I will call the Hunt," the Basilisk said. "Send them to
Griffinhome, let them have a fresh scent." He gripped
the small bone ornament that hung around his neck on
a chain. His hands were trying to tremble again. "Send
me—no, let this one stay and attend upon me," he said,
holding his hand out to the short Moonward Rider
nearest him.

"Yes, my Prince," said the Captain of the Guard. "And
Honor of Souls and her people?"

"Give everyone you find to the Hunt. Burn her fortress,
cleanse the Land."

They had been Riding for most of the morning, and Max
swallowed for what felt like the tenth time in as many
minutes. Now he knew why everyone here always re-

ferred to the place as the "Lands"—plural—and how it was "always midnight" at the Lodge where they'd slept. They'd gone back the short distance through the moon-lit landscape to the Morganite Ring, where it had taken them only seconds to pass through to the Quartz. From there, the small party had set out to Ride around the gap in the Road—*though it isn't a Road,* he reminded him-self—that was formed by the broken Carnelian Ring. Al-most immediately after Riding into what he'd thought would be a clearing in the trees Max found himself bal-ancing on a ledge halfway up a mountain face, just wide enough for him to lead his horse. After that, they'd Rid-den through a rain forest, which had changed abruptly into a wide beach in a windstorm, with waves crashing and salt spray stinging their eyes; and he'd watched a cornfield turn into a foul-smelling swamp in a space no greater than the length of one of the Cloud Horses. These and other changes had been accompanied by cor-responding shifts in air pressure, temperature, and, what was worst for Max, direction. He'd always had a perfect sense of direction, able to navigate even underground with-out difficulty, and twice this morning alone he'd found himself queasily disoriented as the compass inside his head had spun for a few seconds before coming to an abrupt halt in a new—and very unlikely—setting.

And he couldn't even complain, because no one else seemed to notice the way the landscape changed all of a sudden from one step to the next, like the panels in a newspaper comic, although Max would swear he'd seen Cassandra flinch a couple of times.

"When I was first in the Shadowlands," she said, after they had left a forested hillside and entered a prairie grassland, "I thought I would never get used to how *gradual* everything was, how you could ride for days across a prairie, how a meadow would slowly become a forest, or a beach ease into a mountain range."

"Is the whole land like this? Aren't there any . . . normal bits?"

"This isn't an ecosystem," Cassandra said, her eyes focusing on the horizon. "It isn't a coherent whole, like the Earth. The Lands are more like a network of separate places, connected by *dra'aj*." She indicated the prairie grass they were currently riding through, already springing up behind them to show no trail. "Each place is and remains always itself," she smiled at him, "forever touching and forever separate like the pieces on a patchwork quilt."

That made a lot of sense, Max thought. Considering the abilities of the Riders to transport themselves, why should the world they inhabited be coherent, each physical location blending and connecting with others?

"There are places one cannot reach by walking or Riding." Lightborn, unnoticed, had fallen back to take a position on Max's left, leaving Moon alone in the lead. She hadn't been much company as they Rode, constantly singing or humming snatches of tune to herself, matching the lines in her head to the landscape around them, or, for all Max knew, calling up the landscape with the Song.

Lightborn laughed, and tugged on Max's shirtsleeve. "Do you remember," he said, "the time you swore we would find a way to Ride around the Shaghana'ak Abyss . . ."

Max saw Lightborn's clear blue eyes cloud over as the man fell silent. He felt his own smile stiffen on his face. *No,* Max thought, *I don't remember, though I suppose I will soon.*

"Some say that *Ma'at,* the Stone of Virtue, may be such a place, that one can only Move there, and that only the Prince Guardian knows the way. Is that so?" Moon's voice was startlingly loud. She had stopped singing, reined in her horse, and sat waiting for them.

Cassandra spoke into the silence. "He doesn't know."

"Oh, yes," Moon said, drawing her brows together in a frown, "I forgot."

They rode for some time in relative silence, each of

them lost in their own thoughts. Cassandra drew in deep, stimulating lungfuls of air that tasted like rich wine aged in oak barrels. This was home. She had spent years deliberately putting the Lands from her thoughts, knowing she would not return to it for hundreds of human years. And this wasn't the same place she'd left, no matter how heartbreakingly familiar the smell and feel of the air. She would have to be careful and not fall into the same kind of mistake that she had made in the Shadowlands. More than once she would revisit some treasured place only to find the people she knew gone, fields where there had been forests, roads where there had been fields, busy harbors in quiet coves where she had once gone swimming. Even here, things had changed, and the Lands were no longer the world of her childhood.

Between one step and the next, the country turned hilly, and they slowed, letting the horses find their own footing on the increasingly rocky ground. There were no real paths or trails, but like all of the Lands, it was always possible to find going, however rough, for either feet or hooves.

"Are we anywhere close?" Max said, as Cassandra and Lightborn joined him and Moon at the bottom of a particularly tricky slope.

"I believe so," Moon said, looking at Cassandra as if she had asked the question. "We should enter into a forest soon, and come upon a lake with an inn beside it. The Jade Ring is nearby."

"Do all the Rings have places to stay?" Max got down off his horse to walk it carefully around a steep stretch of gravel. Cassandra smiled as the Cloud Horse nudged him playfully in the back, as if to demonstrate that it didn't need Max to watch out for it.

"I don't know that I've been to all of them, but many do," Cassandra said. "Before the Great War—"

"Go back before that," Lightborn suggested. "Back not to your youth, but to mine. Do you know how we traveled then?" His eyes looking at a distant image, Lightborn looked relaxed for the first time since they'd left Griffinhome. "On foot, sometimes," he said, smiling, "or by coach or horseback; each journey would have its particular delights, sometimes by day, sometimes by night, depending upon which would best bring out the special beauties of the places in which we Rode, whether soft meadow, roaring waterfall, or silent and forbidding crags. My favorite places were those that brought the lightening of the spirit that comes when you round the shoulder of a hill, expecting only another hill, and instead you find the world spread out before you."

"I know what you mean," Max said. "There's a place I used to go to in Scotland, and I'd get up early every day I was there, just to watch the sun come up. No matter how often I was there, it was like seeing the whole world laid out in front of you for the first time. There was nowhere else like it." He looked at Cassandra. "At least, I think I was there."

"Many times," she said.

"As a rule," Lightborn continued, when the silence grew strained, "we would not carry provisions with us, unless for a light meal on the grass. When we would rest, or feast, we simply Moved to some convenient and comfortable spot, some favored haven such as the inn we head toward now, and resumed our journeying the following day."

"I have heard my father tell of these journeys," Moon said, her voice a mild reproach. "But no one has done this for some time."

"Why's that?" Max wouldn't have thought that the economy or social structure of a place where magic was the rule would have been affected so much by a civil war.

"There is not *dra'aj* enough now."

"But *dra'aj* has been Fading since even before the Great War," Cassandra protested. "Certainly there were no Guidebeasts, even then."

Moon shrugged. "There are no Guidebeasts except in the Songs."

"Not so," said Lightborn. "When I was a child, there was a Wild Rider—one of those who came on occasion with your father," he said, turning to Max, "who had seen Guidebeasts when *he* was young."

Moon shrugged again. Cassandra smiled, remembering that shrug from when they were younger. Moon wasn't going to argue, but she wasn't convinced. "There is always some elder to tell you how the Lands were better in his youth," Moon said.

"And that's put you in your place," Max said, laughing.

"It is said that the Basilisk has *dra'aj* enough to manifest his Beast," Lightborn said, the ease dying out of his voice. "It is said that some have seen it."

"*Dra'aj* Fades for all except the Basilisk," Moon said in a voice that answered all questions.

They continued in silence, Cassandra concentrating on the birdsong, seeing if she could identify it after all this time, until Moon drew rein sharply at the summit of a hill thick with rocks. She looked downslope with a worried face, a crease forming between her perfect brows.

"Look," she said, as Max and Cassandra drew up next to her.

At first, Cassandra saw nothing amiss, but Lightborn's quick intake of breath made her look more carefully. At the bottom of a gentle slope, she saw a good-sized plain, long grass feathering back and forth as the wind played. In the middle distance, the dark dolmans of the Jade Ring stood out clearly.

"Well?" she said.

"Where is the forest?" Moon said. "The lake? The inn? We should not be able to see the Ring from this ridge."

"What color is that grass?" Lightborn said, leaning forward.

Cassandra narrowed her eyes. She couldn't be sure,

given the uncertain light, but there was something besides the color that seemed odd. . . .

"I've got a bad feeling about this," she said. "Isn't the Jade Ring surrounded by the *Mara'id*? It's not impossible for Naturals to shift, over time, but . . ." She shook her head.

"Are you sure that's the Jade Ring?" Max said. "I mean, we're not, ah . . ."

"No need to be tactful, Max," Lightborn said. "We are not lost and that *is* the Jade Ring."

"I guess this means no beds to sleep in?" Max said.

"And no lake trout for breakfast," Lightborn added.

"Let us go through the Ring," Moon said. "We will be too late in the day to approach the Tarn of Souls—the Songs tell it can only be found at dawn—but we can camp on the other side."

"What are we waiting for?" Max urged his horse down the slope. Cassandra followed more slowly. For some reason she couldn't take this as easily as Lightborn and Moon did. Perhaps, living here, they were used to finding this kind of change. It was different for Max; everything here was strange to him, what was one more thing? She found it profoundly disturbing that a piece of the Lands she remembered so distinctly should change so much. It was one thing to hear about shiftings and distortions, it was quite another to see a familiar place so completely unfamiliar. Would she know her own home, she wondered, or would Lightstead, too, be changed beyond all recognition?

Max, clearly impatient, was out in front by several lengths by the time Cassandra reached the bottom of the slope. The grass did not grow up the hillside, she noticed, but stopped in a well-delineated edge, as if planted deliberately. It was not as long as she thought either, certainly not as tall as hay, though it did resemble it, rustling in the breeze—

"Max! Stop!"

Max's horse had stepped into the grass by the time

he reined it in. He wheeled it smoothly, though the stiffness of his shoulders showed his impatience at being stopped. Before the turn was complete, the horse whinnied, lifting its feet sharply, almost dancing in its efforts, as if it wanted to lift all four feet off the ground at once. It screamed as first one, then two, then all four hooves became fixed to the ground. Cassandra came close enough to see the sweat break out on the horse's skin, then the screams rang through her head, as if they were more than sound. She smelled blood. She swung her leg over and leaped from her horse, running to the grass's edge, drawing her long sword from her back as she ran.

"Max, jump clear!"

Max had already taken his feet out of the stirrups, drawing away from whatever lurked in the grass, and now gathered himself carefully. He jumped for where Cassandra stood on a moss-covered rock, wobbling in the last second as his horse sank horribly beneath him. Cassandra grabbed his arm as it flailed past her and hauled him bodily from the grass, the razorlike blades scratching at his boots.

Cassandra leaned forward as far as she could without overbalancing and swung her sword once, twice—and the Cloud Horse stopped screaming. Lightborn had flung himself from the saddle as soon as the horse began to scream, and now ran toward the still-twitching body. Cassandra stepped into his path, throwing her arms around him to hold him back.

"I wouldn't, if I were you."

Lightborn nodded, his face white, tears in his eyes as he looked at what remained of the Cloud Horse that he had raised in his own stables, and fed with his own hands. It seemed the grass wanted only live prey; it had stopped its feeding when the horse died. The silence was heavy with the coppery scent of spilled blood.

"What made you stop me?" Max said, wiping his face off on his sleeve. His hands were shaking, and he had to drag his eyes away from swaying grasses. Were they moving closer?

"Look," Cassandra said, pointing. "The breeze blows toward us, but the grass moves right to left."

"I hope we never see what grazes on that." Max put his arm around Lightborn's shoulders and drew the Rider away from the edge of the grass.

Cassandra did not move. "I know what happened here," she said.

The others turned to look at her.

"Didn't you say the Basilisk Prince was cutting down Woods?" she asked. "And this was *Mara'id*. The Basilisk has been here, and cut it down."

# Chapter Twelve

BLOOD ON THE SNOW swept into *He'erid* like the biting crystals of the Frozen Desert from which he took his name, leading his Wild Riders on a charge through the Trees. Some few of the Basilisk's spawn stood their ground, but most fled before the charge, dropping their axes and weapons as they ran. The Trees spread their branches and heaved their roots to better impair the hunted, and aid the hunters.

As he rode through a grove of younger Trees, Blood made careful note of the one or two of the Basilisk's Riders who did not run, but lay themselves prone upon the ground, their faces buried in the sweet grass that grew between the Trees, their hands locked behind their heads in surrender, and in protection against the flying hooves of the Wild Horses. There had always been those among the Basilisk's Riders—though fewer it seemed, as his grip tightened—who would willingly switch allegiance, for whom these assignments, away from the Basilisk's court, were opportunities to change their colors without risking either *dra'aj* or throats.

Or so they thought. Blood on the Snow was too old, his Guidebeast too wily, to be caught by so simple a stratagem.

Blood had seen that for some the defection was genuine, whether it stemmed from a change of heart or simple fear, and these the Natural of the Trees would take, and keep safe. But he had also seen that, for some, the surrender was a pretense. Of these pretenders, there were a few who waited to see if the Wild Riders carried the day; they intended to become traitors and spies for the Basilisk. And if the Wild Riders were driven off, they would betray those of their comrades who had been too quick to lay down their weapons. Blood on the Snow did not concern himself with such as these; he left them to the Wood.

Such things were the legacy of the Great War, which, for the Wild Riders, had never ended.

As he Rode, as his *gra'if* blade rose and fell, a soft joy hummed in Blood's heart, a joy quieter and more gentle than that which usually came with battle against the Basilisk. Like all Wild Riders, he rejoiced in the return of the Prince Guardian, to know that once more they would play their part in the turning of the Cycle. But this Prince was of his own blood, second in his *fara'ip* after his lost beloved, and Blood's whole body sang, muscle and bone, to know that his son was safe. It did not matter that the boy did not know him, Blood told himself; that would come. His Warden took him to meet *Saha'in,* Lady of the Tarn of Souls, and difficult as that meeting might be, all would yet be well.

Or they would all be dead and beyond caring.

His *dra'aj* felt the loss of the Troll Hearth of the Wind, but his Wild heart beat content. The Troll had died the way Blood himself expected and hoped to die. Fighting the Prince Guardian's enemies. Truthsheart, she who was Sword of Truth, her message was even now on its way, passing through the network of Wild Riders, Naturals, and Solitaries who opposed the Basilisk, reaching everywhere some member of the Troll's own *fara'ip* might be.

The day's chase was swift, and once the hunted were

slain or captured, *He'erid,* the Natural of the Trees, appeared. She took the form of a Rider woman, tall, pale mottled green, slender and delicate as willow whips. Even seated on his horse, Blood was able to look her directly in the eyes without lowering his own.

"I greet you, Brother." Her voice was the leaves shivering in the wind. "And I thank you for your aid."

"It is nothing, Sister. Can you Walk to safety?"

"Alas, no." The Natural lowered her head like a branch weighed heavy with snow. "I am but young in the ways of my People, and many Cycles must turn before *He'erid* will walk far."

Blood nodded and signaled to one of his men. "Star at Midnight, choose a squad to remain here with *He'erid.*"

"And if we are needed?" the young Starward Rider asked, even as he came forward to obey.

"The wind will take any message I send," *He'erid* said. "So long as thou art here, Star at Midnight, the wind will speak for thee as well. Blood on the Snow has only to step into any *fara'ip* of Trees and thou shalt hear his message."

Blood nodded at the small group of purple-clad Riders on foot under the Trees. "Help my sister with the captured ones," he said, smiling. "And do not fear, I will send for you when it is time."

As a courtesy, Blood on the Snow and his Wild Pack Rode to the edge of *He'erid* before Moving. As they approached the ending of the trees, they were followed by the sound of hooves, and Star at Midnight overtook them.

"My lord," he called as he came within earshot. "My lord, there is news!"

Blood pulled up his horse and waited as his Pack gathered around him and the messenger.

"My lord, Solitaries have come. The Hunt is in Griffinhome."

Blood shut his eyes and drew in air. So much loss.

When he could trust his voice, he spoke again. "And the Lady Honor of Souls?"

"The Solitaries tell us that the fortress was empty when the Hunt arrived," Star at Midnight said, "but the Lands on which it stood . . ."

Blood nodded very slowly. He hoped his old friend was safe—and that it was not her scent the Hunt was following. "Thank *He'erid* for giving us this message. Ask her to be so good as to make sure that Wind-watcher receives it as well, and tell him to bring his Riders to the place we have spoken of."

"As you wish, my lord."

Cassandra woke to see Moon's silhouette outlined against the star-filled sky. Her muscles ached, and there was a dull pain under her left collar bone that she knew was the residue of Lightborn's wound. She was sorely tempted to just roll over and go back to sleep. When she had this kind of feeling at home—and she was surprised to find that she missed her Toronto apartment, now that it would never be home to her again—she would have spent the day in front of the fire with books, newspapers, or maybe watching movies. Instead, she had to get up and take her turn at watch.

They had Moved past the carnivorous grass right into the Jade Ring, and from there in rapid succession to the Tourmaline and into the Hyacinth, where they were now camped in a shallow depression among the rocks, waiting for the sun to rise so they could approach the Tarn of Souls.

Cassandra rolled to a sitting position and stretched her arms up over her head, rotating her shoulders, and reached for her insteps with both hands. She held the position for a long slow count, until her muscles finally felt loose, before reaching for her boots. There was blood on the soles, she noticed as she pulled them on. They'd been far too slow to figure out what the grass was, and slower still to see any danger. That would have to stop.

As disturbing as the idea of change was, it was much more disturbing to think that it had come about through a deliberate act. Both Lightborn and Moon had disagreed with her suggestion that the cutting down of *Mara'id* had created the carnivorous grass. And yet she somehow knew she was right about the grass' origin. As the Troll Diggory had said, she knew Truth when she heard it, even from her own mouth. The twinge of sadness and nostalgia she'd felt when she first realized the *Mara'id* Forest was gone had been her warning. If only she'd listened instead of wasting time feeling sorry for herself and what she didn't have. What she'd felt was lack of health, lack of . . . *trueness* was the only real word. She'd felt the same kind of distortion in the very ill humans she'd Healed over the years in the Shadowlands, especially plague victims, and, more recently, those with HIV. And there was also a special feel to the beaten and the poisoned. She had never associated her revulsion at tainted water and polluted soil with that same lack of *trueness,* but it was the same, she now realized. When she had looked at the carnivorous grass, she had felt the injury to the Lands the same way she could feel it in a body.

Cassandra stood and settled her sword at her hip before drawing on her gauntlets and lifting her helm over her head, feeling it mold and form itself around her face. She had considered simply sleeping in all of her *gra'if.* She'd done it before, but only when there was no one to keep watch and the need for sleep had demanded it of her. Even so, after the grass, it had taken real discipline to remove the protection the *gra'if* gave her. She stepped silently around the banked fire, careful not to disturb either of the sleeping men. It would be Lightborn's turn to watch in a couple of hours, even though she'd tried to persuade him to let her and Moon divide the night between them. He had lost a great deal of blood, and she would have preferred Lightborn to rest after so much Riding, but he'd pointed out that Max wouldn't be able to take a turn, and that short as the night was, three to keep watch would give everyone more sleep.

As if he felt her gaze come to rest on him, Max's eyes opened. He frowned, likely wondering what had woken him up, and then his focus narrowed, and his eyes fixed on Cassandra. He smiled, closed his eyes again, and fell back into sleep.

Cassandra felt her heart turn over and she looked away, pushing her feelings back to where she had tried to keep them tightly locked since she'd seen Max Ravenhill at that cocktail party and felt again all that she had always felt on seeing him. What she now knew she would continue to feel when even Max was gone.

She sighed. Time to concentrate on something she *could* do.

Moon looked up at her as she sat down. Cassandra put her arm around her sister and hugged her, finding some relief from her feelings in the gesture. At first, Cassandra had felt nothing but joy at holding her sister once more in her arms, but she was finding it hard to think of this serious young woman who rarely smiled as the little girl who used to sit on her lap, begging for Songs and a ride on a Cloud Horse. That child had grown up in a strange world, and Cassandra would have to get to know her all over again. If events allowed.

"Do you think he will save us all?" Moon said. No need to ask her who she meant, Cassandra thought, glancing back over her shoulder at Max.

"Isn't that why we're here?" she said finally, more to herself than to Moon.

"We none of us know what the Prince Guardian will want done," Moon said. "Unless Lightborn knows and does not tell. He is the only one of us who knew the Prince. Who knew both Princes, when they were but Riders."

Both women looked at the sprawled heap of clothing that was Lightborn.

"We all assume that the Exile will fight the Basilisk Prince as he did before." Moon's words came as if from a great distance and lured Cassandra back from the circling of her own thoughts. "But do we really know what he thinks, or what he wants, now that he has been in Exile all this time?"

Cassandra looked at her sister's profile, dark against the starlit sky. "Did we ever know?"

"His concerns are his own, his reasons his own. So it is with all Guardians. So the Songs tell us." Moon shrugged, and then turned to Cassandra, laying both her hands on Cassandra's arm. "This is all the world I have known," she said. "Has anyone thought of that, I wonder? I do not remember the great and golden world that was before the Great War. I doubt very much that anyone does."

"There were problems even then," Cassandra allowed, "or the War would not have happened. There would have been no reason for anyone to seek a High Prince."

"You see? So what will happen when the Banishment ends and the Guardian is restored? If he refuses to give the Talismans to the Basilisk, we will only have war again."

Cassandra found Moon's steady stare unsettling. "Perhaps the Talismans themselves will act," she said.

Moon smiled sadly, folding her hands in her lap and swinging her feet. "They did not act before."

"Why are *you* here?" This attitude seemed unaccountable in someone who was helping to bring the Prince Guardian back from Exile.

"I am here for you," Moon said matter-of-factly. "Someone will be High Prince. Or not. Perhaps it will be the Basilisk, perhaps not. There is only one good, one sure thing that comes from restoring the Prince Guardian, my sister, and that is that you will be free of your Oath, and you shall be my sister again. That is all that concerns me in this." Moon leaned over and kissed Cassandra's cheek before rising and going to her bed.

*I will be free,* Cassandra thought. She stared unseeing into the darkness before her. She hardly remembered what it was like to live unbound by her Oath. Had she been free then, she wondered, or merely bound in a different way? No wonder she hadn't wanted to get up, she thought. Even back in Toronto, even when she was doing such a good job at avoiding the Exile that she could live in the same city as Max Ravenhill and never see him, her Oath had given her purpose, had shaped her life. What shape would her life have when that purpose was gone? It had been so long since that shape had been called "sister" or "daughter."

It seemed only moments had passed when Cassandra heard Lightborn wake up and get to his feet, huffing and rubbing the sleep from his face, before he joined her on the outcrop of rock above their campfire. Lightborn had found very little to say to her since his Healing at the Turquoise Ring, but he'd been studying her out of the corners of his eyes when he thought she wasn't looking. He was good at it, very casual, but the light glinting off the small green jewel in his earring whenever his head turned toward her gave him away. Whenever she'd met his glance, however, he'd looked away, or made some other motion to show that he had only been accidentally looking in her direction. But Cassandra hadn't been fooled. The only thing she hadn't figured out was why he should want to look at her without catching her eye, why he seemed alternately puzzled and thoughtful.

She wondered whether it could be simply Lightborn's lack of familiarity with the Healing itself, something he had likely never experienced before, given the rarity of Healers among the Riders. Max, child of penicillin, flu shots, and morphine, had taken it much more in his stride.

Still, she'd figured that Lightborn would come to speak to her as soon as he'd thought of a way to do so that wouldn't sound as though he were thanking her. So when he sat down beside her, much as she had done with Moon, Cassandra made room for him on her rock and waited for him to begin.

"Would you have saved me, if *he* hadn't asked it?" he finally said.

Cassandra looked at him sharply. The man had unexpected complexity. "I don't know," she admitted. "I could say yes," she shrugged, "but that's easy to say now."

"Moon would have left me without hesitation, and she has known me now for some time."

"You aren't needed," Cassandra said. It wasn't much, but it would do for an explanation.

"I think I would have left you, if the situation had been reversed," he said, brushing something he could not possibly have seen in the darkness from the front of his cotte. "Is it a human thing?"

"Not leaving people to die?" Cassandra thought over all she knew of human behavior. All the years of war and pillage, Mongols and motorbikes, the Crusades and the Inquisition, the Holocaust and the Gulag Archipelago. Human history was full of examples of those who had abandoned their nearest and dearest—and of those who hadn't. Human literature, on the other hand, that was full of stories of heroism and self-sacrifice. Maybe it wasn't so much what humans *did,* but what they hoped they *would* do. "Yes, you could say so. I think humans don't like to leave people to die."

"You wouldn't have been leaving me to die, had you left me there in my home. It is not our way to kill prisoners."

Cassandra wished she could be as sure as Lightborn was. "Tell that to the thing that was stuck on the wall," she said finally. "I would not leave anyone to the mercy of someone who would call the Hunt."

Lightborn straightened, with a sharp intake of breath. "I did not think of that, Truthsheart. The Shadowlands must not be such a very pleasant place after all, to be putting such thoughts into your head." He looked back down at his boots, as if he were admiring their polish. Something else he couldn't see in the dark.

"Tomorrow will see the end of all this wondering," she said.

Lightborn nodded. "Tomorrow. And half a Sunturn till the Banishment ends. I pray we have sufficient time."

"He is not Dawntreader," he added, after he had been silent for a while. "He is not my friend. And yet he is." Lightborn looked up into Cassandra's eyes. "He is like a shadow of the Prince that was. I cannot feel *dra'aj* in him, but it is more than that. It is rare to feel the *dra'aj* in anyone these days." He looked away again. "I can feel yours."

She hadn't thought of that. "It is the Healing. Don't be concerned, it will wear off." Her words dried in her mouth. Was that what lay behind Max's feelings for her, too? she wondered, stricken. Could he feel the connection the Healing had made in their *dra'aj*? Would it wear off? She squeezed her eyes shut. Not that it would matter after tomorrow. One more thing she could stop wondering about.

Lightborn was still nodding in response to her words.

"Will his life among the humans have changed him? From what you have told me, I believe it has changed you."

"How do you know I've told you the truth?"

"Your sister says you always do."

"My sister is concerned that the Prince's plans may not match ours, that he may have some plot of his own."

"Ah, but if you would use your influence on him—"

"You forget," Cassandra said, standing up. "I have no influence on the Prince. If I have any influence at all, it is on Max Ravenhill, and we are doing our best to make that influence obsolete. As soon as the Prince is restored, my influence disappears."

As she walked away, Lightborn called after her, his

voice as soft as the moonlight, "Dawntreader would not have risked everything, his life, yours, the whole of the Lands, to save me."

---

" 'Dawn, opens the Window of Day;
Sun, clears the Edge of Sky—' "

"Those lines are repeated three times," Moon said, opening her eyes and looking around at them. "Marking their importance." She frowned at the crest of the hills before them, her lower lip between her teeth. "The timing is important." She glanced back at her sister.

Cassandra nodded, her face solemn. "Yes, I think that's clear." Max was careful not to catch her eye, sure that laughter showed in his own. Moon was as serious and as solemn as a twelve-year-old, and it would never do to laugh at her.

He took a deep breath of air filled with the scents of dawn, the warming limestone and scrub brush, the sharp animal smell of the horses. They stood on the crest of a small ridge, one of many surrounding the crystal-blue water Moon had said was the Tarn of Souls. Even from this small elevation, the Tarn was as surreal as a body of water seen from an airplane, preternaturally still, and the wind that tugged at Max's cloak and blew his hair into his eyes did not disturb the glassy surface of the water. Now that the moment had come, Max was glad that everything looked so calm.

"From here it is best we go on foot. The Songs tell that the water may give madness to animals," Moon said. "They do not, however, limit the numbers that may approach the Tarn of Souls, nor do they tell which of us may speak to the Lady."

"My vote is for Moon to speak." Cassandra's voice was so quiet Max had to strain to hear it.

"As I am the eldest here," Lightborn said, "I believe it should be my task."

Max rolled his eyes to the heavens, whatever calm he'd felt slipping rapidly away. "Look, people, I'm willing to sit back and let you guys argue about it. But I understood there was a time element here." He turned to Lightborn. "Were *you* the one out in front getting us here? Have *you* made a study of the Songs that deal with this?"

"No, however—"

"The 'no' suffices, as the judge said to the rapist. What do you want the rest of us to do, Moon?"

But the young Rider was still shaking her head. "I do not believe the choice is ours," she said. "I believe we must all approach the water."

"Done." With more resolution than he really felt, Max dismounted, tossed the reins of his mount over its head in the way that said "stay here" in any land, and started down the grassy slope toward the water. After a few seconds, Cassandra was at his side. He smiled at her, but while her face lightened a little, he couldn't really say that the look she gave him back was a smile.

"I guess this is good-bye," he said under his breath, as soon as he could hope that the sounds Moon and Lightborn made in their own descent would lend them some privacy. "It's been a great pleasure knowing you."

Cassandra nodded, her jaw set, her gaze turned downward to watch her feet. Instead of speaking, she reached out and touched him on the arm with the tips of her fingers. Max nodded also, certain that she could see him, and made no move to touch her in return. What could he tell her that wouldn't make both of them feel worse?

Not that he could imagine feeling worse.

When they were gathered at the edge of the water, Max watched as Moon knelt, lips moving as she repeated the critical Verses to herself. Finally she looked up, and at her sister's nod, placed her palms three times, lightly, on the surface of the Tarn. There was no wind, Max decided, and no current; no ripples moved out from Moon's hands, and yet her reflection dappled as if dancing to the splashing of an unseen fountain.

At the instant Moon lifted her hands from the water the third time, a woman's head broke the surface far out in the center of the Tarn, as if Moon's movement had drawn it up. The Lady rose as if she had been kneeling and was just getting to her feet, right foot, then left.

Max felt a sudden pressure on his left wrist and looked down to see Lightborn's hand gripping him. His own hands were clenched and he flexed them, consciously willing himself to relax. Cassandra, several paces to his right, had drawn her sword, and pulled her helm down so that the dragon's face looked out from between her brows, and the *gra'if* mail hung long enough to brush her shoulders.

Moon got to her feet, as if unwilling to meet the Natural kneeling. As the Lady approached, it became apparent that she was a small giantess, easily twice as tall as Max. Her eyes were a solid gray with no whites or pupils, like a mountain pool on a cloudy day, and her feet Max could not see, as she seemed to be walking ankle-deep through the water. Somehow, Max found the idea that there was something just under the surface that the ordinary eye could not see more frightening than if the Lady had been walking on the water's surface. The Tarn of Souls was bottomless, Moon had told them.

The Lady stopped three paces from the edge of the water and folded her arms. She shimmered as if she were a reflection herself, and not a solid being. And yet she must be. Max could see droplets of water clinging to her skin, her hair, there was even one on her eyelashes.

Moon straightened even further and, her voice wavering for the first time, began. "I am one who comes—"

"I know." The Natural's voice was cold and clear as a stream in winter. "Thou art Walks Under the Moon. Thy mother was Clear of Light. Manticore is the Beast that guides thee. Your soul is burdened. Still I will not speak with thee, as thou art no kin to me, and I know thee not." She turned her sightless eyes to Max. "*Him* I know well, Guardian Prince. I will speak with him."

Max's blood pounded in his ears, his mouth suddenly dry.

"What do you want of me, Dawntreader?"

The Basilisk Prince had asked him a similar question, Max thought. Would the Lady of Souls make him the same kind of promises?

"I want to be freed of the Chant of Oblivion," Max said.

"*Herra'aj,* the Chant of the Moon," the Lady said, inclining her head slightly. "You will pay my price?"

Max looked at Moon. She hadn't said anything about a price, but even as he thought that, he realized she didn't have to. This was the Lady of Souls, and suddenly Max was certain he knew what she was asking for.

The Natural cocked her head like an inquisitive bird. "Shall I take one of these you bring me?"

Max gripped his own sword hilt, the *gra'if* metal bruising the palm of his hand. This was why no one else knew how to get here. The Basilisk Prince had used whoever was with him to pay the price. Like a pirate captain killing the men who helped him bury the treasure.

"You can have mine," he said. *What the hell,* he thought, *I'm a goner either way.* "If you'll wait until I have helped these people."

Max saw Cassandra step forward out of the corner of his eye. Moon made a moaning noise, but the Lady of Souls answered before anyone else spoke. "I must have my price today."

"You may take mine!"

Max jerked round to Cassandra, his mouth frozen open, and whirled back to face the Lady.

"You may not," he said. "I won't trade anyone else's soul."

Without pupils, it was impossible to tell what she was

looking at, but the Natural spoke to Max as if she simply hadn't heard any other voices.

"I may take the souls of any who find their way here and offer them," she said. "There are always those who do not wish to Fade. Who prefer to become one with me, with the Lake, and through me live from Cycle to Cycle."

Max shuddered. Would it be immortality if you weren't yourself? One thing to give up your identity to save the world, he thought, another to do it for that kind of forever.

"She retracts her offer." He turned back to where Cassandra stood, a white-faced Moon hanging on her arm. "Tell the Lady you retract your offer. I'm still the Exile," he said when she didn't speak immediately. "You're still my Warden, and you can't ... you *can't* ..." He shook his head. It was one thing for him to give up his life, but not Cassandra.

"I retract my offer," she whispered.

"Name another price," Max said.

"I care only for souls." The Lady turned to go.

"Wait!" Shaking with reaction, the only thing Max could think of was Diggory's dismembered body, glued with its own blood to the cold wall of the Basilisk's dungeon room and turned to stone. What had happened to the Troll's soul? "What will you do for souls if the Cycle is not renewed?"

The Lady stopped, as if moving against her will, and turned her head over her shoulder to listen.

"Though, of course," Max used the voice he saved for first-year lectures, "that's not the only thing you should consider."

"What, then?"

"You're not the only one who can give me what I want," Max said. "I could go to the Basilisk Prince and get what you won't give me. His bargain might be a little easier for my friends. Then again, if he gets the Talismans and makes himself the High Prince, what stops him from coming after you? What stops him from dealing with you the same way he's dealing with other Solitaries and Naturals?"

"He would not dare." But the Lady spoke speculatively, as if she was considering it.

"Oh, he'll dare," Max said. "He won't like it that you can give to others what you've given to him. He'll come here and drain your Lake."

"He cannot. Even he has not *dra'aj* enough."

"Really?" said Cassandra, stepping forward, her toes inches from the water. Max should have known she'd see where he was going. "Maybe there's not *dra'aj* enough here, in this world, but what's to stop him going to the Shadowlands and bringing heavy equipment that *dra'aj* can't stop?"

Max didn't know whether that was possible. With any luck, the Lady wouldn't know either.

"I do not know this 'heavy equipment.' "

"And there again, the Shadowlands itself is full of *dra'aj*," Cassandra said. Max was not the only person to look at her in surprise. "A whole world full, enough for the Basilisk to use against you, if we do not stop him."

"And even if you strike some kind of bargain with him, and the Basilisk doesn't come after you, that still doesn't make him the true High Prince," Max continued, "and that means the Cycle won't be renewed, even if he does get the Talismans. That leaves my original question: What will you do for souls then?" Now it was Max's turn to be looked at in surprise. He was a little surprised himself that none of them had thought of this.

"All Cycles end," the Lady said, but she had turned to face him again, and her head was tilted, as if she listened to the whispering of someone Max could not see. Finally, she straightened.

"You like to ask questions," she whispered, almost as if she spoke to herself alone. Her eyes narrowed. "Do you like to answer them as well? Let us play Three Questions.

If you win, I will give you the Chants that will free you. If I win, you will give me your soul."

Max hesitated, searching the faces of his companions for what his response should be.

"You may consult your advisers," the Lady of Souls said, with a hint of sarcasm in her tone. "If you would play the Game, place your right hand on the water's surface." The Lady of Souls turned and walked back to the middle of the Tarn. This time, she appeared to be walking down a staircase, submerging step by step until she had once more disappeared below the flawless expanse of water.

Max turned to Cassandra and grasped her by the upper arms. "Idiot! What if she'd taken you seriously?" He trembled with reaction, and could barely stop himself from shaking her in his anger.

"I spoke seriously," Cassandra said, making no move to free herself. Her smoky eyes flashed at his until his hands finally relaxed and fell from her arms.

"It is the Oath which spoke." Moon put her arm around Cassandra's shoulders. "She is your Warden, she must come to your aid. What?" she added in response to the look that Max felt pass over his face. "Surely you knew this."

"Yeah, I knew it," Max said. But he managed to keep forgetting it. He rubbed his face with his hands as he stepped away from the sisters.

"*He* is *not* the Prince," Cassandra said, turning to Moon, "yet he gives up his very self, all and everything he believes is real, to help us. Why should any of us do less?" She turned back to Max. Now her eyes were the gray of storms. "You agreed to this on my urging. Oath or no Oath, did you think I could do less than I asked of you?"

*That doesn't mean it isn't the Oath,* Max thought, but he nodded acceptance of her words. He wanted to believe her. Time was running out for them, and, god knew, he wanted *something* from Max Ravenhill's life to be real.

"Oaths or no Oaths, one of us must pay the Lady of Souls, or Max must play the Game . . ." Lightborn broke off as Cassandra shook her head.

"He cannot possibly win."

"No one pays." Max didn't say what he knew they were all thinking. They only had half a Sunturn—not quite three days, until the Talismans appeared and the Basilisk used the Chant of Binding.

"Cassandra is right," Lightborn said. "If you play the Game and lose, where will we be?"

"Exactly where you are now." Max looked at him. "I won't be dead, exactly. At least if the Lady of Souls was telling the truth?" He glanced at Cassandra and she nodded, looking away from him as she did so. "So I'll still be alive, and the Talismans will appear on time." Max took a deep breath. "And you people will have three days or so to work out a new solution. No one goes into the Lake for me, are we straight on that?" He turned to Cassandra. She was the closest thing to human in this place, and certainly the only one who would understand. "Don't you see? This is how the Basilisk Prince got the Chants in the first place, he must have paid her price. I can't do that. If I were willing to do something like that, give up someone, even someone willing . . . *use* their soul . . ."

Max fell silent, sure of what he wanted to say but unsure of how to say it without sounding like a fool. Finally, Cassandra nodded.

"Then there would be no difference between you," she said. "The end does not justify the means."

Moon watched them, her face impassive as she clung once more to her sister's arm, as if ready to drag her away from danger.

Lightborn looked at him with narrowed eyes, puzzled and a little afraid. "There must be another way."

"If there is," Cassandra said, "I doubt we have time to think of it."

"What shall we do, my Prince?"

Max took a deep breath. "Tell me about the Game."

———

CRACK!

Windwatcher rolled out of bed and was on his feet, sword in hand, before he saw that it was no enemy who had Moved into his bedroom, but Honor of Souls.

"My lady," he stammered, tossing down his sword and picking up the robe that lay on the chair nearest the bed. He was suddenly aware that he had slept in nothing more than his *gra'if* mail shirt. "How is it . . . ? Your pardon, my lady, but I do not remember that we, that is—surely I could not forget—"

Honor of Souls threw back her head and laughed, though Windwatcher could easily see the tears glistening in her eyes. "Rest easy, my lord, rest easy. You have not forgotten some former intimacy. I am much older than you, and this room was not always your bedchamber. I am not insulted. On the contrary, I thank you. I have need to be amused."

"What has happened?" he pushed a chair forward and led her to it. "Blood on the Snow sent word that the Hunt found Griffinhome empty, but when no one heard from you . . ."

"We fled," Honor said, sitting down in the backless chair Windwatcher used when he put on his boots. "Eight others and myself." She looked at him, her brows drawn low over her eyes, the lines of exhaustion in her face. "The single Hound sent after the Guardian, we had killed that one. Truthsheart showed us how. But this," she shook her head, "this was no single Hound, but the Hunt itself."

"It will follow you." Windwatcher was relieved to hear no fear in his voice, no reproach. He picked up his sword once more. What had Sword of Truth said? Keep striking, no matter what form it took. It was past time for him to fight.

"I think not," she said. "The Natural who lived in my courtyard fountain Moved us, in the way that Water Sprites can. It was," she drew in a deep breath, "interesting. She said that the Hunt cannot follow."

"And Griffinhome?" Windwatcher put down his sword again and sat on the edge of the bed.

The lady shook her head. "It is no more."

Windwatcher gritted his teeth. It pained him to see her this way, but he knew it was no more than he would likely be feeling himself, very soon, if the Basilisk was not dealt with once and for all. The only thing he could offer his friend was action. He hoped it was enough.

"Blood on the Snow has need of us," he told her. "He has asked us to help him make his stand."

Honor of Souls sat up straighter, the vacant look gone from her eyes, though the sorrow remained.

"Then let us go."

# Chapter Thirteen

CASSANDRA FORCED HER EYES to look away from the sight of Max kneeling alone at the edge of the Tarn, his right hand extended to the surface of the water. There was nothing she could do to help him now. Whatever the outcome of the Game of Three Questions, her part in this was over. She squeezed her eyes shut against the sense of loss.

When she opened them, she found Lightborn looking at her, his blue eyes like pale sapphires in the morning light.

"I did not think to see you so detached," he said, a wrinkle forming between his platinum brows.

Cassandra blinked, surprised; detached was the very last thing she felt. But then, nothing was easier than the appearance of calm. You only had to be very, very still. And of course she would seem detached; that was what stillness looked like.

"It's a human thing," she said. "They learn how to stand apart, watch, and wait." Riders rarely stood apart, literally or figuratively, though she hadn't noticed this until she was in the Shadowlands, among humans. As Travelers—what humans used to call Trouping Faerie, Riders were usually with their *fara'ip*. The custom of the troop, the *fara'ip,* had grown so strong that for many among the Riders it had gained the force of instinct.

It was not the practice among Riders to seek solitude, she knew, quite the contrary. Those who did so were the very great, and the mad. Part of the age-old distrust of the Prince Guardian that Windwatcher had spoken of, Cassandra now realized, was the subconscious incomprehension, bordering on fear, brought about by the Prince's solitary—in both senses of the word—upbringing. The fear of the unknown, and for many, the unknowable.

Life among humans *had* changed her, she thought. The stillness that Lightborn found so incomprehensible was born of the ability to be alone, to be inside herself, whole and complete, even while in the middle of a crowded city. She had learned this from humans, who couldn't know each other's *dra'aj* and who were always alone.

She looked back to the edge of the Tarn, where Max stood with the Lady of Souls. Would this be something that he also would bring with him from the Shadowlands, she wondered. Or was it something he'd always had? Had it been, in fact, what had set him apart from other Riders, what the old Guardian had seen when she chose Dawntreader to be her successor? Had the Prince Guardian always been among the great, or the mad, as many suspected?

"Good-bye, Max," she breathed.

Moon watched Truthsheart watch the Exile and gritted her teeth. This would be the last time—surely it *must* be the last time, that her sister would look at the Exile that way. Moon snorted, wrinkling her nose. Look at him there, calling the Lady of Souls to come to him. And what was worse, the Lady would come. Oh, she'd come when Moon called, too, but then she wouldn't talk to Moon. Oh, no, not good enough, not while the Exile was here. No one was good enough while the Exile was here.

Moon shivered, remembering the Lady's eyes on her, and for a moment, she felt again the measuring, the weighing, and the cold shock that followed the Lady's dismissal of her. She covered her mouth with her hand as the flood of uncertainty that had rushed over her chilled her once more. The Lady's glance had seemed to weigh Moon's soul and find it wanting, setting it aside as if the Lady saw no value in it. What had Moon done, the Lady's glance had said, that the Lady should deal with her? And what *had* she done? Moon wondered. If she looked at her life the way she had looked at the Basilisk's, the way she looked at the Exile's—if she examined her own life, what would she see?

She dropped her hand, clenched her fists. No. She would not think that way. She was saving her sister, there was nothing more important than that—even if no one else understood. So the Lady of Souls thought her of no account? So the Lady would choose others over her? Well, it would not be the first time.

But it would be the last, Moon vowed, clenching her fists. Never again would Walks Under the Moon take second place. Never again. Even Truthsheart, even the sister who loved her, taught her, held her, Sang to her—

No. She would not think that way. She had always had first place in her sister's heart until the Exile and his followers came. Moon looked at Lightborn and almost spat. Another one who thought the Moon, Stars, and Sun turned around him. She would show them all just how important a piece she was in this game of Guidebeasts. She would show *all* of them.

Even Truthsheart.

～

Max lifted his hand from the water, and once again the sleek head of the Natural of the Tarn broke the mirrored surface, this time only inches from the shore, as if the Lady had been waiting for him. This time the waters lifted under her, forming a throne in which she sat

composed, her face as expressionless as the water itself.
Her head turned for a moment toward Cassandra and
the others, where they stood halfway up the hill, before
her pupilless eyes returned to rest on Max.

Seated, she seemed both more and less human. The
effect of her immense height was softened, but she
seemed all the larger, more imposing. Water still beaded
on her thick skin, white as a drowning victim, showing
a faint green in the shadows beneath her chin and
breasts. Her fingers were long and delicate; her feet, as
well as the base of her thronelike chair, were under the
surface of the water, which had returned to its glassy
smoothness.

Three sets of questions, Moon had told him, each in
three parts. Nine questions altogether. At the end of
which he'd either walk away someone else, or . . . What
would it feel like if the Lady took him for not answering properly? Would his soul become another drop in
the cool peacefulness of the Tarn? For a moment Max
understood the call of such serenity. Just give it all up,
lie down, and sleep, rest. Nothing more needed from
him, no one after him. Just the cool, calm stillness.

Max shivered in the sudden chill. Answer with the
truth, Cassandra had said to him. The truth is always
safest. But would he know the truth?

Max cleared his throat. "I'm ready."

"What have you decided, Phoenixborn?" The Natural's voice was still and cold as a stream in winter,
her mouth showed pointed teeth. "What do you want
of me?"

Once more, Max felt the lure of the water's stillness,
but he shook away the distraction. He knew what he
wanted. The same thing he'd always wanted. *I want to go
home,* he thought. *I want for none of this ever to have
happened.* The longing for *Max Ravenhill,* his own
apartment, his own life, his books, his crowded office, his
students, even his committee meetings, closed his throat
and stung his eyes. In that moment he knew that if he

gave her this answer, truthfully as Cassandra had advised, the Lady of Souls could somehow make it so.

A movement, a noise, made him aware of the people behind him, and he drew in a harsh breath. He saw that the Lady's question was like the wish a genie offers you. There were always strings attached, consequences you couldn't foresee. Except he knew what the Lady's price would be, for that as for any other gift. He would see it in Cassandra's face every time she looked at him. And he would see it in his own face. Souls.

And that he couldn't live with. Take what you want, and pay for it. That's what the old proverb said. So if you found you couldn't pay the price, would that mean that you didn't really want it?

It took a conscious act of will to loosen the muscles of his throat enough to speak. "I will play the Game," he said.

The Lady closed her eyes and leaned back in her watery chair, her long fingers dancing on the arms.

"Hear the first question," she said, and her voice took on the cadences of recitation.

"What sees the edge of the blade?" she asked, and paused until Max nodded.

"What are the final words spoken?

"What seals all bargains?"

Okay, Max squeezed his eyes shut. One at a time, think about this. What sees the edge of the blade? Knife blade, sword blade, blade of grass? What? "You don't look at the blade," Cassandra had said, "you look at the opponent." But it isn't the blade, Max thought, it's the *edge* of the blade. What sees the *edge?* The guy sharpening the knife. The butcher. The animal being killed. The wound? There were too many answers, and all of them felt right. "Trust your instincts," Cassandra had said. Their lives unnumbered Cycles long, no Natural would trouble to deliberately trick you as Solitaries would; no Natural cared enough, not even this one. But they would let you trick yourself. Of the answers he'd thought of, the one that *felt* the most likely was the last, the wound. Except the wound couldn't see, in the usual sense, so what if he looked at the question metaphorically? What had edges? The landscape around here, for one thing. It had nothing *but* edges. It was easy to tell where one thing ended and the next thing began. He pushed his hair back out of his face. He wished he had one of Cassandra's hair clips. His hair seemed to be growing more quickly than usual, it was brushing his shoulders already. He dragged his thoughts back to the questions. It wasn't always so easy to tell where the edges of things were. To tell the difference between things not apparently different. The two sides of the coin of discerning, one of his old professors used to say, are wit and judgment. Wit sees the similarities in things not apparently similar, while judgment—

"Judgment," he said. "The first answer is judgment."

"Yes," the Lady of Souls said. "What are your explanations?"

Sweat broke out all over his body and Max shivered in the sudden chill. Explanations? Plural? "Judgment" answered all three questions? So it really *was* the Game of Three Questions, even though nine questions were asked. Why hadn't Moon or one of the others told him this? What if he couldn't explain how "judgment" was the answer to each question? What else didn't he know? He drew in a deep steadying breath and flexed his hands. For a second his mind went blank. What were the other questions? Now that he had the answer, would he be able to think of the explanations?

*Start talking,* he thought, *moving the mouth oils the brain.*

"Judgment sees the edge of the blade, because it sees the fine distinctions between things that seem not to have any differences, so it can see the exact point where one thing ends and another begins." The Lady said nothing and Max swallowed. "Judgment is the words spoken if something is being contested, like in a court."

The last one was bargains, what about bargains? Bargaining is like a contest. "A bargain is concluded when both parties feel they've gotten the best they can out of it, when it is their judgment that further bargaining won't change anything."

The Lady sat, eyes closed, for long enough that Max felt the sweat trickle down his back. What would happen if she didn't agree with his explanations? How much warning would he have? At least he was ready for the other questions now. She was looking for abstractions, so all he had to do was find the right one for each set of questions.

"Hear the second question."

Max's lungs stopped hurting as he released the breath he was holding.

"Who is the last man standing and the first to be seated?

"Who is the first man to eat and the last man fed?

"Who is not lost until found?"

*Honor, courage*—Max cursed under his breath and stopped mentally ticking off abstractions; there was no point in hoping to hit on the right one. He should have known it wouldn't be this easy. These questions sounded more like regular riddles, the kind he'd never been any good at. He ran over the questions again in his mind, but got nothing—they were just words.

He took another deep breath and let it out slowly, trying to steady his spinning thoughts. Too many possibilities, that was always his problem with this kind of question. Without some hint, some nudge from instinct, how would he know which of the many possible pathways would lead him to the answer? All he needed was to answer one question, then he could compare his answer to the other questions and see if it fit.

Okay, who sits down first? Ladies, not men. The president? But why would he be the last man standing? Okay, so who was the last man standing? Bruce Willis in a mediocre movie—stop that and *think!* Last man to eat and the first one fed. That sounded familiar. Except the way he remembered it, it was the first man in battle and the last in retreat. *Who* was? Would it help if he could remember the battles he'd fought in when he was the Prince?

No, not the Prince. The King.

Would it fit? The King sits on his throne while everyone else stands, so he's the first to sit down. But he's the last to be standing on the battlefield, because when he goes down the battle's over. The first to eat when there's plenty, the last to be fed when there isn't? Well, yes, if he was a really good king. But what about the last bit? Not lost until he's found? Like the battle again? That wouldn't be it, Max felt certain that he couldn't use the same explanation for two different sections.

This just wasn't his kind of game. He frowned. That was it, something . . . Max unclenched his fists and forced his shoulders to relax. He couldn't go mentally haring off after the thought that just wouldn't jell. In fox hunting, the fox didn't lose until he was found, that would be true for anything that involved prey. But when was the King prey?

Oh.

"In my world, in the Shadowlands," Max corrected, "the answer would be the land's ruler. We call that a king, I think here you call it the High Prince." He gave his explanations before she could ask, before she could tell him he was wrong.

Again he watched as the Lady closed her eyes, otherwise immobile on her water throne. When her eyes opened again, Max found that he was smiling, and he tried to stop. But he couldn't help it. He'd answered two thirds of the questions successfully. There was only one set of questions left.

"Hear the third question," the Lady said, still with her eyes closed. "Will you wear the smile or the veil?

"Will you hear the eyes or the tongue?

"Will you choose the Head or the Heart?"

Max felt suddenly cold and fragile as glass. All the confidence, all the hope emptied out of him. She had tricked them after all, the Lady of Souls. She had always meant the game to end this way, with an unanswerable question. He knew this kind of death-riddle; this was one of those "feathers or lead" questions. The kind the gods asked when there was no right answer, no answer that reason or logic could give you. The right answer was the one the god had decided it would be, and your only hope was that the god would play straight.

Who would ask such a question if they meant to play straight?

Well, *he* was going to play straight, goddamn it. At least he'd have that much, he thought, as the heat of his anger warmed him. Answer with the truth, just as Cassandra had said. He wished more than anything else that he could turn around and look at her right now. One last time. That's what he would choose, if he had the chance. That's what he'd been choosing all along, he realized. What he'd chosen when he walked across that crowded cocktail party to speak to her. What he'd always wanted. Cassandra. Truthsheart.

And just that easily, he knew what he would answer. All the choices the Lady of Souls had given him asked him to choose between reality and artifice. And he knew which he would choose, every time. And his choice would be a kind of pun, too, and so he might as well go out with his sense of humor intact. Max took a deep breath. He wished he wasn't letting them down. He wished he could have become the Prince for them.

"Truth," he said. "The answer to your question is Truth."

The Lady put out her hand. Max felt a tingling in his hands and feet. Involuntarily, he took a step forward into the water and extended his own hand. As if from great distance he heard what might have been Cassandra's voice. Heat spread from his skin inward, as if eating into his body. This was not the healing warmth of Cassandra's breath, but a destructive flame, burning through his body, searing the air from his lungs. Max felt cold wetness and realized that he had fallen forward into the Tarn. His last thought was to wonder if he had at least disturbed the mirrorlike perfection of the water's surface.

# Chapter Fourteen

"FIND WALKS UNDER THE MOON. I need to know what this means." The Basilisk Prince spoke through stiff lips. "And bring the Hound who waits."

Only a very few moments passed before the guard escorted a Hound into the Basilisk's presence and bowed his way out into the passage again. The Basilisk concentrated on the beast before him. He was no longer made uneasy by the way the creature flickered constantly from shape to shape, sometimes this, sometimes that, but always taking on the form of a Rider to speak. One day, the Basilisk thought, he would like to know why that was. One day, he would be at leisure to pursue that kind of interest again.

In front of the Hound he could relax, let his hands tremble if they would, let himself sink with shaking knees to the chaise where the Exile had lain. The strain of hiding his uneasiness from his servants was wearing on him. He had expected to be informed before this as to Dawntreader's whereabouts. If one of his spies did not come quickly with the information he needed, he would have to loose the Hunt again.

Except now they said there was no scent.

The Hound flickered into the shape of a Rider casually leaning against the Basilisk's map table. "We have not the scent," it said in a voice like ground glass. "Among the ashes of the fortress of the one you call Honor of Souls there was his smell. The smell of one of the Shadowfolk. That smell we could find, did it exist in this Land, but it does not."

"Is he dead?" The Basilisk's hands formed into fists. If the Banishment did not end . . . He must have the Talismans, he *must*. The Chant of Binding pushed at him to be used. He had thought there was time in abundance, but now that there was nothing to distract him, no building, no planting, the Chant of Binding burned like a bonfire in his head. He had to have the Talismans and soon.

The thing lifted its shoulders and spread its hands in a grotesque parody of uncertainty.

"Give us a scent," it said.

The Basilisk resisted the urge to smash the Hound across the mouth. It would only amuse the creature. He could not have Dawntreader dead. He it was who had been Banished, and the Banishment would not end without him. But if he was not . . . if they had reached the Tarn of Souls, if the Lady had helped them, and the Guardian was returned . . .

Then the Talismans were found. They would soon be his.

"My lord?"

It wasn't the voice of the Hound. The Basilisk Prince looked up to find his guard had returned.

"Those who were felling the wood of *He'erid* have not returned."

"And?"

"N–nothing, my lord."

The Basilisk nodded. "Come here to me," he said to his servant, whose eyes had focused on the flickering of the Hound.

With her soldier's training, Cassandra had been aware of all the ambient noises of the Tarn, the twitters of unseen birds, the rustle of clothing as she breathed, the sound the wind made as it whispered through the heather, the soft whickers of the Cloud Horses as they spoke to one another up on the ridge, the click of their hooves on rock as they fidgeted, and the chink and ring of their jeweled harness. When Max took a step forward into the water and touched the Lady's hand with his own, all sound stopped—snapped off like the sudden silence when someone touches the CD player's OFF button in the middle of a piece of music. And if that piece of music was loud enough, the listener would be left for just a second with this numb feeling that she had lost the ability to hear. Except that now, the feeling didn't go away. Lightborn touched her arm; his lips moved, but Cassandra heard nothing.

*It's shock,* she thought. *It must be.*

She saw the Lady of Souls reach up to touch Max's face and stepped forward herself, sword lifted. And again, when she called Max's name she heard nothing, not even the sound being conducted to her ears through her own bones. It was as if she had never had ears. Max had fallen to his knees before the Lady's watery throne. The Natural of the Lake was leaning forward now, her long-fingered hand on Max's face, her own sightless eyes fixed on his, as if they looked into each other's souls.

Cassandra threw herself toward the water, but straining as hard as she could, her muscles bunching, teeth gritting with concentration, it was as if the air around her had suddenly turned solid.

Abruptly, the Lady rose to her feet, and in one sweep of motion, deliquesced, disappearing completely as if she had never had solid substance, and Max fell face forward into the water.

Cassandra heard the splash.

She ran forward and with shaking hands pulled Max

back from the edge of the Lake, until he was completely out of the water. His eyes were closed, and he did not seem to be breathing, but as soon as her hands touched his skin, her own heart, frozen in her chest, began beating once again.

"He's alive," she called over her shoulder.

While a young boy fans the flies away, he sits cross-legged in a loincloth on the shady side of the market-place and tells how the dragon swallowed the sun on the day of creation, and people toss coins and handfuls of dried fruit into his bowl.

He sits on his heels on the sunbaked sand, listening to a Solitary, gray-skinned and gravel-voiced, explain where the water was hidden and how he might bring it forth.

He stands beside his king on a beach and draws a horse in the sand with the point of his sword.

He stands beside his king on a French hillside and argues with him about where the longbow men should be placed.

A very tall Rider with crow-black hair, bone-white face, and eyes the cold gray of iron touches his face. "I am Blood on the Snow," the Rider says, "and you are my son."

He sits behind the scenes at the theater and watches his friend Will's play, thinking that his beloved would do a better job of the swordplay, and that he must suggest it to Will.

A Sunward Rider, hair and skin bleached colorless with age, puts *Sto'in,* the Cauldron of Plenty, into his hands and tells him to look within it.

He looks up from the scroll he's painting and sees his beloved, naked under her dragon-patterned silk kimono, bringing him tea. He wishes they didn't have to go to Kyoto tomorrow.

He climbs over the stone sill to where a woman, her golden hair turned amber by the torchlight, waits with a drawn sword in her hand, next to packed saddlebags, riding cloaks tossed on top. He's been to check their horses. "You were right," she says to him, "they didn't listen to me." "They never do," he says, taking his cloak from the top of the packs. "We'd best be off."

He feels the flutter of the Phoenix in his chest, its fires burning.

He swims frantically against the current, but it's too strong for him. Any minute now he'll run out of air, any minute now his screaming lungs will force him to open his mouth and inhale. He feels a warm hand on his face, his body, and he relaxes, allowing his lungs to breathe.

Cassandra ran her hands over Max's body, checking for injuries. He was alive, but until—and unless—he recovered consciousness, they wouldn't know whether he'd failed the test, whether the Lady had indeed taken his soul and left them only an animate shell. Just as she was beginning her examination for the third time, Max gasped for breath, drawing in air and coughing as if he had indeed been drowning.

He caught her searching hand in one of his.

"You're always checking for broken bones," he coughed nonexistent water out of his lungs, "and you never find any."

Cassandra's mouth was open, the words she'd used to answer him a hundred times already on her lips, when the realization of what he'd said struck her still and silent. She sat back on her heels, her hand still trapped in his. He knew what she always did. This wasn't the first time during his long Banishment that Cassandra had checked him for injuries, and it wasn't the first time she hadn't found any. And he *knew* this. Nor was it the first time that he'd brushed away her examining hands and he knew that, too. Max Ravenhill couldn't have known it. The Prince couldn't have known it. *Who was this?*

Again she tried to pull away, but he held her.

"It's me," he said, sitting up and drawing the hand he still held to his lips, pressing his mouth to her palm in the way that always made the skin on her belly contract. "I'm here. I'm *still* here. *I'm* still here. I remember you. I remember . . . everything." His lips smiled and his eyes danced.

Cassandra tried to draw air over the lump in her throat, to blink away the tears in her eyes. She found herself on her knees, held so tightly to his chest that even through her *gra'if* and his she could feel the thumping of his heart next to hers, the uneven shudder of his breath, the skin of his face on her lips, the taste of his tears mingled with her own.

Some inexpressible time later Max—she couldn't think of him as the Prince, she'd never known the Prince— helped her to her feet, brushed the hair back from her face, tucked her hand through his arm, and turned with her to face the others.

Moon stood with her fingers on her mouth, her eyes wide open above them. She looked from Max's face to Cassandra's and back again. Cassandra smiled at her, and Moon slowly lowered her hands.

Lightborn had his hands outstretched, and stood with one foot in front of the other, as if he'd been coming to their aid. His face was a strange mixture of hope and fear, a smile trembled on his lips.

"Well, Lightborn. I asked you once if you were my brother, *Cousin.* I can answer that question myself now." Max let Cassandra's hand fall but didn't move away from her.

Lightborn took another step forward, his hands still reaching out toward them. "Dawntreader—"

"Still my cousin but no longer my brother, isn't that right? Not my *fara'ip* and not for some time. You know, I'm not surprised you'd work against me, Lightborn. But to bring the Basilisk's men to your own mother's house, that's an act of betrayal few have the spine for."

Cassandra looked between the two men, shocked.

Max stepped away from Cassandra, one pace closer to Lightborn. "Why look at me like that?" he said to his cousin. "Did you think I wouldn't remember? Or did you think I didn't know?"

Cassandra drew her sword.

"Small wonder you did not offer to give the Lady your soul to restore my memory," the man who had been Max Ravenhill continued. "You knew that you had but to wait and your master would do it for you. How far behind us are they?"

As Max drew his sword, Lightborn took a quick step back, and CRACK! He was gone.

"You're lucky he didn't draw; that's a sword you're holding, not a dog's leash," Cassandra said, relieved to find her voice steady.

To her surprise, the Prince whirled around, laughing, and scooped her into his arms, somehow managing to avoid both her sword and his own.

"It's better to be lucky than good."

"So you've always said." Cassandra felt her lips trembling and tried her best to smile.

With one last kiss, he set her down and looked at the Lake, his eyes narrowed and his brows drawn down until a line formed between them. He inclined his head in a short bow before turning back to Cassandra and her sister.

"Let's be off before he brings the Basilisk down on us."

"Will he?" Even as she spoke, Cassandra started back up the hill to where the horses still stood. "Surely he could have brought them at any time in the last three days?"

"He had no need to. With Lightborn here, the Basilisk was already with us. But now, without a spy in our camp, they have no choice but to come after us."

Cassandra shook her head, biting her lower lip as she followed Max up the hillside to the horses. She hadn't liked Lightborn much to start with—after so many years among the Shadowfolk she'd forgotten the casual arrogance of the Rider Lords—and yet she'd found herself changing her mind. It was hard not to like such an engaging man. True, his counsel had always been one of waiting and delay—had his insistence on going to his mother's aid in Griffinhome been genuine or a tactic to delay Max's escape? But there were many people whose natural caution made problems worse, not better. Still, he *had* tried to talk them out of coming to the Tarn, even if he hadn't tried very hard, and he had tried to delay them once they were here. It *could* have been in the hope that the Basilisk's Riders would catch up to them.

She paused as she put her booted foot into the stirrup. But Lightborn had let Max play the Game, and what did *that* mean? She reined in her horse—Lightborn's horse, she reminded herself, as they all were—with more force than she intended. It wasn't easy to see the truth of all of this.

When they were all once again on horseback, Max turned to Moon.

"We have followed your lead this long while, sister of my love. Now I ask you to follow mine."

# Chapter Fifteen

THE GUARDIAN'S KEEP WAS the closest thing to a home he'd ever had. Not Hearth of the Wind's desert rocks, not his father's temporary camps with his band of Wild Riders, not Honor of Souls' fortress, Griffinhome. Though he'd lived in all these places, this was the only place in all the Lands, or the Shadowlands now that he thought about it, that belonged only to him. A thick tower of rough-worked stone, its large circular rooms were stacked atop one another, each one comfortably but sparsely furnished. The furniture was placed, and the lighting arranged, in such a way that it had taken him some time to realize, when the old Guardian first brought him here, that the Keep had no windows or doors. It could not be found by accident or by Riding. It was the safest place he knew.

The layout of the tower was so simple that it had taken him only minutes to show Cassandra and Moon everything they needed to know to make themselves comfortable. The instant he could, he'd thrown himself into his favorite darkwood chair, still drawn up to the fireplace, exactly as he remembered leaving it, angled so that he could rest his heels on the raised hearth.

He pushed his hair back from his face and rubbed his

eyes with the heels of his hands. The Sun was almost turned, but he needed time to think, to sort out the jumble of thoughts and feelings that tumbled through him. He was Dawntreader, no doubt, but he was also Max Ravenhill, as well as all the other humans he had been over that long life. Would he really have killed Lightborn? Or was that just the shock of seeing him so close at hand? His sword had been in his hand. He remembered learning of his cousin's betrayal, and in one sense that discovery and the feelings that went with it were only a few weeks old. But between him and that hurt, that shock, was the distance of all his human lives, all their pettiness and all their glory.

Was this distance, this perspective, going to help him now that he was the Prince again? Or would it hinder?

He could see now exactly what Cassandra had meant when she'd told Max Ravenhill that they hadn't been able to change his fundamental character. But he could also see differences, differences that she couldn't know about, that, if anything, undermined his confidence now when he most needed it. He'd known exactly what he was doing when he'd surrendered himself to the Basilisk Prince to stop the War. Buying time. His decision had been based on all there was to know, after weighing every strength and every weakness. As Guardian it was his *job*, for god's sake, to weigh every action against the good of the Lands, the People, and the Talismans. Trust his instincts, sure, but—

He shook his head, chewing on his lower lip. Max Ravenhill had known nothing, weighed nothing. He'd made his decision based on a woman. Not even a known and loved woman, because Max Ravenhill hadn't known Truthsheart, not really. He'd acted solely on trust. He'd made his decision to go to the Tarn even before he'd experienced the Basilisk Prince firsthand. Where had *that* decision come from? Max Ravenhill had won the Game of Three Questions. How? As Max, he'd chosen the right path, but how? Instinct? Luck? His Guardian's training taught him to be wary of the former, and his human experiences that there was no such thing as the latter.

If he could no longer trust in his own judgment, what could he trust?

He tried to relax, but he was distracted by an old sensation made new. He could feel the Lands now, the directions that weren't directions, the space that wasn't space. It was this awareness that made it possible for Riders to Move, but he had never been conscious of it before the Banishment, before the amnesia. He hoped to god it would fade again. It was no more natural for a Rider to be aware of this sensation than it would be for humans to feel the blood moving through their veins. Riders didn't Move consciously; their focus gave them destination, not Movement. "We don't *do* magic," Cassandra had told him once, back in the Shadowlands when they were both pretending to be human. "We *are* magic." She was more right than she had known, he thought. Only a human perspective could have given Cassandra that insight.

He steadied his breathing until his inhales and exhales were the beat of the Phoenix's wings—his wings— as he floated through the currents of *dra'aj* that were the Lands. His heart opened in the old way, and immediately he felt them, his true *fara'ip*. He would always feel them, close or far, hidden or exposed. This was what had brought the old Guardian to him when her time was ending, and this what he would look for in the next Guardian when his time came. The *dra'aj* worked differently in all Riders, in all of the People for that matter, Naturals and Solitaries, too. Some it made Builders, or Singers, or Trees. Some it made Lakes, or Warriors, and some it made Healers. Some it made Guardians. And, only once in each Cycle, the *dra'aj* made a High Prince.

The Talismans stirred as they felt him, but not enough. Only his Phoenix flames kept him from feeling the chill of fear. He had only agreed to the Banishment to buy time, to allow the Prince to appear, to allow the Talismans time to be ready. But now . . .

The end of the Banishment *was* near, he knew it, he could feel it, and the Talismans should be dreaming, close to awakening, and he could indeed feel the echoes of those dreams; *Ma'at,* Stone of Virtue, dreaming its slow visions of earth, always and never sleeping. Solid and still, always waiting for the Time of Princes. *Porre'in,* Spear of War, dreaming of flight, waiting for the Call. *Ti'ana,* Sword of Justice, dreaming of battles, waiting for the Trial. *Sto'in,* Cauldron of Plenty, tasting the wind and the earth, waiting for the Feast. And with himself, the fifth Talisman, they should be dreaming of the Prince, all in their own ways ready for the Cycle to turn.

But they were not. None of them were dreaming of the Prince. They were no more prepared to greet the High Prince than they had been, though the Sun, Moon, and Stars had turned so many times since the Banishment began. But the Cycle *was* ending. Of that, there was no doubt. He had seen the signs of it himself, though as Max Ravenhill he hadn't fully understood what he had seen. Beyond manifestations like the carnivorous grass, there had been signs in every place they had Ridden. Leaves turning where usually there was the green of high summer; skies overcast or raining where in the past had been only spring sunshine. Even at the lodge, he realized, the winter's night had been colder, the snow and wind more biting that it should have been. That the Talismans remained dormant could only mean that there was still no High Prince, that the Cycle might end without turning.

"Be ready, my brothers," he pleaded with them, determined to be wrong, "I come."

As he withdrew, he floated once more through the net of *dra'aj* that was the Lands, his heart and his hope sinking as he went. There was no doubt that the net was weakened and broken, in some places crumbled and gone. Fading more and more as the Cycle turned. With the end so near, where was the Prince?

⟿

If she were human, Cassandra thought, she'd have a headache right now. Human or not, what she most wanted to do was take the Prince Guardian and shake him until he coughed up some answers. He'd whisked them away from the Tarn of Souls and told them he needed time to think, no explanations, no discussion. Time they didn't have, she'd wanted to point out.

And what about Lightborn? Cassandra bit down on her lower lip. She was certain, as certain as she was standing here, that the Rider hadn't said one thing that wasn't true. And he'd sworn fealty, hadn't he, along with Windwatcher and Honor of Souls. Cassandra shook her head. Right now, when nothing was as she'd expected it, she couldn't be sure of anything.

The Guardian said he remembered everything, and maybe he did, but he didn't act like it. Did he really remember her? And if he did? What did she want that to mean? Dammit, there was no time for this!

"What does he do?" Moon said, her head tilted to one side as she studied the Guardian in his chair.

Cassandra drew her sister to the door of the tower room with a jerk of her head. "He's thinking," she said as they gained the staircase. She knew from experience that no sound they made could disturb him while he was meditating, but she was too restless herself to sit and watch sedately while the great Prince Guardian organized his thoughts. There were things that needed doing no matter what he might decide. Supplies to be checked, horses to be soothed, defenses to be investigated and learned, things that she couldn't do if she were sitting in the tower room, waiting for him to decide to speak to them.

The staircase wrapped around the outside wall of the tower, warm despite the fact that it was walled in stone on both sides. A quick examination showed Cassandra that the Guardian's Keep had all the comforts—stabling for horses, a stocked pantry, linen on the beds that smelled as fresh as if it had just been removed from a scented chest, and even kindling ready cut. Below the room where the Prince sat was a combination kitchen and storage room. It was evident that the kitchen was actually used for cooking rather than just as a place to store the traditional food servers that were never empty. The fireplace was large enough to roast a small pig whole and there were signs that such a thing had been done in the past. There were cupboards built into the walls beside the fireplace, and in them Cassandra and Moon found a full supply of travel bags, spare clothing, even weapons that were still serviceable, bows with their strings still sound. Other open shelves held baskets of various sizes and stone bottles filled with wine. So they didn't need to cook if they didn't want to.

"Ugh," Moon said, peering into a shallow basket. She pulled out a loaf of bread as long and as thick around as her forearm. "Look," she said, holding out the bread to Cassandra. "What kind of food is this?"

Cassandra's nose told her what was wrong even before she saw the small dots of blue and white on the crust.

"The *dra'aj* fails," Cassandra said, lifting her eyes to meet her sister's gaze. "Even here, the *dra'aj* fails. The bread is spoiling," she told Moon. "Put it down and wash your hands."

"Food does not . . . 'spoil,'" Moon said, dropping the bread back into its basket and scrubbing her hand on her thigh.

Cassandra remembered her own shock at what happened to uneaten food in the Shadowlands, and how long it took her to get used to containers that didn't refill themselves.

"But why? I have not seen this spoiling of food before," Moon said. "Why should this be happening *here?*"

Cassandra shook her head. "Perhaps because no one

has been here since before the Great War. If all the *dra'aj* is Fading, as I've been told, perhaps it Fades faster where there are no People. Are all the containers like this?" Great, she thought. All safe and sound and hungry as rats. She lifted the lid off a small crock and was pleased to find a round of cheese carefully wrapped in large leaves resting inside. After a few minutes of searching, she and Moon had collected a bottle of wine to go with the cheese, a basket of warm yeast rolls, two peaches, and several pears which, while blemished, were still edible.

At least Cassandra could eat them. Moon wrinkled her nose and chose one of the peaches instead.

"What do you know of the Guardianship?" Cassandra asked, as she sat down at the oval table in the middle of the room.

"Only what the Songs tell," Moon said, pouring out two glasses of wine.

"And that isn't much?" Cassandra tore a yeast roll into four pieces, spread cheese on one, and popped it into her mouth. She chewed slowly, following her own thoughts. Interrogating Moon wouldn't give her the answers she needed anyway. She needed to know the kinds of things the Songs couldn't tell her. His bringing them here was not what was bothering her. They had needed to leave the Tarn, and quickly, once Lightborn's treachery was exposed. And, undoubtedly, the Prince needed time to think. But she didn't like the way the Prince had Moved them here without explanation and without discussion. In the past, in the Shadowlands, he'd always been ready to share his plans and stratagems, always ready to consider the experience and ideas of others, especially her own. Clearly, he no longer saw himself as her comrade-in-arms, but as the Prince Guardian, as an elder lord.

Nothing else could have shown her as clearly as this that she had no relationship with this man, whatever he might think. Even if he did know her, even if he did remember everything, all that his human selves had known and felt, this person, this amalgam of memories, wasn't someone she knew.

"Is he . . . is he well?" Moon said, breaking into Cassandra's thoughts.

"Is he mad, do you mean?" Cassandra shook out her napkin and mopped up a few drops of wine from the table with more care than was needed as she considered the question. She laid the napkin back in her lap. "He feels True to me." And that in itself was true, she thought.

"Would you be able to tell?"

Maybe that was the problem, she thought. Even if he did remember her, and love her, he wasn't human anymore, he was a Rider now. And not just any Rider, but the Prince Guardian. She could hold her own with any human—*and any elder lord,* she thought—but she couldn't expect to have the same easy partnership with the Prince that she'd had with his human selves. Even Max Ravenhill. That companionship was gone, and the Prince couldn't bring it back, even if he wanted to.

And what would she do about that?

"I'll go and check the horses," Cassandra said.

When they came back to the sitting room, the Prince was kneeling in front of the cold hearth, arranging lengths of ash wood over kindling.

"My lord Prince—" Cassandra began.

He turned and smiled, his eyes warm. "Call me Max," he said. "I'm serious," he added when she hesitated, eyebrows raised. "I'm not sure I can explain it, but it feels right to me."

Cassandra nodded, her eyes narrowed. "You've had good instincts in your human lives," she said. "Let's hope that's true now." She leaned against the arm of the other chair, stretched out her legs, and crossed her ankles. "What do your instincts tell you about Lightborn? Will he bring the Basilisk here?"

Max shook his head. "He's never been here. No one

has. I wouldn't have brought even you if there had been anywhere else we could be safe." He stood, dusting off his hands, as flames began to lick at the wood on the hearth. "Besides, the Basilisk Prince isn't important. What matters right now is the Talismans."

Moon sat down in the chair Cassandra leaned against. "The Basilisk Prince is not important?" she said, her eyes on Max's back as he watched the flames.

"Time's running short, and the Basilisk Prince isn't our primary problem," Max said, as he turned to face them. "I must go to the Talismans."

Cassandra's head snapped up when it became clear that Max wasn't going to say why.

"So you know where they are?" Moon leaned forward.

Max nodded. "They're in the Vale of *Trere'if*."

"Oh, fuck," Cassandra said, her annoyance blown away. She glanced at Moon and saw her own fears confirmed by the look on her sister's face.

"What is it?"

"Honor of Souls told us the first day," Cassandra said. "Don't you remember? The Basilisk has built his Citadel in the Vale of *Trere'if*."

"Oh, fuck," the Prince Guardian said.

---

Lightborn picked up the little malachite Cauldron and held it a moment, considering his move, before he set it down on the square next to one of the Basilisk Prince's Guidebeasts.

"Did you tell him?" he asked.

"Why would I tell him?" The Basilisk toyed with his glass of wine, swirling the liquid slowly and inhaling the bouquet. In the corner of the room a large white dog with liver-colored ears stopped scratching and watched them, head canted to one side as if it could understand their speech. Lightborn had the uneasy feeling that the dog changed shape when he was not looking.

"I would have wasted my great weapon, had I told him anything of you," the Basilisk said, after reaching for his own Cauldron and withdrawing his hand without making a move. Lightborn was relieved to see the Basilisk's hands were steady, and that his skin was bronze with health.

Lightborn waited while his opponent chose his piece and moved it. He saw that there was a way for him to win the game, and he wondered whether he should use it.

"He guessed," the Basilisk Prince said, when he had moved his Spear and released it. "His instincts were always very sound."

"And still you sent me to him?" Lightborn kept his voice light, watching the board, as if his only interest were the game.

"Is not the Griffin Lord mine to send?" The Basilisk's voice was sweet and sharp. "And as it happens, he did not remember."

Lightborn glanced up, and saw that the Basilisk still studied the board, smiling. "You knew," he said. "You knew all along that his memory was gone. You sent me to speak to him without telling me. Was this a test?"

"Did you need to be tested?" The Basilisk narrowed his eyes and Lightborn felt his throat tighten. "Do you wish to be tested again?"

A servant entered, a Moonward Rider Lightborn had never seen before, and he breathed again, but not easily. It seemed that more and more of the Riders he saw around the Basilisk's court were new to him.

"Your pardon, my lord Prince," the young Rider said. "But Walks Under the Moon wishes to speak with you."

Once in the room, Moon waited with unconcealed impatience for the Basilisk Prince to dismiss the servant. She was white as alabaster, her hands and lips trembled, and Lightborn felt his own tremor of fear. She would do well to control herself, he thought; in such a state, she could be a danger to herself . . . or to others.

"They are here," she said, as the door swung shut behind the departing servant. "The Talismans are in the Vale."

The Basilisk closed his eyes and smiled. In that smile lay all the sweetness and humor that Lightborn remembered from their youth, when they had been only three young Riders, before Dawntreader had become the Prince Guardian, before Dreamer of Time became the Basilisk Prince. Almost, Lightborn could forgive the Basilisk when he saw that smile.

"I can take you to him now. Give me a squad of men and we can kill him."

"Do not be so hasty," said the Basilisk.

"But what stops you? You no longer need him. The Talismans are here, and at the Sun's turn they will manifest." Her voice was thick, and Lightborn realized that she was very close to crying.

"So long as he is still alive," Lightborn said.

They both turned, and looked at him.

"He must be alive for the Banishment to end."

"But they are here, they can be found without him." Moon reached her trembling hands toward the Basilisk. "Let me show your men, and we can take him as he sleeps."

The Basilisk stood, nodding slowly, turning toward the window of the room.

"He will not wait for them to manifest," Lightborn said.

The Basilisk left off staring into space and looked at him. "You have an idea?"

Lightborn shrugged. He knew better than to make too much of this. "Dawntreader knows where they are. Why should he wait for the Sun to finish turning?"

"That he might remove them is all the more reason for you to take him now, to hold him against the time it will be safe to kill him." Moon looked between the two Riders.

Lightborn shook his head, focusing on the Guidebeast

board, as if he didn't particularly care, as if he were merely considering which piece to move. "In the Vale they may be, but if they were easily found, you would have them already. There is no part of the Vale where you or your people have not been. Let him find them for you," he said. "If Moon returns to him, you can put your hand on him at any moment. Once he has them, you can easily take them from him. Before the Sun turns, they would already be yours."

"I tell you—"

The Basilisk raised his hand and Moon subsided. When Lightborn leaned back in his chair, picking up his own glass of wine, the Basilisk came to stand close over him, staring into his face. When he saw the calculation begin in the Basilisk's look, Lightborn spoke again.

"And there is still the matter of the Stone," he said. "The Stone will not manifest because it was not hidden, except that it is always hidden. The Stone would proclaim you, given the chance to do so." He leaned forward, and reached as if to take the Basilisk's hands in his own without actually touching him. "Let us give the Stone that chance."

Lightborn repressed a shudder as the Basilisk stroked his hair back from his forehead. "You were always the sentimental one," the Basilisk said, his voice a soft murmur. "I shall give you your chance."

"But, my lord, he still holds my sister, he speaks to her in a voice like the sun and she turns to him. She will not be free until he is dead, and you promised me this, you promised me." Her hands had formed fists, but Lightborn could still see them trembling.

"Be patient, you must not blame your sister," the Basilisk said, drawing Moon to his own vacant seat, and pouring wine for her into his own glass. "It may be that she has spent too much time in the company of the Exile, exposed to his own peculiar glamour. I well remember how convincing and persuasive he can be. He draws you in to him before you even know of it, until you are ready to stand with him forever."

*He could be speaking of himself,* Lightborn thought. The Basilisk, too, had his own peculiar glamour.

"This he has done to my sister."

"I will not lie to you," the Basilisk said. "It may be more than her Oath that holds her. It may be that she cannot listen now to another's voice. It may be that only death will free her."

Moon's face went very still, then hardened, the child-like softness that had always been there gone. Lightborn knew that look. It was the look of someone who steeled themselves for the hateful but necessary task. He had seen that look on Cassandra's face when she had killed the horse in the carnivorous grass. He knew what it felt like, that look.

The Basilisk raised his hand. "Go back before they miss you. When the Exile has the Talismans, then we will come for him," the Basilisk said, his eyes on the dog. "Then will everything be as you wish."

"We'll have to go after them."

Cassandra looked up over her cup of wine and saw that he had turned from the fire and was watching her.

"You're giving me that look again," he said.

Cassandra smiled despite herself. "You only say that to show me that you remember."

He held out his hand to her, but she sat down on the low chair to the right of the fireplace to stop herself from crossing the few paces of flagstone to join him. He let his hand drop.

"Here your sister has been tactful enough to leave us alone together, and all you can do is sit there looking grim."

"Here I was thinking that you looked remarkably cheerful, all things considered."

He crossed the short space between them in two

strides, took her hand, and kissed it. " 'I were but little happy if I could say how much,' " he quoted. "If being human taught me nothing else, it taught me to enjoy today, for tomorrow may never come. You used to know this lesson very well yourself. Have you forgotten it?"

"Perhaps I've had less reason to be content with today."

Max's face became more serious and the light in his green eyes darkened, though it did not fade away entirely. "Perhaps so. Still, I would change nothing of the past, since it has brought us to this moment. And because we have this moment, I fear nothing from the future."

Max released her hand and pulled the other chair forward, tugging at it until it faced her. He nodded his satisfaction and sat down. He'd left a little distance between them, but a hand outstretched by either of them would close it.

"Come," he said, "our circumstances have not changed so much."

"Haven't they?"

Max exhaled noisily and sat back in his chair, pushing his hands through his hair. "I understand why you stopped telling me who you were. You did the right thing."

Cassandra almost smiled. "You know, for a smart man, you can be remarkably dim. Perhaps *we* haven't changed. Perhaps it doesn't matter that we two people have never really met, despite all the past we've shared. Maybe it wouldn't matter that you now have a whole life, a whole past, that I never shared with you. It isn't those circumstances that have changed."

"What, then?"

Cassandra struggled to put into words what she'd been feeling since their arrival in the Keep. "In the past, we were just two wanderers, you and I. Now, you are the Prince Guardian, and I am ... what? A soldier, perhaps. A Healer." She shrugged. "I need to find out."

Max leaned forward, his elbows on his knees, and

stared a long while into the flames, the dancing lights calling echoes from the green fire in his eyes. Cassandra began to think that he was meditating once again when he heaved in a sigh, like a man awakening.

"I am not forbidden," he said, speaking to himself. Cassandra frowned, but before she could ask, he had turned to her again.

"If I had known you before the old Guardian came to me, I would have refused the Guardianship."

Cassandra smiled at his certainty but shook her head. "We would have been different people," she said. "You can't know what you would have done."

"No," he said, his voice rough. "Fundamentally the same you found me always, and therefore always yours." He leaned forward on his elbows, his fingers reaching out to touch her knee. "My mother didn't wear *gra'if,* did you know that?"

Cassandra blinked at the change of subject. "Not many do."

Max looked at her, without raising his head. "If she had, my father would have been able to find her, he would have been able to Move to her."

"Fewer still can Move to another's *gra'if,*" Cassandra said.

"I don't offer you everything a man should offer, everything I offered you when we were just two wanderers together. I am not wholly my own to give you," he continued, his voice showing more velvet now, "but I will give you all I can. Among the Wild Riders, when two who bear *gra'if* would marry, they exchange . . ." He lifted his hands to his neck and pulled off the Phoenix torque that circled his throat. He held it out to her.

"Fundamentally the same, I swear it." Cassandra could not look away from the warmth in his green eyes. "I *am* the only person you've ever known. I feel the same thing every time I see you. I felt it as Max, and I feel it now. You are the still center. The world comes into focus around you. Be patient, trust me a little longer, you will see."

"They say the Prince Guardian has a voice like the Sun. It would make all things turn toward him."

"Of a certainty this was so. Until the day they all turned away." His whisper had a wintry chill. "Look in your heart," he said. "Don't you know that I speak the truth?"

Cassandra shut her eyes. Wasn't this how everything started, with Diggory the Troll coming into her office and asking her the same question? She knew the answer now just as well as she'd known it then. She knew the truth of her own heart.

She pulled the dragon torque from her own neck and held it out to him.

Some time later, when they lay together, her head tucked into the curve of his neck, Max could tell that Cassandra was still awake. He shifted, raised himself on one elbow, traced the edges of her lips with his fingers.

"I don't think I ever heard Lightborn say anything that was not the truth," she said.

"There is nothing more likely, sword of my heart. Tell me, did he know your lineage, your Guidebeast? No, never mind. Knowing Lightborn, he knew all this and more about every Warden."

"So? A Rider's lineage is no secret."

"All Dragonborn are truth seers, though they may deny what they see. That is why you have the name you bear. Your parents were of the old lineage, even as I am myself, and kept up the old ways, even though no Guidebeast has been seen since my youth. Lightborn knows these things as well or better than I, growing up as he did in his mother's house. He would know to be careful what he said to you."

"Do all Guidebeasts have such meanings?"

"More than that, much more."

She nodded and rolled over, snuggled into him.

"We'll have to go after them," she murmured into the dark.

Yet she might be right not to trust him, Max thought, as he felt her breathing slow, her muscles relax into sleep. Like Lightborn, he had spoken only the truth to her. But, like Lightborn, he had left many truths unsaid. He had almost told her, but he could not burden her with the weight of his fears. If the Cycles were ending, this might be the only bit of happiness they could have. The Talismans had not denied him, had not forbidden his joining with her, but no one could be told all the truths about the Talismans. And though it bruised him, heart and soul, he was Guardian of the Talismans first, and the man who loved her second.

# Chapter Sixteen

MOON LIFTED THE CLOUD Horse's saddle from its stand and tossed it over the back of her horse. The animal shied slightly, shifting its delicate hooves. Moon tried stroking its flanks as she had seen the others do, but her trembling hands only seemed to make the animal more skittish. She glanced to where her sister and the Exile stood, Truthsheart checking how he had stowed his weapons. Moon's jaw clenched. It did not escape her that they were never more than an arm's length apart. If the Talismans *could* be found without him . . .

"How is it the Basilisk Prince has not found the Talismans?" Moon asked, pleased with how smooth and easy the words sounded. "The Vale is not so large a place, and he has his artisans working everywhere."

At least that made the Exile lift his eyes from her sister's face. Still, he hesitated as if he did not want to answer.

"They are not hidden in the sense you mean," he said finally in his rough velvet voice.

"In what sense, then?"

"On the morning of the final battle, I took them to *Trere'if* that they might be safe. When I submitted to the

Banishment, it was on condition that they remained where I had left them."

*Submitted.* Moon turned her face into her horse's shoulder so that the Exile would not see the contempt she could not disguise. Submitted. As if he'd had a choice. He would not be so arrogant much longer. She would see to that.

"Were you so sure that it was the final battle?" Truthsheart left the Exile's side and came to Moon, patting her on the shoulder and reaching around her to attend to the saddle leathers Moon had left dangling.

"I knew from the beginning that I couldn't win a war."

"But then why fight it?" Moon let Truthsheart help her into the saddle, finding herself calmed and comforted by the touch of her sister's hands. Curiosity warred with caution. There were a few of the old Songs that excused the Prince Guardian on the basis of madness. Was it possible that they told true?

"I didn't think I was fighting a war." The Exile pulled the last buckle tight on his own saddle, pushing his Cloud Horse's interested nose out of his face as he did so. "I thought I was safeguarding the Talismans. That's my task as Guardian."

"But you could have died at any time. How could you protect the Talismans then?"

The Exile stepped into the stirrup and pulled himself up into the saddle. For a moment it seemed that he would not speak, but finally he smiled, though Moon noticed that the smile did not touch his green eyes. "If I die, and the Talismans are safe, then I have succeeded."

"That's madness." This time Moon spoke aloud, unable to contain her thoughts.

"Do *you* think so?" Clearly he now spoke to her sister. Moon held her breath, waiting for Truthsheart's response.

"Once I may have done," Truthsheart said. "But, 'the way of the warrior is death,' " she quoted.

The Exile nodded. "I would—I will—destroy myself

and the Talismans also, rather than have their use perverted. And thus, I would succeed."

"The Talismans are not yours to destroy!" The startled jerk of her hands caused her Cloud Horse to toss its head, whinnying.

"On the contrary," the Exile said, "they are. People have always believed that I refused Dreamer of Time, the one you now call the Basilisk Prince, because there was bad blood between us—which there was." This time the Prince's smile did reach his eyes.

"And that wasn't it?" Truthsheart leaned from her own seat on her mount's back and tucked a curl of hair behind Moon's ear. Again, Moon relaxed under the cool touch of her fingers, as she had done when she had been a child and her sister had soothed her. *She is* mine, Moon thought. *I must save her. If I can.*

"If all one had to do to become High Prince was offer oneself to the Talismans, there would be lineups around the block—people constantly vying for the privilege," he added as Moon frowned at him. "But only the Talismans choose the High Prince. I would have turned down anyone who came, because the Talismans had not told me to seek anyone out."

"The humans say that the best leader is the one who doesn't want the job," Truthsheart said.

"Humans are fond of speaking in metaphor, but in this instance they are right."

"But why was this not explained? Why start the War?" Moon found herself unable to hide her anger. Was he saying that none of this need have happened? That her sister could have been at home all along?

"What makes you think I didn't explain it?" The Prince looked at her with puzzlement, his brows drawn close together.

Moon shook her head. The Exile could no more answer a question straightly than could the Basilisk. They were two of a kind, partners in a dance that would destroy everything. "But we Move to the Talismans now?"

He gave a heavy sigh. "If they were exactly where I left them . . ." He closed his eyes. No," he said, after a time. "The Vale has changed too much . . . and they might also have drifted in hiding themselves further." He shook his head. "We'll go to the Pass of *Welu'un,* and try entering the Basilisk's Vale from there."

The Pass of *Welu'un* was high in the mountains to the windward of the Vale of *Trere'if,* and should have been a bare place of stunted heather and rocky outcrops. Max blinked back sudden tears when he saw the place thick with Trees and understood, from the strength of his relief at finding *Trere'if* alive if not whole and in his place, how much he had been dismayed by the news of the Natural's destruction. It had been so large a blow, he now realized, that a part of him had simply put it aside, refusing to believe it. Naturals such as *Trere'if* were immeasurably old, living from Cycle to Cycle. The idea that *Trere'if* was gone had been too much for him to contemplate.

Even from the one large rock he had used as his guide in Moving, Max could feel the *dra'aj* of the Wood, cool, thick, vibrant, and yet a mere shadow of what they would be able to feel once they Rode their Cloud Horses under the Trees.

"Is this the Great Wood?" Moon seemed to be especially nervous this morning; even her hair refused to lay flat where she had combed it.

"This is *Trere'if,*" he said. Something drew his eye upward and he saw, far overhead, an oddly familiar ribbon of motion as a flock of geese trailed across the sky, shifting leaders in midflight. The season was turning. More evidence, if he needed it, that the Cycle was reaching its cold end. *Let this be the Winter that comes before Spring,* he prayed, though he wasn't sure to whom, *and not the Winter of all things.*

A murmur of voices drew his attention back to Cassandra and her sister. The two sisters had been acting a

little differently toward one another since they had shared
their quick breakfasts that morning. Cassandra seemed
more relaxed, smiling more easily, and touching her sister more than she had before, he thought, but Moon's
nervousness had increased, and her dislike of *him*
seemed, if anything, worse. Contrary to what the Songs
might tell about the effect of his voice, Max was used to
finding that people disliked and distrusted him. His father had wanted him to know and understand his
mother's people, but often, as a young Rider, he'd
thought that life would have been simpler if he had
stayed with his father's people, the Wild Riders, and
kept to their ancient ways. At least, he thought with
some amusement, they had a better understanding of
what Solitaries really were, and he would not have been
constantly explaining things.

Though, of course, none of that had mattered after
the old Guardian came.

Max had thought that the Choosing would change
everything for him. Before that, he hadn't known what
his place among his own people might be. His upbringing by Solitaries was too strange for most Riders to understand. His mother's kin did not find it easy to accept
him; no one doubted that he *was* his mother's child—his
*dra'aj* was proof of that—but his life was too sharp a re-
minder of her death. Even though most Riders did not
actively distrust him, only a few, like Lightborn and the
Basilisk himself before the Choosing, had been his friends,
the beginnings of a *fara'ip*.

At first, after years of living as the Solitaries do, it had
been fun to have companions of his own age, of his own
species, and he'd delighted in the similarities between
himself and his friends, attitudes and abilities he had
never found in the Solitary who had raised him, or the
others he had met over the years of his early life. He remembered the special feeling of contentment that came
from being within the group, a member of a troop. But
it had taken him a while to realize that by such simple

things as seeking solitude for his meditations, as he had been taught by his foster father, the Troll, he was regarded by his own people as eccentric at best, and deranged at worst. As time passed, these differences became more important to the other Riders, and Max found himself increasingly alone.

He'd thought that being chosen as the Guardian would change all that, would give him a real place in the Rider world, allowing people to accept him, giving him position and responsibility, a voice in affairs. He'd found, on the contrary, that the Guardian was the one Rider who was *truly* set apart, the one Rider who could not share his soul with any other, because he shared it with the Talismans themselves, becoming one with them. For the Prince Guardian, his *fara'ip was* the Talismans.

Except he'd changed that now, he thought, touching the dragon torque around his neck, and catching Cassandra's eye as she turned to him and smiled. Hadn't he?

Walks under the Moon did have reason to dislike him, however, Max knew. He had all of the memories of his human personae, and many times Cassandra had told him of how she had left her family to become a Warden, of what she hoped to gain for them by that, of her father's withdrawal and the need to provide for him and for the young child, her sister. Of course, it had meant leaving the child Moon behind with a man half mad with grief. It was obvious that the child had made an idol of the missing sister, longing for her return. Max wondered if Moon was aware that her present behavior most resembled that of a jealous lover. Even now, as they were riding in the dappled light to be found under the great Trees of *Trere'if,* Moon had managed to insinuate her horse between those of Max and Cassandra. Ah, well, he thought, she loved her sister, and resented that even now she did not have her for herself. From what Cassandra had told him over the years about the home she'd left, the child Moon could not have had an easy time of it, even with the privileges that Cassandra's becoming a Warden would have brought them.

And knowing the Basilisk, as perhaps few left in the Lands could know him, Max was certain that the Wardens' families had not actually gained all that much.

He couldn't blame Moon for distrusting him; he *did* have his own agenda, or his *fara'ip* did. Marrying Cassandra by the code of the Wild Riders—permission or no permission—was the single most selfish thing he had ever done. Once more his fingers lifted to touch the torque. If this was the end of all things, then he'd wanted to bind her to him, and it seemed that the rest of his *fara'ip* had agreed. For the moment he would not examine the reasons for that agreement too closely.

"Where go we now?" Moon was whispering to Cassandra, but Max answered her.

"We must find *Trere'if.*"

Moon slowed her horse. "But you said *this* is *Trere'if.*"

"Not the part we can speak to." Max stood on his stirrups and tried to get a view through the Trees. They were thicker here, cutting off his line of sight. "*Trere'if* is a who as well as a what and a where. Be warned, he is perhaps the oldest living being in the Lands, and his ways may seem very strange to you."

"How can he be the eldest?" Moon asked. "The Lands were made for Riders."

"Riders don't live all that long—a little over a Cycle at the most. Naturals," Max shrugged, "no one know how long a Natural can live. Each segment of the People thinks itself the oldest and believes that it understands the true nature of the Lands, what lives, what changes, what ages, and what does none of these things. None have all the answers—neither Rider, nor Solitary, nor Natural."

"And you are the only being that does, I suppose?"

"No, not even I."

"Max."

Something in Cassandra's voice made Max put his

hand on his sword hilt before he looked around to her. "Yes?"

"I don't think we're going any deeper in. The trees have closed in behind us. We're trapped."

"Steady," Max said. "Wait for it."

Pathways disappeared, and the clearing shrank until the Cloud Horses began to snort, realizing that they no longer had the space to turn. Only Max, expecting it, was not startled by the sudden appearance of a Green Man. This was a Tree Natural, tall, thick of limb and body, his skin mottled shades of green, brown, and black, resembling nothing so much as the bark of an oak. His fingers and toes were long, tapering to delicate threads, and his hair was made up of mosses and oak leaves, tiny and delicate as if just opening in the spring. Max was only mildly disappointed when he did not recognize this particular member of *Trere'if's fara'ip*.

"I am Dawntreader," he told the Treeman, "the Prince Guardian. My mother was Light at the Summit, my father is Blood on the Snow. The Phoenix guides me."

"*You* are welcome, Prince of Guardians." The Natural's voice was a whisper of wind in branches, with a hint of the creaking of boughs. A young one indeed. "Your father warned us of your coming and we have been on the watch. Who are these others? It has been long since Riders had the freedom of *Trere'if*."

"These are my companions. Where I go, there must they go also."

The Green Man shook his head, hair rustling. "That is for *Trere'if* to decide. If they would be brought to him, they must be bound."

"Your hospitality has greatly changed," Max said, trying to keep the anger from showing in his voice.

"That also is for *Trere'if* to decide, Guardian. If you wish to come to him, your companions must be bound."

"Don't worry, Max," Cassandra said, laying her hand on his arm. "We won't be offended, I promise you." Cassandra turned to the Green Man. "Is it a long journey?"

"By our ways, it is not far," the Green Man said.

Before he had finished speaking, the wood around them transformed; more than half of the Trees and Bushes disappeared, replaced by Naturals, until they were standing not in a forest glade, but in a crowd of Tree people, though at first there seemed little difference. The Naturals were all like the Green Man, more than half Tree, their skin bark of every texture and color, their hair the same mixture of leaves and branches. There were few smiles among them, Max noticed, though some of the younger ones looked at him with interest and sketched bows in his direction.

The Green People bound Moon's wrists with no trouble using vines they pulled free from their bodies. They held her gently in their delicate long-fingered hands, treating her with great courtesy, but the strictures on her wrists were tight and sure enough for all that. Cassandra presented more of a problem, for the forest people seemed unwilling to touch any part of her *gra'if*. They let her keep her sword and other weapons, sheathed, but managed to bind her wrists only because she willingly removed her gauntlets. Cassandra caught Max's eye and raised an eyebrow, lightly shrugging her shoulders. His frown relaxed. Of course, so long as one of them was free, they were all as good as free.

Or so he told himself, as the forest formed once again around them.

They hadn't gone more than another mile or so, following the slow walk of the Green Man, when the trees began to thin again, the sunlight shining strongly through the branches.

"Is it you, Dawntreader?" the voice was the growl of green wood twisting and tearing, the rubbing together of branches, the hint of falling leaves. Cassandra could just make out an enormous shape in the shadows, made larger somehow by the sudden stillness of the air.

"It is, *Trere'if,* and more than glad to see you. When I heard the Basilisk held your Vale, I feared the worst. I cannot say, however, that I think your hospitality much improved since we last met."

"I had heard it said you were captive. I do not know the ones you bring with you. Are you captive, still?" Trees shivered where the voice was coming from, as if something moved toward them. Cassandra wondered how long it had been since *Trere'if* had taken on a form that could speak to Riders.

"I am not. These are friends and companions."

"Let them speak for themselves, that I may hear and judge of their spirits." The Natural of the Wood finally stepped clear of the other Trees. He was smaller, more delicately built, than Cassandra had expected. Slim, slight, his skin pale green, with the faintest, almost imperceptible mottling; silver-gray hair made up of long, thin leaves, fine and flexible. But then she saw that his size, his coloring, even his shape altered between one step and the next, indeed between one breath and the next, as if he were a ghost seen in a light that filtered through leaves blowing in a fitful wind. He was not *a* tree man, but *the* Treeman.

Cassandra cleared her throat and, lifting her right leg over the saddle horn, slid off her horse to the ground. She took a short step forward and bowed from the waist, as she would have done to her sensei. Her hands were still bound, but that was the least of her worries. It looked as if they were all standing in a pretty forest glade, but she already knew better than to trust what her eyes told her.

"I am Sword of Truth," she said, her voice sounding soft and hollow in the wood-smelling air. "My mother was Clear of Light and my father Moon upon Water. The Dragon guides me. I was one of the Wardens of the Exile in the Shadowlands, and now I follow the Prince."

"Well-named thou art, Truthsheart. I hear the Dragon in thy voice, though I see you wear a Phoenix torque."

Moon stepped forward until she stood elbow to elbow with Cassandra. "I am called Walks Under the Moon," she said, her voice trembling in the twilight under the trees. "I am the full sister of the Sword of Truth, and the Manticore guides me."

"I hear thee, Moonwalker. Thy spirit is heavy. May I lighten it for thee?"

Cassandra felt Moon's barely repressed shudder against her arm. The Lady of Souls had commented on Moon's spirit as well, she remembered.

"I thank you, but no, Old One," Moon said.

"At thy wish, then, but I fear that without this lightening thou may'st not bide within the Great Wood."

"I do not wish to bide here, Old One." Moon's polite inclination of her head made her words less harsh.

"So long as this is so, thou may'st be unbound with thy sister." More of the long-fingered, pointy-nosed people came gliding out of the trees to stroke their bonds until they loosened.

The Natural of the Wood turned its head to Max. "I see that your spirit is also heavy, Dawntreader. Would you be lightened?"

"I am surprised by my reception, *Trere'if.* Are we not welcome here?"

"You are welcome, Guardian Prince. But none but the Wild Riders may enter here, or any other Wood, without hindrance and explanation. Do you not know that now and for many turns past, the one we fought, the Basilisk Prince, has drained Lakes and cut down Woods, in his ignorance turning the Cycle faster?"

Max's thoughts spun. If the actions of the Basilisk were speeding up the Cycle, that could explain why the Talismans weren't ready. There might be a High Prince after all, if only he could buy more time. A knot of tension in the back of his neck that he hadn't been aware of loosened.

"I have been in Exile, Elder Brother. There is much I do not know."

"Then you must marvel to see the People gathered here," the Old One continued. "So many, all in *Trere'if?*

They have come from long distances throughout the Lands, fled from their own places before the axes could come. Those who could. Ah," he turned as Moon made a sound in her throat, "thou did'st not know that this was possible? Many do not remember the lessons of the Great War, when my people fought at the side of the Guardian against the would-be prince." He turned back to Max. "Many among my people regret the day they joined you, Guardian, thinking that their ills began at that time, or that present ills come as a consequence of that conflict, saying that we should not have involved ourselves in the affairs of Riders."

"Are you among those?"

"What affects the Talismans affects us all, Dawntreader. That is as true now as it was when first I gave you my aid. But you must know, that since he has come to power, the Basilisk has turned many of my kind against your people. Few will now help you willingly— even you who are Guardian for us all—and there has been talk that we should rid the Lands of Riders once and for all."

"An action, and indeed an attitude, that will persuade many that the Basilisk's actions against you are justified," Cassandra observed as neutrally as she could.

"As always, Daughter of Dragons, thou speak'st truly, and thy words are as a sword."

"I will be guided by you in this as in other things." Max bowed, spreading his arms wide. "It is not our intention to intrude on your spaces for long."

"It is well. Your father awaits you."

The Natural's words died away into a silence so still that for a moment Cassandra thought she had once again lost the ability to process sound, as she had when standing next to the Tarn of Souls. Then she realized that she could hear her heartbeat, her breath as she drew it in.

It was *Trere'if* which had fallen silent. The Great Wood was poised between one breath and the next, listening.

"Go, Guardian," the Natural said. "Take your friends and go. Now. The Hunt comes. It enters my Sunward borders. The Hunt comes."

Cassandra drew her sword and motioned to Moon to stand on her left side. It felt strange not to automatically protect Max, but even out of practice he was armed and in *gra'if* and better able to defend himself than Moon could ever be.

"Go," *Trere'if* said again. "The Hunt will not stay within my borders if you are not here."

"Will you be safe from it?" Max said, his sword still in his hand.

"Nothing is safe from the Hunt," the Natural said. "But then, the same may be said of the Great Wood. Leave us, take the paths we show you. We will deal with this old enemy in our own way."

"Is he very angry?" Moon kept her voice down as they passed through the Wood.

Cassandra looked up but suppressed her amused response when she saw her sister's face. "He's worried about his friends," she said. "And he's wondering what to do next."

Moon nodded, but she didn't look convinced. There were very few noises now in the Great Wood, but even the wind in the branches was enough to make Moon start and look around her, to the annoyance of her mount. She kept twisting the fingers of one hand in the other, as if her hands were cold and she was trying to warm them.

Cassandra looked ahead to where Max led them along the paths that formed before them as they rode.

"If I thought you would believe me," she said to her sister, "I would tell you that all will be well."

"His goal is death," Moon whispered.

Cassandra leaned over and squeezed her sister's hands. " 'The way of the warrior is death,' " she quoted. "That doesn't mean that the warrior seeks death out."

"Then what does it mean?"

"It means that the warrior is not motivated by the fear of death. Death comes for everyone, and the warrior neither runs toward it nor flees from it. You cannot turn him from his path, nor make him break his oaths by threatening to kill him. You *can* kill a warrior, but you cannot make him afraid to die."

"And will he let his friends die? Will he let his beloved die?"

Cassandra looked at her sister with sadness. "Each must choose his own path," she said. "We are not all warriors." And that, unsatisfactory as it might be, was the only answer she had.

# Chapter Seventeen

THEY RODE OUT FROM the sunshine under the last of the Trees of *Trere'if* into a cold fall day, overcast and gloomy, a chill wind blowing old dried leaves across their path. Max looked behind him and the Wood was gone, lost in mist. Well, that was one way to deal with the Hunt, he supposed.

"We greet you, Prince Guardian."

Two Moonward Riders—Wild by their battered leather clothing—appeared from behind a rocky outcrop, on foot, armed with bows and short swords, with daggers at their belts. They pushed back their hoods with identical graceful motions and revealed *gra'if* helms with the shapes of Unicorns.

"You are known to me," Max said, a smile forming on his face. "Wings of Cloud and Bird in Flight, sons of the same mother."

The twin Riders looked at each other and grinned.

"*Trere'if* gave us word of your coming. If you would attend upon us, my lord Prince," they said in unison, "we will bring you to Blood on the Snow."

Max nodded, gesturing the twins forward. He remembered meeting with his father at the Turquoise Ring, remembered how the older Rider's look of shadowy disappointment had been quickly covered by the impassive mask of the soldier. Max no longer needed Lightborn to tell him the story of his life, but he thought about that telling now, and the feelings that the human Max Ravenhill had felt. As Dawntreader, he had long forgiven his father—in fact, it had never occurred to him that there had been anything to forgive. His mother's death was no one's fault, and as for his early life . . . he glanced at Cassandra, listening to the chatter of one of the twins who walked beside her Cloud Horse, and pretending that she couldn't tell them apart. He'd meant it when he'd said that he couldn't complain about anything that had brought him to this moment. There had been darkness, and struggles, but he had come through them, and he was content with where he was now. Who he was now. He grinned at the irony in that thought. That's exactly the point that Max Ravenhill had arrived at in *his* life.

But having lived his human lives, Max thought, he now had a different basis for comparison, and he thought he knew what the problem with Blood on the Snow really was. It wasn't his son's forgiveness Blood needed, but his own. He had never forgiven himself for his wife's death, and that grief had created a gulf between them. As a young Rider, Dawntreader had sensed this gulf, but not understanding its source, his attempts to bridge it had been clumsy, and ultimately futile. Max understood it very well, and shook his head over lost time. Perhaps, having no *fara'ips,* no natural intuitive bonds with each other, humans learned the whys and wherefores of relationships in a way that Riders never could.

The Wild Riders had set up their camp where a fall of rock and a grouping of old pines created a sheltered area under the shoulder of a hill. From between the rocks ran a trickle of fresh water that had formed into a small pool. Max smiled to see a Water Sprite, all pale greens, splashing in the water and laughing with a young Rider dressed haphazardly in the colors of a Singer who knelt close to the pool's edge. Max had seen dozens of such temporary encampments before he became Guardian, on those occasions when his father had taken him Riding from Honor of Souls' house. There was little more than a fire pit dug and lined with found stone, a few skin tents pitched for privacy under the trees. Wild Riders were the nomads of the Lands, carrying little with them, and never staying more than a few nights in one place. They were always on the Move.

As they rode closer in, Max saw other Riders mixed in with the Wild troop, many whose worn leathers were mixed with clothing in scarlet and saffron. Windwatcher's men, he realized. It was several of these Riders who rushed forward, smiling and saluting, to take the bridles of their horses. Max grinned and returned their salutes with a wave of his hand, finding himself a little embarrassed. Many of the faces around him were familiar, but his eyes searched until they found the figure of Blood on the Snow, tall, rail thin, in the rough and dusty leathers which were the only clothing Max had ever seen him in. Blood turned from the small group of Riders he was speaking to and looked toward them. He did not smile, but Max thought he saw a lessening of tension in the way the older Rider stood. Max swung off his horse before his father could move, determined to meet him when they were both on foot, and therefore on equal ground. He had to do this just right, or the coolness between them that even Lightborn remembered would never be defeated.

As Max neared him, Blood's lips parted, but before he could speak the formal words of welcome, Max took his father in his arms. His grip was harsher, more sudden than he intended, and the *gra'if* of both Riders hardened for a moment, as if at a blow. But they were of the same blood, and the same mind, and their *gra'if* finally softened and relaxed as Blood's arms came up around his son, and they held each other, heart to heart, until their trembling stopped.

It took Cassandra a second to recognize Windwatcher in the tough old leathers of a Wild Rider, his *gra'if*—a mail shirt, a dagger, a single gauntlet and vambrace covering his right arm—an obvious and gleaming contrast. The older Rider made his way to her side through the Wild Riders who were very studiously not watching their leader greet his son. "He is restored, then?"

Cassandra turned more fully toward him. At this moment, she, too, was glad to look away from the father and son.

"He is," she said.

"Has he the Talismans? There is precious little time."

"Of course, you have not heard?"

The older Rider grimaced, and Cassandra saw with concern his tired face grow grayer, and the shadows under his eyes darken.

"I have heard news I never thought to hear," he rumbled. "There is more?"

Cassandra told Windwatcher the whereabouts of the Talismans with a hesitant voice, reluctant to burden him further, but to her surprise he started to laugh.

"So what the Basilisk seeks has been under his hand all this while." He shook his head. "By the Wards, we are the toys of chance, that is certain." He looked at her from under lowered brows. "What is the Guardian's plan? Is there still time, before the Sun's turning, to find the Talismans? Find them and bring them away?"

"If he cannot . . ."

"Yes. Then the end has come, Sword of Truth. We win or we die. If we die, the Lands die with us."

"I fear I have other news," Cassandra said. "Is Honor of Souls also among the company? I must tell her what it will grieve her greatly to hear."

At that the older Rider drew himself upright. "Grieve

her, you say? More than the loss of Griffinhome? Yes, it is gone. The Hunt was loosed there, and finding little prey, for Honor of Souls and much of her household had fled, put the fortress to the fire, and cleansed the Land."

Cassandra gripped Windwatcher's arm, his *gra'if* gauntlet stiff and hard under her own metalled hand.

"Does Lightborn know where she hides?"

"She waits with a company of my soldiers, but—"

"Windwatcher!" Cassandra could barely keep herself from shaking the man. "Lightborn has gone to the Basilisk!"

This was the news that made the old Rider stagger. Cassandra had him around the waist, his arm across her shoulders before he could go down.

"It cannot be," he growled, halfway to tears. "And you thought this news would merely *grieve* her?"

"Some warning must be sent," Cassandra said, feeling in the squaring of his shoulders how her words gave Windwatcher purpose.

"There is little time," he said, his gruff voice strong again. "I will send one of my own guard, but we must hope that Lightborn does not know."

After she had seen Windwatcher safe with his own men, Cassandra joined Max where he crouched beside Blood on the Snow, both men looking over the map that Max had drawn from Blood's description on a smooth patch of dirt. Riders had no need for maps, but the older man caught at the idea quickly, fascinated by the concept. They were much alike, father and son, Cassandra thought, both raven-haired, fine-boned, long-faced, and both with the same thin, slightly hooked nose. Max must have his mother's jade-green eyes, for his father's were gray as ash, and her full, mobile mouth, but the thing that really set them apart was Blood's evident age. His health was good, Cassandra saw, but in this light his hair was more silver than black, there were visible lines on his face, and his skin was the color of old bone.

In a way, this man was now her father-in-law, Cassandra realized, doubly part of her *fara'ip*. At that moment, he looked up and smiled, and there again Cassandra saw his resemblance to Max.

"Greetings to you, Sword of Truth." Blood on the Snow took her hand and held it to his forehead in the old way of showing obligation. "My thanks for the restoration of my son and Prince."

"It was my task," she said, the old formal response coming to mind just in time. She bowed her head over their still-joined hands. When she straightened, it was to see Blood's eyes wide, focused on the Phoenix torque around her throat. It wasn't until he smiled that she was aware how tense she had become.

"You became my *fara'ip* when the Troll Hearth of the Wind joined you to us," the old Rider said. "Have you now become my daughter?"

Cassandra cleared her throat. "I have."

"I am old, my days at court are long behind me, else I would have words pretty enough to tell you how much I am pleased."

Cassandra blinked, breathing carefully and tilting back her head a little to prevent her tears from falling.

"And your sister? I am sure she rejoices also."

She looked around her now and saw that Moon was being entertained by the Moonward twins, who had managed between them to make Moon smile. She still wasn't sure what Moon felt. They had not been alone since they arrived at Max's tower, and Cassandra hadn't found the right moment to speak to her.

"Give her time, Truthsheart," Blood said, interpreting her silence easily. "Her whole world changes."

Cassandra nodded and forced a smile. She knew that what Blood said was true, but she wasn't very comforted by it. She was glad to let Blood's voice draw her attention back to the map.

"Let me call one who has been most recently in the Citadel," Blood was saying as he signaled to one of the Wild Riders hovering near them, who quickly returned with a young Starward Rider. She wore Singer's colors, Cassandra saw, but they were made up of bits and pieces of clothing, some very clearly belonging to other, larger Riders. The leggings beneath her tunic were the magenta Cassandra knew to be the Basilisk Prince's color.

"This is Twilight Falls Softly," Blood said, drawing the young Singer closer to the map with a beckoning hand. "She came to us from the Basilisk's Citadel only a short time ago, and can tell us what we need to know."

The Singer frowned over the map as it was explained to her, looking up finally with a smile that brought color to her pale cheeks and brightened the turquoise of her eyes.

"This is like the thing they call 'writing,' yes? Have you—no." She held up her hands. "I have too many questions, and all must await a better time and place." She studied what Max had drawn for a few minutes before speaking.

"The whole of the Vale," she said finally, "except for these sections, here and here," she pointed with the tip of a dagger, "has been transformed, either into the Citadel itself, or into part of the Garden that surrounds it."

"So the walls of the Citadel are here, here, and here?" Max frowned. "The Vale itself has not changed shape?"

"Not if you have drawn truly," agreed Twilight. "But the Talismans need not be within the Citadel proper in order to be behind walls." She rested back on her heels. "The Garden is made up of miniature versions of the Lands. The Walls were not yet in place when I escaped, but they may be now—the Basilisk would not say when exactly, nor for what he waited, only 'soon'—and it was said that once in place, only the Basilisk himself can cross these walls without Moving, and it is only from his tower study," Twilight touched her upper lip with the tip of her tongue before bringing her dagger point down again, "this point here, that all the Garden can be seen."

"A frontal assault is therefore out of the question," Blood said.

"Moving into the Garden is a waste of time," Cassandra said. "Even if we knew the place well enough to Move, if these Walls are up, we'd have to keep jumping from section to section . . ." she shook her head and turned to Twilight Falls Softly. "How did you get away?"

"It was my plan to walk," the younger Rider said, with an embarrassed half smile on her lips. "I had no idea of the real distance. Fortunately, I found a Water Sprite who also wanted to leave, and she brought me with her through the ways of the Naturals."

"There is more to her story than she tells you," Blood said, smiling broadly, "but that, too, must wait a better time and place."

"Are they together? The Talismans?" Cassandra looked across the map at Max. "Maybe we won't need to Move much."

"I put them in the Cave of Sighs, but," Max shook his head, his raven hair falling into his eyes. "I can't see where it should be."

"Don't think the Rider way," Cassandra told him, "think the human way. If you had a map of the old Vale, and you superimposed it over this one . . ."

Max looked at her with raised eyebrows and the beginnings of a smile. Without even looking at the map scratched in the dirt, he brought his index finger down on a spot left of center.

"Here."

"Within the Citadel itself, then," Blood said.

"Allowing for windage," Max said smiling. "They may have drifted a bit, but that is more or less where they'll be."

Blood stood, shaking his head at Cassandra's offered hand. "Can you Move there, Twilight Falls Softly?"

"He will know." The Singer had grown so pale that her eyes looked like bruises in her face. "We were told that the Basilisk could feel Movement to and from the Citadel, and I . . ."

From the trembling of her lips it was obvious the young Singer was terrified. To have escaped once, and to be asked to go back . . .

"There is no one else," Blood said gently. "None of us has been there since the building was completed."

"I have," Max said. "Once I'm that close, I should be able to walk right to them."

"Max." Cassandra couldn't believe her ears. "The dungeon room? And if it's locked?"

"When I first woke up, I wasn't in a dungeon room," he said, his eyes, narrowed in memory, still on the map. "I was in a round tower room, full of windows, maybe even the room that overlooks the Garden."

Twilight nodded, scanning the map. "There was a broad table? Many small carpets? A divan? The Basilisk's workroom. It is at the top of the Basilisk Tower, here." She indicated the same spot that Blood had pointed out before. "There are other towers, though none so high, all along this perimeter wall. Between are public rooms, halls, barracks, and six courtyards." She sketched in these details quickly before looking up at the faces watching her. "The rest of the Citadel is patrolled by soldiers, but none go without permission into the Basilisk Tower. If he knows there has been Movement, the Basilisk may send a guard, but providing the Basilisk himself is not there, you should have no trouble—"

"And if he *is* there?" Blood was frowning.

Cassandra knew her cue. "Then *we* should have no trouble."

"You'll stay here with Blood and his Riders." Max didn't look at her. "It's too—"

"Dangerous, yes, I know." She laughed at his open-mouthed look as she stole his line. "He'll know you're coming, whether he can feel the Movement or not. You can't go alone."

"Look—"

"Fight you for it." She looked at him with her eyebrows raised as far as they would go. What was the point of knowing someone for a thousand years if you didn't learn how to win an argument?

"If you would be guided by me, my Prince," Blood said, his face lightened in what must pass for him as a smile, "do not part from Sword of Truth. Two can pass unnoticed as easily as one. And I fear that you have not held a blade in some time. If it were possible, I would suggest a small company of Riders, but as it is not . . ."

"I may have another use for the Wild Riders," Max said, "if they will consent."

"You have but to ask."

Walks Under the Moon had watched everything closely and behaved as carefully as she could. She had nodded when required, smiled when smiling was called for, bowed her head at introductions as befitted her. But all the time she had been watching her sister, hoping even now that Truthsheart would step away from the Exile, now that he had his own *fara'ip,* his own father, to help him. But no, the solution would not be simple after all. She would have crept into his chamber and killed him in his sleep, Basilisk or no Basilisk, but for the knowledge that they had slept in the same bed. Her sister and the Exile. Moon could see now that Truthsheart must indeed be mad. All those years in the Shadowlands, among the people she called humans . . . of course her poor sister was mad.

There must be a way to save Truthsheart from this madness, to set her feet finally on the path back to sanity. Moon had thought the Basilisk had promised her this, but she feared now that she could not trust him. *Never mind,* she thought, *I can do it myself.*

And so she had watched and smiled and bowed. And waited until her sister was gone, asked the Wild Rider who was assigned to her care where she might wash herself, and when he walked away to allow her privacy, she Moved.

Max stood back to back with Cassandra, swords in their right hands, left hands linked behind them, grasping wrists. He could feel her bare skin under his hand. For where they were going, and what they needed to do, they had removed all their *gra'if* except what could be concealed under their clothes, and those clothes were the deep magenta of the Basilisk's personal guard. Max hadn't asked Blood on the Snow where the uniforms had come from.

"I could have won the fight," he said.

"With a couple of centuries of practice, maybe."

"You're just saying that to make me feel better."

SLAM!

The smell told him they'd made it, even before he opened his eyes. The air that moved through the round windows smelled of flowers and ornamental grasses, not of rain-swept granite and pine needles. The circular room was exactly as Max had last seen it, the cushioned couch, the small table near it still holding its wine decanter and jeweled cups.

He walked over to the couch, fingered one of the tassels on the edge of a cushion, remembering when he'd lain here, talking with the Basilisk.

"Could you Heal him?" he asked without looking up.

"I can only Heal the addiction, not the cause of it." She was shaking her head, frowning. "I don't remember any Song that tells of addiction to *dra'aj.*"

Max tossed the cushion back onto the chaise. "Few people know of it, but that's where the Hunt—"

Cassandra held up her hand in a shushing motion and jerked her head. "They're coming up," she whispered.

Max pointed at himself and then at the door; pointed to her and then to the backless stool in front of the work-table. Cassandra nodded as Max flattened himself against the wall behind the door. Max might be known, but no one would recognize her, and that might buy them some time. She sat down and crossed her ankles like a student awaiting the arrival of the vice principal. She held her sword low down at her side, where it could not be seen from the doorway.

The swift, tapping footsteps halted in the open door-way. Cassandra looked up, widened her eyes, and gave the Sunward guard, drawn sword in his hand, a small smile. She knew that Max had his hands up, ready to push the door into the guard if anything went wrong.

"What are you doing here?" the guard said.

"The Basilisk sent me," she said. "He told me to wait for him here." The tremble in her voice wasn't faked, but she hoped she sounded convincingly proud of her-self. She'd heard many young women, noticed by their princes, sound just that way.

Evidently the guard had, too. He swallowed and looked away, suddenly unable to meet her eyes.

"You know you're not supposed to Move within the Citadel," he said brusquely.

"Well, I know, that is, they told me that, of course, but when the Prince himself ordered me, I thought . . ."

The guard nodded. "See you wait quietly, then." His eyes flicked up and away from her again. For a mo-ment, Cassandra thought the Sunward Rider was going to say something more, but he jerked his head at her again, turned on his heel, and started down the stairs.

Cassandra relaxed her grip on her sword hilt and stood up as Max stepped from around the door, rolling his eyes skyward. She shrugged.

"Where to?" she mouthed.

Max closed his eyes, felt for the flames within him,

though he wasn't surprised when he felt in which direction they pulled him. Where else could they go? "Down."

Cassandra nodded, gesturing for him to take the lead with a mocking half bow.

He paused at the next landing, keeping his heart open, feeling for the flames of the Phoenix's nest. Here, a wide archway opened into what could only be a conference room. Wall hangings embroidered and brocaded in Guidebeasts of all kinds, ten chairs around a long oval table, the chair at the head elevated slightly above the rest. Everything in the room elaborately decorated—each chair carved and painted, the table a mass of marquetry. Even the floor was parqueted with both stone and wood—and not, as Max saw with a twist to his stomach, in darkwood. Nothing could express his relief at not having to enter the room. It would have been like walking on rugs made from the skins of friends. He felt Cassandra's grip on his arm, and met her eyes, dark and stormy gray in a face set hard as stone. He swallowed and motioned her on.

The bottom of the tower had two exits. Max went without hesitation to the double doors at the left of the stair. Cassandra took hold of his sleeve in her fingers.

"Outside?" she whispered, a worried frown creasing her brows.

He nodded, and mouthed the word "courtyard." She shrugged and went to the left leaf of the carved wooden door. Again, this was Wood, not darkwood, and Max felt his stomach lurch with nausea. The door's bolts and hardware were darkmetal, new, and perfectly fitted. Cassandra grimaced, lips pulling back from her teeth as she reached for the door. Managing not to touch the Wood, she slid the bolts back, taking such care that Max only heard the smallest "snick" as the last bolt slid free.

The doors opened into an interior patio, a large rectangular space surrounded by a pillared arcade. The pillars held up a covered gallery fronted with an elaborate lattice, as if there were a harem to be hidden from public view. Colored flagstone paths radiating out from a central fountain divided the patio into sections. Each section was itself a different color, created by a careful choice of flowers, small shrubs, and a single tree. Stone seats invited people to rest and listen to the beauty of the water.

"Is there anyone in the water?" she breathed as she followed him down the path.

Max shook his head. "This is plumbing, not a Natural, and there's not enough water to hide anyone else."

The tree farthest from the doors was a slim ash, and Max approached it slowly. He knelt before it, and placed his palms on the silver-gray bark. The tree shuddered, exactly, Cassandra thought, as a woman might shudder under her lover's hands.

Max stood, and the tree was gone. In his hands was an ash wood spear.

"It's a war spear." Cassandra's hand was out before she was aware of moving, already imagining the feel of the spear's time-smooth shaft under her fingers. Its head, gleaming like *gra'if,* though she couldn't guess whose *gra'if* it might be, was fully the length of her forearm.

"Hence the name," Max said. "*Porre'in,* Spear of War."

Cassandra looked at him, her mouth twisted sideways. "I meant," she said, drawing back her hand, "that it is actually a war spear. For some reason I expected it to be," she held her hands a few feet apart, "symbolic in some way." It was, in fact, longer than the human war spear, almost a lance. "It seems so ordinary," she added.

"Touch it," Max said.

Cassandra took hold of the shaft in the middle, between Max's hands, and for a second, he let her bear the weight of it. At once she felt it warm and pulsing, like a living thing, and felt herself flying through the air, not like a bird, but like a missile, the rush of wind created only by her own forward movement intoxicating, sucking the air away from her before she could breathe it in. Her blood sang, and she felt herself gasping. She took a step back to keep herself from falling, met Max's shining eyes above the spear he held between them.

"Did you feel it?" he said.

"It's in flight," she said, clearing her dry throat with difficulty.

"It always is," Max said. "It's a true symbol."

"Who holds it can call the People to War," Cassandra said.

Max shook his head, his lips pinched thin. "You heard *Trere'if.* The People won't fight. And they're right. I used this once already, thinking I was doing the right thing, and you know how well that worked out. There's a lesson in that bit of history, and I have to listen to it. Whatever else—" he paused. *Ravenhill would go with his instincts,* he told himself, *and you are fundamentally the same.* "I believe the Talismans have their own plan and I—we—will have to wait and trust in them."

She scanned the covered gallery uneasily, took in the slant of sunlight on the flagstones. "Max, where to now? I think the Sun is turning."

Walks Under the Moon had gone home, to Lightstead, to where she could think without soldiers and Wild Riders and Exiles to distract her. She could not stay seated in her workroom chair more than three heartbeats before she was once more pacing about the room. If her movement could even be called pacing as she edged around the crowded dusty furniture, twitching her skirts out of the way as her hands touched, turned over, and replaced long disused objects. Bowls, stones, knives for paring fruit and cutting leather, hair ornaments, misplaced shoes, and on one table by the door, scraps of paper from the Shadowlands and old pens, the ink long-dried, remnants of her failed experiments in adapting the Shadowfolk's invention of writing to the Rider language.

Finally, she made her way to the windows and sat there, stared unseeing out of the window, and thought of her father. He had sat thus for months after the death of his wife, their mother, and after Truthsheart's departure to the Shadowlands he had continued, dozing in his chair, barely touching his food, responding to his remaining child less and less until one day his chair was empty and he was gone. Faded.

Moon sat now in her own chair. Was this what she had without her sister, she thought. A chair. A window looking out on nothing?

Moon could see now that she had not thought about the Exile in the right way. She had thought of him, when she thought of him at all, as a piece in the Basilisk's game. But he was real. Living, breathing, and real, and the hold that he had on Truthsheart—though based in falsehood and trickery—was a real hold. Merely separating them would not be enough. If her sister would not—or could not, a softer voice said inside her—listen to reason, the Exile would *have* to be killed. Then her sister's eyes could be opened. Moon shivered with more than cold. It might not be what the Basilisk wanted, but she could do this, and more, to save her sister.

She must go again to the Citadel, and await her chance.

---

The other doors, darkwood Max saw with relief, and as elaborately carved but nowhere near as heavy as the ones leading onto the patio, opened into a large room, sunlight streaming in from openings high in the walls. After Cassandra's words outside, Max automatically measured the angle of the light. There was still time, he thought. Just. He studied the room, frowning. The space was not large enough to be the great hall of the whole Citadel, and Max thought it was more likely a throne room or audience chamber as yet unfurnished. Here, again, the decor was crammed with details. From their vantage point at the doors, a few steps above the floor, he could see that every inch of it was covered with mosaic tiles, like a great Velazquez painting laid down to walk on. It was a battle scene, not conventional Riders with Cloud Horses, however, but a battle of Guidebeasts, as if this was taking place early in the Cycle, when the *dra'aj* was so great that Guidebeasts were commonplace. Even so, Max knew that this wasn't a battle as old as the use of Guidebeasts might suggest. He recognized the central figures. A Phoenix was raising its sword in one flame-tipped claw, just as a Basilisk was bringing its petrifying vision to bear. The Phoenix was turning to stone even as it lifted its sword.

This was a rendering of the final battle of the Great War. The final encounter of that battle.

Max walked out into the center of the floor, drawn by the tiled depiction of himself.

"Is this how it was?" Cassandra whispered from behind him.

Max looked around, shaking his head. "I never crossed swords with Dreamer, but otherwise it's accurate enough, I suppose. Look, there are the Trolls and Elementals, and there a few Naturals, both Springs and Trees, on my right flank." The artist, Max saw, had played with the perspective somehow, so that though the participants were not shown as life-size, or even as properly proportioned relative to each other, somehow the sizing worked, and the field of battle looked natural. Or as natural as a field of battle can look.

He nodded again. Yes, accurate enough. Except . . . Max squatted, traced the outline of the Phoenix with his fingertips, feeling a hot flush rise from the cold tiles. He was not, after all, raising his blade to strike. He was reaching for it. It had clearly been knocked from his hand. Now Max frowned and reached out to touch the mosaic sword and found the warm pommel of *Ti'ana* in his hand.

"Max?" He could hear the awe in her voice. "Is it . . ."

He could understand her hesitation. It seemed no more than any old sword, a bit longer than a rapier, with a broad, double-edged blade, and a plain hilt covered with braided leather. Not so long as the great two-handed swords made for those who wore *gra'if,* the swords they had left behind in Blood's camp, but with the same kind of curved cross guard. It fit into his hand like his own *gra'if.*

Max reversed his grip and held *Ti'ana* out to her. "See for yourself," he said.

"It's not just a thrusting blade," she said as she reached for the rounded hilt.

"No," Max agreed. "It cuts."

With her hand inches from the grip, Cassandra froze and lifted her head.

Max didn't argue when she pushed him toward the tapestried wall. He'd heard the footsteps, too.

⟶

Lightborn's orders were very clear. "Follow them," the Basilisk had said. "Be prepared to take them once the Talismans are found. Until that moment, keep them under your hand, but lightly." Lightborn knew perfectly well that the Basilisk was once again making sure of him. The Basilisk never let Lightborn forget that he was a traitor, he lost no opportunity to use Lightborn against Dawntreader, to remind him that he had betrayed his friend. Even now, when his treachery was known, it would be Lightborn who would follow the Prince Guardian at a distance, Lightborn who would capture him once the Talismans were found, and Lightborn who would hand him, and the Healer Truthsheart to the Basilisk.

The Basilisk trusted no one's loyalty, but asked for proof after proof. Lightborn touched the spot over his heart where the scar from his arrow wound still puckered the skin. What, Lightborn wondered, would the Basilisk use to make him prove his devotion when Dawntreader was dead?

Lightborn had left his own instructions that if Walks Under the Moon presented herself, she should be brought to him, and not to the Basilisk Prince. No one would see anything unusual in that. Over time, Lightborn had fallen into the habit of giving instructions and orders, in part to remind the Basilisk's followers that he could, and in part to check that his authority still existed. The Basilisk did not always tell you when you had fallen out of favor, sometimes you found out when it was too late. It paid to be very careful, and to take nothing for granted.

The last few sunwidths Lightborn had spent talking to certain guards and soldiers. Talking so carefully that many would not even be aware of the real purpose behind their discussions. When Walks Under the Moon was ushered into his salon, Lightborn was ready.

"I have been thinking," she said, "and the Basilisk will not give me what I want."

"How then can *I* help you?" he said.

"I want the Exile dead," she said. "What if the Basilisk does not kill him? What if they make some pact? I want only my sister, and while the Exile lives, she will never turn away from him."

That was very true, Lightborn thought. More true than perhaps anyone but himself would understand. However, Walks Under the Moon refused to see that even without the Prince Guardian, Truthsheart would not necessarily be the person that Moon wanted her sister to be. But would any of them be themselves for long, if the Basilisk bound the Talismans? He indicated the chair to his left. "What do you propose?"

Max stood frozen with Cassandra's hand on his arm, his shoulder blades pressed tight against the wall behind them and the tapestry inches from his nose. Was he trembling? He wondered if she could feel anything through the layers of leather on his forearm. She seemed not to be breathing at all, but Max was certain that the Riders who were now standing in the great hall, perhaps right on the figures of Dawntreader and the

Basilisk Prince inlaid in the floor, would hear the pounding of his heart, and the rush of air forcing itself through his lungs.

Would the soldiers notice the hole in the mosaic?

They seemed to take hours to stroll through the hall. Their murmuring voices faded away as they finally reached the doors on the far side. Cassandra released her grip on his forearm.

"Which way now?" she whispered as they emerged from behind the tapestry.

The hall had three exits. The door they'd come through would lead back to the tower or the patio. The set of wide double doors had the look of a ceremonial entrance, but they could see a smaller passage at the far end of the room, through which the three soldiers had gone.

"Let's follow the crowd," he said.

～

"They have just left the battle chamber, my lord Prince," the young Sunward Rider bobbed her head in a short bow. When the Basilisk merely nodded, his gaze fixed on the distance, the young Rider continued. "The Exile now bears two swords."

That brought the Basilisk's eyes to her. For a moment, the dark depths flickered, fascinating her, and the young Rider lowered her own eyes, her courage briefer than she'd hoped. Perhaps it was better not to come to the Basilisk's attention after all. How could eyes so dark burn so brightly? Her legs felt stiff, but she was afraid to move, to be seen fidgeting under the Basilisk Prince's eye.

"Continue following," the Basilisk said. "Stop them if they try to leave the Citadel, but otherwise, follow."

The Sunward Rider bowed low and left the room. She was several paces away before the stiffness left her legs.

～

The short passage led to a small courtyard. Two soldiers were sparring with staffs while several of their comrades

watched, yelling out encouragement, or insults, as
seemed called for. Only one glanced over at them as
they walked through, but she turned back to the combat
quickly enough, wincing in sympathy as a particularly
heavy blow landed. As they'd thought, the Basilisk's
men must be used to seeing new faces and to not asking
where the old ones had gone.

The passage on the far side of the courtyard was
smaller and plainer than the ones they'd come from, the
stone walls smooth but undecorated. This part of the
Citadel was clearly the area for servants and men-at-arms.
The passage led first to an armory with racks of bows, arrows, swords, pikes, and axes in orderly rows. Beyond that
was a barracks room, and just beyond the barracks was a
larger room clearly used as a dining hall. Soldiers, it appeared, did not eat with their lord in this Citadel. Cassandra thought that was probably all to the good.

She waited in the open doorway, leaning on the Spear,
as Max entered the room and approached the sideboard
on the left of the entrance. It bore the customary baskets, platters and bowls, cups, bottles and jugs, which the
Basilisk's soldiers would find always filled with breads,
meats, soups, wines, and ale. Max ran his fingertips over
the sideboard itself, almost as if he were checking for
dust, before coming to a stop in front of a deep, covered
ceramic dish.

"Don't tell me they're keeping soup in it," she said.

Max laughed without making any sound. But as he
looked up to answer her, the light around them changed,
turning brighter, warmer, thicker. Max paled, and put
his hand to his chest, as if to feel his heart beating. Cassandra stepped forward as he fell to his knees and felt
the Spear of War leap once in her hand, as the Prince
Guardian sat back on his heels, drawing in a deep
breath, smiling. He, too, seemed brighter, warmer, his
pale face flushed with color, his green eyes glowing jade.

The Sun had turned, Cassandra realized. The Banishment was over.

*I am free of my Oath.* She smiled. *I don't feel any different.*

A cracking sound made them both turn to the sideboard, where the soup tureen was gone, replaced by a cauldron twice its size, made of greenish-gray stone inlaid with the same bright metal that shone from Spear point and Sword blade. Max took his hand from his heart and placed it on the rim of the Cauldron.

"This is *Sto'in*," he said. "Cauldron of Plenty. The Font of *dra'aj* for the whole of the Lands, and for all of the People." He lifted the lid.

"Well, what do you know?" Max flicked the edge of the Cauldron with a fingernail, and the bowl rang with a note as pure as the finest crystal.

"Don't do that again," Cassandra said. "Someone will hear it."

"Too late," said a familiar voice from over her shoulder.

# Chapter Eighteen

"MOVE AWAY FROM him, Truthsheart."

Using the Spear as a pivot, Cassandra swung herself around to face the door and stood braced, *Porre'in* held like a quarterstaff across her body. Not for the first time, she thanked the gods that her reflexes were as well-trained as they were. Her heart was pounding, and her hands were damp on the ash shaft of the Spear. She didn't know what had startled her more, the sight of her sister with a dagger in her hand, or the fact that Lightborn was standing behind Moon, his sword drawn.

"Moon, what is this?" she asked, backing toward Max as she spoke.

"Truthsheart, stop, go no nearer to him. Can you not see? He has bewitched you, but it is not too late. Come with me now and Lightborn will free us all from his glamour."

Cassandra felt the sting of tears in her eyes. *Oh, my poor sister,* she thought, seeing once again in her memory's eye the younger Moon pressing her face against her side. This was her own fault. She *had* neglected Moon, not then, not when she had agreed to be a Warden, but since her return. She had seen—she had been told, in no uncertain terms, how important she was to Moon, but there had been no time. And now there never would be. She had driven Moon to someone who *would* listen to her, someone who would take her seriously. If she had only looked beyond the surface, Cassandra thought, she could have seen what she now saw very clearly, that Moon's *dra'aj* was far from True. Even now there was no time. The Banishment was over, the Talismans were revealed. They had to get them away.

Still, she had to try.

"There is no glamour," she began.

"There is!" Moon took a step closer. "He does not care about you, he never did. All he cares for are his Talismans. Leave him and come with me."

"I cannot." Cassandra backed away until she was at Max's side. Out of the corner of her eye she saw that he had sheathed *Tai'na* and drawn his own sword. She understood his hesitation to use the Talisman as a true weapon, staining it with the blood of the very People it should serve; she felt just as reluctant to use the Spear she held in her own hands. But if ever there was a time to use weapons that could not be defeated, this was it.

"If you cannot free yourself, then his death will free you. Move away, my sister."

"I won't let you kill him." Cassandra took another step back, but shifted her hands on the Spear, picking out the best spot to hit Moon, to knock her out without killing her.

"Do you not see what he has done to you?" Moon stamped her foot. "He uses you, he would let you die for him. I have waited my whole life for you to return to me, and now," Moon held out her hands, seemingly unaware that she still held the dagger, "now I will not let you slip through my fingers. His glamour stops you from loving me again."

"My sister, my own, you have my love. You've always had it. You're my sister. Nothing and no one can take that away." Cassandra waited, but her sister's face did not change; it was set, jaw jutted forward in stubbornness. Moon did not believe her, Cassandra saw, and she never would. Cassandra took a step closer to Moon and Lightborn, her heart heavy with what she must do now. If she could keep their attention focused on her, then Max could still escape. She would have to live with what she'd done to Moon, but she would not let Max, and the Lands along with him, pay for her neglect of her sister.

"There is only one way you can be free of him, and I will give you this gift."

"It is no gift. If you try to hurt him, I will kill you myself."

"Do you hear yourself?" Moon looked to Max, spitting out her words. "Is this what you wanted? Not only will she die for you, but she would kill me, her own sister, her only *fara'ip*. The Basilisk was right! You are no Guardian, Prince of Death! Everything you touch is poisoned and destroyed. Give me back my sister!"

Moon threw herself at Max, dagger raised, but even as Cassandra raised the Spear to club her sister down, Moon's words cut through her mind, dripping misery as they went. *The Basilisk was right?* Oh, god, it was *Moon* who had betrayed them to the Basilisk, *Moon* who had told the Basilisk where they were, who had brought the Hunt to Honor of Souls' home. Not Lightborn, but *Moon*.

And it was Lightborn now who lunged for Moon, tackling her, knocking her off her feet and rolling over until she was twisting in his arms. Cassandra took another step back and began to circle them as they struggled on the floor. If she could get a blow in . . .

Lightborn cried out, and the coppery smell of blood filled the air. He rolled free, pushing away from Moon, his left arm clutched in his right hand. Moon staggered back to her feet, white-faced and pale as her namesake, blood marking the edge of her dagger.

"Go!" Lightborn said to Max. "Quickly."

Cassandra threw herself between Max and her sister,

but Moon ran, not toward Max as Cassandra expected, but back, toward the door.

"Guards!" she called.

They must have been waiting in the passage.

The first guard brushed Moon aside as if she had been no more than a curtain. He ran straight for Cassandra, but just as she changed her grip on the Spear to sweep his legs from under him, he spun around and hacked at the man coming behind him. At this several of the other guards also turned on their fellows, not, as far as Cassandra could see, in a true attempt to kill them, but as if to drive them from the room. Cassandra glanced aside at Lightborn. He was on his feet again, blood darkening the sleeve of his left arm and dripping from his fingers to the floor. His sword was raised in his right hand, and he stood his ground to the left of where Max stood before the Cauldron.

"Heads up," she called, and threw the Spear. It embedded itself in the wall a handspan from Max's head and he nodded at her, smiling. Best that he have all the Talismans within his own reach.

Cassandra drew her sword, stepped lightly around the soldier with his back to her, and cut down the man in front of him with two swift slashes at his hamstrings. The Rider she'd helped nodded his thanks as he turned to the next enemy. Cassandra, untroubled by the worry of telling friend from foe, simply struck back at anyone who attacked her. She worked her way around the room, trying to get closer to where Max and Lightborn stood, their backs against the sideboard. Like her, Lightborn did not hesitate to kill the attackers, he must know which of these guardsmen were his own followers. But was this a trick? Would he appear to save them only to betray them?

And where was Moon? Cassandra thought she saw a flash of red color in the doorway, but focused her efforts on killing the Rider in front of her, sweeping his sword to the side, the palm of her hand against the flat of his blade, and thrust forward with her own. The Rider moved his left arm as if to copy her parry, and her blade went through his forearm. She wished she could believe that Moon had simply run away. But she knew, sickened, that was too much to hope for. Moon had gone for help. Could Cassandra do anything else wrong?

Apparently she could. She had forgotten she was not carrying her *gra'if* blade, and when her opponent twisted aside in the last moment to keep her sword point from entering his chest, his foot slipping in a pool of blood on the floor, she did not bother to compensate, and her darkmetal blade jammed, wedging in the bones of the man's elbow and pulling her forward as the Rider went down. She let go of her sword before she could be pulled off her feet, just as a blast of cold air struck her, pushing the breath from her lungs and replacing it with the smell of old blood and rot. She put out a hand to steady herself, grabbing the sleeve of a nearby soldier without thought as to whether he was friend or foe. She heard Lightborn call out a warning, but before she could react, another wave of coldness passed through her, bringing with it a sound so low it shivered in her bones. Now she remembered, they had heard this, felt this, in Griffinhome. *The Hunt,* she thought, *someone calls the Hunt.*

She turned back toward the sideboard, but Max and Lightborn were no longer there. They were farther along the wall now, Max with the Cauldron in one arm, the Spear in his other hand, and Lightborn defending them both. Before she could take more than a step toward them, a net was thrown over her, weighted edges pulling her down. Her knife was already in her hand, but cutting through was going to take more time than she had.

"Max!" she called. "Max!" Through the openings in the net she could see him take two steps toward her, hefting the Spear in his left hand. That wasn't what she wanted. "Go!" she yelled. "The Hunt comes. Go!" As he hesitated, drawn back by Lightborn's hand on his arm, Cassandra gave him what she hoped was a confident smile. She tapped the torque at her throat, hoping he could see what she was doing under the net.

"I still live!" she cried out, and had the satisfaction of seeing Max's acknowledging grin before—

SLAM!

At the Wild Rider's camp, Lightborn was quiet a long time when he was told about his home, long enough that Max started to feel a reluctant concern. But he couldn't let Lightborn's obvious shock and sorrow distract him from the explanations he needed. The Wild Riders had seated the wounded Griffin Lord on a rock, well-padded with saddlecloths, while their Healer—a Dragonborn Sunward, Max noticed—bound up Lightborn's wounded arm, apparently without the *dra'aj* to Heal him outright. Max needed to hear what Lightborn had to say, needed to know whether he could trust him again. Now, above all, he needed this distraction, when his whole body shivered with the necessity of going to Cassandra immediately, though he knew it was the wrong thing to do, though he told himself that if they had wanted her dead, they would not have used the net.

Finally, Lightborn nodded, opening his eyes and taking a deep breath that was almost a sob. "I am happy I did not know this when I was with the Basilisk, just now. Not even *my* powers of dissembling could have saved me. But *his*," Lightborn shook his head, lower lip between his teeth, "his are greater than I would have thought possible. Was he so sure of me, then?" He looked up at Windwatcher. "No," he said, in answer to the older Rider's question, "I did not know where my mother hid. We often thought it best that there were things I did not know."

Windwatcher grunted. "Are you saying that your mother knows you are a traitor?"

*Good question,* Max thought.

"I did not think," Lightborn said, gritting his teeth as the Wild Rider helping him tightened the bandage and tied it off, "that I was a traitor." He frowned, looking up at Max. "Though it sounds trivial now, even self-serving, I never meant to choose between you. I never thought there was a need. You had always been at odds, you and Dreamer, when we were young. Too much alike. I thought your dispute with him a mere continuation of this. At first, I told myself I could reconcile you; I saw myself earning a place in the Songs as the great Peacemaker." He shook his head, hissing softly as he let the Wild Rider draw a well-worn leather shirt over his arm.

"I thought you should let the Talismans choose. Either they would choose him, or they would not."

Blood on the Snow looked as if he would speak, but Max held up his hand, and the older Rider relaxed once more. Lightborn needed to do this, Max knew, to purge himself.

Lightborn continued, absorbed in what he was saying. "I did not consider the right or the wrong of the matter. I did not see that there *was* a right or a wrong. I only saw that you were acting willfully, denying something to Dreamer of Time because of old wrongs. I see now that I thought the Talismans *would* choose him. I see now that I always thought he had the right of it, that I let him lead me, decide for me, because I thought he would win. It is . . . easier to be on the winning side.

"I never thought of what I was doing as betrayal. You were both my friends, almost my *fara'ip*. I thought you could speak to each other through me. I told myself I never chose him, you see, so I told myself that I never betrayed you."

"You betrayed them both," Blood said.

Lightborn nodded, his gaze fixed on that long ago, far away time, on the Rider he had been then.

"You could say that finally the Basilisk chose for me," Lightborn said. He looked up at Max, a ghost of his former grin appeared on his face. "One day I found that my ability to say 'no' to him had vanished. That my loyalty to you," here Lightborn shook his head again, a spasm of pain crossing his features, "that what I saw as my loyalty to you, would cost my life, and more than my life. I began to be afraid. Is that when you knew?"

"I guessed," Max said, thinking back to that time.

"Now, of course, many people know that disloyalty to the Basilisk can bring much worse than death. Now he has the Hunt." Lightborn frowned. "The Basilisk Prince. People little understand how well he is named. His heart is a living stone. A hard reflection of a true prince, like an image in a mirror. The calling of the Hunt is not the greatest of the evils he has done. I began to understand, to learn, during the Banishment. You were right, all those years ago. He is a Basilisk, and he will make the Lands a brittle place, as smooth as glass. A reflection of his emptiness, his cruelty. Better we should not be, better we should Fade, if it is our time, than that we lose our nature. I believed myself changed when I became aware of what he really was, I confessed to my mother, but there was little then that we could do but wait for your return. Then came the rumor that the Basilisk had the Chant of Binding, and I was once more afraid. When we met at my mother's house, when you did not know me . . ." Lightborn shrugged, hissing in his breath as his movement jostled his injured arm.

"Once again you did not choose," Blood said.

Lightborn nodded. "How well you see me." He straightened as much as he could, still sitting on the padded rock. "I think that even then I was telling myself I did not need to choose that neither of you knew."

"Have you chosen now?" Windwatcher's growl was menacing, and Max saw that he was not the only one who'd had doubts about Lightborn. But unlike Windwatcher, Max had not seen the ruins of Griffinhome.

Lightborn looked up at Max. "You saved me," he said. "In peril of your life, and more than your life, you waited to save mine. You *are* the Prince Guardian, and you hold the Heart of the People. The Sword of Truth stood at your right hand. I was dying, and at your bidding, that same Sword touched me and restored to me my life. Whether you knew yourself or not, at that moment, you showed me what the Heart of the People truly is, you showed me *your* true nature. That you would risk everything to do what was right. What further signs did I need to direct my path? At that moment, truly, I chose."

Max searched Lightborn's face, as if there would somehow be some mark. He found himself convinced, not by what was there but by what wasn't there. Lightborn was relaxed, Max saw, completely relaxed without any of the brittle tension that had characterized him for so long. Max held out his hand, but when Lightborn took it in both of his and ducked his head to kiss it, Max pulled him to his feet, and into his arms.

"I would have waited for dancing girls," he said gruffly.

"I would suggest that we wait no further," Blood said, after a moment had passed. "This camp is known to Walks Under the Moon, and it cannot take her long to bring the Basilisk's forces down upon us."

"I am not certain that Moon will continue to aid the Basilisk," Lightborn said, "now that her sister has been separated from the Prince. Moon's motivations are entirely personal; her purpose is to restore her *fara'ip,* not to help the Basilisk."

Max nodded, his hand on Lightborn's shoulder. "As you've shown us, people don't always get to choose whether they'll help the Basilisk," he said. "We have to plan for what she *can* do, not for what she *might* do. She has been here, she can bring others." He lifted his hand to his throat and touched the dragon torque resting on his collarbone. "We'll split up, and I'll join you once I've found Cassandra."

"You cannot go, my lord," Windwatcher said. "Send me, I will take some of my men—"

Lightborn turned to speak to the older Rider but

paused when Max held up his hand. "I am the only one who *can* go—"

"My lords." It was one of the Moonward twins. "My lords, Walks Under the Moon has brought the Singer Wait for the Dawn to have speech with you."

Max lowered his hand and looked at the Riders with him. Windwatcher had put his hand on his sword hilt without seeming aware of it; Blood pursed his lips in a silent whistle.

Lightborn shrugged, grinning broadly. "As ever, you are proven correct, my lord Guardian."

Max knew from the borrowed motley that the young Singer Twilight Falls Softly wore in camp that Singers in the Basilisk Prince's court were forced to wear his colors but it was still a shock to see this Starward Singer dressed in solid magenta.

"Since when have Singers worn any colors but their own?" Max smiled pleasantly as the Starward Singer's ivory cheeks reddened. It showed sense to send a Singer to parley. Even Solitaries and Naturals recognized the neutrality of Singers as the keepers of the People's histories, teaching them their own Songs so that nothing would be lost. But to see a Singer in the Basilisk's deep magenta livery rather than in the traditional multicolored clothing . . . Max shook his head. It only underscored what Lightborn had said of the Basilisk's goals.

"My lord Guardian," the Singer said, bowing. His voice was well-modulated and pleasing, but his greater Gift lay in his memory, not in his singing voice. "The Basilisk Prince sends you greetings, and asks that you meet with him."

"No." Windwatcher and Blood on the Snow spoke in unison. Lightborn merely laughed.

"You see how I am counseled," Max said, shrugging and spreading his hands. "I do not believe that the Basilisk has anything to say to me that he has not already said."

"My lord Guardian," the Singer said. "I was instructed

that if you refused, I was to tell you that the Basilisk holds Sword of Truth, and that he wishes to discuss with you how she might be set free."

"And does her sister, who stands with you, have nothing to say to her freedom?"

The Singer turned with a courteous bow to Moon, but the young Rider looked away, studying her feet. It was impossible to tell from the way she shook her head whether she was under coercion herself, or whether she helped the Basilisk willingly. In spite of what she had said, Max found it hard to believe that Moon would actually stand by and let the Basilisk harm Cassandra.

"Wait." Lightborn stepped forward and put his hand on Max's forearm. "What proof can you give us that Sword of Truth still lives?"

Max touched the dragon torque at his throat, its warmth all the answer he needed. Still, let Lightborn's question stand. What would the Basilisk's answer be?

"She has bid me to remind you, if I had speech of you, my lord Guardian, that it is better to be a dead lion than a live jackal."

Max cut off his laughter before the tears under it rose to the surface. He nodded at Lightborn's questioning face. Only Cassandra would have thought of that.

"Tell me his offer," Max said, when he could trust his voice.

"He will free Sword of Truth and allow her to live in peace wheresoever she chooses if you will give him the Talismans."

Max opened his mouth, but no sound came out. Strange how something could still shake you, even though you expected it. Some little part of him still believed, somehow, that the Basilisk would not dare to ask.

"I tell you we waste our time." Moon's voice cut through the cold air between them. "He will not do it. He will let her die before he fails in his Guardianship," Moon almost spit the word out. "Sword of Truth is nothing to him."

Max ignored this, though he wondered how he had never noticed just how much the younger Rider hated him. "You will give me some time to consider?"

"If I may, I will stay and await your answer."

"In spite of the colors you wear, you may stay." Max took a deep breath and expelled it slowly. He pointed at Moon. "*She* may not."

Still not looking at him, Moon made a sneer of distaste, and with a CRACK! she was gone.

Max stood alone in the tent they had put up to house the Talismans. He hadn't looked beyond this moment, beyond having them with him again. Beyond saving them from the Basilisk. Everyone had thought that finding them, keeping them from the Basilisk, would be all that was needed. Did they seem more awake now? He couldn't be sure. It may have been only that they were together now, and he with them. Four now, after so many turns of Sun, Moon, and Stars, instead of only three. He cupped his hands around the Cauldron, bent forward until his face was in the bowl, as if he were dipping his face into a basin of cool water. What if they were five, not four? What if he took them to the Stone? There could be no safer place for them . . .

He felt a stirring, as flames within him rose, and he straightened, his hands still on the Cauldron.

Clearly, this was what they wanted. Was it possible? Was there now a High Prince to be brought to the Stone? But what had changed in the last few sunwidths? Unless Lightborn . . . Max sat down heavily on the small folding stool that stood before the chest holding the Talismans. What about Lightborn? It was possible. Max grinned and shook his head. Lightborn had changed since the time before the Great War, when the Basilisk Prince had asked for the Testing. He had changed and grown even since Max's own return to the Lands. Was that what the Talismans had been waiting for? Would they now Choose?

Max closed his eyes, reached out again with his Phoenix heart, but this time there was no answering surge of flame. The Talismans had told him all they had to tell for now. Perhaps he grasped at straws. Perhaps, after all, there was to be no High Prince, and the Cycle would not turn . . . perhaps it was only that the Talismans wished to be joined with the last of their *fara'ip*. Well, then, he would do that much for them. And for himself. And if there should, after all, be more than that? Well and good, he would be ready.

But there was something he had to do first. Max closed his eyes and curled his fingers around the dragon torque at his neck, the scales warm and pliant. She was alive. Alive and presumably safe, though unable to Move. Well, he could think of two reasons for that. Unconscious or Bound. Either way, even the Basilisk would not offer to trade him anything other than a live Cassandra. He hoped they were keeping her in the tower room and not the dungeon.

He reached out to stroke the Dragon helm sitting next to the Talismans on an old piece of embroidered silk that Blood on the Snow had given him. The rest of the *gra'if* she couldn't wear into the Citadel was here as well, her gauntlets and greaves, her swords and daggers. Cassandra had Moved to him using his own *gra'if,* but he didn't think he could do that. Her ability to Move to him had more to do with her being a Healer, he knew, and specifically with having Healed him many times, than with her having used his *gra'if*.

As he pulled his own gauntlets on, he remembered the darkmetal shackles, and tucked her thin mailed gloves into his belt.

"You will go to her, then?"

Max hadn't heard Blood on the Snow enter the tent behind him. "I must," he said without turning around. "She came for me." Even if it was just the Oath that brought her, he thought, even if that was all it was, he had to go after her now. He touched the Dragon torque again. He had bound her to him the only way he could, so that the end of the Banishment wouldn't separate them. He hoped it would be enough.

He turned to face his father, unprepared to find the Wild Rider smiling.

"I will not stop you, my son." Blood's voice was a soft thread of sound. "On the contrary. I came to be sure that you understood what this," Blood touched the torque around Max's neck with the tip of his index finger, "bound you to."

"I understand," Max said. In the look he exchanged with his father, Max saw all the words that neither of them could say, as the ghost of the woman they had lost stood between them.

"Go to her," Blood whispered, stepping back from him.

Max emptied his mind of everything except his missing torque. He knew where it was the same way the he knew where his feet were, where the tips of his fingers touched the inside of his gloves. It was a part of him, he had only to Move toward that part of his fire that was— There!

He was in a broad passageway, a part of the Citadel he had never seen. The walls were paneled in darkwood, and the floors were dressed in reddish stone, polished mirror smooth. His Phoenix torque lay under his right hand, on top of a hall table. Of course. As it was really *his gra'if,* they would have been able to remove it. The table also held a vase filled with apple blossoms and the weapons Cassandra had been carrying, several daggers, a throwing knife, and a sword with blood hastily and poorly wiped off. Max hooked the Phoenix torque—he no longer thought of it as his—through his belt to leave both hands free.

Next to the table was an ordinary darkwood chamber door, such as might lead to any bedroom or sitting room. This door, however, had a gleaming inlay, bright and silvery and hard to focus on. The door was Signed. Max knew who was behind the door, and even though he knew there was nothing he could do about it, he flattened himself against it, his cheek pressed to the door's tooled surface, hands reaching as if he could force his fingers through the wood, as if his thoughts, his love, could pass through. He couldn't move, unwilling to go without her; unwilling to face the decision he now had to make.

He didn't Move until he heard the sound of approaching feet.

Max looked across the makeshift table at Blood on the Snow, Lightborn, and Windwatcher, studying each Rider in turn, assessing the different strengths he would find in them. Exactly as if they could help him. But they were Riders, he knew what they would say. He knew what he would have said himself, before he had lived his human lives. One Rider's life was a small price to pay to keep the Talismans out of the Basilisk's hands. A very small price when weighed against the good of the Lands and all the People. Cassandra would tell him the same thing herself. Everything they had done had been done with the purpose of keeping the Talismans away from the Basilisk. One Rider's life.

But Cassandra's life?

Even he might consider—for a moment—Cassandra's life a fair exchange if it bought the good of all the Lands and all the People. If sacrificing her life meant the start of a new Cycle. But if he were wrong about the possibility of a High Prince, if his hope about the change in Lightborn was nothing more than that, hope born of desperation . . . then giving up Cassandra wouldn't buy them anything. If the Cycles were ended, if he was the last Guardian, Cassandra's death at the hands of the Master of the Hunt would buy him and his followers nothing more than a little bit of time. Time they would spend running from Hounds.

Max looked at the faces across the table again, but there were still no answers there for him.

"My son," Blood said, getting to his feet. He had always looked what he was, Max thought, the oldest among them, but this was the first time he'd seen Blood move like an old man. "I know what you are thinking. You are wondering whether you can live with yourself when you have chosen your duty over your love. I once made such a choice, and I tell you, you can. But I tell you this, also. While it is possible to live with the decision should you choose duty, you will wish it were not. Do not speak hastily. Weigh what you must do." He gathered up the other two Riders with a sideways jerk of his head and led them out of the tent.

Max took a deep breath. His father's understanding was more comforting than he could have imagined, though it didn't help him. It was easy to choose between right and wrong; it was much harder to choose between two things when both were right.

And what, after all, if he were wrong? Would Cassandra's death buy the Talismans the time they needed for the Prince to appear? He had said, arrogantly he now saw, that they could ignore the Basilisk. But the Basilisk would not stop hunting him, would not stop killing his friends, there would always be someone dear to him—he looked through the tent opening to where Lightborn and Windwatcher had joined Blood on the Snow at the far side of the clearing. When they felt his stare and turned to look back at him, he shook his head minutely and lowered his face into his hands. This had to stop, and stop now.

He was in very great danger of making the same mistakes he'd made the first time around. When he'd let his own arrogance and his own pride make his decisions for him. This time he'd better think. All those years in the Shadowlands, planning other people's campaigns, testing strategies. What had he learned? What were his goals? What did he want to happen?

He could not let the Basilisk have the Talismans. He could not let the Basilisk kill Cassandra.

He could kill the Basilisk.

Max's laughter hurt his throat. It was so obvious he felt stupid. He saw exactly how he could do it, too. And if things went wrong, well, the Talismans would be where it seemed they wished to be. It was worth the risk.

He strode to the doorway of the tent, looked around the Riders outside until he caught the waiting Singer's eye and nodded. He motioned toward his father and Lightborn and waited until they were all gathered around him.

"I have made my decision," he said. "But I will tell it only to the Basilisk himself."

The Basilisk's Guidebeast set was the most intricate Cassandra had ever seen, each piece carefully carved and inlaid with stones of different colors to make them as lifelike as possible. The little ruby-and-bloodstone Dragons that were her pawns even seemed to feel warm. Cassandra picked up her Cauldron and moved it two spaces to the left, where it could protect her High Prince. The long sleeves of her red, silver, and black gown didn't quite cover the darkmetal cuffs on her wrists, and the chain that shackled them together swung, tapping against the edge of the table.

Cassandra leaned back in her chair. They had taken all her weapons from her, but her *gra'if* mail shirt they could not remove without killing her, and she had deliberately left the high collar of the gown open at her throat to let it show. She didn't worry about her lack of weapons. Even the manacles didn't trouble her, though they were threaded through a darkmetal bolt on the floor at her feet. Eventually, the Basilisk would get careless, venture too close, and she would kill him. She looked around the small chamber at the Signs embedded in the walls, then back at the Rider across the table who had powered them. But perhaps she would save killing him for a last resort.

"What are your plans for my sister?"

"I have no plans," the Basilisk said, studying the board. "I have fulfilled my bargain. I have taken you from the Prince Guardian."

Cassandra looked around the room, at the darkmetal and onyx embedded in the walls. "Somehow I don't think this is what Walks Under the Moon had in mind."

"My dear," the Basilisk looked up at her from under his brows. "I said she could have you. I never said she could keep you."

Half an hour, more or less, they'd had together, in this room, before the Basilisk came to play Guide-beasts. No, Cassandra was sure that wasn't what Moon had had in mind when she'd made her bargain. At first, when Moon had knelt at her feet and put her head in Cassandra's lap, she'd held herself stiffly away from the younger Rider. But a memory of the little girl who'd sat like this so often relaxed her spine, and a half-forgotten habit brought up her hand to stroke Moon's hair.

"Do you remember the Fair at Vareye'vo?"

"Hmmm." Cassandra had kept stroking Moon's hair.

"The pageants, the Cloud Horse races, the tournaments of fencing. Singing. That is what I want. I want us to have those days again."

"Do you think the Basilisk Prince will give it to us?"

"He is the only one who makes an attempt."

"But he is not the High Prince; what he's attempting is wrong."

Moon turned her face up to look Cassandra in the eye. "I am not so certain he is not the High Prince," she said. "The Songs say the identity of the Prince will be as clear as a sound from a bell, and there is no other obvious candidate. It *must* be him."

The "him" who sat across the table from Cassandra now.

"I would be interested to hear about your experiences in the Shadowlands, when we are both at more leisure," the Basilisk said. He picked up his goblet of wine from the small side table next to his chair.

"I doubt there will be much leisure in my future."

He raised his eyes to her as he set his wine down again. "It can be arranged. We must know more about them, and soon, if we are to assume our rightful rule over them. I know you could give me valuable insights into that world, and the value of its peoples."

Cassandra lowered her eyes, pretending to study the board. Only years of discipline kept her from launching herself across the board at him. She couldn't afford to show him her reaction to his words. She'd seen the effects of his interest in Malcolm Jones' home—seen the remains of Mal's human wife and children spread throughout his house. Did the Basilisk really expect her to help set the Hunt on humans who had not even the possibility of Moving to delay the inevitable? Who could never have *gra'if?* Nausea twisted through her stomach, and she forced herself to swallow.

The Basilisk made his move, pushing one of his own pawns, a small golden version of his Guidebeast, ahead one square. Cassandra slowly released the breath she'd been holding, sat forward, and took his Spear of War with her Prince Guardian.

"The people of the Shadowlands are not so very different from our People," she said. "As thinking, feeling beings, we are motivated by similar things; we love for similar reasons, and we hate for similar reasons as well. We fear different things, but we fear."

"This does not surprise me, though I believe it would others." The Basilisk leaned back from the game and picked up his wine again, turning the goblet in his fingers as he gazed into the air over her head. "There are Songs that say the humans may be our distant kin, debased and degenerate from living in the Shadowlands." He took a sip of wine and nodded. "This may be so. It may be that brought here, as I plan to do for the deserving, they may recover their birthrights as Riders. Once I have restored the Lands, and we Riders are returned to our ancient glories, there may be much I can do for these poor cousins of ours."

"Our ancient glories?"

"You are young, and it is possible that you do not know the Songs as well as you might, living for so long in the Shadowlands. Those Songs which claim that Guardians and Princes may come from the ranks of Solitaries and Naturals have been proven false." By whom, Cassandra wondered. Or was this the result of more of Moon's research? "It is clear that only Riders can be Princes of the Lands, since we alone among the three Peoples can Move."

Cassandra carefully controlled her face. *He doesn't know,* she realized, thinking of Water Sprites and Trees.

"In other Cycles we have been tolerant of the demands and foolish understanding of both Solitaries and Naturals, and it has made them arrogant, caused them to hold us in contempt, and to cheat us of our power. In their defiance and conceit, they drained the Lands of *dra'aj,* and brought about the lessening we see around us."

Cassandra glanced up, and her fingertips froze on her High Prince's dragon. For a moment, she had seen not the Basilisk Prince sitting across from her, but *a* Basilisk, its snaky cock's head turned to one side to fix its eye on her, its dragon's tail curving up over the back of his chair, like a stinger on a scorpion. Then a flicker of something else, something darker, and then it had been the Basilisk Prince again, turning a captured Spear over in his hand as he watched the board. Cassandra dropped her gaze and forced her hand to finish moving her pawn. No one of her generation had ever seen this, few would believe it possible. A Guidebeast. Even the Basilisk Prince did not seem to be aware that he had transformed. It was true, then, she thought, the absence of the Beasts *was* due to insufficient *dra'aj,* a problem the Basilisk Prince evidently did not have. She'd seen something else, though, in the last moment, just before he had resumed his Rider's shape. And that was something she *had* seen before. Not a Basilisk exactly, but something scaly and leathery, something familiar.

When she killed the Hound, she remembered, her stomach sinking, it had taken on the shape of a Rider, the last shape it had before it Faded.

"They cannot be allowed to continue," the Basilisk was saying. Cassandra finished her move. "The Lands must be saved. Those who agree and will conform themselves will be allowed to do their parts to aid the efforts of restoration, as those who have helped me with the Garden. Those who do not are the enemies of all of us, and the enemies of the Lands."

The most horrible thing, Cassandra thought, was that the Basilisk believed what he said was the truth. But so had Lightborn, and so had Moon, and she had been wrong about them. Max had said the Dragonborn could sense "trueness" in people, but surely there had to be more to it than just knowing when people believed what they said?

She shut her eyes and breathed deeply, as if she were preparing to Heal. Instead of touching the Basilisk, however, instead of looking at only his body, she looked deeper, trying to do consciously what she did without thought when Healing. When Lightborn had said he could sense her *dra'aj*, she had told him it was because she had Healed him. The Healing normally used the *dra'aj* of both parties. She had never bothered much with the *dra'aj* of humans; in most cases there was so little of it that it often had no effect on the health. But if she could see the Basilisk's *dra'aj* ... She could feel herself flushing, as flame began to rise in her. When she touched an addict, she thought, she touched more than the damage done to the body, she touched ... there. She gripped the arms of her chair. This was like stepping to the edge of the sidewalk and instead finding yourself on the rim of the Grand Canyon. Vertigo, nausea, and—

"There are people like you in the Shadowlands," she said, relaxing and opening her eyes. "They are called psychopaths." She moved her Guardian into a space three squares from the Basilisk's High Prince.

"I believe it's my game," she said.

# Chapter Nineteen

"I UNDERSTAND YOU WISH to speak to me." The Basilisk looked beyond Max at the Wild Riders spread out on the hill behind him. "You seem to have fewer followers than when we last met on the field."

Max steeled himself to appear as calm and relaxed as the Basilisk seemed to be. Dreamer of Time had always been at his sunniest, his most expansive and generous when he thought that things were going his way. Max resisted the feeling that if he only explained once more, if he only tried again, the Basilisk would hear him, and this time it would be different. The time that he could have reached Dreamer by speech alone was long past.

"I wish to discuss your offer, and to make a counter-offer of my own."

"I am happy that you would discuss this," the Basilisk said. "I grow fond of Sword of Truth; I would prefer not to punish her for your stubbornness."

Max took a deep breath and forced his fists to open. He didn't need to be reminded that failure to comply would mean Cassandra's death. Or worse. The Basilisk could use the Chant of Oblivion and leave Cassandra stranded in some inhospitable part of the Lands, helpless and immobile, or he could simply feed off her himself until she slowly Faded, feeling her *dra'aj* drain away, unable to prevent it.

"You say that if I give you the Talismans, you will free Sword of Truth, and let her go safe."

"I do."

"If I agree," Max gritted his teeth against the murmur of sound behind him. "If I agree," he said, raising his voice, "I would want further conditions."

"The life of Sword of Truth is not sufficient?" The Basilisk Prince smiled. "Perhaps Walks Under the Moon was right after all."

*Don't let him distract you,* Max told himself. "I would want an amnesty," he said. "I would want freedom and safety for all who have followed me, whether Rider, Natural, or Solitary."

"I think not." The Basilisk shook his head. "I think that is too much. I will kill your lover and take the Talismans from you another day."

"What if I bring you to the Stone?" This time there was silence behind him.

"I do not need the Stone. I have the Chant of Binding."

"But you claim to be the High Prince. If that is so, the Stone will proclaim you, and you will not need the Chant of Binding. Both Naturals and Solitaries must acknowledge and obey you, if the Stone proclaims you."

Even the wind seemed to have died down; no leaves blew across the ground. Lightborn had said this might be enough. Was he right, Max wondered. Would the chance to be proclaimed tempt the Basilisk? Had he read the man right, finally, after all these years?

"This is all it takes?" The Basilisk's voice was at its most musical. "All that time ago, all I had to do was find someone you loved? You would have given me the Talismans then?"

Max clenched his jaw tight, knowing that to answer would undo all his plans.

"Very well, I agree to your bargain, Dawntreader,

Prince Guardian. You will give me the Talismans, and take me to the Stone of Virtue, in exchange for the lives and freedoms of all your followers." The Basilisk Prince tilted his head coyly. "Your followers, Dawntreader, not you."

Once again Max ignored the murmur of sound behind him. He was neither surprised nor concerned by this detail. His own freedom had never been part of his plan.

"Will you send me Sword of Truth now?" was all he said.

"I am not so trusting as that."

Max nodded, it had been worth a try. "Once again, it is I who must trust you."

"This is a small thing, Dawntreader, it costs me nothing to give it. Especially if I gain all."

That was the difference between them, Max thought. The Basilisk could consider Cassandra's life a small thing. He could give it up, and it would cost him nothing. He wouldn't spend the rest of his life regretting it, wondering if he'd done the right thing.

The Basilisk held out his hand. "You will not lose by this, Dawntreader. I will not shut you out of the great work. All that I promised you, I can still do, if you would but join me."

Max kept his hands at his sides. "Be here at dawn."

Later, he sat cross-legged beside the fire they had built in front of the tent that housed the Talismans.

"I'm not so sure what I would do in your place, but I believe that I know why you do this," Lightborn said, his hand on Max's shoulder. "You did it once for me. Better we all die, than that we desert one another."

"What profits us if we all die, and the Basilisk has the Talismans?" Windwatcher said. "My Prince," Max looked to where the Sunward Rider sat on the far side of the fire, "you cannot do this. No one honors Sword of Truth more than I. I would have welcomed her in my *fara'ip,* blood of my blood. But the price of her life is too high."

Max nodded, his neck creaking with stiffness.

"No." Blood's voice cracked across the space between them like a whip. "The Talismans are his. It is not for us, and most especially, Watches the Wind, it is not for *you,* to tell the Prince Guardian what he can and cannot do." He looked at Windwatcher with a face as cold as his name. "Do we forget so quickly how we came to be here? Do we forget so quickly what occurred the last time the Guardian told us what must be done and was not heeded?"

It was Windwatcher's turn to nod his head. "You are right, Old One. I spoke out of fear and uncertainty." The old warrior turned to Max. "I ask your pardon, my Prince."

Max grinned. He only hoped he seemed more confident than he felt. "Trust me," he said. "I have a plan."

"He has a plan," Blood said, his chuckle rusty. "Shall we do less than the Basilisk does? Let us trust him."

⌒

"He will trade for your life."

Her first feeling was elation. He loved her that much, he would give up everything, the world itself, for her. But following close behind that elation, so close that it was almost the same feeling, was horror at what he had done. Her knees gave way and she sank down into the cushioned seat next to the gaming table, now with its board reset for a new game. Max would save her, but at what cost? No matter how much he loved her, how could he do this? Didn't he realize that this was proof of love she would spend her whole life regretting? Did *she* have no say in this?

*Get a hold of yourself, woman,* she thought grimly, gripping the arms of her chair. *He's got a plan.* She almost smiled. *He's* always *got a plan.*

"You have no reason for so much fear, Sword of

Truth. It is not only his agreement that could save you. I will not harm you unless I must. You have other uses."

She should have seen that coming. Why kill her when keeping her alive would be so much more useful? Amazing that he thought this would reassure her. As long as she was alive, she was a warranty for Max's good behavior. As long as she was alive, the Prince Guardian was vulnerable.

And that was the real problem, wasn't it? Because Max's plans had been known to go wrong in the past. There was that time in Florence, when they'd had to let themselves down the castle walls at the ends of knotted sheets, minutes ahead of the men coming to put them in the dungeons. If there was any way, any way at all that the Basilisk could end up with the Talismans . . .

It was too risky. She couldn't let Max risk everything to free her.

The Troll Diggory had been bound rather more than Cassandra was, at least at this moment. His only option had been to force the Basilisk to kill him. She could do that, too. Or she might have another option. Hers was not the only death that would free them. Psychopath she'd called him, and the thing with psychos was . . .

"I find myself disinclined to part with you," the Basilisk was saying. "Once I have the Talismans, why should you not stay and help me?"

"Help you?" she said, her voice as sharp as she could make it. "You don't even know how badly you need help." She turned up her eyes and shook her head. "Fool! You stink of Hound. You transform into your Guidebeast without even being aware of it. Do you even know what that means? Or maybe you have a Chant to fix it?"

The Basilisk gripped the back of his chair, his knuckles white against his bronze skin. "If I change into my Guidebeast, it is a sign of my *dra'aj*. It is a proof that I am what I intend to be, High Prince over all the People."

"*Your dra'aj?* Really?" Cassandra pitched her voice to

its most sarcastic. If she could get him angry enough . . . "You think stealing it makes it yours? And is your Guidebeast twisted and scaly? Are its eyes filmed over with webbing? Does poison ooze from its joints?" Cassandra took a deep breath while he looked at her in shock, disbelief warring with fear in his eyes. "You are draining the *dra'aj* from others, everyone knows this. I don't know how or why you started, but now you can't stop, and you need more and more of it." She stopped to take a breath. "It's turning you into a Hound, you stupid fool. And what good will your Talismans do you then?

"Let me help you," she said, holding out her hands to him. "Let me Heal you. You have fallen from the True, but it may not be too late." *Come a little closer,* she thought. I'll *help you all right.* It would mean her death either way. The Basilisk might kill her, or he might come close enough that she could kill him. Since the Room was Signed, killing the Basilisk would lock her into it forever. But she told herself that death from starvation was an easy price if she killed the Basilisk first.

"You should not say such things to me, Dragon spawn."

"Why? What are you going to do? Kill me?" she said with a sneer, looking him up and down and curling her lip. "You can't, you need me for your little trade. So go ahead and threaten me, Hound spit, see if you can frighten me."

White-faced, the Basilisk picked up the Guidebeast board, scattering the pieces over the floor, and struck her across the face. She had meant to let him hit her, to lure him closer, but her reflexes for once betrayed her. They had her arms up in time to take the sharp edge of the board on her forearm, but not fast enough to grab the board while he still held it. She felt the sharp pain of the bone snapping. *Just the ulna,* she said to herself as she allowed momentum to carry her to the floor, softening the blow. The Basilisk aimed several kicks at her ribs. Her *gra'if* shirt hardened, saving her from the worst of it. She rolled into him, hoping to knock him down and get her hands around his throat, but her chains stopped her short, allowing the Basilisk time to grab the small table that held his wine and stun her with a blow to the head.

He grabbed her by the hair and shook her. The pain was tight and hot, but pain alone would not kill her.

"You are wrong," he said. "I *can* frighten you." She did not see what he did, but even with her eyes shut, and even with the throb of pain in her arm and head, she could feel the difference in the room as he deactivated the Signs. He stomped to the door and threw it open, lifted the bone ornament he wore on a darkmetal chain around his neck to his lips and blew.

Here, so close to the Horn, Cassandra felt the call pulse through her body like the blast wave of an explosion. Only the manacles prevented her from being flung against the wall with the fury of the sound. Did she feel the bolt which fastened her chains to the floor give a little?

The Basilisk came back to where she lay and grabbed her by the hair again, giving her head another shake. "You know so much about Hounds, you will enjoy the company of one. Perhaps you could try to Heal it."

~~~

The sun was long gone, the moon had risen, and the fire had died down to coals. Soon they would have to either go to sleep or put more wood on the fire. Scattered throughout the clearing were other fires, around which other small groups of Riders were equally wakeful, talking, eating, polishing weapons. A few were singing softly. They all knew that the Basilisk would be back at dawn, and it was as if no one wanted to spend what might be their last hours asleep.

"You should not go alone," Lightborn said, as if continuing a conversation.

Max sat up and poked a branch into the fire, watched

as it flared up before adding another. "Don't worry," he said, "that's not the plan." He turned to where Blood on the Snow's profile was limned by the flickering firelight. "The Troll Hearth of the Wind, was part of your *fara'ip.* Have you any other Solitary that you can call on?"

The Wild Rider's gray eyes sparkled. "I do. The Ogre Thunder Under the Mountain is a part of the same *fara'ip.* What is your need of her?"

"It is customary, when a candidate is taken to the Stone, that it be witnessed by representatives from all the People. As he has Singers with him, there could be quite a few among the Basilisk's followers who would know this, and we should be prepared, or he may think we're bluffing. I think we can be sure the Basilisk won't be bringing any Naturals or Solitaries with him. We'll have to provide the witnesses ourselves."

"But the Stone will not Sound? You have said the Basilisk is not the true Prince. We *do* bluff?" Lightborn sat at attention, straightening from where he had been lounging on his elbow, looking back and forth between Max and Blood.

"Witnesses witness," Max said. "That's what we want them for."

"What of *Trere'if?*" Blood said. "You must have a Natural as well, and there are few within dawn's distance of us that can Walk."

"Good. Can the Moonward twins call him?"

Blood nodded. "*Trere'if* will carry my message to Thunder Under the Mountain as well."

Blood rose smoothly to his feet, crossed to where the twin Riders lounged beside their own fire, and hunkered down to speak to them. Max waited until he saw them nod and Blood returned.

"Father, can you choose ten of your Riders, all *gra'if* wearers, to go the Stone?"

"I can choose any number. Any and all of them will stand with us."

"I don't doubt it. But I don't think more than ten will fit where I need them to be." Max smiled at his father. "You'll understand when you see it."

Blood nodded, lips thinned, considering. "I would choose the Moonward twins."

"No problem. There's time for them to get back from *Trere'if* before dawn." "And the others?"

Max added another piece of tree branch to the fire. This time the wood, too green to burn properly, smoked until he'd pushed it to one side.

"Windwatcher, will you take charge of the remaining Riders?"

"Willingly. How shall we attend upon you?" The gruff soldier showed his pleasure in his smile.

Max laid his hand on the older Rider's shoulder. "Take the remaining Wild Riders, your own people, and any others who will follow you. Go to the Portals. If you do not hear from any of us before the Sun rises again in this place, destroy them."

"But, my lord—"

Max held up his hand. "The Solitaries will show you how; there are those among them who saw the Portals made. There is *dra'aj* in the Shadowlands. In this, Sword of Truth was correct," he said aside to Lightborn, "and if the worst should come, if we should fail, I would like to keep that *dra'aj* from the Basilisk." *And perhaps,* he said to himself, *the Shadowlands will survive the end of the Cycle.*

"It shall be as you wish, my lord Prince," Windwatcher said. "Lady Honor of Souls awaits with the greater part of my people. She will aid in this."

"When you see my mother," said Lightborn, looking fixedly into the fire, "give her my heart, tell her . . ."

"I will tell her you have chosen," Windwatcher said.

Lightborn smiled, and for a moment Max saw again the friend of his boyhood. *He would make a good Prince, that boy, now that he's back.*

Windwatcher bowed to Max and followed Blood on the Snow through the camp, going from Wild Rider to Wild Rider, speaking to each one, sending some for their Horses, returning others to their interrupted tasks.

Max turned back to Lightborn. The Starward Rider was leaning forward, frowning, his eyes full of a question.

"Go ahead and ask," Max said, "while there's still time."

"Why did you not take the Basilisk to the Stone before? If you knew the Stone would not proclaim him?"

Max leaned back and squeezed his eyes shut. "Humans have a saying: 'Hindsight is twenty-twenty.' " Lightborn went on looking at him and Max sighed. "I thought I shouldn't have to prove it. And I was right, I shouldn't have. I speak for the Talismans in this and all things. He is not the High Prince." The words he could use to tell Lightborn what he suspected leaped into Max's brain, but again he kept silent. "I might not know who the High Prince *is*," he said instead, "but I do know who he *isn't*. My word should have been enough. So all my critics are right. The Great War was not the Basilisk's fault. It was mine. I hadn't yet learned that there are more important things than my pride."

"And you have learned this now."

Max looked up again, but Lightborn was watching the fire. It hadn't been a question, Max realized. He wished he could be as sure as Lightborn seemed to be.

"These witnesses—others have been to the Stone in the past, then? Other Riders?" Lightborn was thinking again, his brows drawn together over eyes made sapphire by the glow of the fire.

Max nodded. "The Songs tell of Riders who have witnessed the proclamations."

"Moon is a Scholar of the Songs," Lightborn said, grasping Max's arm. "And if others have been there, she will know of them, and how to find them. They may be there already."

Max patted the other Rider's shoulder. "There can't

be anyone waiting for us, if that's what's worrying you. The Stone isn't part of the Lands."

"But then how do we Move there?"

"*You* can't Move there," Max said. "Any more than you can Move to the Shadowlands without a Portal."

"Then how . . . ah, *you* are the Portal to the Stone," Lightborn said, his voice soft. Max nodded. Was Lightborn's quick understanding a good sign? Or was he still just clutching at straws?

"Without you, the Basilisk could never be proclaimed."

"I want him to know that."

"And I said you had learned to do without your pride."

Max grinned, holding up his hands. "Wait a minute. He thinks the Stone will Sound. And if it doesn't? Well, I think he'll take the Talismans and use the Chant of Binding on them as he intended to do all along. And tell the People that the Stone did proclaim him."

"But then why take him there? What is your purpose?"

Once again the words, the explanation hovered on Max's lips. Once again he kept silent. If he was wrong, if Lightborn was *not* the High Prince . . . Max couldn't raise anyone's hopes that way. This might be their only chance to kill the Basilisk, and he didn't want anyone distracted from that. Better they all thought they Rode to their deaths.

"I'll get him away from his followers. The Stone is the only place in all of the Lands, and even the Shadowlands, where I alone control who Moves there. The only place we can outnumber him."

"And if that is not enough?"

Max looked down. "No one has ever been to the Stone, or left it, without a Guardian to Move them."

"So, if you are dead . . . ?"

Max inclined his head once, his eyes fixed on Lightborn's.

"So this is a trick?" Lightborn's smile was joyous. "We will lure him to the Stone, and we will kill him."

"Or die ourselves, yes."

"A simple plan. I like it."

―――⌐⌐―――

Cassandra smelled the Hound the moment it entered the room and redoubled her efforts to pry loose the ring that fastened her darkmetal shackles to the floor. Using the chair leg was awkward, especially with her broken arm, but she thought she felt some give to the bolts that held the ring in place. What she did not feel was the distinctive movement the air would make as the Signs reactivated, and for a moment her heart leaped and the adrenaline surge gave her strength enough to pull the bolts free. She brought her concentration to bear, pushing aside the pain in her head and the throbbing in her arm. Even if the Hound followed her through the Move, if she could focus enough—

—a bruising grip on her ankle jerked her leg up and swung her around, letting go not when she was in the air as she half expected, but back on the floor so that she only slid across the flagstones and came to a jarring stop against the hearth of the fireplace, the chains of her manacles bruising her ribs and back. *Damn,* she thought, fighting the urge to clear her head by shaking it. Leaving the Signs open had been no oversight on the Basilisk's part, but a calculated ploy. She couldn't both defend herself *and* Move. And the distraction of freedom would be enough to make her defense a poor one. Or so the Basilisk might think.

She couldn't hope to kill the Hound. The Basilisk Prince she could have managed, even with the cracked ulna, but the Hound was a different matter. She wasn't even sure that it could be killed without *gra'if,* and her mail shirt made a poor offensive weapon. If she couldn't solve Max's dilemma by killing the Basilisk, she had to do it by dying herself. Normally, you could count on a Hound for that. But this time . . .

*He's been told to scare me,* Cassandra thought, drawing in slow careful breaths to save her ribs. *So how can I get him to kill me instead?* She could start out by seeming more injured than she was. Because it had to be a kill, a clean kill. No sane person would choose death by Hound as a good method of suicide. She remembered very clearly Nighthawk's advice when he'd taught her how to kill Hounds. "Don't let them feed," he had said to her, "if it seems to you that you will not prevail, kill yourself before it begins to feed." Good advice, she was sure. Sound. She shut her eyes tight against the throbbing in her arm, a counterpoint against the ringing in her head.

Forcing air out of her lungs, she used the hearthstone and then the mantel of the fireplace to pull herself to her feet, kicking the heavy skirt of her gown out of the way. She was just straightening her knees when the Hound swept her feet out from under her and pounced on her, landing lightly on all four clawed feet, crouching over her with jerky flaps of its stunted wings. She managed to get her arms up to protect her head, but the strain on the broken bone, weighed down by her manacles, was telling. Her forearm moved as if it was not a part of her, but a dead weight. If only it were as numb as dead weight usually was, then at least it wouldn't cost her so much effort to ignore the pain.

If she couldn't concentrate enough to Move, could she concentrate enough to Heal herself? In the past, she had often Healed humans with little more than a touch, almost without thinking of it. She wasn't human, but perhaps she could Heal enough—ooof!

The Hound had pounced again, this time giving her a savage bite that might have broken ribs, except that under her clothes her *gra'if* mail shirt hardened, protecting her from the Hound's teeth. Frustrated, the Hound batted her with its spiked tail, sending her sliding partway across the room until she came up against the divan with a jarring thump.

It was playing with her like a cat, she realized, as it

morphed into a leather-and-furred dragon, deformed and wingless. But cats sometimes were careless enough to kill their prey before they intended to. Somehow, she had to get this one to do that. The Basilisk was counting on her to react to the Hound like any Rider, with fear and loathing. But she wasn't any other Rider. Either the Basilisk had forgotten that she had killed a Hound in the Shadowlands, or he had never been told. Cassandra strongly suspected it was the latter.

Could that be her approach? She swallowed and tasted blood, spat it out on the floor. Could she taunt it with the death of its pack mate? It had worked with the Basilisk, and the Basilisk, she now knew, was more than half Hound. Could she get this one angry enough, or careless enough, to kill her?

"What were you to start with?" She cleared her throat and spat out another gob of blood. "Chimera? Griffin? Just some big kitty cat, huh?"

This time, when it batted at her, she clutched at the limb—she couldn't be sure whether it was arm or leg. The scales under her hands morphed to feathers, to skin, to soft wet flesh, to rough fur and back to scales again. She clung, pain numbing her right hand, trying to bring her teeth to bear, until the Hound shook her free by the simple expedient of banging her against the wall until her grip loosened and she let go. She looked up right away, tossing her head to clear her hair from her eyes, even though it set her head to clanging like a bell.

"What's the matter? Can't keep your shape?" It circled her more warily now, pupilless eyes blinking, spiked tail lashing like a big cat's. "I've killed one of you already," she said. "Maybe you knew him? Looked like he might have had some cat in him. Or her."

The Hound snarled and sprang for her, wings sprouting from its leathery back, scales changing to feathers even as it hovered over her, claws snatching. Cassandra picked up a chair, forcing her numb right hand to close over a leg, and heaved it at the distortion hovering, wings beating, above her. The momentum of throwing the chair unbalanced her, and as she was teetering, the Hound landed on her shoulders and knocked her to the floor. Again her *gra'if* shirt hardened, saving her from having the air knocked out of her. She twisted, feeling the Hound's shardlike talons dragging through the skin of her arms, and closed her hands on its forelimbs, digging through the feathery layer to touch the skin beneath. It was not, as she somehow expected, burning hot, but cold, clammy, as if the Hound were injured or dying. Cassandra felt heat rising in her blood to answer it. She felt the heat pouring from her into the Hound.

*No,* she thought.

His Signed Room was dark and quiet, even the fire in the hearth had gone out, ashes cold now and half-burned bits of kindling spread across the singed floor. The first thing the Basilisk saw, when his eyes adjusted to the darkness in the room, was broken furniture. He drew his brows down. His Guidebeast set was scattered over the floor and several of the pieces were crushed and broken. It was not until he had peered around the room twice that he saw the body of Sword of Truth lying in a heap by the far wall, what he had taken for shafts of light her *gra'if* mail shining bright as flame through the tears in her dress. The Basilisk motioned with his hand, halting the guards at the door. His hands shook and he told himself it was rage. If the Hound had killed her, after being given strict instructions that Sword of Truth was not to be seriously harmed . . . He forced himself to breathe deeply. Her words had troubled him, but only for a moment. What she suggested was not possible. Riders did not *become* Hounds. The Hunt was the Hunt, and always had been, Cycle through Cycle. She had wanted to strike at him, that was all. To destroy his confidence. But she had chosen her weapon badly, her accusation too wild to be believed—though not too wild to punish. He strode forward, avoiding the broken furniture and crumpled rugs, and mindful of the game pieces still whole on the floor. His hand went once more to the Horn he wore around his neck. If she were dead . . .

But she was not dead. And neither was the naked Rider asleep in her arms.

"Well," the Basilisk said, his voice a bare whisper. "Perhaps I will keep her after all."

He swung around and went back to the waiting guards.

"Bring them both."

---

Dawn had the clarity that only comes on a cold fall day. Max's breath fogged in the early light. The air actually seemed colder, now that the sun was up, than it had the night before. Blood on the Snow and Lightborn flanked him. Behind them stood the Ogre Thunder Under the Mountain her green-gray bulk overshadowing the Natural *Trere'if* who seemed almost delicate beside her. Beyond them was a semicircle of Wild Riders on their Cloud Horses, all that were left after Windwatcher had taken the others to the Portals.

"If this turns out badly," Max said, "I'd like to say I'm sorry now."

"Good to hear you are so confident," Lightborn said. Blood merely shook his head, smiling.

Max grinned back. *Here we go,* he thought, as— SLAM!

The Basilisk had brought with him a full troop of mounted soldiers, all conspicuous in their soft purple clothing. One or two of the host's Cloud Horses tossed their heads as their Riders reacted to the presence of the Ogre and the Wood. It was clear from this, and from the muttering that passed through the ranks like a breeze and was almost instantly checked, that most

of them had not been told who and what they were
going to meet. The Basilisk Prince himself was flanked
by two Starward Riders, standing one at each of his
stirrups, looking like pale flames in the dawn's light.
One of them was Walks Under the Moon, and the
other—Max let out the breath he had been holding.
The other was Cassandra.

Her face was dirty, bruised, and her *gra'if* mail shirt
gleamed through tears in her clothing. There were
darkmetal cuffs around her wrists, joined with a short
chain. Max felt a flood of heat as the anger and fear
he'd carefully suppressed surged to the surface. In that
moment he wanted nothing more than to kill the
Basilisk Prince with his own hands for no other reason
than that the stone-sucking Basilisk had dared to
touch her.

But he pushed the fires of his anger back, forcing
himself to be calm, as calm as she appeared to be,
glowing in the cloudy day like torchlight, her pale skin
a golden cream, her gray eyes almost as brightly silver
as her *gra'if*. The sight of her took Max back to the
night Cassandra had killed the Hound, when she'd made
the streetlight pale by comparison. There was a young
Moonward Rider on her left, his purple cotte and leggings badly fitted, looking around him with small jerks
of his head, holding her tightly by the forearm, not like
a captor, but like a small boy who holds to his mother
in an unfamiliar place. When Max caught her eye, Cassandra smiled and gave him a "thumbs up" sign with
her left hand. Max bit the inside of his lip to keep his
face straight, blinking furiously against the tears that
threatened his eyes. He knew that look. *I'm ready,* the
look said, *let's go.* Didn't matter that he'd had no
chance to explain his plan to her, she knew he had one,
and she was ready to back him up. She was ready.

Max hoped she didn't remember that time in Florence.

The Basilisk urged his horse forward a pace, motioning to Cassandra.

"I have brought you Sword of Truth," the Basilisk said, his voice smooth and cool.

Max took a step toward her before he could stop himself.

"Not so quickly, Dawntreader. Where are the Talismans?"

"I have taken the precaution," Max said with a slight bow, "of Moving them to the Stone." He indicated the men standing behind the Basilisk. "It seemed like a prudent course."

The Basilisk inclined his own head, his gaze moving across the Wild Riders assembled behind Max. "Suppose I take you now?"

Max shrugged. "You cannot force me to Move you to the Stone," he said.

"I still have Sword of Truth," the Basilisk said, eyes narrowing.

Max held up his hand, index finger extended, as both Lightborn and Blood in the Snow stepped forward.

"How many times can you play the same card?" he said to the Basilisk. "I would have no reason to take you to the Talismans if Sword of Truth is dead."

Cassandra still smiling, eyes bright, made a noise as if she might laugh.

"Then I am ready," the Basilisk said, with a mocking bow.

"There must be witnesses," Max said.

"My guard can be our witness."

Max shook his head. "No more than a score can go, and afoot. Custom requires that the Stone's proclamation be witnessed by representatives of all the People."

The Basilisk looked over his shoulder at where Moon still stood, near the soldiers. She inclined her head once.

"So the Songs tell us," she said. "The High Prince is Prince for all the People, as the Talismans are for all the People."

"Thunder Under the Mountain will witness for all Solitaries, *Trere'if* for all Naturals," said Max. "Blood on the Snow will witness for the Wild Riders, and Lightborn for all the Riders you have given your word to leave safe. Sword of Truth I will have as well."

The Basilisk looked around him, quickly calculating. "Half a score of my men will go with us."

Max bowed. "Choose them."

Moon and Cassandra stepped forward immediately and waited to one side while the Basilisk's guards divided themselves into two groups, the smaller of which dismounted and joined Cassandra and Moon. A commotion broke out when two men from the mounted group that would be left behind tried to separate the young Moonward Rider from Cassandra. He was not armed, but he clung to her with one hand as he snarled and struck out with the other. Even their Horses were reluctant to approach him, and the guards backed away, glancing uncomfortably at one another. The mounted commander approached the Basilisk and addressed him quietly. The Basilisk, his eyes never moving from where Max stood, shrugged, and smiled.

"Very well, let him come." Max didn't understand the Basilisk's twisted smile. "Let *all* of my People be represented."

Max waited until those chosen to go were ready, standing in a rough circle in the middle of the Wild Riders' camp. He managed to insinuate himself so that he stood between Lightborn and Cassandra. She had the unknown Moonward Rider to her left. On the other side of Lightborn was the Ogre. If he didn't mind leaving everyone else to die, Max thought, he could take Cassandra now and go.

"Join hands," Max said, taking Cassandra's warm hand in his own and returning her squeeze. He had an instant's wild desire to laugh as he looked around the circle. Ogre and Wood, Wild Riders and the Basilisk. They could be the guests at some expedient but distasteful political marriage, forced by custom and against their inclinations to take part in a round dance.

He looked at Cassandra again, and her smile caught the breath in his throat.

"I will take you to the Stone," he said.

# Chapter Twenty

THE STONE WAS A PINNACLE of rock, thrusting upward through banks of bright cloud hanging miles below its edge, as solid looking as any alpine meadow. The uneven platform of its summit was no more than fifty meters square, limestone gray, without grass or bush or tree. Rough and irregular, it looked like a block of clay squared off by a giant child. Three of the edges dropped off sharply into the bottomless gorge, and even the fourth side was only slightly rounded over. The sky was a cool azure, clear and bright, the light constant, casting no shadows. There was nothing else to see.

"It does not sound." The voice was *Trere'if*'s, branches groaning. "No matter what you may do from this moment forward, Dreamer of Time, we are all witness to it. *Ma'at* does not sound. The Stone of Virtue rejects you. You are not the High Prince."

*No*, Max realized, *and Lightborn isn't either.* He'd told himself all along, since the idea had first come to him, that it was only a chance, one in a million. But his hopes had been higher than he'd known. Only the rush of standing on the Stone itself for the second time this morning saved him from being crushed with disappointment.

It was impossible to remember, between visits, what it

was like to stand here, with the rest of the Talismans, and be whole and complete. Not just the mouth that spoke, but all of the body together. This was what no one knew, that there were five Talismans, not four. The Stone, the Spear, the Sword, the Cauldron, and the Guardian. He could feel the blood hammering through his veins, the air sliding through his lungs. He could sense every rock, every crevice; he knew without looking that the Sword, Spear, and Cauldron were behind him on the fold of rock that formed the table waiting always for them here, on *Ma'at.*

Where they would wait forever, now that there was no High Prince. Now that the Cycles were at an end.

"How can it sound? I have not yet seen it. Bring it forth." The Basilisk's musical voice brought Max's attention sharply back to the matter at hand. The Cycle wasn't over yet.

"This *is* the Stone," Max said, using his most condescending smile. "We stand upon it."

The Riders behind the Basilisk murmured uneasily.

The Basilisk spun, jerking his head back and forth, clearly wishing to deny it. *Let him try,* thought Max. This was a place like no other, and it was showing its effects on all of them. Even one or two of the Riders among the Basilisk's men were relaxing, soaking in the extraordinary silence. *Trere'if* looked as though he might put down roots, and the Ogre had hunkered down, rubbing the Stone's surface with the palms of her rough hands. The young, unknown Moonward Rider had finally let go of Cassandra's arm and was looking around him, an expression of peace relaxing his face.

"You are here, the Talismans are here, the Guardian is here, and the Stone does not sound," Blood said, his rough silk voice ringing in the still air. "You are not the Prince." Another stir of movement ran through the Basilisk's men and one or two eyed the edge of the Stone and shifted closer to their fellows.

Max saw a look of puzzled indecision pass across the

Basilisk's face. With nothing to lose, he stepped toward the Rider who had been his friend, almost his *fara'ip,* holding out his hands.

"Dreamer, you see the truth now. Let the past go."

Moon pushed forward and grabbed the Basilisk's arm in both hands, clinging when he tried to shake her off. Her eyes looked indigo dark in her pale face. Max could swear she was sweating.

"Do not listen to him," she said, tense as a cat. "He is trying to trick you, son-of-Solitaries as he is. This is not the Stone."

The Basilisk relaxed, the look Max had seen fading, to be replaced by another, the eyes overly bright now, the smile strained and stiff.

*He* will *deny it,* Max thought unbelieving, *he's going to deny it after all.*

"Of course," the Basilisk said, his head nodding in little jerks as if in answer to Max's thought. He flung Moon off and turned toward the rock where the Talismans sat.

". . . . . . . . . . ." the Basilisk said.

Max put his hands up to his head. What—? He had *heard* that. Almost. A musical whisper tickling inside his head. The Basilisk went on speaking. Max backed away until he bumped into Blood on the Snow behind him. He was aware that Cassandra was calling out to him, that she was trying to reach him, her chained hands stretched out toward him, but that two of the Basilisk's men had her by the arms and were pulling her away. The young Moonward Rider had fallen to his knees, and was covering his face with his hands. *Trere'if* stood suddenly still, his mouth open in a soundless scream, his head thrown back, his arms thrusting into the sky and spreading into leafed branches, his legs twining together, the tendrils of his toes thickening as they rooted, cracking and shivering the rock as the Natural took on his true form.

The Basilisk went on speaking.

Max's knees gave way, and he felt Blood's hands and Lightborn's, lowering him until he was kneeling, leaning against the Table of the Talismans, head pillowed on his arms. As his eyes closed, Max saw Blood draw his *gra'if* sword, but he did not hear the sound of the metal clearing the sheath.

The Basilisk went on speaking.

*The Chant of Binding,* Max thought, ice forming in his veins, as the Basilisk's voice, perfectly audible now, indeed the only sound he could hear, rang through his head, dancing through his thoughts like a black Sprite, shutting doors and fixing chains, bolts and locks as it went. He shook his head, but couldn't clear out the sound. And now he couldn't open his eyes again. He felt himself dissolving as the Basilisk's voice washed through his mind, felt his bond with the Talismans strengthen and harden, felt the chains moving to circle them all. *Oh, god.* His thought was a scream, despair rising like the head of a snake to strike at him. *The Chant of Binding. I should have killed him right away . . . I didn't think it would work so fast . . .*

<hr />

Cassandra hardly felt the hands of the Riders holding her, bruising her arms as she struggled forward against them. All she saw was Max sagging against the rock that held the Talismans, changed and lambent now in this extraordinary light. Was Max losing color? Did he glow with an echo of their luminescence? What was it she'd been thinking earlier about plans going wrong?

Suddenly, her head cleared, and she had an instant to feel embarrassed, and glad that none of her students could see her making such an amateur's mistake, dragging against the combined strength of two Riders. Use your opponents' strength against them was practically the first lesson she taught anyone. She abruptly stopped fighting her captors and threw herself in the direction they were forcing her to go. Startled by the sudden lack of resistance, it was easy for her to yank them farther off balance and knock them into each other, the impact sufficient to free her from their hands.

Lightborn was shaking Max, and Blood was whistling a high, two-note signal as Cassandra launched herself into the Basilisk, striking him just below the knees and knocking him down. If only she could get her hands around his throat . . .

Riders in rough leather and *gra'if* came boiling up over the rounded edge of the Stone like wasps out of a nest. Wild Riders, she thought, seeing the Moonward Twins, her mouth widening into a grin. She *knew* Max would have a plan. Max *always* had a plan. He was no mean strategist after all. He could only Move a score, he'd said. But he hadn't said how many times he'd already done it.

Cassandra shifted her weight, heaving herself over the prone Basilisk Prince, reaching around to get a better grip on his throat—these manacles weren't attached to anything, and she was sure she could crack his neck for him even at this angle—suddenly her hands were pulled away by the darkmetal chain that hung between them. The Basilisk rolled away and smiled at her as he held up the chain, wrapped once around his own fist. It had not even occurred to her that her chains had been put on by the Basilisk himself and that, Keyed to him, they bound her to him also. She struggled anyway, digging in her heels and twisting her body against the uneven ground, but ultimately she was unable to resist the pull of the darkmetal. The Basilisk dragged her across the surface of the rock until all she could see through the hair that had fallen over her eyes was empty space.

Max felt a surge of power and clarity as the Chant stopped, and suddenly he could hear the sounds of fighting and one thin voice—he thought it was Moon—screaming. His heart tightened, and he struggled to his feet. He could think of only one thing that might make Moon cry out like that, and he ran toward the noise, pushing Riders, both friend and foe, out of his way. Thank god, either Blood or Lightborn had seen what was happening in time to call the Wild Riders he had hidden on the ledge under the rounded edge of the Stone.

Max stopped running.

The Basilisk stood at the brink of the abyss, Cassandra on her knees at his feet. Moon lay crumpled to one side, a red stain, brighter than the red of her dress, matting her hair on one side. She had tried to save Cassandra at the last, Max thought; whatever she had said before, she had tried to save her sister. The Basilisk looked up at Max and smiled. For an instant, Max thought he saw a cock's head on the Basilisk's shoulders, but then the image was gone.

"It appears you cannot be trusted after all, Dawntreader," the Basilisk said, with a nod toward the Wild Riders. "I know your own death will not bother you, but perhaps this will." He gave a jerk to the darkmetal chain he held, and before Max could move or call out, the Basilisk threw Cassandra over the edge and into the gorge.

"No!" the scream tore at his throat. *Oh, Christ, there's no bottom.* Max flung himself to his knees at the edge of the precipice and found the retreating speck of darkness that was Cassandra's body against the whiteness of the clouds. He imagined he could smell saffron flowers in the air where she had been.

Out of the corner of his eye, Max saw the strange Moonward Rider run to the Basilisk and attack him, lips drawn back from his teeth in a silent howl. The Basilisk rounded on him fast as a cat, but then Max's focus narrowed. He concentrated on Cassandra, pushing aside the images his fear tried to show him of her falling until she starved to death, her body drying and wizened, still falling, days passing, weeks—

Max shook himself and gritted his teeth. He subtracted the sounds of battle behind him, subtracted the edge of the precipice under his hands . . . *stop,* a small, calm voice in his head said. *You can't help her if you Move to her; you'll only die with her.*

Cassandra's body fell into the clouds below him and disappeared. Dying with her didn't seem like such a bad idea.

*No,* he said, perhaps aloud. He felt the bond of the Talismans, the elegant grace of the Spear, the cold strength of the Sword, the rich fullness of the Cauldron, and the solid clarity of the Stone beneath his hands. *Please,* he said to them, showing them what he intended. *Let her live. Don't let her die like this, not like this. Alone. Let me help.*

He felt the Talismans respond, each in its own way, to the desire of his heart, to what was, in a way, their own desire, since he was a part of them. *WE AGREE.*

Heart beating again, Max took a deep, preparatory breath, gathered his own *dra'aj,* all that he had apart from his link to the Talismans, and *MOVED* it, flung it out toward that dark falling speck. *Dra'aj* enough would transform you, the Basilisk himself was proof of that, if nothing else. The Basilisk Prince's *dra'aj* was taken by force, and his Basilisk was tainted by addiction. But Max would give Cassandra, his Truthsheart, all that he had himself; given willingly, as his own mother had given him hers, it would be pure. Would it be enough? That the Talismans had given their consent gave him hope. Cassandra was Guided by a Dragon. Dragons could fly.

Max felt in the core of his being the Phoenix that was Dawntreader, that was the Prince Guardian, that was Max Ravenhill, leap up from its nest of fire and, closing its wings, plummet over the edge of the precipice, flying like a thrown spear to where he could hear the air whipping away from her mouth as she struggled to breathe against the rush of wind, heard the rush as it swept past her ears. Felt the struggle within her as she fought to turn her body, to make the air hold her up, to deny the powerful draw of the empty spaces beneath her.

Looking at her with his Phoenix eye, Max saw a hot blast of flame in her Dragon's mouth, and reached out like a lover to the aid of the Dragon struggling to be born. His Phoenix poured its fire into hers, fed her *dra'aj* with his, and hoped it would be enough, as he felt his bond with the Talismans sustaining him, strengthening him, and then pulling him back with a SNAP! to feel his knees and hands bruised by the stone under them.

Cassandra tried to flatten her body as she had learned to do when skydiving, and though she knew that nothing and no one could save her from falling until she died, she tried not to think of it. She wished she could have said good-bye to Max; his anguished cry would be the last living sound she would ever hear. For that alone, she'd like another chance to kill the Basilisk Prince. *Oh, please, Max*, she called aloud, her words taken upward by the wind as soon as they left her mouth, *Dawntreader, my Prince, get up and kill the bastard*.

She wished she could have taken Moon in her arms one last time, to try to mend the broken thing between them. And what would happen to the poor Hound, now that she was not there? The air whipped past her mouth so quickly she barely had time to breathe it in. She tried turning over, but she could not stay flat unless she was facing down, limbs spread. The rush of air chilled her except where *gra'if* covered her chest and back.

Her *gra'if*. Where was it? Could she Move to it? She tried to clear her mind. There was no pain to distract her; in Healing the Hound she had Healed herself. She tried to block out the rushing air, subtract the cold, add the Dragon—she could use her Guidebeast's wings right now—add the feel of her scaled gauntlets on her hands, the face of the Dragon resting over her face as she slipped the helm down. She felt a hot breath of fire as it passed through her throat. She rolled over after all, and thought she could see Max, reaching out for her as she

floated, Dragon-bright, through the clouds. She saw the
Phoenix streaking toward her, hot red and yellow-
orange, with its great flame-tipped talons outstretched,
its heat reaching for her, and she reached back with her
great clawed hands for the Fire Bird.

   And caught it.

—◆—

Max felt someone pulling him back from the edge, shoving a sword into his hands. A Moonward Rider—but he
was gone, back to the fighting, before Max could tell
who it was. His body felt different, and the strange enhanced perception that he associated with the Talismans
was gone, though the connection was still there, thin as
a thread. So *his* Binding still worked. He was still the
Guardian, though his *dra'aj* was gone. It *had* to be enough.
If his gift had worked, if she had become her Guidebeast, Cassandra, more than Dragonborn now, could do
more than fly. She would be the only one of them able
to Move from the Stone, since there was no barrier to a
Guidebeast's Movement, not even the barrier of the
Talismans. *If he kills me,* he prayed to her, *come back
and eat the son of a bitch.*

   Max put his hand to the ground, bracing to push himself to his feet. He had half expected to die, as his mother
had died giving him all her *dra'aj*. He was drained, but
alive. His emptiness was familiar, he realized. He had
lived with this for years as a human, and he would be
able to live with it now. Thank all the gods he could remember being without *dra'aj*; it would have been more
than an unprepared Rider could tolerate. He laughed,
startling himself with the harshness of the sound. He
wondered how the Basilisk would feel if he knew that
the Chant of Oblivion he'd once used on Max was the
thing that ended up saving his life. He had been the
Prince long enough to feel a little disoriented, now that
he was without *dra'aj* once again, but that was the worst

of it. Would any of them be able to leave this place, he wondered, now that he could no longer Move them?

He looked around as a Rider stepped to his side, and he saw that the young Moonward Rider who had helped him was the stranger, the one who had clung to Cassandra. The young Rider was deathly pale, and his face was drawn as if by long sickness.

"Is she safe?" he said, his voice a harsh growl.

"I don't know," Max said. "I hope so."

The young Rider nodded, looking over the edge. "I am her Hound," he said, matter-of-factly.

Max didn't have a chance to ask him what he meant, jumping to his feet just in time to block a blow aimed at the young Rider by one of the Basilisk's men. In minutes they were fighting back to back, pushing their way toward the Table of the Talismans, where Blood, Lightborn, and a few of the Wild Riders still held off a knot of Riders dressed in purple. Max cut once, twice, lunged for the wrist of the man who faced him and pulled him onto his blade, yanked the blade out, and stepped over the body as it fell.

In seconds, he and the young Rider had joined the others around the Talismans, as the remaining purple Riders regrouped around the Basilisk's flickering form. Max could see the Ogre's body lying still, massive—dead or injured—he could not tell, on the far side of the Stone, beyond where *Trere'if* swayed, still rooted to the rock. The few bodies he could see wore purple. Where were the rest of the Wild Riders?

"Faded," Blood said in answer to Max's question, as he tied a strip of cloth around a small wound in the thigh of one of the Moonward twins. Max couldn't tell whether it was Wings of Cloud or Bird in Flight. "We could have prevailed, but the Basilisk has taken them. As we grow weaker, his strength increases."

"Father, I am sorry. I'm afraid we're all going to die here."

"There is no better place to die, nor any better people to do it with," Blood said, getting to his feet and giving the remaining Moonward twin a rough pat on his shoulder.

Max shook his head. "I haven't been completely open with any of you. I didn't want—I still hoped and I didn't want to take from you what hope you might have." He looked away, seeing that the Basilisk and his men were grouping for another charge. He had less time than he thought. "When I was restored, the Talismans showed no signs of expecting the High Prince. But, when the Banishment ended, they wanted to come here, and I brought them, hoping," Max put his hand on Lightborn's shoulder.

*"I?"* Lightborn choked out his laughter, wiping blood from his face with the back of a filthy hand. "You thought the traitor might be the High Prince?"

"Enlightened traitors sometimes make the best princes. I thought—your joining with us was the only real change that took place after the Banishment ended. I hoped it might be what the Talismans were waiting for," Max looked around again, "but the Cycles end with us," he said. "There is no Prince."

It was Blood on the Snow who finally spoke. "Do not despair so quickly, my son. Among the Wild Riders it is known that the Cycles end with the death of the last who knew the High Prince of old." Blood looked at Max, his eyes narrowed. "I am the last of the old Cycle," he said. "The last Wild Rider still living who has known a High Prince. Old he was, ancient beyond seeming, and I but a child. With my death, for good or for ill, the Cycle ends. It may be, as you have said, my son, that we will die here. But we are not dead yet."

"Father." Max found himself unable to say more. He cleared his throat and looked away. His father was right. No better place to die, or better people to do it with. The Talismans were safe, where they wanted to be. He searched the tiny flame left within him, and felt it burn true. Whatever their purpose might be, Max had accomplished it.

"My lords," the Moonward Rider who had called himself Cassandra's Hound said. "They come." Max shook himself. It was a bit early for self-congratulations, he thought, if the Basilisk still lived.

The Basilisk Prince approached them, preceded by the remainder of his men. This time there was no denying that flickering appearance of the Basilisk beast as he came nearer. He even seemed to stumble a little, as if on unfamiliar feet, and turned his head from side to side, as if he saw through a bird's eyes.

"Whatever else happens," Max said, pushing himself away from the rock table that held the Talismans, "kill the Basilisk. Those with *gra'if* come with me to the front. Don't let him live," he said, unsure whether he spoke to anyone besides himself. "Don't look him in the eye, and keep striking no matter what you see. Nothing else is important."

Yelling at the top of his lungs, Max charged forward. He forced the Rider guarding the Basilisk's right flank back three steps. They weren't outnumbered, but even as he thought this, Max saw the Basilisk Fade a Starward Rider he did not know. Out of the corner of his eye, he saw his father go down on one knee, and Lightborn leap to stand over the older Rider. "Watch my back," Max called to the young Moonward Rider who still stood near him, and turned his eyes to the Basilisk. What he had said was true, only the Basilisk mattered now. *Let the Talismans be free,* he thought, *let the Cycles end in peace.*

Max shoved a Sunward Rider out of his way to bring himself face-to-face with the Basilisk. Flushed with color, and almost vibrating with energy, the Basilisk Prince *flickered,* and this time stayed a Basilisk long enough that the sword dropped from his Beast's claws.

Max bared his teeth. "Oops," he said, and struck.

The Basilisk morphed back to his own shape, ducked the blow, and ". . . . . . . ." he said.

Max laughed as he became aware of his advantage. That Chant had no power over him; he had no *dra'aj* to bind. "Try something else," he said, laughing, "I've heard that one already," and he cut at the Basilisk's face, open mouthed in surprise.

But again the Basilisk ducked the blow, recovering his sword in an easy sweep of his hand. Max's heart sank. Full of stolen *dra'aj,* he was much stronger, and much faster, than Max could have anticipated. Even when they were young, he had needed all of his wits and his speed to beat the Basilisk with a sword. Hacking away at men-at-arms in a melee was one thing, but except for an hour or so of practice with Cassandra, he hadn't faced a master with a sword in his hand for centuries. And without his own *dra'aj . . . ?*

Was Cassandra alive? Did her Dragon float among the clouds? Would he ever know?

His ankle turned under him, and he felt the point of the Basilisk's blade enter him, stabbing his lower left side, just under the edge of his *gra'if* mail. The Basilisk Prince would have remembered that vulnerable spot from when they'd sparred together all those years before. This time, instead of the blunt blow of the practice sword, Max felt a sharp pain, and he smelled blood and saw Cassandra's face haloed by the light of a streetlamp. He sank to one knee. *Full circle,* he thought, as for a moment he felt oily pavement beneath him, and not the Stone of Virtue. Dead from a gut wound. He had no *dra'aj,* none that would keep him alive long enough to be saved by anyone not a Healer. Killed by a Hound. Don't let it take you alive, he remembered Cassandra saying. Had he dreamed everything between that moment and this? Was Cassandra a Dragon, or was she lying dead in the alley? The cold was beginning to spread even as he pushed himself back to his feet.

There was a roar of flame as a Dragon—red with a silver breast, each perfectly formed scale outlined in a delicate line of black—soared over the edge of the precipice, breathing fire. The fighting stopped as everyone looked up at the Guidebeast hovering over them with slow sweeps of its red-and-black wings. The young Moonward Rider howled in triumph, tossing his sword in the air, and Max had a moment to think how beautiful she was, before he flung his arms around the Basilisk, trapping his sword arm.

"Now! Now!" he called, knowing the Dragon that was Cassandra would hear him, would understand.

She turned her delicate muzzle toward him, and Max saw himself reflected in her gray eyes. Saw that she knew him, that it *was* Cassandra, truly the Sword of Truth that he knew and loved. His heart swelled until he thought it would explode.

"Now!" he yelled again, as the Basilisk struggled in his grasp. He saw the Dragon take breath and closed his eyes against the blast as the Basilisk writhed, screaming, in his arms, and suddenly what Max held was not the Rider, but the true Basilisk, its red eyes blazing, desperately struggling to free itself from the searing bite of the fire, its wings beating him about the head, its clawed feet raking at Max's heart. But Max gritted his teeth and hung on, keeping the Beast in the heart of the dragonfire, the *dra'aj* fire that enveloped them. Max braced himself against the blast, determined not to flinch at this final moment as Cassandra breathed, and her flames washed him, pure *dra'aj*, not consuming, but filling him completely with heat and light and sweetness, and still she breathed, until he thought he might empty her, her flames burning clean until he himself was shedding light and fire; until he himself ignited, the Phoenix in his nest of fire, the Fire Bird rising from his death, and Max found that the Phoenix, too, had claws, and he added his freshly fed fires to those filling the Basilisk, and the stone-eyed beast filled with fire, swelled with heat, and exploded outward, over him, through him, the blast deafening him, stunning all his senses until Max knew that it was too much, that even his Phoenix self could not hope to contain the fires, the *dra'aj* now set free.

But even as he felt himself on the brink of melting with the force of *dra'aj* pouring through him, the blaze found his link to the Talismans and flowed through it, the flames singing and crackling in triumph as they fed through him to the Talismans and they, too, caught fire, absorbing, awakening.

"Dreamer of Time," the Talismans said through Max's lips, "Are you not content? Do you not now feel the Truth?"

The Basilisk's face relaxed; for a moment Max saw the real Dreamer of Time once more, and the Phoenix in him rejoiced. Max released him, taking a step away, ready to welcome his friend.

". . . . ." the Basilisk said, his lips curving in a smile. He lunged for Max's throat, the skin on his cock's head morphing from feathers to scales to tiny snakes.

Max fell back under the Basilisk Prince's weight, pulling the Rider off balance. Without thinking, his body remembered what Cassandra had painstakingly taught him over the centuries. He brought up his feet as he fell back, catching the Basilisk Prince in the stomach, and straightened his legs until he catapulted the Basilisk, morphed now to a lumpy griffin, over his head.

And over the edge of the Stone. They had been closer to the precipice than Max had thought.

And he was once more kneeling on the Stone, the Talismans bright and alive behind him, the Basilisk gone, tumbling his eternal changes through the bottomless sky.

Max saw the Dragon, wings aloft, blazing in triumph, delicately touch its silver claws down on the Stone near him.

The Stone sounded.

# Chapter Twenty-one

THE LIGHT NEVER CHANGED on *Ma'at*, the Stone of Virtue. It was still midday, and the only shadow cast was that under the ash tree rooted in the center of the Stone where there had never been plant or tree before. Still, a part of Max knew that it wasn't just hours, but a whole Cycle that was passing as they bore witness. Some of the Riders grouped under the tree were wearing purple but looked as if they no longer quite remembered why. The others wore the dusty, well-worn leathers of Wild Riders, with here and there a *gra'if* helm or sword catching the light with its peculiar silver gleam. The Ogre Thunder Under the Mountain had been unconscious, not dead, and now sat near them, leaning her cheek against the bark of the ash tree that was part of her *fara'ip*.

Max was dimly aware of Lightborn's hand on his shoulder, as he was dimly aware of the hard rock under his knees, but the full force of his attention was focused on the High Prince.

The High Prince of the People had shed her Guidebeast's form and sat in her *gra'if* shirt and a pair of worn leather breeches borrowed from one of the dead, cradling in her arms an old Wild Rider who was not quite dead.

"Can you free *Trere'if?*" Blood on the Snow was whispering, his voice a faint thread, but clearly audible in that cool silence that once more prevailed on the Stone.

"I can," the Prince said in her dark chocolate voice, "but let me first—"

The old Rider placed trembling fingers on her lips. "Your Healing is not for me, my lord Prince," he said. "Your Healing is for the Lands. Make them True again, my Prince," his hand fluttered upward toward the branches above them, "free *Trere'if.* I am the last of my kind, the last to have seen the High Prince of old. It is my time to die, and this is a good place. I have reached the end of my journey; with me the Cycle turns."

The High Prince raised her eyes from the old Rider's face to look at Max, her eyebrows slightly lifted. Max nodded, while his heart tore.

"My son." Blood turned, his profile sharply etched against Cassandra's *gra'if.* Max took his father's hand.

"Father," he stopped and cleared his throat, forced a smile to his lips. "When did you know?"

Blood smiled, his lips pale against his bone-white skin. "I only guessed," he said, touching the tip of his finger to the Phoenix torque Max had restored to Cassandra's neck. "When I saw this. They were wed, the High Prince and the Guardian, in my time. I thought—I hoped, it might be so."

Max nodded. Now he knew why his father had not stopped him from going after Cassandra, had almost encouraged him to bring them all here, to the Stone. To give the Talismans a chance to Test her.

"Why did the Stone not Sound when she arrived?"

Max did not even glance up at Lightborn's question; he already knew the answer. He had known it as soon as the Stone *did* Sound.

"There was the Testing," he said. "She didn't leave when she could have, she came back for us, emptied herself of *dra'aj* to fight the Basilisk, to fill the Talismans." He looked up. "And to save me."

"The Heart of the People," Lightborn said, his soft voice husky and full.

Max nodded, his eyes once more on his father's face.

"Your Dragonborn Prince is very beautiful," the old Rider whispered. "A pity I will not see your children."

Max shut his eyes, clamped his teeth against the words that pushed against his lips. He felt it as Blood on the Snow Faded, his *dra'aj* passing through Cassandra, the High Prince, and Max himself, to the Talismans, and from them to the Lands. As it should be. As it had not been for many turns of Sun, Moon, and Stars.

He was standing, and Cassandra had her arms around him, and his face was buried in her saffron-scented hair, and her lips felt cool against his neck.

"My Prince."

They both looked up at the soft whisper, though Max knew that there was only one person who could be addressed that way when the High Prince was present.

"Here is another who is dying." The Moonward Rider who had been helping them came forward, with a red-draped body in his arms.

"Oh, god," Cassandra said, stepping toward them with her hands raised. "Moon?"

Cassandra gathered the girl into her own arms, knelt and bowed her head, laying her cheek against the blood drying on Moon's.

Max touched the Moonward Rider on the arm, drawing him away from the site of Healing. The first Healing of the new Cycle.

The Sun had turned three times when the High Prince and the Guardian rode their Cloud Horses through the Pass of *Welu'un* to where it opened into the Vale of *Trere'if.* The Vale was full of the Wood once more, all traces of the Basilisk's Citadel gone with the turning of the Cycle and the coming of the High Prince. The wind blew from the Vale, bringing with it the dark earth forest smells, the small sounds of life and death in the wild Wood. Behind them the Pass was full of brightly colored tents, dominated by the black, red, and silver pavilions that were the court of the High Prince.

Cassandra liked to make sure that they rode alone together for some part of every day. For one thing, it was a way for them to be just Max and Cassandra again. They pulled up, their Cloud Horses dancing, as they came upon Moon sitting on a boulder, looking out over *Trere'if,* her arms circling her drawn-up knees. The Moon-ward Rider, Stormwolf, was nearby, looking at a flower he'd picked out of the grass, brows furrowed, but a small smile on his lips.

Moon turned and stood when she heard the horses, a smile blooming on her own face. She and Stormwolf were the only two Riders who wore Cassandra's colors, and both were very proud of that.

"I have been trying to remember exactly why I hated you so much," she said to Max, "but," she shrugged, "it feels like it was someone else."

"Glad to hear it," Max said, smiling. "Do you know that Honor of Souls is looking for you?"

"I'm safe here, and besides, Stormwolf is with me."

"And Honor of Souls looks for him as well," Cassandra said.

Stormwolf, who had once been a Hound and who—like Moon—was learning to be just a Rider again, had turned at the sound of his name and came wading through the waist-high grass, still holding the little blue flower.

"Are we wanted, my Prince?" His voice had become less harsh, and he now spoke routinely above a whisper, but his past still cast shadows in his gray eyes.

Cassandra watched them walking slowly back toward the pavilions with a smile. It was one of her better ideas, she thought, to give her sister and the ex-Hound the task of watching out for each other, and to have Honor of Souls look after them both.

"The Wild Riders are having the last laugh," Max said, when they had urged their Horses forward into *Trere'if.*

"How so?" Cassandra turned to smile at him, bringing her thoughts from her sister back to the Lands.

"With so much of the Basilisk Prince's work undone by the Talismans," Max said, nodding at the Vale before them, "many of us are wanderers and travelers again. Restoring harmony among us all may be your biggest challenge."

"I've got a feeling that's going to be the least of my problems," she said, frowning.

"Really?" Max shifted in his saddle to face her completely. "So what do you think the challenge of this new Cycle will be?"

Cassandra smiled, looking back at *Trere'if* again.

"The Shadowlands."

Now available in trade paperback from
DAW Books, the first novel of
Violette Malan's new fantasy series,

# THE SLEEPING GOD

Read on for a sneak preview.

PARNO LIONSMANE RESTED his elbows on the ship's rail and watched as his Partner, Dhulyn Wolfshead, led her mare Bloodbone from the deck of the *Catseye* down the ramp to the pier. The spotted mare was snorting just a bit, and putting her feet down delicately, but Dhulyn kept her moving with soft murmurings and a steady pressure on the bridle. The *Catseye* was a small coastal trading ship, wide and low in the water, and the horses had spent the four-day trip from the Isle of Cabrea secure in an enclosed horse-box on deck, but there were few horses who traveled happily by sea. Dhulyn had taken Warhammer, Parno's big gray gelding, down the ramp first, claiming that Bloodbone would be ashamed to be more frightened than his gelding, and would come the more quietly for the bigger horse's example. Parno believed her. He believed any and everything that Dhulyn told him about horses.

"Good trip then, mercenary?" Captain Huelra left off directing his sailors and joined Parno at the rail.

"Calm and quiet, thank you, captain, just how we like it." Parno hunched his shoulders against the chill breeze that was blowing off the water. The harbor at Navra was sheltered—the salt flats which made the town important—were off to the east—making it the best place to dock this early in the year, when most travelers were still waiting out the last of the winter storms.

"Don't usually like horses onboard," captain Huelra was saying, "but your Brother is a good hand with them. It is natural to her, eh? Being an Outlander and all?"

Parno looked to where Dhulyn stood with the horses, bloodred hair dull under the cloudy sky, rubbing their faces and caressing their ears while they became accustomed once again to the feel of land underneath their hooves.

"You could say that."

Captain Huelra planted his elbows on the rail next to Parno and looked around. "You're late getting started. Thought you'd changed your minds, eh? Decided to stay aboard after all. The season of the salt caravans is almost a moon away, and if it's work you need . . ."

"We won't be staying in Navra," Parno said, straightening to face the captain. "As soon as Dhulyn Wolfshead finds us a decent packhorse we'll be going on to Imrion."

"Imrion? Work there aplenty, if what the gossips here in Navra tell me is true. But you could take ship from here, eh. Not mine, of course," Huelra added, gesturing with obvious pride at the *Catseye*. A perfect craft for the inner sea, it was much too small to venture out into the open ocean.

Parno laughed and jerked his thumb at Dhulyn. "The Wolfshead didn't win *that* much off your crew playing tiles," he said. Not that his Partner would agree to an ocean journey in any case, even if they had the money, but Parno saw no reason to tell Huelra that.

The captain nodded again, looking at Parno slantwise, from the corner of his brilliant blue eye.

"Ah. Should have known. They're saying Imrion's on the brink of civil war, eh, and if the Mercenary Brotherhood is gathering, they must be right."

Parno leaned forward again, hands lightly clasped, hoping the shock he'd felt at Huelra's words hadn't shown on his face. They'd been out of touch, for certain, but not so out of touch surely that he had to hear what rumor spoke of from outsiders. When he was sure his voice would be normal, he turned his head toward the man.

"The Wolfshead and I came almost without stopping from Destila," he said, naming the city at the far end of the Midland Sea. "Changing ships only at Cabrea. Does rumor say what it's about?"

"The Jaldeans are on the one side . . ."

"A bunch of harmless old priests?"

"You've been away to west, you say, Lionsmane, but you're from Imrion yourself, eh?"

"You know better than that, captain. We're Mercenary Brothers, Dhulyn Wolfshead and I, and *that's* where we're from."

The captain nodded, tongue flicking out to the corner of his mouth. "Still. If it were anyone else . . . I don't mind telling *you,* mercenary, I'm not from Imrion myself." He shrugged.

"It's not the old priests you remember, asking for alms for the shrines of the Sleeping God, it's the New Believers, younger men trying to win the people away from the foreign gods that've been gaining a following here in the east."

"And who on the other side?" It would be strange indeed, Parno thought, for civil war to break out because of a dispute over religion. Minor scuffles certainly, but while the Sleeping God was certainly the primary god here, the whole Letanian peninsula was known for its tolerance of all religious views. Even the Cloud People were open-minded on this point if on no other.

"They say the Tarkin himself," Huelra answered, "but only a few of the Great Houses have declared themselves one way or the other. And all on account of the Marked," the man continued, reading the question off

Parno's face. "The New Believers're saying the Tarkin doesn't see the danger—"

"*Danger?* From the *Marked?* How dangerous can they be? There's not one in five hundred who are Marked." Parno was almost smiling in his relief. This time rumor had to be wrong.

Captain Huelra opened his mouth to speak, and snapped it shut again with a frown. Parno turned to see what had drawn the man's attention. A woman in an elaborately folded green headdress had stopped to say something to Dhulyn. His Partner listened, nodded, and jerked her head toward the ship, clearly indicating where Captain Huelra stood beside him. Parno glanced back at him when the man sucked at his teeth.

"There's one now, from Imrion like so many others, and she'll be asking for passage, eh, and I'll have to turn her down."

Parno raised his brows. "She looks like she has money."

"That woman's Marked, or her husband is. They're to wear green headdresses now, and there's a curfew for them and all." He looked back at Parno, the muscles of his face gone hard. "And *that's* your New Believers as well, eh? It started in Imrion, but it's spread here, as you can see, maybe in the last moon or so. I don't know what it is they hold against the Marked—not my business, Truchara's a good enough god for any sailor—" Huelra spit over the side, giving water to his goddess as he spoke her name.

"When did this start?" Parno said, frowning in his turn. If there could be dress codes and curfews even in a Freeport like Navra, the status of the Marked was changing indeed. "The Wolfshead and I haven't been in Imrion since they took the field against the Dureans at the battle of Arcosa."

"Arcosa? That would have been in Nyl-aLyn's time, the old Tarkin."

Parno nodded. The Marked woman had left Dhulyn

and was making her way toward the gangplank, and the section of deck on which he and the captain stood. "This business with the Marked, would that be the new man's idea?"

"Not from what I hear, eh? But it's all he can do to prevent an open breach between those as support the New Believers and those who would just as soon let be. I'll tell you straight, since it's you I speak to Lionsmane, and I leave here on the next tide, no good will come of any persecution of the Marked, it's madness, pure and simple."

Huelra turned, fixing his eyes on Parno's. "I tell you plain, it goes against my heart to let you off here. Money or no money, I'd rather you stayed aboard. The whole of the west country was flooded last spring, an earthquake leveled Petchera in the summer—and there's rumors the Cloud People are looking to break their treaty. Imrion's luck has turned bad, you mark my words."

Parno laughed to cover the chill that had come over him, raising the hairs on his arms. "Why, captain, we're Mercenary Brothers looking for work. What better place for us to go than a country with trouble coming?"

Anything else the captain might have said was cut off as he turned to greet the Marked woman, who, having made her way up the gangplank was hovering at the captain's elbow. Parno nodded to them both and stepped aside, knowing he'd learn nothing more just now, and thinking it was high time he joined Dhulyn with the horses.

Bloodbone and Warhammer showed every sign of putting their sea voyage behind them. As Parno walked up, Bloodbone was snuffling Dhulyn's shoulder, but both horses were alert, flicking their ears, bobbing their heads and generally taking an interest in what was going on around them, as battle-trained mounts tended to do.

Dhulyn was doing the same, though in her own peculiar way. Still holding fast to the horses' bridles, she was watching a group of children play a skipping game farther along the pier, not far from where she stood with the horses. Having had no real childhood herself, it had always seemed to Parno natural that Dhulyn showed a great curiosity in the childhoods of others. She smiled as he neared her, her eyes still watching the children's game.

"It's the same rhyme," she said. "That sweeping rhyme the children were singing in the street in Destila."

"You sure? Those kids were playing a game with blindfolds."

"Nevertheless, it's the same rhyme, same cadence, same consonance. I'm curious, how do these rhymes and games get transplanted from one place to another?"

Parno shrugged. Dhulyn had spent a year in a Scholar's Library before taking her final vows to the Mercenary Brotherhood, and she'd never lost the habit of making these scholarly observations. "Adults like you see them, I would suppose, and carry them home for their children, like new toys."

"It would be interesting to trace the songs and the games back, try to find the point of origin from which they spread."

"You think such a point could be found?" Parno said, smiling. His years with Dhulyn had taught him that many the countries of the eastern continent told folktales and stories of amazing similarity. Why, it didn't take a Scholar to see that the God Dreamer of the Western Horde was the same deity known as the Sleeping God here in the Letanian Peninsula.

"Unless it goes back to the time of the Caids, then it will appear to have sprung up everywhere at once." Dhulyn shrugged one shoulder. "Ah well, a dissertation subject for some Scholar no doubt. And meanwhile, here we are back in the land of the Sleeping God."

"The Sleeping God's worshiped everywhere," Parno said, taking Warhammer's rein from her.

"But here, on the Letanian Peninsula, he is the first god, is he not?"

"The Brotherhood recognizes all gods," he reminded her.

"And all gods recognize the Brotherhood." She turned fully to look at him. "I told Huelra where to send our packs. Has the place changed very much? Do you remember the way to the inn you've been telling me about?"

"What do you think?" he said, grinning as he took Warhammer's bridle from her.

"I think you got lost in our cabin last night."

Parno swung, Dhulyn ducked, and the children looked over from their game, excitement plain in their faces— as was the disappointment when no fight broke out. Dhulyn, grinning for the benefit of the children, tilted her chin toward the *Catseye.*

"What's that about? The woman in green?"

"When we get to the inn," he answered, turning away.

They led the horses away from the *Catseye,* dodging seamen and dockworkers loading and unloading from the ships and fishing boats tied up along the pier. It really was too crowded, Parno told himself, to tell Dhulyn what he'd learned from Captain Huelra. That could wait until they could find some private corner at the Hoofbeat Inn. And besides, he needed to think a bit, find a way to tell her what they were heading into so she wouldn't just turn around and get back onto the ship. Dhulyn had been uneasy with the idea of returning to Imrion ever since he'd suggested it, looking for a reason not to come. And he couldn't be sure where a civil war might weigh on the scale of come or go.

The horses were spoiling for exercise, but the streets close to the docks proved to be so uneven that Dhulyn suggested they continue afoot. Parno was just leading the way down a narrow lane when his Partner froze.

"Did you hear that?" she said, her rough voice unusually loud in the cold air.

"The market?" Parno said dryly, bracing his feet as Warhammer, not as well trained as Dhulyn's Bloodbone, shied slightly, pulling him forward.

Dhulyn held up one finger to silence him and listened again, eyes narrowed, head tilted. Parno shrugged, wishing he'd worn his heavier cloak, and waited for Dhulyn to agree with him. The main market, if he remembered correctly, was off to the east, closer to the saltworks, but the barrows and stalls of the fish market, the one that served the docks and the ships, could be seen off to the other side of the pier they'd just left. Even this late in the afternoon, the buzz of the buyers and sellers, the calls of the merchants hawking their wares, even the sound of an optimistic flute, were still clear in the crisp air. But if Dhulyn thought she'd heard something else ...

"There!" Dhulyn's head jerked up and she swung herself into the saddle urging Bloodbone with her knees into an opening between two houses, turning away from the docks. Parno was mounted and only half a length behind his Partner before Bloodbone's tail disappeared from view.

The alleys between the houses and buildings in this quarter of Navra were none too clean, and the streets were not much better, Parno found as he followed Dhulyn out into a wider avenue. The freezing and thawing of early spring had heaved the cobbles and paving stones and left them slick underfoot. Even the dirt lanes were more than half slippery mud. Not the best conditions to be racing your horses, but Parno knew better than to argue with his Partner. He ducked an overhead sign with a swallowed curse. He was willing to wager practically anything he owned that it wouldn't be her horse that went down as she rode it much too fast around the next tight corner.

And he still had not heard anything out of the ordinary.

The laboring breath and clattering hooves of their horses made enough noise that the few people they encountered had plenty of time to get out of their way. Market day it might be, but away from the market itself and the busy areas around the docks, most townspeople finished their business early in weather like this; the day was turning cold, and the sky promised snow. One tall old man, well-wrapped in a red wool cloak, looked up in surprise as Dhulyn Wolfshead galloped past him, and called out angrily, not noticing the tattoos of their Mercenary's badges, even though both she and Parno were bareheaded from habit.

They turned into a street of better class houses, a few of them as much as four stories tall with the featureless lower walls that spoke of interior gardens or courtyards, or both. Not so fine as nobles' houses, to Parno's experienced eye these looked like the homes of well-to-do merchants. And suddenly Parno smelled smoke, and saw as they rounded yet another corner a three-story house with flames dancing in two upper windows that gave on the street.

Even now, he could not hear the sound of the fire, and he knew that Dhulyn—Outlander or no—could not possibly have heard it either. This burning house must have been some Vision she had Seen.

The usual crowd of people who gather out of nowhere at any sign of trouble were milling around in the irregular square in front of the burning building, but something was wrong—more wrong than just a house on fire. Parno frowned as he urged Warhammer forward. He'd seen many a mob in his time as a Mercenary, and this one wasn't behaving normally. Those closest to the fire acted as he would expect, some craning for a better view, others pointing and yelling—shock and excitement apparent in faces and stances. As for those farther away, far too many were standing far too still, hands hanging limp, heads all, as he now realized, at the same angle. And aside from some shoving, and what looked like a fistfight breaking out on the far side of the crowd, no one was doing anything. Not putting out the fire, not bringing water, not even helping to drag out furniture. In fact, two men seemed to be preventing someone from coming out of the house. Parno edged forward into the opening Dhulyn had made in the crowd just as a man put his hand on Warhammer's bridle. Parno bared his teeth as the man looked up. His eyes widened when he saw the red and gold tattoo reaching from Parno's temples to back above his ears, and he backed away.

Closer now, Parno could hear the flames as they ate through the house wall, blistering the stucco to the right of the doorway. A woman at the front of the crowd threw a stone at the upper window on the left, screaming something Parno couldn't make out.

Flames or no, Dhulyn rode Bloodbone right through to the front of the house, swung her leg over the pommel of her saddle, and jumped off, knocking the two men who'd been blocking the doorway sprawling over one another. The darker of the two sprang to his feet, a cudgel ready in his fist. Dhulyn stepped in close to him, knocked his arm away with her left forearm, brought her booted heel down sharply on his instep, and drew her sword from the sheath that hung down her back. All without taking her eyes from the doorway.

A young girl burst out of the now unguarded door, but was choking too much to actually speak.

"Children upstairs," Dhulyn called out to him as Parno drew rein beside her, using Warhammer's size and wickedly rolling eyes to push the crowding people farther back.

"I'll go," he said, tossing her his reins. Demons and perverts, he thought, not for the first time thankful that he didn't See what Dhulyn sometimes Saw. Children. He pulled his feet from the stirrups and, steadying himself with his hands on the pommel, hopped up on the saddle until he was balancing on Warhammer's back, wishing he was wearing something with more grip than his boots.

"Keep your eyes open." He didn't have to tell her to watch the crowd. She'd have noticed before he did that something was amiss.

Out of the corner of her eye Dhulyn Wolfshead watched Parno make the small jump that got his fingers hooked on the windowsill above them. The muscles in his arms bulged as he drew himself up, swung one leg over the sill, and was gone into the smoky darkness within the house.

# Violette Malan

# The Sleeping God

### *A Novel of Dhulyn and Parno*

Masters of weapons and the martial arts, mercenaries
Dhulyn and Parno have just saved one of the Marked,
one of those with special powers, from a mob under
the influence of the Sleeping God. Dhulyn's own gift
may make her a similar target, so the pair takes ship for
safer shores. On a seemingly simple escorting mission,
not even Dhulyn's talent can warn them of the threat
lurking at the end of their journey.

0-7564-0446-8

*Raves for Violette Malan:*
"Believable characters and graceful storytelling."
—*Library Journal*

"Fantasy fans should brace themselves:
the world is about to discover Violette Malan."
—*The Barnes & Noble Review*

To Order Call: 1-800-788-6262

www.dawbooks.com

DAW 58